# The Last
# Great Dance
# on Earth

# The Last Great Dance on Earth

## SANDRA GULLAND

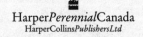

HarperPerennialCanada
HarperCollinsPublishersLtd

History is a story, as told by the victor.
—*Napoleon*

The Last Great Dance on Earth
*is a work of fiction based on (and inspired by)*
*the extraordinary life of Josephine Bonaparte.*

THE LAST GREAT DANCE ON EARTH
Copyright © 2000 by Sandra Gulland.
All rights reserved. No part of this book may be used
or reproduced in any manner whatsoever without
prior written permission except in the case of brief
quotations embodied in reviews.
For information address
HarperCollins Publishers Ltd,
55 Avenue Road, Suite 2900,
Toronto, Ontario, Canada M5R 3L2

www.harpercanada.com

HarperCollins books may be purchased for educa-
tional, business, or sales promotional use. For information please write: Special Markets Department,
HarperCollins Canada,
55 Avenue Road, Suite 2900,
Toronto, Ontario, Canada M5R 3L2

First HarperPerennialCanada edition

Canadian Cataloguing in Publication Data

Gulland, Sandra
The last great dance on earth

Includes bibliographical references.
ISBN 0-00-648562-6

1. Joséphine, Empress, consort of Napoleon I,
   Emperor of the French, 1763–1814 – Fiction
I. Title

PS8563.U643L37 2001   C813'.54   C2001-900697-7
PR9199.3.G7915L37 2001

02 03 04 RRD 5

Printed and bound in the United States

*For Chet and Carrie,*
*prince and princess*

I will not stand before you as time passes;
I will stand before you eternally.

—*Oscar Bearinger, "Masks and Shadows"*

# The Last
## Great Dance
### on Earth

# I

## La Bonaparte

I was not born for such grandeur.
—*Josephine, in a letter to her daughter Hortense*

## In which peace seems an impossible dream

*March 2, 1800—Tuileries Palace, Paris.*
"Josephine . . . Come see the moon."

I woke with a start. A man was nudging my shoulder, his face illuminated by candlelight. "Bonaparte, it's *you*," I said, clasping his hand. I'd been dreaming of home, of my beautiful Martinico, dreaming of the sea. But I was not on a tropical island. I was in the dank, opulent palace, in the bed of Marie Antoinette and King Louis XVI—the bed of the dead. I pressed Bonaparte's fingers against my cheek. "What time is it?"

"Almost three. Come outside with me."

"Now?" I asked, but threw back the covers.

"It's a little chilly," he said, draping a cape over my shoulders.

A full moon hung over the river, bathing the gardens in a radiant light. "It reminds me of something you once wrote to me," I said, taking Bonaparte's hand. "That we are born, we live and we die—in the midst of the marvelous."

"I don't remember writing that," he said, heading toward the steps that lead down to the flower beds.

The fertile scent of spring was heavy in the air. Bonaparte brushed off a stone bench for us to sit on. I leaned my head on his shoulder, overcome with a feeling of longing. It is the season of renewal, yet I remain barren—in spite of love, in spite of prayers.

"I think best in the open air," Bonaparte said. "My thoughts are more expansive." By moonlight, in profile, he looked like a Roman statue. "See those shacks down by the laundry boats? Every citizen should have a proper home—and clean water. I'm thinking of a canal system to bring it in. And more hospitals—there should never be more than one patient to a bed. And bridges across the river would be beautiful as well as practical. Imagine it! I intend to make Paris the most beautiful city of all time."

"You will do it," I said, with confidence. What could stop him? Already so much has changed. Before Bonaparte, everything was chaos, and now prosperity prevails and France is made whole again—*I* am made whole again. Not long ago I was a widow, a survivor of the Terror, a frightened mother of two children. Now I look upon my life with wonder, for everywhere there is abundance—of wealth, certainly, and even glory, but mainly of heart. As Madame Bonaparte—indeed, as *Josephine*—I have felt my spirit blossom. This intense little man I married has inspired me to believe once again in heroes, in destiny, but above all in the miracle of love.

It was at this moment that I found the courage to voice the question I have long been afraid to ask: "Bonaparte, what if . . . ?" What if we can't have a child?

An owl's plaintive call pierced the night silence. "We must not give up hope," Bonaparte said gently. "Destiny has blessed us in so many ways."

Blessed me, certainly—blessed Hortense and Eugène, my fatherless children. "*You* have blessed us," I told him truly.

*Je le veux*, Bonaparte so often says. I will it!

If only he could will a child into being.

*March 6.*

Tonight, after a performance at the Opéra, Bonaparte was thrown a bouquet by a girl in a revealing gown, her plaited straw bonnet tied with blue ribbons. "I'll hold that," I offered.

Later I discovered a note tucked in it, inviting the First Consul to a rendezvous. I threw it into the fire. Daily, it seems, Bonaparte receives an invitation from some young maiden eager to sacrifice her virtue to "the saviour of France."

*March 7.*

I knew from the way Bonaparte pitched his battered tricorne hat across the room that the news was not good. "They refused my offer of an armistice," he said with a tone of defeat. His hat missed the chair and fell onto the carpet, startling the three pugs sleeping on a cushion by the fire.

"Again?"

"Refused to even consider it." Bonaparte threw himself into the down-stuffed armchair; two feathers floated free. "Refused to even *discuss* it." His cheek twitched. "*Pacem nolo quia infida*," he said, mocking an English accent.

"The English said that?" I rescued Bonaparte's hat from the pugs.

"No peace with . . . the infidel?" Hortense translated slowly, looking up from a charcoal sketch she was working on. She pushed a flaxen curl out of her eyes, leaving a smudge of black above her brow.

"And *we're* the infidel?" I asked (indignant).

Bonaparte got up and began to pace, his hands clenched behind his back. "The British flog their own soldiers and accuse *us* of brutality. They violate international agreements and accuse *us* of lawlessness. They pay every Royalist nation in Europe to wage war against us and accuse *us* of starting conflicts! If they don't want war, why don't they try to end it?"

"Papa, you must not give up," Hortense said with feeling. Peace is something my daughter has never known, I realized sadly. When has France not been at war with England?

"I will never give up," Bonaparte said with quiet intensity, that spirit his soldiers call *le feu sacré*: the will to be victorious—or die.


*March 9—Malmaison, our fourth-year anniversary.*

We stayed all morning in bed. Bonaparte's hopeful enthusiasm for conceiving a child makes me sad. Every time we have marital congress (often!) he names the baby—a boy, of course. This morning it was Géry—Napoleon Géry Bonaparte. Last week it was Baudouin, Gilles, Jean. Tonight, who will it be? Jacques? Benoît? Donatien?

I go along with this game, yet I know I'll not conceive. I had a hint of a show several months ago, but no longer, in spite of the tincture of senna I take to keep my body open, the endless restoratives and expulsives I consume—birthwort boiled in beer, syrup of savin, powdered aloe and iron—all bitter to the taste and bitter to the soul.

*2:45 P.M.—a lovely spring afternoon.*
"I have the perfect cure," Madame Frangeau said, pulling her cap so that the lappets would hang properly. "It has never failed."

I observed the midwife with astonishment. She was as eccentrically dressed as I'd been told to expect, her shirred gown covered with the fringes and tassels that had been the fashion before the Revolution. "Ergot?" I guessed. The mould was said to be infallible (except in my case).

"No, not ergot, not jalapa, not even scammony. Come with me."

I followed her out of her modest abode and over the cobblestones to the door of a house on a narrow street. "Madame Frangeau," I protested, "I don't think I should—"

"Madame Bonaparte, I am the midwife," she informed me with authority, pounding on the door.

And indeed, she did have authority, for all the household jumped at her command. I followed her into a bedchamber where she told a woman in bed, "Don't stir! I have need only of your infant." She instructed me to sit in the nursery, to slip my gown off my shoulders, whereupon, having cleansed me, she put the swaddled infant to my breast. "I will return in a half hour," she said, and abandoned me.

I was shaken by the beauty of this week-old baby at my breast—its milky sweet smell, the silken down of its skull—but also by the humiliation I felt being tended in this way.

Dutifully, the exuberant and confident midwife returned, dispatching me with salves and herbs and instructions to "congress" at *least* once a day. "You must drown in your husband's vital fluid."

It is my tears I am drowning in! On return I broke down, exhausted by all the "cures" I've tried, frustrated by my body's stubborn refusal to respond.

*Evening, not yet 9:00 P.M.*

Bonaparte pulled the cord of a little silk sachet, trying to unknot it. "Zut!" he said, slicing it with a meat knife. He shook the contents out over the dinner table. An enormous diamond glittered among the dirty china, the chicken bones, the half-empty plates of peas, plum pudding and cod-liver canapés. "A bauble for our anniversary," he said, flicking it toward me, as if it were a plaything.

"How many carats is that?" Hortense asked, her eyes wide.

"One hundred and forty," Bonaparte said. "King Louis XV wore it in his coronation crown. The police finally found it in a pawnshop."

"So *this* is the Regent diamond," I said, holding the translucent gem between my fingers, losing myself in its light.


*March 10.*

Time is a woman's enemy, it is said. This morning I sat before my toilette mirror, examining my face. I am thirty-six, six years older than my husband. On impulse I sent for "my" diamond. The embroidered blue velvet case was placed reverently before me. Gently, I edged the gem out of its nest.

"Hold it at your ear," Hortense whispered, as if we were in some sacred place.

I sat back, examining the effect in the glass.

"Pour l'amour du ciel," the maid said, crossing herself.

By diamond light, I seemed transformed: younger. I glanced uneasily over my shoulder, imagining the spirit of Queen Marie Antoinette looking on. She knew the irresistible lure of a brilliant—and now, alas, so do I.


*March 29, 1:15 P.M.—Tuileries Palace.*

I am writing this by the light of three candles. It is afternoon, yet dark in this room, the curtains drawn against the curious eyes of the men and women in the public gardens outside.

Hortense is to join me soon. We're going to Citoyen Despréaux's annual—

*Much later, after midnight, everyone asleep (but me).*
—Citoyen Despréaux's annual dance recital, that is.

I was interrupted earlier by Bonaparte, who showed up unexpect-edly—as he does so often—humming "la Marseillaise" (badly). "I have an idea for Hortense," he said, sitting down in his chair beside my toilette table. He picked up a crystal pot of pomade and examined the etched design, the details. "General Moreau," he said, sniffing the pomade, rubbing some on his fingertips, then putting it back down and picking up a silver hair ornament. (Bonaparte is never still!)

"Ah," I said, considering. General Moreau *is* a possibility—a popular general, dapper, always in powder, with the manners of a gentleman. "But too old for Hortense, perhaps?" General Moreau is close to forty, a few years older than I am, and a good ten years older than Bonaparte.

"Did I hear my name?" Hortense asked, appearing in the door.

"Your mother was telling me what a charming young lady you've become," Bonaparte said with a fond look at his stepdaughter.

"Indeed! That gown looks lovely on you." The cut flattered Hortense's lithe figure. The silver threads shimmered in the candlelight.

"That isn't English muslin, is it?" Bonaparte asked, frowning.

"Of course not, Papa." Hortense made a neat pirouette.

"Bravo!" we cheered.

"But I'm having trouble with the minuet," she said. "In the first figure, when passing, I'm to do a temps de courante *and* a demi-jeté."

"Instead of a pas de menuet?"

"Only on the first pass, Maman. Otherwise, it looks affected—or so the dance master says. And *this* pas de menuet has two demi-coupés and two pas marchés en pointe."

"Bah," Bonaparte said.

"Why don't you show us," I suggested.

"Papa, I need you to be my partner," she said, tugging on Bonaparte's hand.

"I'll play one of Handel's minuets." I took a seat at the harpsichord.

Reluctantly, Bonaparte stood. He placed his feet in a ninety-degree turnout and stuck out his hand. "Well?" he said to me over his shoulder.

"First Consul?" Bonaparte's secretary interrupted from the door. "Citoyen Cadoudal is here to see you." Fauvelet Bourrienne's chin quivered in an attempt not to smile at the sight of Bonaparte attempting a plié. "I suggest we not keep him waiting—he's an ox of a man, and spitting everywhere."

"Cadoudal, the *Royalist* agent?" I asked, confused—and not a little alarmed. Cadoudal is the leader of the rebel faction—the faction intent on putting a Bourbon king back on the throne. The faction intent on deposing Bonaparte.

"He's early," Bonaparte said, putting on his three-cornered hat and heading out the door—relieved, no doubt, to escape the minuet.


Bonaparte's young sister Caroline was standing outside the recital hall when Hortense and I arrived. She was dressed in a short-sleeved ball gown more suited to an evening fête; only a thin froth of organdy ruffles served for a sleeve. "Joachim will be here in five minutes," she said, chewing on a thumbnail. "I made him practise cabrioles for a half-hour this morning."

"Why cabrioles?" Hortense asked. "I thought you were to demonstrate a gavotte."

"Le Maudit! We are?" Caroline took a snuffbox out of a gaudy bead reticule.

The dance master opened the door. "Ah, Madame Bonaparte—mother of my *best* pupil! How kind of you to honour us with your presence." Citoyen Despréaux patted his brow with a neatly folded lavender handkerchief.

"My husband will be here any moment," Caroline informed him, taking a pinch of snuff. "General Murat," she added, in answer to the dance master's puzzled expression.

"Of course!" Citoyen Despréaux exclaimed, casting a concerned look at Caroline's exposed arms. "You are to perform the gavotte. Mademoiselle Hortense, if you would be so kind? I'd like to consult with you regarding the layout of the room." With a studied balletic motion, Citoyen Despréaux gestured my daughter in.

"I'll see you after, sweetheart," I told Hortense, blowing her a kiss. "Is your mother inside?" I asked Caroline, lingering. She seemed forlorn, all alone.

"She's not coming," Caroline said, snapping the snuffbox shut. "She's visiting Pauline today." This with a hint of chagrin. Of Bonaparte's three sisters, beautiful (and spoiled) Pauline is clearly the favourite. Elisa, although plain, is lauded as "literary" . . . and young Caroline? Poor Caroline is illiterate and, although not plain, with her common extremities, thick neck, muscular build and what Bonaparte calls a "warrior spirit," she is certainly not what one would ever call *engaging*.

"Ah, there's your husband," I said. It was all I could do not to smile watching Joachim Murat swagger toward us, a big, muscular soldier dressed entirely in bright pink: a pink velvet coat with tails, pink satin knee breeches, even a flat pink hat embellished with pink-and-black striped feathers.

Caroline opened the timepiece that was dangling from a heavy chain around her neck. "He's three-and-a-half minutes late."

Citoyen Despréaux positioned himself before the twenty or so assembled guests—the family and friends of his students. "Bonjour! We will open our recital with the most regal of dances, the traditional minuet, a dance whose very simplicity reveals *all*: the education, the grace and—dare I say it?—the *class* of the performer. But first, the walk: the cornerstone of good breeding." He motioned to his students, who circled self-consciously.

"Observe how perfectly *this* young lady moves," he said, indicating Hortense. "The very essence of unaffected fluidity! Now, perhaps if I could have a young man to—Ah, Citoyen Eugène, fantastique."

I turned to see my son at the door, a black felt hat on his head, his unruly curls escaping. Grinning sheepishly, he approached the dance master. "But I'm in boots," I heard him whisper to Citoyen Despréaux. "I didn't expect to—"

"I only wish you to demonstrate a bow, my good fellow."

Dutifully, Eugène raised his right arm to shoulder height, clasped his hat by the brim and, slipping his left foot forward, bowed deeply.

"Voilà, the *perfect* bow," Citoyen Despréaux said, touching his lavender handkerchief to the outside corner of each eye. "Merci, Citoyen Eugène, you may be seated."

"It's a good thing he didn't call attention to my walk," Eugène whispered, taking the seat beside me. I smiled—his *lumbering* walk, Bonaparte and I call it.

Overall, the recital went well—Hortense performed brillantly. Eugène and I were so proud! Even Caroline and Joachim managed, although Joachim made too many circles and ended up at the wrong end of the room—a common error, certainly, but one Citoyen Despréaux unfortunately felt called upon to note.

After, Caroline, Joachim, Hortense and Eugène went out for ices. I pleaded fatigue and returned to the Tuileries Palace, only to find Bonaparte in a temper, pacing back and forth in front of a blazing fire. The Minister of Foreign Affairs was sitting in front of the fire screen, watching him with a bored expression.

"Madame Bonaparte," Talleyrand said with a catlike purr. "It is always a pleasure to see you, but especially this evening. The First Consul is in need of your calming influence."

"Do not mock me, Talleyrand," Bonaparte barked. "It's not *your* life on the line."

I put my hands on Bonaparte's shoulders (to calm, yes) as I kissed each cheek. "The meeting with Citoyen Cadoudal did not go well?"

"He would strangle me with his own hands given half the chance."

"I don't know why this comes as a surprise to you, First Consul," Talleyrand said. "Citoyen Cadoudal wants a Bourbon king back on the throne and you're rather inconveniently in the way."

"The French people are standing in the way—not *me*. Two hundred years of Bourbon rule was two hundred years too many." Bonaparte threw himself into the chair closest to the fire, his chin buried in his hand.

"The Bourbons, of course, argue that two hundred years of rule confers permanence," Talleyrand said, lacing his long fingers together with a fluid motion. "They created that red-velvet-upholstered symbol of power in the throne room; they consider it *theirs*. And so long as it remains empty, I venture they will do everything in their power to get it back."

"And England will do everything in *its* power to help them."

"Correct."

"You both make it sound so hopeless," I said, taking up my basket of needlework. "Is peace an impossibility?"

"'Impossible' is not a French word," Bonaparte said.

"There is peace, and there is lasting peace," Talleyrand observed philosophically. "History has proven that the only lasting peace is a blood knot, the mingling of enemy blood—and not on the battlefield, First Consul, but in the boudoir. Peace through marriage: a time-honoured tradition."

"What are you getting at, Minister Talleyrand?" Bonaparte demanded. "You know I don't have a son or daughter to marry off to some lout."

"You have a stepson, the comely and honourable Eugène Beauharnais—"

"A boy yet, only eighteen."

"—and a stepdaughter, the virtuous and accomplished Mademoiselle Hortense." Talleyrand tipped his head in my direction. "Who, being female and nearing her seventeenth birthday, is at an ideal age to marry."

"I'm beginning to think you are serious, Minister Talleyrand," Bonaparte said. "Marry Hortense to an Englishman? The English would never condescend to join one of their blue-blooded ilk to anyone even remotely related to me. Have you not read the English journals?" He grabbed a paper from a pile on the floor and tossed it to the Minister of Foreign Affairs. "Top right. It will tell you who I am in the eyes of 'Les Goddamns.'"

"Ah, yes. 'An indefinable being,'" Talleyrand read out loud in English, a hint of a smile playing about his mouth, "'half-African, half-European, a Mediterranean mulatto.'"

"Basta!" Bonaparte grabbed the news-sheet and threw it into the fire, watching as it burst into flames.

"I wasn't thinking of mating your daughter to the English, frankly," the Minister of Foreign Affairs said evenly. "I was thinking of Georges Cadoudal."

"Oh, Minister Talleyrand, I trust you jest," I said faintly, my embroidery thread knotting.

## *In which we have reason to fear*

*April 9, 1800, 2:20 P.M.—in the downstairs drawing room at Malmaison, a lovely afternoon.*

We made the four-hour journey out to Malmaison seeking country quiet—only to find everything in a state of chaos. The hothouse is almost but not quite roofed, the drapes almost but not quite hung, the fireplace mantel in Bonaparte's cabinet almost but not quite completed. And now, as if all that isn't enough, the first cook is upset because the second cook put away a jelly-bag wet, and the second cook is upset because the first cook expects him to empty the hog pails. (It's a sign of what my life has become that I have *two* angry cooks to contend with—and this at our country château.) Then my flower gardener—not the kitchen gardener or the groundskeeper—tremulously informed me that three cartloads of lilac bushes had been delivered: could he leave them in the front courtyard? Put them behind the farmhouse, I told him. "We're expecting guests."

As soon as he left, Hortense and Caroline came into the room with their fête gowns on, which they paraded for me to admire.

"How much did Hortense's gown cost?" Caroline wanted to know, swishing the gold fringe at the hem to reveal a spangled satin petticoat underneath. "Mine was four hundred and twenty-three francs."

"I believe Hortense's gown was less," I lied, to satisfy Caroline. Hortense's simple gown of fine ivory cotton was draped to imitate a toga.

"Your gown is beautiful, Caroline," Hortense said, in an attempt to appease.

*You* are beautiful, I wanted to tell my daughter. Slender, graceful, her head crowned in golden curls, Hortense reminds me of an angel.

"Madame Frangeau says I have the look of a boy-producing woman." Caroline positioned herself in front of the full-length mirror and pushed up her bosom.

"Madame Frangeau, the midwife?" Hortense asked, her voice filled with awe. Caroline is only one year older than she, but Caroline is married and knows the secrets of women—secrets that mystify (and frighten) my daughter.

"But just to be sure, I drink plenty of red wine." Caroline leaned close to the mirror to examine her face—that flawless rosebud complexion that gives her a girlish countenance quite at odds with her masculine neck and shoulders.

"But isn't it the man who is supposed to drink wine?" Hortense asked. "Before . . ." She flushed.

"I'm not convinced one can determine the sex of a child." Four years of trying to conceive had made me a reluctant expert on the subject.

"Madame Frangeau says you can," Caroline said. "She knows all sorts of tricks. She says it's a wife's duty to produce a child, that a woman who fails to do so has been cursed. Maybe you should talk to her about your problem, Aunt Josephine."

My *problem*. "I already have," I said, chagrined, leaving the room to get my basket of embroidery threads.

"Maybe it's not my mother's fault," I overheard Hortense say on my return. I paused at the door. "After all, she had me and Eugène."

"There's one way to find out," Caroline said. "If Napoleon got another woman pregnant, then it would be clear that—" (The gall of that girl!)

"Caroline!" my loyal daughter objected.

"I didn't say Napoleon should do it, just that that's how one could make a determination. And speaking of making a determination, now that you're going to be seventeen, don't you think it's time you married?"

My cue to enter. "I happen to know a few young men who would love to be considered by Hortense—Citoyen Mun for one."

Caroline made duck-lips. "He's a gabbler and a boor."

"There are other qualities to consider," I suggested, but thinking, I confess, that *gabbler* and *boor* well described Caroline's own husband, Joachim Murat.

"I am going to marry for *love*," Hortense said, clasping her hands to her heart.

"There are many forms of love," I said cautiously. Hortense's romantic notions concern me. "An arranged marriage will often blossom into sincere devotion, while a romantic union withers with age."

"My husband loves me," Caroline said. "He does anything I tell him."

I heard footsteps approaching, a rustle of silk. Mimi appeared in the door, her hands on her wide hips. "Yeyette," she said, addressing me by my childhood name,* "the architects said to tell you the hothouse will be finished next week." She rolled her eyes up, as if to the heavens. "But it won't be finished for two months, I'll wager you."

"And we *know* that Mimi can tell the future," Hortense said, smiling at her former nanny.

"But can she say when someone's going to die?" Caroline demanded. "In Corsica, there are women who go out at night and kill an animal, but before the animal dies, they look into the animal's eyes and see someone's face and then that person dies. It's true! Any Corsican will tell you."

"No doubt, but that's not the type of thing Mimi does," I said, with an apologetic look at Mimi.

"So what *does* she do? My mother had a Negress who could predict the weather with sticks." Caroline took the last three macaroons on the plate.

"Mimi predicts the future from cards," I said.

"Then get her to tell us our futures," Caroline persisted. "I want to find out if Joachim and I will make a *you know* before he leaves on campaign in two days. Hortense could find out if she's ever going to marry, and—who knows, Aunt Josephine—maybe *you* could find out if you're ever going to be able to—"

"Do you have your cards with you?" I asked Mimi, interrupting.

"First, the birthday girl," Mimi said with a good-natured grin, pulling the worn pack out of her apron pocket.

"Oh no," Hortense said, as if faced with her doom.

---

* *Josephine's childhood name was Rose and her nickname Yeyette. Mimi had been a slave on Josephine's family's sugar plantation in Martinique ("Martinico"). She and Josephine grew up together and had a sisterly relationship. It is possible that they were, in fact, half-sisters; Josephine's father may have been Mimi's father. Josephine had purchased Mimi's freedom a few years previously.*

We watched in silence as Mimi laid out the cards in rows, seven cards wide. The Death card with its ghoulish skeleton turned up in the fifth row—but that can mean many things, I thought: *transformation, change*. The Lovers card was in the row above it. "I see a husband, and I see love," I said. But not necessarily together.

Mimi nodded slowly, pulling at her lower lip. "You will have four babies."

Hortense beamed.

"By two men," Mimi added, frowning.

"Aha!" Caroline opened her snuffbox and inhaled a pinch.

"Two marriages?" I asked. How did Mimi see that?

But Mimi had already pulled in the cards and handed me the deck to shuffle. "How about I do yours now, Yeyette?"

"Why am I *always* last?" Caroline brushed snuff off her bodice.

"Patience, Madame Caroline, we'll get to you," Mimi said, taking the cards back and laying them out. "Oh-oh—there she is again."

"You jest." But there it was: the Empress card, the Empress with her weary, unhappy eyes.

"My mother is often told she will be queen," Hortense explained to Caroline. "Even when she was a girl in Martinico she was told that—by a voodoo priestess."

"Oh, let's not talk of it!" The memory of that afternoon disturbs me still.

Caroline shrugged. "She lives in the Palace of Kings. That's almost like being a queen."

I heard a horse approaching at a gallop. "Palace of the *Government*, we call it now," I reminded Caroline, going to the window. "It's Bonaparte," I said, relieved to see his little white Arabian racing through the gate.

"I was accosted by hooligans," Bonaparte exclaimed, sliding off his horse.

Mon Dieu, no! "Near the quarry?" His hat was askew and there was dust on his uniform—but then, Bonaparte always looks a shambles. "Did you outrace them?" I asked, brushing off his frayed jacket. Bonaparte's horse is small, but fast.

He laughed and tweaked my ear. "Bandits wouldn't dare lay a hand on me. Don't you know that? Where is everyone?"

Everyone: the Bonapartes, he meant—his Corsican clan. Mother Signora Letizia, jolly Uncle Fesch and all his brothers and sisters: Joseph "the Elder" and his wife Julie, Elisa "the intellectual" and her husband Félix, Pauline "the beauty" and her husband Victor—and Caroline and Joachim, of course. Is that everyone? Oh, how could I forget young Jérôme—"the scamp"? (Bonaparte has decided to send the rambunctious fifteen-year-old to sea soon because of his extravagant debts, inclination to duel and absolute disregard for any form of study.)

Lucien "the fireball" is at his country estate and Louis "the poet" is in Brest, so that makes eleven Bonapartes. Hortense, Eugène and I bring the total to fifteen. I'll have a word with my quarrelling cooks.

*April 10—a balmy spring morning at Malmaison, cows lowing, lambs bleating.*

My daughter is seventeen today! "Now you are a woman," I told her. Her eyes filled with apprehension. I pulled back the bed-curtains to reveal a mountain of parcels, an entire wardrobe in the latest fashion—a wardrobe such as a woman wears.

My chatterbox girl was momentarily speechless. Then oh, what pleasure, opening one parcel after another, exclaiming over the laces and trimmings, the flounces and frills on all the gowns. There were quite a number: three for morning wear, two for afternoon (but suitable for receiving), two silk gowns for evening, a walking gown, a ball gown and even a lovely riding habit—accompanied, of course, by a parasol and numerous bonnets, gloves and slippers.

"This is like a trousseau, Maman," Hortense said, overwhelmed. "One would think I was getting married."

"As you will *soon*, no doubt." At this her expression darkened.

It was a beautiful afternoon for a birthday fête—we dined off tables set up on the lawn. We had just finished sherbet and syrup when who should canter up the driveway but Bonaparte's young brother Louis, holding a bouquet of hyacinths aloft like a torch.

"Louis is back from Brest already?" Bonaparte asked, squinting.

Louis dismounted his lathered horse and presented the flowers to Hortense. "Love is nature's cloth, embroidered by imagination," he said, bowing like an old-fashioned knight.

"Have you been reading romantic novels, Louis?" Hortense gave him a mocking look.

"Voltaire," he said, flushing. He looked comely in a bottle-green riding jacket, his wavy chestnut hair cut to shoulder length in the style now popular with the young.

"Who is Voltaire?" Jérôme "the scamp" asked, throwing a bread roll at one of the pugs, hitting it hard on the head.

"Maybe if you listened to your tutors once in a while you'd learn," Elisa said, between hiccups.

"The flowers are lovely, Louis," I exclaimed, to soften my daughter's teasing—and divert the argumentative Bonapartes.

"You made excellent time," Bonaparte said, embracing his brother.

"Louis is a good rider," my ever-cheerful Eugène said.

"When he's not falling off," Caroline said, helping herself to the last of the cream.

"Magnifico!" Elisa's husband Félix exclaimed. (Why?)

"A fearless rider," Bonaparte said. "I owe my life to him."

"Blood is everything," Signora Letizia said, taking out her knitting.

"Salúte!" pink-cheeked Uncle Fesch said in Italian, emptying his wine glass before a servant refilled it.

"Louis has a fast horse," Joachim Murat said, twirling a pink silk tassel. "He paid a lot of money for it—several thousand francs."

"I *love* a horse with a big chest," Pauline said, pulling down her sleeves to better display her perfect white shoulders, "and *strong* flanks."

"I have dispatches for you, Napoleon," Louis said, pleased to have met with his older brother's approval. "As you thought, English warships are blockading Brest. Our ships can't get out to sea."

"Maudits anglais," Bonaparte swore under his breath.

"Maudits anglais," Pauline's husband Victor echoed.

"You've arrived just in time," I said, inviting Louis to take a seat between me and Hortense. "We're having a ball tonight."

"At which even Papa will dance," Hortense said.

"Napoleon?" Louis asked with a sceptical look.

"I can dance perfectly well." Bonaparte looked disconcerted when we all burst into laughter.

"Other than *country* dances?" Hortense teased.

"Bah! What's wrong with country dances? They're jolly—and at least one gets a little exercise," Bonaparte said, and with that he pulled Hortense to her feet and spun her about the lawn, humming loudly (but tunelessly), while two pugs scurried after. I turned to see the servants hiding behind the bushes, doubled over laughing.

*April 11, early evening (beautiful weather).*
Proudly, we bid our soldiers adieu this morning—Eugène, Louis and Joachim, each sitting on his horse so proudly, riding off to join their regiments. (Joachim has embellished his uniform with pink gewgaws—even his horse's saddle blanket is pink. Bizarre.)

It is sad to see so many empty chairs around the table. Bonaparte mopes. He wishes he were riding out with the men. He will be joining them soon enough, I know.

*April 12—back in Paris (alas).*
Caroline has been miserable, stomping from one room to the next. I have been trying to console her, assuming that she was melancholy because her husband was gone, but it turned out she is furious because he hasn't been assigned an army of his own.

"Maybe she's a little sensitive right now because she's . . . *you know*," Hortense whispered to me from the harpsichord bench.

"Is she?"

"She must be. She told me they . . . *you know*, all night long." Hortense struck a chord, flushing furiously.

*April 28—Malmaison.*
I am writing this at the breakfast table to the sound of Caroline retching.

*Noyon*
*Chère Maman,*
   *We were days in the rain from Corbeil. Soon I expect we'll be setting out over the Alps to Italy.\**
   *The renovations at Malmaison that you described amaze me: arcades and moving mirrors? I like the idea of one big room on the ground floor instead of three little ones—better for a ball.*
   *I'm surprised Hortense has rejected Citoyen Mun—I thought he was an excellent choice. I'll think of some other possibilities.*
   *A million kisses,*
                              *Your loving son, Eugène (Captain Beauharnais)*

*April 30.*
At a salon last night, Caroline's singing was received with audible snickers. "Someone should tell her not to perform with such zest," a woman whispered to me. "People will think her impure."
   The comment angered me, and I rose to Caroline's defence—Bonaparte "zest," after all, has saved the nation—but, in truth, someone does need to have a word with the girl. She tries so hard to be noticed, but her dramatic grimaces, her quivering lips and panting sighs are only viewed as laughable.

*May 1—Malmaison, blowing rain.*
When I suggested to Caroline that her "wonderful" singing would be better appreciated if she were to perform quietly, without embellishments, she turned on me!
   "I don't need *your* help," she said with such spite that I was left speechless.

---

\* *"Italy" in 1800 comprised various independent states, including several northern territories claimed by Austria.*

"Sometimes I don't know what to make of Caroline," I told Mimi later.

"She's dangerous, Yeyette," Mimi said. "I saw it in her cards."

I had to laugh. When I think of Caroline, I imagine a plump powder-puff of a girl. Jealous, yes, and temperamental, certainly—but *dangerous*?

*[Undated]*

Mimi slipped me a folded note with my morning cup of hot chocolate. "Just as I thought," she said.

*I workd in the Dineing Room all week. Shee say to her Husband they wood have Everything but for the Old Woman & her 2 Children. Shee say the 1st Consul must get rid of Her. Shee say Shee will find a way.*

"I don't understand," I said, perplexed. The note was crudely written on the brown paper used to wrap fish in. "Who is this 'shee'?"

"Madame Caroline." Mimi looked smug. "I told you she's not to be trusted."

I reread the note. Was I "the old woman"? "Who wrote this?"

"One of Madame Caroline's footmen."

"You've got a *spy* in Caroline's household?"

"Old Gontier's nephew. He can be trusted."

"Mimi, that's not a good idea! Please—don't do it again."

"So I have to pay him myself?"

"How much?" I said with a laugh. (Fifty francs—mon Dieu.)

*11:20 P.M.*

I keep rereading the spy note, puzzling over it. Can I believe it? Can I afford not to?

*May 3.*

I am writing this in the downstairs drawing room at Malmaison, at my lovely new escritoire—mahogany, with Egyptian touches in gold, *very* elegant. It is after three o'clock. Soon I'll go down to the kitchen to see how the dinner preparations are coming along. Quite well, I suspect, from the fragrant scent of roast chicken (Bonaparte's favourite) that fills the air. I just sent two of the domestics to ride out to meet Bonaparte on the road. I worry about his safety, frankly. "But whatever you do, don't let on that I sent you to meet him," I warned them.

*May 4—still at Malmaison (we return to Paris in the morning).*
Old Gontier, my man-of-all-work, informed me around one this afternoon that the stonemasons had left, that the mantel was finally finished.

At last, I thought. The stone dust has been driving us mad.

"But Agathe says to come see," Gontier said. "There's something she wants to show you."

The mantel looked excellent, although the scullery maid had quite a job to do cleaning up the dust. "You wanted me to see something, Agathe?"

She got up off her knees, wiping her hands on her stained apron. "This." She pointed to a snuffbox on the desk.

I recognized the intricate mother-of-pearl inlay in a Roman motif. "It's Bonaparte's."

"But the First Consul's is chipped on one corner."

She was right. All Bonaparte's possessions are scarred in some way. "Perhaps someone left it here," I suggested, feeling its weight. But why an exact replica? "Agathe, could you ask the groom to send for Fouché?" I said, carefully putting the box back down.

"The Minister of Police?"

Yes, I nodded. My old friend—the man who knows everything.

"Poison," Fouché said, prying the snuffbox open with his long yellow thumbnail. "When inhaled, it will cause the victim to expire within one revolution of the minute hand."

Poison! I sat down, opened my fan. If it hadn't been for Agathe's apprehension, her sharp eye . . . ! "Are you sure, Fouché?" Had murderers been in our midst—in our *home*? The masons, perhaps? I'd offered them refreshment, inquired after their well-being.

"Someone went to some trouble making a replica." Fouché traced the inlay with his finger. "The First Consul must be notified immediately."

"He's here now," I said, hearing a horse. Only Bonaparte comes through the gate at a gallop—he knows no other pace.

"*Poison* in my snuffbox?" Bonaparte scoffed.

"It's not really yours, Bonaparte," I told him. "It just looks like yours."

"It's an excellent reproduction. Who made it?"

"One of the stonemasons, likely," Fouché said.

"But *why*?"

"Certainly, there are any number of possibilities, First Consul. Revolutionaries long for a return to anarchy and the Royalists for a return to monarchy. Extremists of every persuasion want you dead. It is, one might say, the price of your popularity."

"It looks like snuff." Bonaparte started to take a pinch. I grabbed his hand. "I'm not *that* easy to kill off," he said, laughing.

"Bonaparte, at the very least you shouldn't ride alone," I told him. "You should have someone with you." And guards at all times, and . . .

"Bah!" Bonaparte said, glowering.

"First Consul, with respect, I suggest you consider it," Fouché said. "A minimum of precaution would put your wife at ease. For some reason, she prefers you alive."

"I refuse to be coddled like some feckless ninny!"

"Don't worry," Fouché told me later, on leaving. "We'll protect him. We'll just have to make sure he doesn't know it."

*In which I try (but fail) to accept*

*May 5, 1800, 11:45 P.M.—Tuileries Palace.*
Bonaparte and I had just returned from the Opéra when his sister and brother were announced.

"Joseph has something urgent to discuss with you before you go," Caroline said. Bonaparte's older brother Joseph stood behind her, dressed entirely in pale yellow brocade.

"Before I go where?" Bonaparte demanded.

"To Italy," Caroline answered, offering her snuffbox to her brothers before taking a pinch herself. (She claims it calms her sickness of the stomach, which has been violent throughout her first month.)

"How did you find out I'm leaving? No one is supposed to know."

"What we want to know is what happens if you get killed," Caroline said, refusing my offer of a chair. Joseph sat down instead, his hands pressed between his knees.

"If I die—or rather, *when* I die—I'll be put in a coffin," Bonaparte said evenly, reaching for a paper knife and slicing open an envelope.

"It's not a jesting matter, Napoleon! Who would run this country?" Caroline paced with her hands behind her back (as Bonaparte so often does), her masculine movements at odds with her ensemble: a gauze creation wildly embellished with bows and wired flowers.

"According to the Constitution, the Second Consul," Bonaparte said, looking up from the letter.

"Cambacérès?" Joseph's voice was tinged with disgust.

"*That* would set an interesting example for the nation," Caroline said scornfully. "Imagine—the French Republic led by a man who claims that a country is governed by good dinner parties, whose passions run to food, expensive wine and young men."

"Second Consul Cambacérès is a highly capable individual." Bonaparte crumpled the letter and hurled it into the roaring fire.

Oh-oh, I thought. I rang for the butler: a collation. *Anything*.

"Your successor must be within the clan," Caroline said, squaring her shoulders.

"And I am the eldest," Joseph said, scratching the end of his nose.

Bonaparte looked at his brother and laughed. "*You* want my job, Joseph? You don't know what's involved. You'd have to rise before eleven. You might actually have to work a day or two."

"It is our right!" Caroline said, her cherub cheeks pink, her eyes blazing.

"*My* right," Joseph said.

"The French Republic is not a family fiefdom!" Bonaparte exploded.

By the time the butler arrived with a tray of wine and sweetmeats, they had departed in a temper. Mon Dieu.


*6:30 in the morning (cold).*
Bonaparte left before dawn. "I'll be back in a month, I promise," he said, pulling a greatcoat on over his consul's uniform.

"Please, Bonaparte, take me with you." My trunk was packed!

"I need you in Paris, Josephine. No matter what you hear, you must act as if all is well."

"Even if I hear what?" I asked warily.

"Even if you hear that I've been defeated, or that I've been killed. Even if you hear that your son has been—"

*No!* I put my fingers over his mouth.

"The public will be watching. They will assume that you know. *Always* tell people I am victorious."

"But what if the rumours are true?"

"I'm not going to be defeated. I have you, don't I? My guardian angel," he said, kissing me tenderly—his good-luck kiss, he calls it.

*Le 21 Floréal,\* Geneva*
*I love you very much. My Josephine is very dear to me. A thousand kindnesses*
*to the little cousin. Advise her to be wise, do you hear? N.*


*May 14—Malmaison.*
Hortense squinted to make out Bonaparte's messy scrawl. "I think that
says 'little cousin,' Maman." She frowned. "What little cousin?"

"Are you sure that's what it says?" I asked, taking the letter back—
flushing, I confess. Bonaparte has a habit of referring to a very private
part of me by code name. "It must mean something else," I said, turning
so that she might not see my smile.


*May 24, 1800, Aosta*
*Chère Maman,*

*A quick note just to let you know that we are over the Alps. The passage*
*took five days. It was icy—we literally slid into Italy! So large an army has*
*not crossed the Saint-Bernard Pass since the days of Charlemagne. It made*
*me realize how much can be accomplished by a leader who has perseverance*
*and knows his own mind. You know of whom I speak.*

> *Your devoted son, Eugène*
*Note—Citoyen Henri Robiquet is a good possibility.*


*May 30—Paris.*
"My brother has requested that I give you thirty thousand francs out of
his account, Madame," Joseph said with a hint of a bow. "I thought it
wise to take care of the matter before I made my departure." Belatedly,
he removed his hat and stuck it under his arm.

"You're leaving, Joseph?"

"I'm departing for Italy this afternoon."

---

\* *May 10. A new calendar had been established during the Revolution. The months were
named after the natural world. (Floréal, for example, meant month of flowers.) The weeks
were ten days long and ended with "Décadi," the day of rest. Confusion resulted because people
continued to use the traditional calendar.*

"You'll be seeing Bonaparte? If only I had known—I could have accompanied you."

"It was an abrupt decision."

"Is there a problem?" I asked, suddenly fearful.

"My brother Napoleon may die."

I felt for the back of a chair to steady myself. "Whatever do you mean?"

"And Lucien has claimed the right to succession."

"Lucien *Bonaparte*? What right?" I asked, confused. Anyway, wasn't Lucien in mourning for his wife?

"Exactly! Lucien may be Minister of the Interior, but I am thirty-two and Lucien has only just turned twenty-five. I am the eldest. It is *my* right, not his. This must be settled immediately, before Napoleon is killed in battle."

"Oh," I said weakly. "Of course."


*June 14, Saint-Germain-en-Laye*
*Chère Madame Bonaparte,*

*I know how busy you are these days with official and unofficial duties, but perhaps you could spare a moment of your time for your poor aunt and her ailing husband? The Marquis has taken a turn. If you are unable to call, at least pray for him.*

*Your godmother, Aunt Désirée*


*June 17—Saint-Germain.*
Aunt Désirée met me at the door, her face white with rice powder. "Thank God you're here! The Marquis is dying—from strawberries, of all things."

"Aunt Désirée, please don't alarm me. Are you serious?" I don't know why the possibility of the old Marquis's demise surprised me. We'd celebrated his eighty-seventh birthday not long ago. It was a miracle he was alive, but because he had lived so long, I'd come to think he would always be with us.

"Oh yes, I assure you, he is at the heavenly gates. My goodness, but it's a hectic business. The doctor has been here three times today already, and each time costs eleven livres—I mean francs. What *do* we call money now? I wish they'd stop changing the names of things. Perhaps you could have a word with your husband about it."

"It is francs now." The air was as thick as that in a hothouse. There were fresh-cut flowers on every surface. "Did you get my letter about Eugène being safely over the Alps?"

"And that's another thing," Aunt Désirée said, her hand on the stair railing. "If we're at war with England, why are we fighting Austria? And if we're fighting Austria, why are we fighting in Italy?"

"It's hard to explain," I said, following Aunt Désirée's ample posterior up the stairs. How did we get onto politics? And what about the Marquis! "The flowers are beautiful," I observed, changing the subject.

"The mayor of Saint-Germain sends us a fresh bouquet every day," Aunt Désirée said, her taffeta skirts swishing with a voluptuous languor I found disconcerting, under the circumstances. "Monsieur Pierre, we call him. He and the Marquis played piquet together every evening—until the Marquis ate all those strawberries and started dying, that is," she said, coming to a stop in front of the Marquis's bedchamber, catching her breath. "Monsieur Pierre won every game, and so that's why he sends flowers."

"Oh," I said, trying to figure out the logic.

"The doctor applied leeches to the Marquis's stomach and then a laxative blister, which very nearly carried him off right then and there," Aunt Désirée hissed, so that a maid dusting the wainscotting should not hear. "Frankly, the doctor is a simpleton! He objects to the turpentine enemas I give the Marquis, when it's perfectly obvious that I've been keeping my husband alive all these years with them."

*Turpentine?*

"Mixed with snail water," she assured me, her hand on the crystal doorknob, "which I make with sweet wine from the Canary Islands—but where am I supposed to buy Canary wine now? If I'd known there was going to be war with England again, I'd have bought a supply. Maybe next time your husband decides to make war, he can let me know ahead of time."

Aunt Désirée had so many misconceptions, I didn't know where to begin. "Bonaparte tried to get England to agree to a peace, but—"

"The solution is plain to see, my dear. If we gave the Pretender his rightful throne back, England would leave us alone."

Put a Bourbon king back on the throne? Had we gone through the Revolution for nothing? "Aunt Désirée, it's not—"

"I don't care what people say," Aunt Désirée said with conviction. "Too much freedom is not a good thing. What's wrong with feudalism? It's impossible to get good help these days, for one thing. Marquis de Beauharnais," she yelled, throwing open the door. "It's Rose to see you. You remember: *Yeyette.* Or Josephine, as she's calling herself now."

The Marquis, sunk deep into the centre of a thick feather bed, turned his head slowly. "You know—Madame *Bonaparte*," Aunt Désirée yelled in his ear.

"Bon à Part Té!" the dear man croaked.

*June 18—still in Saint-Germain.*
I'm taking a quiet moment to reflect (strengthen). The Marquis went quietly—"Like a lamp without oil," Aunt Désirée said—in the arms of his wife and his son François. Even dear old Aunt Fanny managed to arrive "in time," dressed for the occasion in a sequined ball gown of tattered ruffles.

The Marquis's last words were whispered to me: "Marry Hortense to a man with good teeth." I told Aunt Désirée that he said, "I married a good woman."

I'm surprised, frankly, to feel so overcome. The Marquis had a good long life, and he didn't suffer. May God be with him, may he rest in peace.

*June 21—back in Paris.*
A mounted courier sent by the Minister of Police brought me back to Paris in a state of alarm. "You look pale," Fouché observed, on greeting me.

"I'm anxious, I confess." Paris seemed deserted. "Why are the streets so empty?" And why had he sent for me?

"Everyone has headed south in the expectation of hearing news from

Italy," he said, tugging at his stained cuffs. My friend was expensively attired, but even so the effect managed to be shoddy.

"What news?"

"The city is rife with rumours. In every café in the Faubourg Saint-Antoine idlers are claiming that your husband's army has been defeated in Italy. The opposition is openly making plans to snatch the Republic from the grasp of 'the Corsican'—as they call the First Consul."

"Bonaparte has been defeated?" How was that possible?

"As well, there are rumours—false, no doubt—of the First Consul's death."

I put my hand to my heart. *Rumours*, he'd said. "Is nothing known? Have there been any reports?"

"There *has* been a setback, apparently."

"Fouché, *please*, be honest with me," I said, my voice tremulous. "Is it possible that the stories are true?"

"It would be misleading to deny it." Fouché cleared his throat. "You should know that there is also talk of your son—of his death," he added quietly.

I clasped the arms of my chair. I would not be able to endure such a loss!

"It's only gossip," Fouché assured me, handing me a crumpled cambric handkerchief. "You must not dwell on it. All eyes will be on you tonight."

The reception for the foreign ambassadors! "Minister Fouché, I can't possibly go. I've already sent a message to the Minister of Foreign Affairs explaining that there has been a death in my family, that I am unable to do the honours. And now, what with this news . . ."

"But you *must* be there. The factions are poised, ready to attack. At the least hint that the First Consul has fallen, the nation will be plunged into civil war." At this Fouché's eyes widened. "Which is why we are counting on *you* to play the part of Victory."


*Nearly 2:00 in the morning.*
I recalled Hortense's acting lessons as I spoke my lines, presenting the backs of my hands, elevating them on the word "victory," my eyes

sweeping the room as my arms gradually ascended to the highest point. "The First Consul is not only alive, but victorious!"

Following a measured applause, I turned away (trembling). Had they believed me?

"I think so," Fouché said, without moving his lips.

It was into this strained atmosphere that a messenger was announced shortly after midnight. My heart jumped when I saw that it was Moustache, Bonaparte's courier. Grinning under the impressive facial appendage which had earned him his nickname, the mud-splattered rider laid two tattered Austrian flags at my feet. Bonaparte *had* been victorious!

*June 22, Sunday.*
Salvoes of artillery announced the victory at noon. Giddy with delirium, the servants danced down the halls. "The Funds have gone up seven points," Mimi announced, calculating an excellent profit.

*Milan*
*Chère Maman,*

*Before the Austrians knew it, we were upon them! I led a charge and captured an Austrian officer—che buona fortuna! Papa has promoted me to head of my squadron.*

*We had a good skirmish in spite of the difficulties. The plains of Marengo were not very good for cavalry—too many streams and ditches. Pegasus was cut on the flank but will heal—luckily, for many horses were lost. I was fortunate to get away with only two sabre cuts on my saddle cloth.*

*The citizens of this country have hailed us as heroes—you should see the celebrating!*

*Papa said to tell you he will write soon.*

*A million kisses,*

*Your proud son, Eugène*
*Note—It's true what they say, Maman: Italian women are very pretty.*

*June 24.*
"I'm told that the people of Milan have gone mad with gratitude, that the women literally throw themselves at the feet of our soldiers," the artist Isabey said, studying his cards.

"Italian women are *so* hot-blooded," the actor Talma said.

"All women have a weakness for a conqueror," the writer Madame de Souza said, artfully using her cards as a fan.

"Oh?" I said, pulling in my winnings. Bonaparte has not been writing.


*July 2, or rather July 3, after 3:00 in the morning (can't sleep).*
Bonaparte returned quietly, before midnight. Within an hour, crowds had gathered in the gardens, men, women and children waving flambeaux: an eerie, ghostly sight.

"We rejoice in you," I said, wrapping my arms around my husband, holding him. Holding him.


*July 4.*
Bonaparte is home; he is victorious, all is well. Why, then, do I feel so melancholy—so alone?


*July 5—Malmaison for the day.*
"How *are* you, darling?" my dear friend Thérèse asked, straightening her wig of infantine blond—her disguise.* I must have sighed heavily, for she spread her bejewelled fingers and exclaimed, "Mon Dieu, that bad?"

"Can't I hide anything from you, Mama Tallita?" Thérèse and I have been through much together. One might even say she saved my life. Certainly, she enriches it with her wit and wisdom—and abundant heart.

"You know better than to even try," she said, tapping my knuckles with her painted fan.

---

* *Thérèse was separated from her husband (Tallien) and living openly with a married man (Ouvrard), by whom she had a number of children. Publicly, she was perceived as a "fallen woman," and Napoleon did not want Josephine to associate with her. Nevertheless, the two friends continued to meet secretly at Malmaison.*

I confessed the reason for my depression of spirits: my suspicion that Bonaparte was having an amourette with another woman. "Since his return from Italy, he has been curt with me, impatient without reason." Thérèse winced. "You've heard something?" I asked.

"It's just a rumour—something about that Italian singer from Milan."

"La Grassini." Of course! Young and voluptuous, La Grassini is renowned for her passionate nature, her angelic voice. Two years ago I arranged for her to sing for us in Italy. I remember Bonaparte's enthusiasm, remember the buxom Italian singer's caressing eyes. Bonaparte had been oblivious to her all-too-obvious invitation—then.

*July 6, 4:15 P.M.—Paris.*
"Is it true that the prima donna of La Scala has come to Paris?"

"La Grassini?" Fouché withdrew a battered tin snuffbox from his vest pocket. "She arrived in a carriage drawn by eight black horses, rather hard to miss. All the people of Paris saw her."

"And what else have all the people of Paris seen?"

He gazed at me with his heavy-lidded eyes. "Perhaps you should first tell me what you yourself see."

"It is natural to become watchful, when suspicions are aroused." I paused, turning my wedding ring. It had become oblong, rather than round; it fit my finger perfectly. Too perfectly, perhaps. I could no longer remove it. "Do you know what I would dislike? I would hate to be the last person to know if my husband were . . ." I felt my cheeks becoming heated.

"Exercising the right of kings?"

I nodded. More and more, I was learning about the "right of kings." I counted silently to three and then looked up at him. "No doubt you would know."

"It is my business to know." Fouché spit into a spittoon. "As you suspect," he said, wiping his mouth on his sleeve, "your husband has fallen for La Grassini's charms."

"A soldier's wife understands these things," I managed to say. "It will blow over, like a squall."

"You are wise, Madame, the perfect wife."

*[Undated]*
The perfect wife is angry! The perfect wife spent a fortune this afternoon, ordering five hats, six pairs of gloves, four pairs of slippers and two pairs of boots, not to mention a number of small linens in fine cambric, embroidered and laced and beribboned. Not to mention a new gown by Leroy, the most celebrated designer in Paris.

*July 7, 3:45 P.M.—hot!*
"A Bastille Day ensemble? A gown for the wife of the victor?" Leroy's eyes glazed over, as if a vision had come to him, a vision of mystical dimensions. "Mais oui! I see antique ivory gauze, *swirls* of cascading silk with appliquéd gold laurel leaves, a *plush* golden velvet shawl, embroidered in gold and edged with ermine. Laced slippers, long gold gloves with pearl buttons—of course!—a bandeau of laurel leaves made of pearls . . ."

"Perfect." *Wife of the victor.*

"But Madame Josephine," Leroy said, tugging on the knot of his starched azure neckcloth, "the First Consul is frugal, and . . ."

The *frugal* First Consul is spending twenty thousand francs a month on a mistress, I happen to know. "You were saying, Citoyen?"

"Well, it's only fair to warn you that ermine is . . . Well, right now I'm afraid it is perhaps a little *dear*, perhaps too . . . ?"

"Spare no expense."

*July 9—Tuileries.*
Madame de Souza announced at whist this afternoon that after the age of thirty a woman cannot expect to have first place in her husband's heart, that she should be content to be second.

"That would be worse than death itself," I said heatedly (losing the round).

*July 10—Malmaison (bright moon, dark thoughts).*
"I hate to tell you this, darling, but she's right," Thérèse said, giving me a vial of Compound Spirit of Lavender—a remedy for women feeling a

great sinking. "If it's not La Grassini, it's bound to be some other trollop. Husbands are like that. It's one of the things a wife must accept. Has he been doing his duty by you?"

I nodded. If anything, Bonaparte's attentions have been more ardent than before.

"Then what do you have to complain of? Just because he has a mistress doesn't mean he doesn't love you."

Love? Bonaparte had not loved me—he'd *worshipped* me. "You don't understand!" How could I possibly explain what it was like to be loved by a man such as Bonaparte, to be his muse, his angel, the object of his all-consuming passion? Am I to lie beside him now while he dreams of La Grassini, smell her musky scent on him, hear the joy in his voice as he sings, knowing that it is love for another that inspires him? "Accept it, Thérèse? Never!"

"Do you want your husband's enduring love?"

"Of course," I said angrily.

"Then repeat after me: I *accept*—with love, grace and magnanimity." She laughed. "And no gritting of teeth."


*[Undated]*
Three hats, two gowns, seven pairs of slippers, five pairs of silk stockings, two shawls, a necklace of rubies and pearls.


*July 14, Bastille Day, almost midnight.*
It was almost time to leave for the Bastille Day fête when Eugène arrived from Milan. "You made it!" I threw my arms around my son. He smelled of horses—horses and campfire smoke.

"Oh là là, Maman!"

"Is something wrong?" I asked, alarmed by his outburst.

"No, not at all. It's *you*. You look . . . beautiful!"


Eugène and his chasseurs escorted Bonaparte and me to the Invalides. A deafening cheer went up as we pulled through the gates of the Champs-de-Mars, the enormous field a sea of faces.

Inside, the Invalides was packed, the air oppressive. I was moved to tears as Eugène solemnly presented the captured enemy flags. Then Mademoiselle Grassini sang, filling the vault with (I had to admit) heavenly sounds. It pleased me to note that she has developed a double chin and was wearing too much Spanish Red.*

* *Spanish Red: red dye in a horsehair pad, used as a blusher.*

• *36* •

# In which we are very nearly killed

*July 22, 1800—Paris.*
At the Théâtre Français tonight, the police apprehended a man aiming at Bonaparte with a peashooter.

Bonaparte laughed when Fouché informed him. "You're serious—a peashooter? They're going to have to do better than that."

*August 7.*
I can't sleep. This morning ruffians were caught lurking in the quarry on the high road to Malmaison. Their intention was to attack Bonaparte as we returned to Paris.

*August 9—very hot.*
Fouché sidled up to me at tonight's salon. "No, don't tell me," I said, my heart jumping in my chest. "I can't take it!"

"Calm yourself. I merely wish to inform you that La Grassini is discontented with your husband."

"Oh, thank God! I thought perhaps there had been another attempt on Bonaparte's life." In every shadow I saw a man with a knife. The slightest noise confirmed my fears. "What did you say about La Grassini?"

"She complained of the First Consul at the salon of the Minister of Foreign Affairs last night."

"*You* were at Talleyrand's?" Talleyrand and Fouché are arch-enemies.

"My spies keep me informed. La Grassini confided to those assembled at the whist table that the First Consul's lovemaking was . . . *unsatisfying* was how she put it." He pronounced the word "unsatisfying" with unseemly relish.

"I take no comfort whatsoever in her indiscretion." How dare she!


*October 10—Paris, very late.*

On returning from the Opéra tonight, Bonaparte and I found Fouché waiting for us in the Yellow Salon, tapping his foot. The Minister of Police was not happy. The commotion we'd heard during the performance had been his men apprehending assassins armed with daggers and pistols—men intent on murdering Bonaparte!

I scooped up my train and sat down on the edge of a stool. "Assassins?" But what shocked me even more was that Bonaparte had known about the plot for weeks, but had not informed Fouché, thinking that he would lure the conspirators out into the open himself. "Bonaparte, you knew those men would be at the Opéra?" I was stunned—and *angry*. How could he be so cavalier? Not only had he put himself at risk, he'd put *me* at risk as well.

"Your husband not only knew the assassins would be there tonight," Fouché said, "he arranged to provide them with the money they needed in order to carry out their scheme. Have you any idea, First Consul, how close you came to getting murdered?"

I trembled for Fouché. Bonaparte does not take a scolding well, however justified.

"The plan worked, Minister Fouché." Bonaparte paced under the crystal chandelier. "I'm fed up with Revolutionaries intent on my demise—and so I took action. If this little episode proved anything, it proved that there is a great deal going on in this city that you are entirely unaware of. You don't know anything!"

"Respectfully, First Consul, I know a very great deal," Fouché said, his lips thin. "I know, for example, that a man in a greatcoat regularly emerges from the palace, gets into a hired fiacre and goes to 762 Rue Caumartin, an abode which he has leased for the use of a well-applauded

Italian singer. A short time after, the man in the greatcoat reappears and returns to the palace. Within an hour of his departure, a tall young man, a violinist, is seen to enter the home of the energetic Grassini, who—"

"Get out!" Bonaparte kicked a burning log.

I followed Fouché into the antechamber. "How could you do that to him!"

"Devotion wears many masks. The First Consul endangers himself by such conduct."

"You humiliate him in the name of duty?" I turned on my heel, trembling with emotion.

I found Bonaparte in the bedchamber, sitting on our big bed, unlacing his boots himself. "We can pretend I was not witness to that scene," I said, sitting down at my embroidery frame by the fire.

"Just as you have pretended not to know, Josephine?"

I picked up my embroidery needle, checked the colour of the thread, a shimmering light blue, the colour of a summer sky. My hand was shaking. "Yes." I put down the needle. "*Please*, Bonaparte, get up and pace the way you usually do. I don't like it when you are so still."

"I'm surprised you aren't angry."

"I've been angry. Now I'm angry at *her*." La Signorina Grassini had not only seduced my husband—worse, she had made a cuckold of him.

"I've been a fool."

I put aside my frame and went to him. "Don't be angry at Fouché," I said, taking his hands in mine—his soft, feminine hands of which he is so proud. "He spoke out of devotion for you."

"Do you know how much I love you, Josephine?" The firelight danced in his grey eyes.

Later, in Bonaparte's arms, I took advantage of his gratitude to persuade him to take at least a few precautions against attack. And no more trying to ferret out assassins on his own! Reluctantly, he consented. "You love me too much," he complained.

"We all do!"

*October 18—Tuileries Palace, Paris.*

Early this morning, Fouché was shown into our bedchamber. I sat up, alarmed. It was dark still. "This must be urgent, Citoyen Minister of Police," Bonaparte said, instantly alert.

"A bomb stuffed with nails and grapeshot exploded behind the Salpêtrière convent a few hours ago. The culprits got away, but I have reason to think they had you in mind, First Consul. I thought you would want to know."

"Mon Dieu, Bonaparte—a *bomb*?" Would there never be an end to it?


*Christmas Eve—Paris.*

The worst has happened. At least we are alive, I remind myself.

It is three in the morning now as I write this. I'm in the little sitting room next to our bedchamber. The embers cast a dying light. I've given up trying to sleep. Perhaps if I write it out, the memory of this evening will stop haunting me.

Caroline, eight months along now, joined Hortense, Bonaparte and me for dinner. We were looking forward to going to the opening of Haydn's *La Création*—all of us but Bonaparte, that is, who announced that he'd changed his mind, he had work to do. (Even on Christmas Eve.)

"Please come," I begged him, knowing how disappointed the public would be not to see him, how unhappy they would be to see only *me*. "You've been working so hard lately." Day and night, his energy was boundless. "It's going to be splendid." (Oh, recalling those words! If anything had happened to him, if he had been killed!) "It would please me," I said finally, knowing he would not refuse.


The coaches were lined up in the courtyard in readiness. A footman jumped to open the door of the first carriage for Bonaparte and his aides. "The ladies will follow with Colonel Rapp," Bonaparte instructed César, his coachman, who grinned broadly, clearly in his cups. César cracked his whip and the horses charged out the gate.

"We do not need to follow *quite* so quickly," I instructed our driver as Hortense and Caroline were handed in. I was about to follow them when

Colonel Rapp suggested that my shawl, which is embroidered with an Egyptian motif, would look lovely arranged in the Egyptian manner, tied at the waist. I paused to change it. We owe our lives to this delay!

This next part is painful to recount. As our carriage turned the corner onto Rue Nicaise, we were thrown into the air by an explosion. Colonel Rapp yelled at us to cover our heads. I remember the sound of timbers cracking, the strong smell of gunpowder.

"It's a plot to murder Bonaparte!" I cried out. (I'm ashamed to admit that I lost my head.) There was rubble all over the street, and what seemed to be a very great number of people, some writhing, some lying still—*bodies*, I realized with a shock. And then, slowly, a chorus of cries filled the air.

Suddenly our coach was flying pell-mell. "Stop!" I heard myself scream. The horses had bolted, taken the bit. "Turn back, they've killed him!" The memory of it makes me tremble even now.

Our carriage finally pulled to a stop in the Tuileries courtyard. "You will excuse me, ladies?" Colonel Rapp said, struggling with the carriage door mechanism. He hit it with his fist and jumped out.

It seems a dream to me now—much of it in fog, yet other scenes sharp, the memory painful. "There has been an explosion on the Rue Nicaise," I heard the coachman say. "Grand Dieu, things were flying!"

I recall someone asking if the First Consul had been injured.

"I don't think so," our driver answered. "He went on ahead."

"Are you all right?" I asked the girls, my voice shaky. Hortense appeared calm, though pale. "Caroline?" What a terrible thing to happen to a young woman in her delicate condition!

"Where's a footman?" Caroline said, looking out the shattered window. "Why doesn't someone come to hand us down?"

Hortense pulled a handkerchief out of her reticule. "Imagine what would have happened if we had left a few seconds earlier!"

If I hadn't stopped to rearrange my shawl, if I hadn't . . .

"It was just a house on fire," Caroline said.

A footman came running. Limping after him was a cavalier with a gash under his chin, leading his horse by the reins. "The First Consul was not injured!" the cavalier said, his voice quavering.

"Thank God," Hortense whispered.

"Are you sure?" I demanded. "Did you *see* him?"

"He is at the Opéra, Madame Bonaparte—you are to join him there. Another carriage is being prepared for you."

I was to go to the Opéra? I wasn't sure I could even walk! "Of course," I said, pulling my shawl around me, as if this was what one did after a violent explosion: one proceeded to the Opéra. A prick of pain reminded me that there was glass everywhere. "What happened? Do you know?" I asked as he handed me down. I felt tremulous, but I could stand.

"Apparently a barrel of gunpowder exploded."

"A barrel?" The explosion had lifted our carriage into the air! "Were many people hurt?" *Killed.*

"I suggest you take a different route," the soldier said over his shoulder, giving Caroline a hand.

People were crowding into the courtyard. I saw Mimi making her way through to us, wiping her hands on her apron.

"There's been an explosion!" Hortense cried out to her.

"Bonaparte's all right. I'm to join him at the Opéra."

"*You're* going, Yeyette?" Mimi asked, frowning.

"I'm fine." I needed to see Bonaparte; I needed to know he was safe.

"I'm coming with you, Maman," Hortense said, her blue eyes swimming.

"What's happened to your hand?" There was blood on her left thumb.

"It's just a little cut, from the glass."

"It has stopped bleeding," Mimi said, examining the wound. She withdrew a patch of plaster from her pocket and secured it to Hortense's hand with a handkerchief. "Stay close to your mother," I heard her whisper as a carriage pulled up beside us.

"What about me?"

"Caroline, you really must—"

"I'll look after Madame Caroline," Mimi assured me, her hand firmly on Caroline's shoulder.

"Best send for the midwife, just to be sure," I called out as we pulled away. "Madame . . . " My mind was in a fog.

"Madame Frangeau," Hortense called back as our carriage pulled into the roadway, the soldier escort riding alongside, his horse wild-eyed.

Bonaparte was sitting in the theatre box drinking an amber liquor. "Josephine," he said, standing and removing his hat. And then, with a little bow, "Is something the matter?"

Did he not know? Talleyrand caught my eye, made a gesture with his hand behind Bonaparte's back: Be quiet, stay calm, the First Consul knows, the audience is watching.

"You're just in time," Bonaparte said, turning toward the stage. Madame Barbier-Walbonne's voice filled the hall—the oratorio had begun.

I wrapped my shawl around me, as if by bundling myself tightly, I might stop the trembling. Hortense put her bandaged hand on my shoulder, to calm. I stroked her fingertips. How close death had come.


Once we were back in the privacy of our suite at the Tuileries, Bonaparte's calm gave way to fury. "Every time I turn around, someone's trying to kill me," he raged at Talleyrand. "Têtes des mules! It's all these bomb-making Revolutionaries, longing for the days of anarchy and violence, the same fanatics who were responsible for the explosion at the Salpêtrière convent, no doubt."

"*And* the Opéra plot," Talleyrand observed, propping his gold-tipped walking stick against the arm of the chair. "And likely the snuffbox plot, too, for all we know."

"This is intolerable." Bonaparte threw a log on the flaming fire, sending sparks flying.

"Did the Minister of Police ever convict any of these Revolutionaries?" Talleyrand asked. "His friends and colleagues, one might note."

"And what is that supposed to mean?" Bonaparte demanded, his fists on his hips.

"It means that Fouché should be arrested and shot, in my opinion."

Shot! Talleyrand's words shocked me.

"There has been enough bloodshed tonight, Minister Talleyrand," I was relieved to hear Bonaparte say, passing off Talleyrand's remark as a joke.

Shortly after Talleyrand left, Fouché himself was announced. "Where have you been?" Bonaparte demanded.

"At the site of the explosion, First Consul," Fouché said, touching the brim of his battered hat. "Seven killed and over twenty injured."

Mon Dieu!

"I suggest you give your drunken coachman a reward, First Consul," Fouché continued, tugging at his stained linen cuffs. "Had he not been so reckless, you would be dead. The keg of gunpowder appears to have been set intentionally."

"Damned Revolutionaries!"

"They would like to murder you, certainly, but they are not guilty of this act."

"Surely you're not going to claim that it was the work of the Royalists," Bonaparte scoffed. "Royalists may intrigue, but they do not stoop to violence."

"I say it, and what's more, I will prove it."


*January 2, 1801—Malmaison.*
"I'm so relieved you're all right, darling!" Thérèse exclaimed, removing a leather mask,* a cloak, a hat *and* a wig. "I very nearly died when I read the news-sheets." She embraced me vigorously, enveloping me in a cloud of neroli oil. "How terrifying it must have been!"

"I'm at the end of my strength," I confessed. Fouché insists that Bonaparte's Mameluke bodyguard follow him everywhere. Roustam even sleeps outside our bedchamber door at night. "As well, Fouché has posted two guards *inside* our bedroom," I told her. Every few hours they wake Bonaparte, who assigns a new password. Accustomed to sleeping on the battlefield, Bonaparte falls quickly back to sleep. I, however, lie awake all night, fears swirling, trying to ignore the presence of the guards.

Thérèse tapped a flower-shaped beauty patch stuck to her chin. "Make sure you have your doctor bleed you, but not much, just a bit. Cooling laxatives are called for—an infusion of senna with salts. It will be over soon, won't it? I heard that the police have discovered the owner of that cart."

A cart with a barrel of gunpowder in it: the "infernal machine" everyone

---

* *It was not uncommon for a woman to wear a leather mask to protect her skin from the weather.*

is calling it. "They know who he is, but they can't find him, Thérèse!" Petit François—a man with a scar over his left eye. "So long as he walks free, I cannot feel safe, no matter how many guards watch over us."

*January 6—Tuileries Palace.*
Given that human temperament is composed of four humours—blood, bile, phlegm and melancholy—I'd say that the members of Bonaparte's family have an excess of bile.

Oh, how uncharitable of me! But truly, sometimes they are too much even for Bonaparte. "I turn into a wet hen around them," he told me last night after Kings' Day with the clan—or rather Cake Day, as we're to call it now.

After sharing the latest news (the scar-faced man has yet to be found), plans for the season, and the usual discussion regarding status, money and bowels, we got onto that other clan favourite: my fertility—or lack thereof.

It began innocently enough, with Caroline announcing that her midwife had told her that her baby-soon-to-be-born is a boy.

"Because of all that red wine you've been drinking," Pauline said, resplendent in a revealing gown of white satin.

"It's the man who is supposed to drink the wine," Bonaparte said.

"That's what *I* thought." Hortense blushed.

"What would you know about such things?" Caroline said. Swathed in ruffles and sequins, her big belly prominent, she looked like a carnival balloon.

"What does it matter whether your child is a boy or not?" Elisa asked Caroline. "It won't be a Bonaparte. It will only be a Murat."

"At least that's better than a Bacchiochi," Caroline retorted.

"Magnifico!" Elisa's husband Félix exclaimed. (Why?)

"Blood is everything," Signora Letizia said, frowning at her knitting.

"Speaking of Bonaparte offspring, I have an announcement to make." Joseph pressed his hands between his knees. "*My* wife is expecting a child."

"Our prayers have been answered," Uncle Fesch sang cheerily, swirling wine in his goblet and then holding it to the light.

"Cin-cin! Cin-cin!" Everyone raised a glass.

"That's wonderful news, Julie." I caught Bonaparte's eye. If Julie and Joseph could conceive a child after years of trying, then perhaps we could, too.

"I credit the waters of Plombières," Julie told me.

"Not *my* waters?" Joseph looked pleased with his bad jest.

"Aunt Josephine already went to Plombières—in 1796," Caroline said. "It didn't help her."

"That's likely because of her age," Elisa said, holding her breath to prevent a paroxysm of hiccuping.

"Spa waters can be dangerously exciting," Uncle Fesch observed, his cheeks heated by the fumes of the wine.

"Pauline has been unable to have a child since our son was born almost three years ago," Victor Leclerc said, adjusting the set of his tricorne hat—an exact replica of Bonaparte's.

"And we've tried *everything*," Pauline said, languorously fanning herself with a peacock feather. "The doctors say I'm a mystery."

"Mystery, dear sister? Erotomaniacs are often unable to procreate." Caroline shot her sister a gloating look.

"Erotomaniacs?" Hortense looked confused.

"I'll explain later," I mouthed to her.

"*Or* it could be due to an abnormal state of the blood," Caroline observed. (Addressing me!) "Certain diseases—which I will not mention in front of Mother—are believed to inhibit conception."

"How long before dinner, Josephine?" Bonaparte asked, pacing again.

"I had thirteen children," Signora Letizia said, twirling yarn around her stiff index finger.* "Five of them died."

"A wife has a Christian obligation to produce children," Uncle Fesch said.

"Sons," Joseph said, giving his wife a tight smile.

*January 22.*
Caroline has had her baby—a boy, just as the midwife predicted. I've

---

* Due to an injury, Signora Letizia could not bend her index finger.

sent over one of our cooks. Caroline's cook has resigned in protest because Signora Letizia insists on keeping a live frog in the kitchen in case the baby shows symptoms of thrush. I pray that this does not happen, for if it does, the infant will be induced to suck on the live frog's head.

*[Undated]*
Can't sleep. Still no sign of the scar-faced man.

*January 31—Paris.*
At last! This morning, the police discovered the scar-faced man asleep in a bed in a garret. He confessed, revealing the name of the man who had paid him to explode the bomb—the name of the man who had paid him to *murder* Bonaparte. "Georges Cadoudal," Fouché said with a slow (smug) smile. "Safely in England, regrettably."

The Royalist agent! "So you were right, Fouché—it *was* a Royalist plot," I said.

"It is proverbial," Fouché said, offering Bonaparte a pinch of snuff before taking one himself. "The Seine flows and Royalists intrigue. It is the nature of things."

"Intrigue and murder are not the same, Minister Fouché." Bonaparte paced in front of the fireplace with his hands clasped behind his back. "The devil!" he cursed, halting abruptly. "England's behind this."

*In which my daughter is impossible to please*

*July 5, 1801—a hot Sunday morning at Malmaison.*
It's confirmed: Hortense, her cousin Émilie and Bonaparte's mother are coming with me to Plombières. Colonel Rapp, who is to accompany us, has just informed me that we are to be escorted by a detachment of cavalry and three aides. The last time I went to the spa, I had only Mimi for company. My life has become so complex—now we require a carriage just for our trunks of ball gowns.

*July 8 (I think)—Toul, very hot.*
We have stopped for a few moments at an inn while the horses are changed and the wheels cooled—tempers cooled. The girls are lively, Signora Letizia disapproving, Colonel Rapp ill. I endure.

*July 10—Plombières-les-Bains.*
We've arrived, at last—the trip was harrowing.*

* *Hortense and her cousin Émilie composed the following letter about the journey: "Never has there been a more agonizing journey to Plombières. Bonaparte* mère *showed courage. Madame Josephine trembled in fear. Mademoiselle Hortense and Madame Lavalette argued over a bottle of eau de Cologne. Colonel Rapp made us stop frequently in order to ease his bile. He slept while we forgot our troubles in the wine of Champagne.*

*"The second day was easier, but the good Colonel Rapp was suffering still. We encouraged him to have a good meal, but our hopes crumbled when, arriving in Toul, we found only a miserable auberge which offered nothing but a little spinach in lamp oil and red asparagus*

*July 13—Plombières-les-Bains.*

"Madame Bonaparte," the spa doctor said, regarding me with rheumy eyes, "I, more than anyone, understand the delicate nature of this subject. When the reproductive powers are defective, few women have the courage to speak to a physician. It is evidence of your sincere wish to give your husband the fruit of your love that you have returned to Plombières. The condition can be rectified, but first you must tell me *everything.*"

"Everything?" Flushing, I recounted the efforts Bonaparte and I had made to produce a child—the periods of abstinence followed by periods of coital activity, the techniques Bonaparte had undertaken in order to expel slowly, the herbs I'd taken to increase my "receptivity."

"And yet nothing." Dr. Martinet studied the thick file of papers. "From what your doctor in Paris indicates, there hasn't been a show since . . . "

"For over a year," I admitted. And that merely a hint.

"On your previous visit, we ruled out malformation of the canal. As well, the feminine characteristics are clearly in evidence." He pushed his spectacles onto the bridge of his nose. "It's therefore likely that a morbid condition of the blood is to blame."

I felt my cheeks becoming heated. Did he think I might have some shameful disease?

"A chronic decline! When the blood has become bankrupt, there often follows a failure of the reproductive function, leading to derangement." His spectacles magnified his eyes. "It is generally believed that an enfeebled uterus is the cause, but I am of the opinion that that organ is entirely dependent."

"Oh?" I said, confused.

"The causes of a uterine decline are indolence, nutritional perversion or the taking of drastic medicines."

*simmered in sour milk. (We would have loved to see the gourmets of our household seated at this disgusting meal!) We left Toul in order to eat at Nancy because we'd been starved for two days.*

*"We were joyfully welcomed when we arrived in Plombières. The illuminated village, the booming cannon, all the pretty women standing in the windows helped us not to feel sorry about being away from Malmaison.*

*"This is the exact story of our trip, certified to be true."*

Did he suspect me of indolence? "I eat well," I said, wondering what constituted nutritional perversion and whether Mimi's rabbit-bone remedy might be considered a drastic medicine. Three knife-tips of bone shaved off the ankle of a rabbit shot on one of the first three Fridays in March were believed to stimulate the uterus. (But had failed to stimulate mine, alas.)

"Of course you do, Madame Bonaparte! In *your* case, acute suppression of the menses was caused by a violent disturbance, suffered due to imprisonment during the Terror. Such derangement of the blood calls for *baths*: foot baths, sitz baths, even vapour baths are proven to be beneficial."

"I take baths daily, Dr. Martinet." A practice Mimi considered ruinous.

"And you've been ingesting the uterine tonic I prescribed?"

"The viburnum? Dutifully." I sat forward on the hard oak chair. "Dr. Martinet, may I ask you something?" I ventured hesitantly, clutching my fan. "I'm thirty-seven years old, as you know—far from young, admittedly, but not yet what one could call . . ." I paused, not knowing what word to use. "You once suggested it possible that I was in the turn of life."* And if so, could I please turn back?


*July 17.*

When not taking the waters and all manner of remedies, I'm entirely occupied with delicate and time-consuming discussions sounding out the parents of prospective husbands for my lovely but persnickety daughter. There are a few excellent possibilities. I am hopeful.


*Sunday afternoon, July 26.*

"I don't like him." Hortense crossed her arms over her chest.

"But Hortense," I said, trying not to let my exasperation show, "Eugène even recommends him. Citoyen Robiquet is a gentleman, intelligent and well-educated. He has such good manners." I felt like a fair vendor, hawking my wares. "Don't you like the way he enters a room?

---

* *Josephine began menopause in her early thirties, likely due to the trauma of her imprisonment during the Terror.*

The way he ties his neckcloth? *Very* elegant. And so charming! And from a very good family." *Wealthy.* "What do you not like about him?"

My daughter refused to say, her expression glaring defiance. Later, I learned the reason for her stubborn refusal: she'd discovered the young man rolling on the floor with one of my pugs. "Undignified," she pronounced, refusing to be swayed.

*[Undated]*
"Too short."

*[Undated]*
"Too tall."

*[Undated]*
"Too—"

"No! Don't tell me!" I clasped my hands together—hard. I felt like strangling my daughter. The objection to one young man had been that he could not dance; the problem with another was that he had eruptions on his cheek. (Only two.) And yet another wore a silly hat. (High fashion in England.) All honest young men of good family! "Let me guess." I paced in front of the fireplace, as Bonaparte does when he is angry. "He's too educated, not educated enough. Too wealthy, not wealthy enough. Too aristocratic, too common, too . . ."

Hortense's chin puckered. "My thoughts exactly!" she exploded angrily, and stomped out of the room.

I give up!

*July 29, 1801, Saint-Jean-de-Maurienne*
*Chère Maman,*
*Hortense has rejected all those suitors—even Citoyen Robiquet? I'll try to think of some other possibilities. She's not easy to please!*
*I was elated to learn that England has finally agreed to negotiate. You see?*

Papa's tactic is working: force Austria to sign a peace treaty, and then England will have to follow.

A million kisses,

Your loving son, Eugène

Note—I've sent Uncle Joseph a note of congratulations on the birth of his daughter, although a letter of condolence might have been more in keeping, knowing how much he had hoped for a son.


*August 1, very hot—Plombières.*
We're packing, getting ready to head back home. Hortense slumps about with a long face. Marry she *must.*


*August 8—Malmaison.*
Bonaparte greeted me with a lusty embrace. I feel like a field in spring—plowed and well-fertilized.


*August 17—Malmaison.*
Family gathering here tonight. Caroline brought Achille, who is seven months old already. She is feeling ill, she announced, suffering nausea and vomitings every morning. (Yes, she is with child again.)

Bonaparte held little Achille for almost one hour. My throat tightened watching him. What a good father he would be, doting and proud.

Faith, the water doctor told me. I must have faith.


*August 25, 10:15 P.M.*
Bonaparte was in a playful humour tonight as we gathered in the drawing room before dinner. Hortense (looking lovely in her new spotted silk gown trimmed with lilac ribbons) was sitting on the settee, working at her frame. "Well," Bonaparte said, reaching over to tug her ear, "I've just been to your room and read all your love letters." He often teases Hortense in this way, but this time, instead of smiling and shrugging, she made an awkward excuse and hurriedly left the room.

Bonaparte and I looked at each other: what was *that* about? When she returned for dinner, Bonaparte asked if she had secrets. "No, Papa!" she said, then chattered non-stop about her acting lessons, how much she was learning from the great actor Talma, about the ball she and Caroline had gone to the night before, so charming a fête she "almost suffocated" (the highest praise). "Both Citoyen Dupaty and Citoyen Trénis danced a quadrille with Madame Récamier," she chatted on (and on). *Everyone* said (she said), and *she* agreed, that Citoyen Trénis is a much better dancer than Citoyen Dupaty, that even Citoyen Laffitte is a better dancer than Citoyen Dupaty, and Citoyen Laffitte does not know how to make the grand bow with the hat. Citoyen Trénis's jetés have verve, she said, and although they perhaps lack in grace, his spirit is lively and vigorous, and as for . . .

After exactly fourteen minutes (as usual), Bonaparte threw down his napkin. "You'll excuse me?"

Hortense and I were left in silence. "Now," I said with a smile, passing her some bonbons on a platter, "about running off to your room so mysteriously—is there anything my daughter might want to tell her mother?"

And then, with obvious relief, Hortense confessed that Bonaparte's aide, Christophe Duroc, had slipped a letter into *Lives of the Saints*, a book she had been reading.

"*Duroc* wrote you a letter?" I asked, concerned. I don't care for Christophe Duroc (phlegm), and not just because he is known as "the procurer." He is handsome, in a fashion, and fanatically loyal to Bonaparte, but his manner is cold—I can't imagine him loving a woman. And in any case, it is improper for a young man to write a girl a letter; many a reputation has been ruined for less.

"I did not open it, Maman," Hortense hastened to assure me—but confessing that she *had* tried to read it without breaking the seal. "I only wished to see how a man proposed."

*Proposed!* "Hortense, a gentleman who respects a young woman wouldn't propose without discussing it with her parents first," I said carefully. And a gentleman who respected a girl wouldn't write to her unless they were already engaged.

*September 2—Paris.*
It has been almost one month since I returned from Plombières, and still no change. *Faith*.


*September 3.*
Bonaparte's young brother Louis has taken to joining us in the drawing room evenings, reading aloud from Young's *Night Thoughts* while Hortense sketches and I sit at my tapestry frame. (Bonaparte, of course, is usually in his cabinet immersed in work.) Now and then Louis will look up and gaze at Hortense as she applies charcoal to a self-portrait.

   I wonder—


*September 5, late afternoon.*
Is it possible that Louis is in love with Hortense? He, Bonaparte and I were enjoying a pleasant conversation yesterday evening on the subject of German literature when Hortense came into the room. Abruptly Louis stopped talking. No persuasion on our part could induce the crimson-flushed young man to continue. "The silent one," Hortense teased, oblivious to the powerful effect she has on him.


*Shortly after 2:00 A.M.—can't sleep.*
Why haven't I considered Louis before? He is twenty-four (a good age), serious in his demeanour, not unattractive, intelligent. Educated, literary. Since his fall from a horse in Italy, his health has been a concern—he uses his right hand with increasing difficulty—but it is not a congenital problem and will no doubt improve with treatment. He's a bit moody, sometimes, but gentle (he dotes on his mongrel water spaniel). Generous features, a nice height. Excellent teeth.


*September 8.*
I've been to see Madame Campan for advice on staff. As a former lady-in-waiting to Queen Marie Antoinette, she is invaluable, but as Hortense's

former schoolmistress, she is even more so. I told her all I've been going through trying to find a suitable husband for Hortense, all the excellent young men who have been introduced to my daughter, how she has rejected them all. I told Madame Campan my concerns: that Hortense has formed an ideal in her mind that no man can live up to, that the novels she reads have given her romantic notions, that she is intent on a love marriage, a practice that is becoming more and more common, true, but so often ends in misery.

Madame Campan looked alarmed. "A *love* marriage is out of the question," she said firmly, smoothing her black gown, which was modest in design, without frippery or devices. "Young people are swayed by emotion—they are unable to choose wisely. Your daughter is intelligent. I am confident she will come to the conclusion that the French system is superior to any other. Who do you have in mind?"

I told her that although I'd not yet discussed it with Bonaparte, I was coming to the conclusion that his brother Louis might be ideal.

Madame Campan sat back with a satisfied look. "I was going to suggest that you consider Louis. Even if he were a repulsive candidate, I would recommend him, for the benefits to you, your husband—indeed, the nation—are abundantly clear to all concerned."

*Abundantly clear.* "Certainly, but—"

"But fortunately, he is not a repulsive candidate. Louis is a reflective individual. He is kind and has simple tastes, as does Hortense. They share a poetic sensibility. And his feelings for your daughter?"

"Frankly, I'm beginning to suspect Louis may be in love with her."

"They would have handsome children."

Oh yes! And what a joy it would be for Bonaparte and for me. Their children would unite us, console us if we are never able to . . .

September 8—Paris.
"Josephine?" Bonaparte nudged my shoulder. "Are you awake? I've been thinking: what about Louis? As a possible . . . *you know*, for Hortense."

"What a good idea!" I said, wrapping my arms around him. "Why didn't I think of it?"

*September 10.*

"Bonaparte, we must do something about Hortense and Louis."

"Do what?" Bonaparte asked, closing the book he was reading, a history of the Emperor Charlemagne, holding his place with his finger.

"You know—what you talked about."

"That's a woman's job," he said, opening up the book again. (Breaking its spine.)

"But someone needs to talk to Louis, and really, it should be you."

"What do I know of such matters?"

"More than you think," I said with a smile.


*[Undated]*

"So I talked to my brother." Bonaparte sat down beside my toilette table, examined my gown (approvingly), the embroidered lawn, the décolleté. "Louis *is* in love with—"

"Bonaparte!" I hissed, rolling my eyes in the direction of my hairdresser.

Citoyen Duplan laughed, fluffing out my side curls. He'd persuaded me to try a rhubarb and white wine tint, which gave my chestnut hair a hint of gold. "Madame Josephine, you know me better than that."

"I know you too well."

Then Bonaparte's secretary appeared at the door. (It's always like this now: bustle and turmoil.) "First Consul, Minister Talleyrand wishes to have a word with you."

I took my husband's hand. "And?" What about *Louis*?

"And he agreed," Bonaparte said with a shrug, standing up.

"That's all?"

"I'm not in the room!" Duplan said, digging in his case of combs. "I'm invisible."

"He was going to anyway, he said." Bonaparte lowered his voice. "Now someone needs to talk to you-know-who, see if you-know-who would be . . . you know: *receptive*."

"Nowhere to be seen!" Duplan exclaimed, throwing up his hands, turning his back.

"I don't think I should be the one to discuss it with her." It would put too much pressure on her. "Best to have someone outside the family, I think."

"Fauvelet could do it," Bonaparte said.

"Certainly," Fauvelet said. "Do what, First Consul?" I heard him say as he followed Bonaparte out.

"Citoyen Duplan, I'm serious, don't you dare say a word," I told my hairdresser immediately after the door had closed. "Not even a whisper." *Especially* not a whisper.


*4:30 or so.*

This afternoon, when Bonaparte's secretary came to model the new jacket I'd designed for him (it's excellent—even Bonaparte has requested one), I told Fauvelet our thoughts. "Louis is gentle and affectionate and he cares for Hortense sincerely. Were they to marry . . ." I outlined the benefits to all concerned. "I agree with Bonaparte that you are the ideal person to approach Hortense on this delicate matter." Well—perhaps not ideal, but . . .

"I know, Madame Josephine, the First Consul discussed this with me, but I don't think I could—"

"You and Hortense play in theatricals together. You have a companionable relationship. *Please.* Would you mind? Could you just find out what her feelings might be?"


*September 13.*
"She wept, Madame."

Wept! "Why? What did she say?"

Fauvelet shrugged his thin shoulders. "She didn't."

"Well—what did you tell her?"

"That she owed it to her country."

Mon Dieu.

"And that the First Consul and you had decided."

"Didn't you point out Louis's good qualities?"

Fauvelet looked at me quizzically. "Louis has good qualities?"

"Didn't you point out how gentle and sensitive and intelligent he is?

Didn't you tell her that Louis loves her?" As I had instructed him to say!

"I started to, Madame, but I don't know if she heard me." He pursed his lips. "She was crying awfully hard. Don't worry!" He held up his hands, as if surrendering to an enemy. "She *assured* me she would never do anything to displease you."

Hortense has asked for eight days to consider. Now, alone at my escritoire, I am full of remorse. How difficult this is. Are we doing the right thing?

*September 15—Malmaison.*
I observe my daughter's sad look and have to turn away. "She must decide herself," Bonaparte told me, taking me in his arms.

*September 16.*
Madame Campan is with Hortense now. I can hear the low murmur of their voices, the muffled sound of Hortense weeping. I can't bear it.

*Later.*
I walked Madame Campan to her carriage. "She will be fine," she said. "You must be patient."

"What is Hortense's objection?" Why is my daughter so miserable? We are not asking her to marry a repugnant old man. Certainly *that* sort of thing happens all the time. "Does she dislike Louis? Bonaparte and I were under the impression that she cares for him."

Madame Campan leaned toward me. "I think she expects to feel *rapture*," she said. I frowned. "Exactly!" she exclaimed. "Of course she cares for Louis. He's just not her *ideal*. Hortense has always been very . . . theatrical, one could say, but in the best sense! Sensitive, certainly. Romantic, I'm afraid. She'll come round—you'll see."

*September 17.*
Bonaparte has issued an ultimatum to England: unless a peace treaty is

concluded, negotiations will be broken off. "And as for your daughter . . ." he said, pressing for resolution.

Four more days.


*September 21, early afternoon—Tuileries Palace.*
Fauvelet poked his head in the door. "Madame Josephine?"

I looked up from my fancy-work.

"She has agreed. She said she would not stand in the way of your happiness."

I scrambled for my handkerchief, my chin quivering.

## *In which my daughter finally marries*

*September 22, 1801, almost 10:00 P.M.—a rainy day in Paris.*
Louis looked terrified. "You wish to speak to me, Napoleon?"

"Yes, sit," Bonaparte said, throwing a crumpled paper into the roaring fire. "Hortense has agreed to consider an offer of marriage, were one submitted to her." I cringed. Bonaparte can be so blunt! "I recommend her. She is a sweet and virtuous girl."

Just then Hortense came into the room with a bound music book in her hand. Seeing Louis, she turned and fled.

"A bit timid, perhaps," Bonaparte said, bemused.


*[Undated]*
Now all that remains is for Louis to make his declaration to Hortense. The two are painful to watch, always at opposite ends of a room, always silent. Bonaparte and I wait . . . and wait and *wait.* How long can this go on?


*October 3, 1801, Saint-Jean-de-Maurienne*
*Chère Maman,*

*A quick note (the courier is leaving soon). The news that England has finally agreed to sign a peace treaty is glorious!*

*Victor wrote that he has been put in charge of the fleet sailing to Saint-*

*Domingue.\* What a splendid command! This is his opportunity to prove his worth. Pauline must be pleased.*

*Hortense hasn't written for some time. Too busy entertaining suitors?*

*A thousand kisses, I am well,*

*Your loving son, Eugène*

*October 14.*

"Perhaps you should have a word with Louis," I suggested to Bonaparte. "Encourage him to . . . *you know*." Propose! Simply getting the young man to *speak* to my daughter was going to be a problem.

"What do I know of these things?"

"Would you prefer that I take care of it?" Our big ball was coming up: the perfect setting.

*October 21, 6:00 A.M.—Malmaison.*

Oh, it's early in the morning, but I'm too fraught to linger in bed. My heart is aswirl with feelings of joy, doubt—but most of all, relief.

Bonaparte and I opened the ball last night with a minuet. (He only missed two steps.) "What are you going to say to Louis?" he hissed, for we had decided that the time had come.

Presentation of the right hand: "What do you think I should say?"

Presentation of the left hand: "Tell him to get on with it!"

I induced the shy suitor to sit beside me. "Louis, do you think it would be improper for a woman to request a dance with a man?" A cotillion had been announced and couples were proceeding onto the floor.

"I believe it is the man who must always ask," he said solemnly.

"Pity," I said, with what I hoped would be a giveaway smile. Unfortunately, he didn't understand. "Would you find it shocking, then, were I

* *The preliminary peace treaty with England opened up the Atlantic Ocean, which had been previously controlled by England's fleet. Saint-Domingue (Haiti now) had been in French hands for some time, but France had been unable to sail there. Troops were required in order to quell an insurrection.*

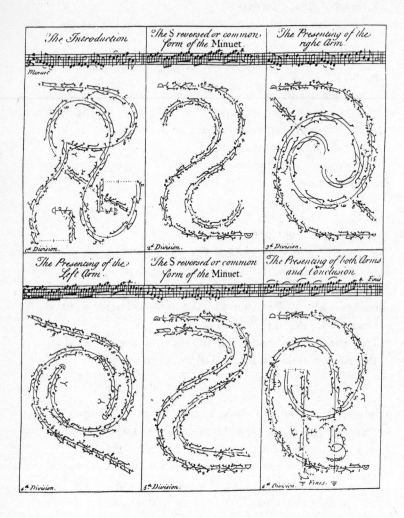

The Introduction

The S reversed or common form of the Minuet.

The Presenting of the right Arm.

The Presenting of the Left Arm.

The S reversed or common form of the Minuet.

The Presenting of both Arms and Conclusion.

to inform you that if you were to ask the honour of my hand in the dance, I would be happy to accept?"

He looked at me in all seriousness, a small frown between his eyes. (*Nice* eyes. Madame Campan is right: their children would be handsome.) "You'd like to dance, Aunt Josephine?"

"I'd be delighted." He led me out onto the dance floor. Hortense was sitting with Caroline near the musicians; I wiggled my fingers at them.

"Your daughter is usually one of the first on the floor."

"She is passionate about dance."

"She dances well," he said as the music began.

"As do you, Louis." Although, in truth, his movements lacked confidence. Perhaps with time Hortense could . . .

"I aim only not to make a fool of myself," he said as we proceeded down.

"You underestimate your abilities." This was true. Louis has exceptional qualities. Turning my head (the old women sitting at the edges of the dance floor knew how to read lips), I said, "Louis, Bonaparte and I have been thinking about you and Hortense. Have you given any thought to *when* you might make a proposal? Tonight might—"

"No! I mean, yes." Louis missed a step, and try as he might, could not correct it.

"I'm breathless," I lied. "I believe I should sit down." It was a faux pas to leave the floor in the middle of a piece, but at least we were at the bottom of the dance.

He escorted me to my chair. "Won't you join me for a moment?" I asked with authority, offering the empty seat next to mine. Dutifully he sat down beside me, his eyes darting about with the look of a captured animal. Men! I thought, so valiant on the battlefield, so timid in the parlour. "As I was saying—" I would have to be firm. "Bonaparte is anxious to settle the matter. He feels you should declare yourself to Hortense—*tonight*. There she is now," I said, pointing with my fan.

Louis looked stricken. "But now she's with Caroline *and* Émilie."

A dance would be too challenging for Louis under the circumstances, I realized. "You could invite her for a stroll in the garden." I touched his elbow, urging him to stand. One step, and he would be committed. But that step! "Go," I hissed.

*[Undated]*

The clan received the news in chilly silence. Slowly, Signora Letizia got to her feet and held up her glass of verjuice, her stiff index finger pointing at Hortense as if in accusation. "Now you will be one of us," she said, and sat down.

After, in the drawing room, as Hortense sang one of her new compositions and I accompanied her on the harp, I sensed an undercurrent of hisses, sharp glances, covert hand movements—a flurry, it seemed, of secretive murmurs.

*October 29, 1801, Saint-Jean-de-Maurienne*
*Chère Maman,*
   *What a surprise! I'm delighted. Louis is perfect for Hortense; they suit each other in so many ways. Has a date been set? Just think—I may be an uncle next year!*

   *Your loving son, Eugène*
*Note—I'm thinking of growing a goatee.*

*November 17, 1801, Saint-Jean-de-Maurienne*
*Chère Maman,*
   *Very well, no goatee!*
   *I've finally decided on my wedding gift: two horses, one a roan mare and the other a bay stallion, both sired by Pegasus. What do you think? Would you mind keeping them at Malmaison until Hortense and Louis have their own establishment?*

   *Your loving son, Eugène*

*December 18, 1801, Saint-Jean-de-Maurienne*
*Chère Maman,*
   *You should know that the details of the wedding gown you are having made for Hortense are lost on your son. What do I know of silk and fine lace? But would it be possible to have Hortense's portrait painted wearing the gown? That, at the least, might console me for not being at the ceremony in person.*

*I've been getting my regiment ready to join you and Papa in Lyons next month. I regret that I can't be in Paris for the big event—too much to do!*

*Your loving son, Eugène*

*Note—Hortense wrote that Pauline is unhappy about having to go to Saint-Domingue with Victor. I've heard it said that Papa wanted to get Pauline out of Paris, away from a number of admirers. (You can see how bored I am: I've stooped to gossip. Forgive me!)*

*December 25—Christmas Day.*

Christmas dinner with the clan. "I'm so happy that Hortense and Louis are getting married, Aunt Josephine," Caroline told me, piling her plate high with pudding and tarts. "Just think, Hortense and I will be sisters, as well as bosom friends—and Napoleon will be Hortense's brother," Caroline said, catching Louis's eye. "That must please him; Napoleon is so *very* fond of Hortense. Everyone is talking about what a *close* family we are."

*December 26, early morning.*

Something in Caroline's expression last night made me uneasy. Against my better judgement, I've asked Mimi to contact her spy. "I was going to anyway," she told me with a grin.

*[Undated]*

Mimi slipped me a note this morning. "From Gontier's nephew?" I recognized the crude script.

"It isn't very nice," she warned me.

I tucked the note into my sleeve.

*This Evinng Mme Carolin told her Brother Louis he must not marry the Old Woman's daughter. Shee told Him Peopl say the 1st Consul is Lover of Mlle Hortens. Louis said that is a Lie, that it is not True, that He will marry Her. Mme Carolin broke 5 dishes Shee so angry.*

I'm enraged! My hand is trembling as I write this.

*December 29.*

And so, in spite of opposition, rumours and suspicion, plans proceed for the marriage of a Beauharnais, the daughter of "the Old Woman," to a Bonaparte. The contract will be signed on January first—in only three days; the ceremony to be held the day after. The wedding gown is almost finished. Leroy has outdone himself.


*December 30.*

Hortense was ill all night. Overcome with hysterics, she raged and wept. She could not possibly marry Louis, she finally confessed. "I have given my heart to another!" she said, falling against the pillows.

I folded and unfolded my hands, folded them again. What was my daughter telling me?

"I love Christophe Duroc," she wailed.


*11:20 A.M.*

"She's very upset. I don't think she can go through with it."

Bonaparte threw down his book in exasperation. "What do you mean? She has to! Everything is set."

"She's in love with one of your aides—with Duroc."

"Christophe?" Bonaparte snorted with amusement.


*Very late—past midnight (can't sleep).*

This evening before retiring, Bonaparte informed me that he'd offered Hortense to Christophe Duroc. "You did *what*?" It took me a moment to even respond.

"As we discussed," he said, pacing in his nightshirt. "I told Fauvelet to tell Christophe that I'd give him half a million and the command of the Eighth Military Division at Toulon on condition that the wedding take place in two days and they leave for Toulon immediately."

*Toulon?* "Fauvelet spoke to him this evening?" I gasped.

"Yes, he informed Christophe of the offer before Christophe left for the Opéra. He gave Fauvelet his refusal on his return."

"Christophe Duroc *refused* her?"

"He wants to live in Paris, he said. He doesn't want to live in Toulon."

My poor daughter! Christophe Duroc entertains no affection for her whatsoever, for he responded to the offer quite crudely, telling Fauvelet that he couldn't be bothered, that he was on his way to a whorehouse.

The air in Hortense's bedchamber was close. "Hortense?" I parted the embroidered bed-curtains. Hortense was sitting against the pillows, the counterpane pulled up to her chin. "How are you feeling?"

"I am fine, Maman," she said, her voice measured. "Thank you for inquiring."

She is young, I reminded myself, subject to moods. I sat down beside her. "There's something I have to tell you." There was no other way, or time. "I know you entertain a hope of marrying Christophe Duroc. I discussed the matter with Bonaparte, and he offered, but . . . Duroc refused," I said, as gently as I could.

"You're just saying that! You don't want me to marry him," she sobbed, throwing pillows. "Where are you going?" she demanded when she saw that I was leaving.

"I'm going to summon Fauvelet," I said, trying to remain calm. "He will tell you himself what Christophe Duroc said."

"Don't go!" she wept, her shoulders heaving.

I took her in my arms. She was so hot! "I'm sending for a doctor."

*December 31, New Year's Eve.*

With considerable difficulty I managed to get Bonaparte to postpone the wedding. "Two days," I said. "Dr. Corvisart feels she will be well enough by then." Dr. Corvisart is the only doctor Bonaparte trusts.

"You don't understand!" Bonaparte exploded. (Everyone is being so temperamental! There is too much going on at once.) "Several hundred Italian delegates are expecting me in Lyons to inaugurate their new republic. All the arrangements are going to have to be changed. Do you have any idea what this entails?"

"She just can't do it, Bonaparte!"

*Almost 10:00 P.M.*

"A two-day delay?" Louis looked suspicious. "It will make a poor impression," he said, drawing his head into his shoulders. "May I inquire why?" He didn't feel that a wedding date should be changed under any circumstances, he said.

"She's really quite ill. Believe me, Louis, it will make an even poorer impression if you go ahead with it. She can barely sit up, she's so weak."

*January 2, 1802, early morning.*

Hortense has recovered—well enough, in any case. And so we will proceed with the signing of the contract, the civil ceremony, the religious ceremony—dragging my reluctant daughter into the holy state of matrimony.

"All girls feel that way," Madame Campan assured me. "Hortense is more expressive than most."

More stubborn than most!

*Sunday, January 3.*

The contract has been signed, so at least *that* ordeal is behind us—and an ordeal it was. Bonaparte's mother scowled the entire time; Caroline and Joseph smiled falsely. In spite of my resolve, I wept, which distressed the groom. Only Hortense seemed unperturbed (aloof).

After the signing, Bonaparte presented Hortense with the stunning diamond necklace set we'd had made for her. "Thank you," she said, but without any emotion. She is *determined* that nothing please her.

*January 4, just after 8:00 A.M.*

I woke with the dawn and have already accomplished a great deal: reviewed the menus, arranged with Leroy to make one last alteration to Hortense's gorgeous wedding gown (it's a surprise for her), sent a letter asking Cardinal Caprara to officiate at the religious ceremony to be held at the little house on Rue de la Victoire after the civil ceremony.

Frankly, I'm in such fits over this wedding that I keep forgetting Bonaparte and I will be leaving for Lyons in a few days and will be away for a month. I'll see whether Hortense and Louis would like to stay at Malmaison, look after all the animals.

Hortense and Louis. Hortense and Louis. Hortense and Louis.

Louis and Hortense.

Madame Louis Bonaparte.

Madame Louis.

Madame.


*11:45 P.M. A long day.*

Shortly before nine I knocked on the door to Hortense's room. She emerged in a plain crêpe gown, carrying a small orange-blossom bouquet. "You're not dressed? It's time to go upstairs. Everyone is waiting."

"I *am* dressed," my daughter informed me.

I looked at Mimi in confusion. "What happened to the wedding gown?" The exquisite gown of white satin. "Was it not delivered?" And what about the diamonds Bonaparte had given her? Hortense was wearing a single strand of inferior pearls.

Mimi rolled her eyes as if to say: I give up. "The bride prefers to be simply attired."

I pressed my lips together, trying as best I could to hide my frustration. It would do no good whatsoever to argue, I knew. "You look lovely," I lied.


It was a grim affair, in truth. We stood solemnly as the mayor joined Louis and my daughter in marriage. The family and the Second and Third Consuls watched the proceedings without any indication of joy. Bonaparte was impatient to have it over with quickly. (He had work to do!) I feigned happiness, but it was difficult: Hortense looked so miserable. Louis regarded her anxiously—my heart went out to him.

After, the cheerless party proceeded to the little house on Rue de la Victoire, where Cardinal Caprara had been waiting in his canonicals for hours. (He'd misunderstood the time.) After champagne, which I hoped would make the gathering at least a little bit gay (it didn't), Cardinal Caprara joined Hortense and Louis in the eyes of God. And so the knot is truly tied, for better or for worse.

Bonaparte wished the two well, and then he and the two Consuls immediately departed—they had much to do to prepare for the trip to Lyons, they said. While waiting for dinner to be announced, Caroline mentioned to the Cardinal that she and Joachim had only had a civil marriage and that someday soon they intended to be married by the Church.

Cardinal Caprara examined his timepiece, a heavy gold instrument dangling on a thick chain. "I could marry you now, if you like. It would only take a half hour or so," he assured me, for the table had been set.

I glanced at Hortense and Louis, sitting glum-faced on the sofa. "You wouldn't object?" It was, after all, their happy day. (Hardly.)

"Of course not," Hortense said dutifully, but then added, "that is, if my *husband* does not object."

"No, I do not object," Louis said, his voice so quiet that it was hard to hear.

"Anyone else wish to marry?" the jolly Cardinal said after he'd rushed Caroline (six months along and already enormous) and Joachim through the ceremony.

"Pity the First Consul isn't here, Maman," Hortense said, and then wisely bit her tongue, for it isn't generally known that Bonaparte and I have never been joined by the Church. At the time, it was not possible*—and now it is awkward.

Then, as dinner was announced, Cardinal Caprara took his leave: "I'm afraid I am expected elsewhere."

"Before you go, Cardinal Caprara, would you mind? If you could . . ." I looked around to make sure no one could hear. "If you could bless their bed." It is an old custom, and who can say? Perhaps it will help. Certainly Hortense and Louis are in need of a blessing.

* *Catholicism had been outlawed during the Revolution.*

## *In which we are all of us blessed*

*January 31, 1802—Paris, home again, 7:30 P.M. approximately.*
We're back, at last. The trip to Lyons was . . . well, surprising. The adulation! But also all the pomp, the tiring ceremonials. It helped that Eugène joined us there, so proud with his regiment.

Speaking of whom—he has just arrived. He's anxious to go see his sister—as am I!

*9:45 P.M.*
Eugène lifted Hortense off her feet in a big bear hug. "Madame Louis! You haven't changed a bit."

"I'm the happiest woman in the world," she said (catching my eye), chatting on about Louis's problematic health, the art class they are taking together, a pug dog's litter, a lame horse, old Gontier's trouble with his back. Then Louis joined us and Hortense fell silent as he talked of this and that, clasping her hand in his, never taking his eyes off her.

I'm *so* relieved.

*February 18—Malmaison.*
Louis looked so proud. I knew right away what he was going to say! "The midwife informs us that although it is too early to know for *sure*, my wife is likely with child."

"That's wonderful!" I exclaimed, embracing Hortense—restraining myself from crushing her, so great was my joy.

Eugène heartily shook Louis's hand. (His weak hand: I cringed.) "I guess this means I'm going to be an uncle." He struck a dignified pose that made us laugh.

"How do you feel?" I asked Hortense anxiously. I feel so protective of her!

"Sick!" Hortense moaned.

"Good, then it will be a boy." Bonaparte tweaked Hortense's ear. "Joseph has a girl. Lucien has girls. It's about time we had a boy Bonaparte."

My daughter is going to have a *baby*—I'm delirious!


*February 23, a chilly afternoon.*

Louis's plan to go to a spa for a health cure is an excellent idea (clearly, he needs it) except for one thing: he expects Hortense to accompany him. I'm ill with concern! Barèges is so far. It would take over a week to get there, and the roads are terribly primitive. I've persuaded Dr. Corvisart to have a word with Hortense about the dangers of such an expedition for a young woman in her condition.


*February 28, Sunday and a Décadi—Malmaison.*

Hortense has dark circles under her eyes. Louis has been waking her in the middle of the night. "He weeps, Maman! He says if I loved him, I would follow him anywhere."

"You explained to him what the doctor said?"

Hortense nodded. "And so I told him I'd go with him, but that if I miscarried, it would be *his* responsibility."

"Hortense, you can't risk that!" I said, my hands clasping her shoulders.


*March 1—Tuileries Palace.*

"He wept as the carriage pulled away, Maman," Hortense said, collapsing into my arms. "He says he can't live without me!"

Oh, the early years of marriage are so passionate, I thought—so *stormy*.

"Bonaparte said things like that when we were first married," I told her, to soothe. "Corsican men are extreme in love—or maybe just Bonaparte men," I added with a smile. Extreme in everything, I might have said: love, hate, ambition, pride. "Louis's health concerns him, I know. The waters will help. And once the baby comes, things will settle down. You're lucky to be married to a man who loves you so much. And something tells me he'll be a devoted parent."

Hortense smiled through her tears. "He has already filled a closet with toys."


*March 27, 11:30 A.M.*
It's official now—England has actually *signed* a peace treaty. "Your island is French again," Bonaparte told me with a kiss, as if presenting me with a gift: my beloved Martinico.

"Ah, just think of the cashmere shawls we'll be able to buy now," Caroline said, eating macaroons by the handful. (She's enormous—only one more month.)

"And gowns of English muslin." Hortense gave me a private wink— we've been wearing English muslin all along, only telling Bonaparte that the fabric is French leno.

"And English plants for an English garden," I mused. I've already written letters to England, to botanists there.


*March 30.*
I've sent a parcel to Martinico, sent Mother portraits of Bonaparte, me and the children along with a gold box beautifully decorated with diamonds. Inside, I've tucked some gold medals and coins in honour of Bonaparte's victories.

Now that the seas are safe to travel, I'm hoping Mother can be persuaded to move to France. I've also suggested that Uncle Robert send my goddaughter, fifteen now. Young Stéphanie would benefit from a year at Madame Campan's school before marrying.

*April 6—Paris.*

Peace was signed with England less than twelve days ago and already Paris is swarming with Lord Such-and-Suches and Lady So-and-Sos, going about town with their quaint umbrellas and their noses stuck in the air. This in spite of the fact that they are incredibly *impressed*, blinking their eyes, disbelieving, taking in the glory of our new Republic—taking in our fine clothes, our glittering entertainments, our vitality, our *pride*. Expecting squalor and disarray, they are stunned to find a well-managed, thriving country, shocked by our fine new hospitals (especially the one just opened for children—the first of its kind), our schools, our roads. Everywhere one looks there is construction: a new quay, bridges, monuments. "I wish to make France the envy of all nations," Bonaparte told me not long ago—and I believe he has already succeeded.

*April 8.*

Wonders upon wonders: now there will be peace with the Church. "We'll celebrate Easter Sunday in the Cathedral of Notre-Dame," Bonaparte told me.

Celebrate in regal style: all the servants to be in livery.

"Easter Sunday?" Leroy exclaimed. The distraught dress designer placed the back of his wrist to his brow and closed his eyes. Only ten days.

*April 18—Easter Sunday in Paris.*

The church bells of Paris are ringing again. What a glorious sound! Bonaparte opened the casement windows and stood at the sill in his nightshirt, as if breathing in the deep resounding peal of Emmanuel, the big bell of Notre-Dame—silent for how long? Ten years?

Our morning reverie was shattered by a salvo of guns that made the windows (and my heart) tremble. "I have everything I could wish for," Bonaparte said solemnly. Peace with England. Peace with the Church. "If only . . ."

If only we could have a child.

*April 26.*
Very busy. Caroline has had her baby—a little girl, named after Signora Letizia. A difficult labour.


*June 4—Paris.*
To the Opéra tonight to see *Hecuba*. The applause for Bonaparte was tumultuous. When Priam said to Achilles, "You fulfill the hopes of the nation," I thought the walls would tumble, the cheering was so great. The audience demanded that the line be repeated, and repeated yet again.

It does not seem to matter how often it happens—the fervour of the people continues to overwhelm me. Overwhelm me and frighten me, for where will it lead?


*June 10—Malmaison, a beautiful summer day.*
Thérèse lifted her veil of white muslin held in place by a crown of roses. "My divorce from Tallien is now official, so I'm dressing as a virgin," she announced. "What's wrong?" she demanded, looking at me closely.

I hesitated—but to whom could I speak truly? "The people are so grateful, they will give Bonaparte anything he should ask for."

"The world! And even then, it would not be as much as he has given us." She laughed at my expression. (Thérèse isn't given to adulation.) "Don't look so surprised. I can see as well as anyone that your husband has accomplished the impossible—and to think what a fool he seemed when we first met him. Remember how we laughed at his toothpick legs in those big smelly boots? Ah, now I've got you smiling. So tell me, what do you fear he will ask for?"

"People are saying that he should be named First Consul for Life—"

"Of course. *Everyone* is voting in favour."

"—with the right to name a successor."

"I didn't know about that part."

"What's the difference between that and a king? Sometimes I worry that in striving to become legitimate in the eyes of the world, we are becoming what we fought so hard to change."

"It's not really the same. It's being voted on, after all—it's up to the people to decide what they want. And even if Bonaparte were voted king, he would be a citizen-king."

"I know, I know," I argued, "but already some people are telling him that the right to name his heir isn't enough—that the office should be hereditary." His *family*, in particular—insisting that the office should fall to one of them.

"Ah, now I understand. You and Bonaparte have no children."

"And I'm beginning to think we never will."

"Have you tried—?"

"Everything!" I've given up animal foods, liquors of a spirituous nature. I've endeavoured to keep my body open by ingesting tincture of senna, Epsom salts and other laxatives. (Oh, the results.) I've even had leeches applied to my temples. "I'm going to Plombières soon for yet another cure, but I confess, I . . ."

Thérèse placed her hand over mine. "Darling, you must have faith."


*July 2—Plombières.*
The water doctor is hopeful. "The waters are making you ill. That is a good sign."


*July 7—Plombières, hot.*
A miracle—I've had a hint of a show! "Return to Paris immediately," the water doctor ordered, prescribing tonics and potions. "Constant relations, and no moving about after. Keep your hips propped up on a pillow for at least two hours."

I'm packing.


*July 14, Bastille Day—Paris.*
I've prepared for bed like a bride. A pagan spirit is in the air: tonight twelve girls, dowered by the city, were married to soldiers at the Bastille Day banquet. Bonaparte looked splendid in his Lyons coat of crimson satin laced with gold. "Like a king," his family told him with satisfied smiles. A king requiring an heir.

*July 29.*
The results of the vote have been published. Over five million citizens voted in favour, less than ten thousand against.


*August 2—Malmaison.*
Today it is official. Bonaparte is now First Consul for *Life*.

"What will this mean?" I asked him as we walked along a path banked by blooming roses.

He picked a yellow blossom, held it to his nose, his eyes closed, as if lost in sensation. "Things are going to change," he said, opening his eyes.

First: we must double our staff. "But Bonaparte—"

Second: Malmaison is too small. We must move to the palace of Saint-Cloud. "But Bonaparte—"

And third: he is to be addressed as Napoleon. "But Bonaparte—"


*August 6.*
This afternoon Madame Campan and I toured the palace of Saint-Cloud, making long (*long*) lists of what is needed, *who* is needed: ladies-in-waiting, torch boys, pages, footmen . . . My head is reeling. I'm writing this in bed.


*August 8—Tuileries.*
"It's a supernatural materialization," Fouché reported. "The Church has found a saint for your husband: Saint Napoleon." From now on, August 15 will be known as Saint Napoleon's day.

"So who is this Saint Napoleon, anyway?" Hortense demanded, looking up from copying out scripts of the one-act comedy she is directing—as well as acting in, in spite of being seven months along. (At least it gets her mind off her long-absent husband, still in treatment at the spa.)

"Some lazy reprobate, no doubt," Eugène said with a boyish grin, ducking Bonaparte's attempt to tug his ear.

*August 11—Malmaison.*

Hortense is frantic. "Maman, what am I going to do? My costume is too small for me *already* and Fauvelet *still* doesn't know his lines."

"Don't worry!" In her condition, it isn't good to get distraught. Calm is required. "We'll get Leroy to make alterations to your costume, and Eugène can coach Fauvelet every night. It's going to be wonderful."

"How do you know?"

"The best actor in Europe happened to tell me."

"*Talma* told you that?" Beaming—for there could be no greater praise.

*Fort de France, Martinico*
*Chère Yeyette, my beloved niece,*

*You must understand—your goddaughter Stéphanie is still a girl. I appreciate the advantages of having her educated in France, and I am certainly not concerned knowing that you and your illustrious husband would make sure that she was well looked after, but her mother and I cannot bring ourselves to send her across that perilous body of water, no matter how peaceful the seas might be at this time.*

*I regret to tell you, as well, that there isn't any hope of persuading your mother to sail to France, in spite of the gracious invitation the First Consul has extended. She remains firmly of the Royalist persuasion.*

*Your most humble etc. uncle, Robert Tascher*

*August 12, late afternoon—Paris.*

Bonaparte threw an English journal into the fire and sat glaring at it as it burst into flames. "Riff-raff!" His expression alarmed me, but also provoked my curiosity. "You don't want to know about this, Josephine," he warned me, sensing my thoughts.

"But now, of course, you must tell me."

He jumped to his feet and began to pace, his hands behind his back. "The English journals are circulating the rumour that Hortense has already given birth."

I shrugged. "They're simply mistaken."

He stopped short, his hands fists. "And that therefore Hortense was with child at the time she married." He paused before he added, "And that I am the father of her child."

I watched an ash fragment float up the chimney. "That's what was in that news-sheet?"

"And they call this peace!" Bonaparte kicked the burning logs.

"We must make sure Hortense never learns of this."

"Nor Louis," Bonaparte said quietly, under his breath.

*August 15, Saint Napoleon's day (!)—Malmaison.*
What a birthday fête! Has there ever been one like it? Saint Napoleon, indeed. (Saint Napoleon, who is only thirty-three today—so young!)

The reception at the palace this morning went smoothly. It was followed by a glorious concert (three hundred musicians playing Cherubini, Méhul, Rameau—heavenly). Then, after a Te Deum at Notre-Dame, we caravanned in flower-festooned carriages out the long road to Malmaison for a garden fête. The weather, for all my fretting, turned out to be perfect: a clear blue sky, not a cloud.

"Our prayers have been answered." Uncle Fesch, who was made a bishop today, raised yet another toast.

"The sun always shines on Papa," Hortense said, ebullient in her gaiety, for her one-act comedy had gone off splendidly, well-clapped. ("Fantastique! Formidable!" Talma was heard to exclaim over the cheers.)

Even Bonaparte enjoyed himself. He insisted Hortense lead a dance with Eugène, in spite of her condition. "Do it for Saint Napoleon," he said with his irresistibly charming smile.

*August 16.*
Hortense is so upset! There's an article in today's *Journal de Paris* about her dancing at Bonaparte's birthday fête last night. "Why did they have to say I was seven months with child?" she demanded.

"May I see it?" Bonaparte's secretary handed me the news-sheet.

"And look, Maman, someone even wrote a stupid poem about me.

'On seeing Madame Louis Bonaparte, seven months pregnant, dance on August 15.'"

"Do you know who wrote this, Fauvelet?" No author was credited, but I had a suspicion.

"Certainly not, Madame Josephine," Fauvelet Bourrienne exclaimed, moving his hand in the epic style of delivery, as if the upper arm—the "oratorical weapon," Talma called it—were completely detached from the body.

"Someone with no literary talent whatsoever," Hortense ranted.

"None whatsoever," Fauvelet echoed, but colouring.

I pressed my lips together to keep from smiling. *So.*

Hortense burst into tears. "Why did they have to say anything at all? I didn't even want to dance. I wouldn't have if Papa hadn't *insisted.*"

Fauvelet looked stricken.

*Don't worry, it's all right,* I mouthed, putting my arm around Hortense and leading her out the sash doors into the rose garden. Clearly Bonaparte had wanted Hortense to dance for a reason. No doubt he had asked Fauvelet to write the poem about her and publish it in the paper—thus proving to the English scandalmongers that Hortense had not yet given birth, quelling the evil rumours. "You're such a lovely dancer, Hortense. That's why people write about you. Don't fret, *please* don't fret."


*September 14—Malmaison.*

"I've come to bid you farewell," Fouché said, standing in the foyer at Malmaison.

"You're going away?" I asked, distracted, for I'd just come from Saint-Cloud, where workmen are trying to finish the renovations before Bonaparte and I move in four days from now. I've been trying to figure out what type of bed-curtains would suit our bed there. Its unique boat-shape makes it a challenge. A velvet in a terre d'Égypte hue would be perfect, I've decided, but it requires something more: perhaps a gold fringe to make the embroidery stand out.

"It appears I've been let go."

Slowly Fouché's words penetrated my harried thoughts. I leaned against a crate. *Let go,* did he say?

"Well—demoted."

"You're no longer Minister of Police?"

"*Senator* Fouché." He spoke the title with contempt. "A perfectly useless position."

"I can't believe that!" Fouché is the best Minister of Police imaginable. How can Bonaparte manage without him? If there is trouble, Fouché knows of it. If there are assassins plotting, Fouché finds them. "Bonaparte did this?" Fouché is the only one of Bonaparte's ministers who has the courage to speak truthfully to him. He has often angered Bonaparte—true!—but Bonaparte owes his life to him.

"Apparently my services are no longer needed."

"I don't understand." But I suspected the reason. Fouché argued against Bonaparte's being made First Consul for Life, and this enraged Bonaparte's family. Too, Fouché is my ally.

"Another clan victory," Fouché said with a smirk.


*Early morning.*

Last night I tried to talk to Bonaparte about Fouché, but it proved difficult. "I was advised," was all he would say. I dared not broach the subject of his family's influence, their greedy nature—their hatred of *me*. Bonaparte is master of Europe—but when it comes to his family, he weakens dangerously. *Blood is everything*, his mother often says. *Blood is our only strength.* Blood is your only weakness, I want to tell him—but do not dare.


*September 18—Saint-Cloud.*

Exhausted! We moved in the rain. The rooms at Saint-Cloud are spacious, but cold. As soon as it clears, Bonaparte and I are going for a ride in the park.


*Sunday, September 19.*

The midwife estimates that Hortense's baby could come as early as the first of October, several weeks before previously thought. She told Hortense that it is easy to miscalculate with a boy.

"She thinks it's a boy? That's wonderful!" A girl grandchild I would love—with all my heart—but a boy would solve so much.

"But Maman, that would be three days *short* of nine months since we married," she said, looking up from a drawing she was working on, a copy of an infant by Greuze. "What would Louis think?" Louis, who was expected home from the spa any day soon.

And what would the English scandalmongers write, I thought—but did not say.


*September 21—Saint-Cloud, sunny and bright.*
Louis returned from the spa yesterday, but alas, all is *not* well. His health, unfortunately, is not improved, to judge by his extreme disability. (His right hand is so crippled he can't use it.) His spirits are tormented, as well, for he threatens to drown himself if the baby is born early!

"But Louis knows that you are virtuous," I told my daughter, looking for a way to make peace between them.

"Of course he knows, Maman, but all he cares about is how it would *look*, what people would think."

"He loves you—you know that." If Louis heard the rumours circulating in England, it would inflame him, no doubt. That he had not said anything to Hortense was to his credit. "Periods of separation are difficult."

We talked as we walked along the rutted cart paths edging the fields. I eased my daughter's fiery spirit—or tried to—by urging her to be gentle with herself, as well as with her husband. "Louis has been away for seven months—a very long time. There's often a period of turmoil on the return." I know this all too well. "It's best not to allow yourself to become heated, especially in your condition." I put my arm around my poor lumbering daughter. It will certainly not help matters if this child *does* come early.


*October 7—Saint-Cloud.*
It is now nine months plus three days since Hortense and Louis married. "I'm saved," Hortense said, her hands clasped as if in prayer.

Hortense has always been given to drama, to melodrama—but in truth, we are all relieved.


*October 10.*

Late this morning a horse cantered up the drive and into the courtyard. I headed out to the terrace to see who it might be, but even as I opened the door, Eugène came bounding up the steps, yelling at me to hurry.

"Is it Hortense?" I cried out, made fearful by his state of alarm.

"It's happening, Maman—I was with her when it started! Louis says to come *quickly*."


I didn't think the drive from Saint-Cloud into the heart of Paris could be made in under two hours: now I know that it can. We left Saint-Cloud at 10:05, and at exactly 11:48 Eugène and I were at the door of Hortense and Louis's town house, pulling impatiently on the bell rope.

"Yoo-hoo!" We turned to see a woman dressed in an old-fashioned red gown covered by an apron festooned with ribbons. She was balancing what looked to be a birthing stool on top of her head with one hand and holding a leather portmanteau with the other. "I can't unlatch the gate."

"Madame Frangeau!"

"The midwife?" Eugène hurried to let her in.

I greeted the good woman, but just then the front door opened. "Madame Frangeau?" Louis said, his afflicted right hand clawed over his heart. (Awful.) "At last."

"Louis, how is Hortense?" And then, from within the house, I heard a cry. Oh no!

Louis held up the index finger of his good hand to silence me, examining a pocket watch that he clutched with the other, counting off the seconds. "Good," he said, dropping the watch into his pocket.

"Dr. Jean-Louis Baudelocque will be here after he finishes his meal, Citoyen," the midwife informed Louis, untying a kerchief.

"*After?*" Louis asked anxiously.

"Truth is, he just gets in the way," she hissed in my direction, stepping aside as the hall porter carried the stool and portmanteau up the stairs.

Louis hurried after the porter, talking over his shoulder to Madame Frangeau. "My wife's pains are coming often now. I think she's near."

"Someone should let Bonaparte know what's happening," I suggested to Eugène, who was standing in the courtyard looking bewildered.

"I will!" he said, relieved to have a task.

"He's working at the palace today," I called out, but my son was already on his way out the gate.


The lying-in room smelled strongly of cloves. Madame Frangeau was closing the windows, barking instructions to the two maids.

"Maman!" Hortense gasped when she saw me. Louis was seated beside her, stroking her hand.

"How are you, darling?" My sweet, my treasure, my heart! She looked like a girl in the big bed, a girl with golden locks, her big blue eyes peeking out from under the lace frill of her nightcap. A frail slip of a girl with an enormous belly.

"She's splendid," Madame Frangeau said. "Now, Madame Josephine, if you could sit yourself here, out of the way, while I take your daughter's measures."

Obediently I sat down on the opposite side of the bed. Hortense writhed as a wave of pain came over her. "Dear God," she cried out.

I swallowed, took a breath as the midwife cheered her on. "That's the way! The louder the better. Let the neighbours know. Let all of Paris know!"

Dr. Jean-Louis Baudelocque didn't arrive until shortly before three. The child—the most perfect I've ever seen—was born shortly before nine. Although it was not a long labour—eight hours in all?—it was not an easy one. My daughter suffered!

I will never forget that beautiful sound—the baby's first lusty wail. "It's a boy," Louis whispered, as if in disbelief at his good fortune.

A *boy*. I felt light-headed, blessed.

"A boy!" I heard a maid yell in the hall.

"A boy!" I heard someone call outside in the courtyard—the coachman likely. Somewhere in the house a bell was rung. Oh, the excitement!

I wanted to run out into the street, ring the bells of Notre-Dame.

"Good work, Madame Louis. You've given your husband a healthy baby boy," Madame Frangeau said, holding the red and screaming infant up for Hortense to see. (*Careful!* I wanted to cry out.) "Wash him up, measure and swaddle him," she told the nursemaid. "He's perfectly well-made," she added, as if speaking of an object, "not a flaw that I can see." Louis followed the nursemaid out of the room in a daze.

Dr. Baudelocque tapped my daughter's knee through the covering sheet. "One more push, Madame Louis, and the business will be done."

"We don't want the womb climbing back up!" the midwife said, as if it were a thing alive.

Hortense winced, but did not cry out. I stroked her damp forehead with a cloth dipped in rosewater. It is early yet, I know, the danger not yet past. Heaven's gates stay open nine days for a woman in childbed.

Louis reappeared with a proud look in his eyes. He knelt beside the bed and kissed Hortense's hand. I was moved to tears—his simple action was so noble.

"He is well, *our son?*" my daughter asked.

"Six pounds, two ounces, and eighteen inches long," he said, his eyes glistening.

"That's an excellent weight," I said.

"He looks small to me," Louis said excitedly, "but the nursemaid told me he's big—and very well made."

The nursemaid appeared with the baby in her arms, tightly swaddled and peaceful now. "Oh, Hortense, he's an angel," I said, a lump rising in my throat. Napoleon-Charles he will be named—so it has already been decreed. Little Napoleon.

"Our Dauphin," the nursemaid said, putting him into Hortense's arms.

"Hold your tongue," I heard Louis hiss at the nurse.

"Bonjour, little Napoleon," Hortense whispered, gazing into the eyes of her son, her cheeks wet with tears.

## In which I have suspicions

*October 13, 1802—Saint-Cloud, a chilly day.*
Hortense is being treated like royalty for having produced the first male Bonaparte grandchild. Even Signora Letizia conferred begrudging congratulations on the mother of "her son's son." And now Eugène has been made Colonel of the Guards (quite an honour—he's only twenty-one), although the title "Uncle" excites him more, in truth.

Unfortunately, such Beauharnais glory has excited clan jealousy—further aggravated by today's birth notice in *Le Moniteur*. Hortense's name is printed in small capitals. "They don't do that for any of *us*," Caroline said, clutching baby Letizia in petticoats, little Achille sitting beside her sucking his thumb. "Don't we count?" She is with child again, but it does not seem to calm her. If anything, becoming a mother has turned Caroline into a lioness.

"Make sure you contact *Le Moniteur*," I suggested to Bonaparte's secretary later. "All family members must be treated *exactly* the same."


*October 14—in Paris for a few days with Hortense.*
Madame Frangeau (*General* Frangeau, Eugène calls her) has ordered Hortense to be wrapped in a feather comforter and the fires in her room kept blazing, "to sweat the poisons out," she said.

"Of course," I agreed, but tactfully suggested that the maids put branches of apple on the fire, for the air in the lying-in chamber has become heavy.

"I'm *drowning* in my bodily fluids," Hortense complained. She maintains her good humour in spite of Madame Frangeau's insistence that she lie flat for one full week, not moving even to allow the bed to be made, or to change her underclothes.

"It would be certain death," Madame Frangeau informed us.

"Only a few more days," I comforted my daughter, gazing upon the precious face of the newborn in my arms (falling in love). "It's wise to be cautious."


*October 15—still in Paris.*
Nine days. Madame Frangeau has allowed Hortense to sit up—but she's not to get out of bed for another five. "If I hear that your feet have so much as *touched* the floor, there will be hell to pay."


*October 20—Saint-Cloud.*
"I've come to bid you farewell, Madame Josephine." Bonaparte's secretary stood forlornly before me.

"Farewell, Fauvelet?" I asked, pulling off my gloves, my thoughts on Hortense and the baby. Little Napoleon is sleeping better now that his wet-nurse has agreed to abstain from fruit and vegetables.

"I've . . . I've been let go."

"Pardon?"

He repeated what he'd said, but even then I could not comprehend. Let go? Fauvelet Bourrienne was not only an excellent secretary, he was Bonaparte's oldest friend. "But why?"

He waggled his fingers. "Oh, I made some investments, and . . ." He shrugged, shoving his hands deep into the pockets of his redingote. "*Indiscretions*, the First Consul said."

"But Fauvelet, everybody plays the Funds."

Fauvelet flushed. "I guess I took advantage of my position."

"I still don't understand." Doesn't everyone "take advantage"? What about the investments that Bonaparte's brothers and sisters have made—even his mother? What about those made by Minister Talleyrand, for that matter, who regularly profits from knowledge of international developments, who considers such "income" his due? "Did Bonaparte's family have anything to do with this?" I demanded. Fauvelet is my ally—something the clan holds against him.

He hunched his shoulders. "Well . . ."


*November 15—still at Saint-Cloud (chilly).*
Little Napoleon was christened this morning. Bonaparte and I, as godparents, held him proudly. He was an angel—not even a whimper. ("Everyone knows that if a baby doesn't cry at his christening he will die," Caroline said later. That girl!)

We returned to Louis and Hortense's house where Louis, entirely on his own and much to my daughter's surprise, had arranged a fête in her honour. Hortense's closest friends were there—her cousin Émilie, the three Auguié sisters and Caroline.

Soon after, Hortense's former schoolmistress, Madame Campan, arrived and then all the other members of the Bonaparte clan. Lucien came with his two girls. Elisa appeared in a bizarre ensemble she'd designed herself, a composite of Egyptian, Roman and Greek styles that she expects every woman in Paris to adopt. "Joseph sends regrets," she announced (but later disclosed that he felt it disrespectful of Louis to celebrate the birth of a son so soon after he himself had suffered such a grievous disappointment in the birth of yet another daughter—a second). And last, jolly Uncle "Bishop" Fesch arrived with Bonaparte's mother. Signora Letizia stood in the centre of the room refusing all offers until Bonaparte led her to the chair of honour on the right of the hearth.

It was as Caroline was trying to get little Achille to show everyone how he can wave that Aunt Désirée—dressed in a youthful Grecian style!—made a dramatic entrance with dear old fusty Aunt Fanny, who appeared shrunken but vigorous as ever, her thick face paint smudged. With the bravado of an author who has just received a literary award, she read aloud a rather drawn-out verse she'd written in honour of her goddaughter's son, "the new Apollo." I was becoming concerned about the length of Aunt Fanny's recitation (Bonaparte was starting to twitch), when Eugène arrived in his new uniform as Colonel of the Consul Guards, and all the girls made a fuss, causing him to blush.

Once all the guests had arrived, and everyone was comfortably settled, and the children were quieted with bribes of comfits, we talked of the excitement in Paris over the coming debut at the Théâtre-Français of Talma's protégée, an actress of only fifteen. Then we exchanged news of Jérôme and Pauline, both in the Islands. Of young Jérôme, not much could be said—only that he had written for more money (as usual)—but Pauline is reported to like Saint-Domingue after all, "in spite of the snakes and savages."

After a collation Louis solemnly presented Hortense with a stunning set of rubies. She was overwhelmed, I believe, for there were tears in her eyes as she thanked him quite sweetly. Then the true jewel of my daughter's crown, her beautiful baby, was brought in by the nursemaid for everyone to admire. He belched quite splendidly, which made us all cheer. The children squealed and jumped up and down to see his pink little face, as Louis and Hortense and the doting godparents—Bonaparte and I—looked on proudly.

I can't remember a gathering when my family and the Bonaparte clan have been so united—if one can call it that. I suspect Aunt Fanny with her careless ways (she sat on the arm of a chair) and Aunt Désirée with her girlish pretensions (flowers in her hair at sixty!) horrified Signora Letizia. Oh, that evil eye! Yet all in all, and in spite of the jealousies, it was a lovely family fête, thanks largely to the children. I induced them to sit quietly near me so that they could stay with the adults. Little Napoleon lay in my arms the entire time.

"Ah, portrait of a mother," Caroline said, holding out her thumb and squinting at me as an artist might. "Pity—"

*Fort de France, Martinico*
*Chère Yeyette, my beloved niece,*

*We promise, we'll consider your offer and talk it over with Stéphanie. She's a spirited girl. You'll be pleased with your goddaughter, should you ever have an opportunity to meet her.*

*The house you purchased for your mother in town is magnificent. Now all we have to do is prise her out of her ramshackle abode in Trois-Ilets.*

*Your well-meaning uncle, Robert Tascher*

*November 17—Saint-Cloud.*

A meeting with Madame Campan this afternoon, regarding the staff required for Saint-Cloud, their duties and functions. "One lady-in-waiting isn't enough," she said, looking over my notes.

I confessed I didn't know what exactly a lady-in-waiting *did*.

"Ladies-in-waiting do just that: wait."

"But for what?"

"For whatever you fancy. To join you for a game of chance, or a walk in the garden. To hold your fan should you care to dance. To call for a servant to bring refreshment, should you suffer a sudden and unexpected thirst. To read to you as you work at your frame. To amuse your guests with intelligent and pleasing conversation. To reflect well upon you, by virtue of their reputation and breeding. In short, to make your life pleasing. I suggest you begin with four."

"Won't that be too many?"

"At the speed at which your husband's destiny is unfolding, Madame Bonaparte, I predict that you will soon require five times that number."

Just then my dame d'annonce opened one of the double doors and exclaimed, "Citoyen Talma!" so loudly that I let out a little shriek. "Madame Campan, perhaps you could help with the training of the staff," I suggested under my breath as the great actor entered with an air of regal authority—made somewhat difficult by the sheepskin cap he was wearing and a silly little muff he had hanging from a cord around his neck.

Slipping off his hat and tucking it under his right arm, Talma looked slowly about the room, his eyes lingering on the bronze chandeliers, the yellow velvet chairs, *us*. With a fluid motion, he placed his right gloved hand behind his back (without letting the hat slip), the other extended, palm up, and bowed deeply. "Ladies," he said, his voice resonant. "My pleasure." Then, with a nervous, almost tragic intensity, he slipped off his gloves and ran his fingers through his unpowdered hair. "How was that?"

"Excellent!" I said, clapping. "Madame Campan, what do you think? Was that not a perfect entry?"

"Commanding," Madame Campan agreed. "But the gloves stay on."

I persuaded Talma to join us for a glass of Chablis. We shared the news we'd each gleaned in various salons, reviews of the various spectacles we'd attended, the excitement about his young protégée, Mademoiselle Georges. The volatile actor confessed that he was fraught with concern that she would fail him. "She's a child, and yet she is to play Clytemnestra! What does she know about maternal feelings? Grand Dieu! I will never survive this debut."

Shortly after Talma was summoned by Bonaparte, Madame Campan took her leave as well. I saw her out through the labyrinth of corridors to her carriage. On return, passing Bonaparte's cabinet, I heard sounds of violence: a terrifying shriek. The guards came running, their hands on the pommels of their swords, and threw open the cabinet door to reveal two startled men: Bonaparte standing about three feet from Talma, who was holding a plumed quill aloft like a dagger.

"What is it?" Bonaparte demanded, turning.

I looked at Talma and then back at my husband. "It sounded as if someone was being murdered!"

Talma burst into laughter. "I told you that you should consider a career on the stage, First Consul."

Sheepishly, Bonaparte showed me the papers in his hand: a play script. "I was helping Talma rehearse a murder scene," he said.


*November 20—Saint-Cloud.*
I've been interviewing applicants for the various staff positions all week. It's exhausting—and I've several more to interview tomorrow.

A wonderful respite today when Hortense came with the baby. Bonaparte and I turned into silly beings, cooing and talking nonsense, making faces and peering into the face of this perplexed little one— notre petit chou.

"You see?" Bonaparte said when the baby made a face. "He knows me."

I *love* being a grandmother.


*November 21, still raining.*
"Madame Rémusat?" I hadn't seen Claire Rémusat for over a decade— she'd been a girl then. Clari, we'd called her. Although she was a young woman now, I recognized her sharp little nose and lively eyes.

"Madame Bonaparte," she said, dropping her head. Her graceful move showed respect, but displayed good breeding, as well.

Short and a little plump, there was something childlike about her; she seemed younger than her twenty-two years, perhaps due to her archaic pleated cap.

I led her to the chair by the fire. "Do you mind if I call you Claire?" During the Terror, she and Hortense had played with dolls together, but that wasn't the only thing they had in common. Tragically, both girls had lost a father to the guillotine. (Oh, those terrible days . . . )

"I would be honoured, Madame Bonaparte," she said, straightening the neck ruffle of her old-fashioned gown, "but most people still call me Clari." She placed her hands in her lap, one hand over another (to cover a stain on her glove).

"Hortense tells me that you are married and have two children."

"Two boys," she said, her melancholy eyes brightening. "One five years and quick, the other two years, but an infant in his growth and mind." She swallowed before adding, with heartfelt emotion, "Madame Bonaparte, you are well-known for your generous heart, for your will-ingness to help the unfortunate. The Angel of Mercy, people call you, because you further the cause of every petition that is made to you—you never turn anyone away. We lost everything during the Revolution. We have not a sou. I beseech you, please help us."

"I am the one in need of help," I assured her. The daughter of an impoverished aristocratic family, Clari no doubt found it humbling to beg employment. "I am in need of someone to accompany me—a lady-in-waiting. The salary is only twelve thousand francs, but you would share the position with several others, so you would still have time for your family."

"You are so kind!"

"And your husband?" I asked. "The First Consul might be able to employ him, as well."

"I will be forever indebted," she said, clasping my hands, her compo-sure giving way.

*November 23, late morning.*

Bonaparte has approved my selection of ladies-in-waiting (except for the Duchess d'Aiguillon,* alas). Madame Lucay, Madame de Copons del Llor, and Madame Lauriston will report in shifts, beginning in a few weeks. Clari Rémusat will begin immediately. Her husband will be one of Bonaparte's chamberlains, as well—which solves their monetary embarrassment.

*November 27.*

Clari Rémusat, her husband and children moved into a suite at Saint-Cloud yesterday. She is quick-witted and cultured, and seems eager to be of assistance—certainly, I can use help.

*November 29—Saint-Cloud, chilly.*

"I picked up your parcel in town, Madame," Clari announced from the door, pushing back the hood of her cloak.

"I'm so glad you're here," I said, making smiling wide-eyes at Clari's two boys, their cheeks red from the wind. "I'd like your advice." I'd been studying a book of Greek statues that my architects had loaned me, and I was trying to get my shawl to fall in the manner of one statue in particular.

"We got held up on the Rue Saint-Honoré," Clari said, handing her youngest child into her nursemaid's arms. "You should see the lineup at the Théâtre-Français! Even at noon there was a long queue."

"A lady got hurt and the police were there," her eldest boy Charles said, one hand clutching the skirt of his mother's gown.

"Oh dear!" I told the boy, putting my hands to my cheeks—or pretending to. I was *not* to touch my face. Citoyen Isabey, Hortense's art instructor, had attended to my make-up and regarded my face as a work of art.

"It's true." The child nodded. He is an exceptionally sombre five-year-old, mature for his years.

"Apparently, there was a bit of a press when Mademoiselle Georges

---

* *The Duchess d'Aiguillon had shared a prison cell with Josephine during the Terror. She was not permitted to hold a position at court because she had been divorced.*

arrived," Clari said. "The Venus of Paris, people are calling the girl. Is it true she's only fifteen?"

It was after six by the time Bonaparte and I arrived at the theatre. "Not a seat empty," the theatre manager told us, escorting us to our box. "And now, may the performance begin," he announced, bowing deeply as the audience cheered.

Over the balustrade I looked to see what faces I recognized, nodding to acknowledge Minister Talleyrand, and the Second and Third Consuls, Cambacérès and Lebrun. In the third tier, way at the back, I thought I recognized Fouché, sitting alone. "*Everyone* is here," I whispered to Bonaparte. Caroline and Joachim (in pink), Elisa and Félix. "*And* Joseph," I said—but not with Julie. "Ah, it's your mother." I made a little wave to them all, but they didn't wave back.

By the end of the first act, the audience was becoming restless, in spite of Talma's riveting performance as Achilles. Everyone had come to see Mademoiselle Georges play Clytemnestra, and she was not to appear until the second act. So when the curtain opened, the claque cheered loudly.

At last the moment arrived: Clytemnestra stepped onto the stage. She *is* beautiful—tall!—but from our close vantage point, I could see that the poor girl was trembling. "Mon Dieu, Bonaparte, she can't speak," I whispered. Fortunately, the appreciative murmur of the crowd seemed to give the young actress courage and she began to recite her lines—somewhat mechanically, however, and without that fire that one senses in the great artists of the theatre.

It was during the third act that the trouble began. My heart jumped at the first hiss. It seemed to come from the benches toward the front. Then increasingly the critics became more and more vocal until, during the fourth and final act, there was a very long hiss during one of Mademoiselle Georges's speeches. Then the pit erupted: shouting, raising canes and umbrellas. Blows were exchanged!

Poor Mademoiselle Georges stuttered out a few lines. She looked as if she might faint. "Courage, Georges!" I heard someone yell out, and at this the young actress's voice became strong—angry even—and the audience fell silent. At the final curtain, the audience burst into cheers.

*December 1, early evening—Saint-Cloud.*

Talma struck a pose, his eyes raised in prayer, his shoulders thrown back, signifying pride. "Even Geoffroy, that idiot of a critic, was impressed with my protégée's masterful performance," he said, crossing both hands on his chest, casting his eyes down slowly and bowing his noble head.

"Bravo!" Clari clapped with delight. The famous theatre critic had recently lashed out against Talma, calling him a "Quaker of dramatic art." Talma's new school of acting, in Geoffroy's view, should be banished for tampering with the incantatory alexandrine.

"That's wonderful," I exclaimed, feeling that perhaps it was Talma who should be commended for a masterful performance. Although certainly beautiful, Mademoiselle Georges tends to speak her lines in a monotonous drawl, and that, to my mind, hinders perfect elocution. Still, she is only fifteen. "We should send her a note of congratulation, Bonaparte."

"I've already seen to it," Bonaparte said, staring out onto the terrace, lost in thought.


*December 16—cold!*

Troubling news from the Islands. Things are not going well in Saint-Domingue—apparently there has been a revolt. "Damn Victor Leclerc!" Bonaparte ranted. "I gave him my best men, our most seasoned soldiers, and even then he can't manage so much as a skirmish."


*December 22—still at Saint-Cloud.*

I confess I'm growing weary of Mademoiselle Georges—weary of the cult of enthusiasm that attends her every move. Or is it simply that I am growing old, and am jealous of her youth?

Bonaparte and I arrived late at the theatre. Mademoiselle Georges was centre stage, drawling a monologue. (There I go again!) The audience applauded our appearance, demanding that the actors start over—which they did.

All in all, it was a passable performance, I thought—at least on the part of the young actress. There was one curious moment when Mademoiselle

Georges said the line, "If I have charmed Cinna, I shall charm other men as well," and the audience craned to look at Bonaparte.

"It appears they think you've been charmed," I said, touching my husband's hand (watching his eyes).


*December 23.*
Terrible news—Victor Leclerc is *dead*. He died in Saint-Domingue of yellow fever. We are stunned to hear it. Bonaparte's beautiful sister Pauline is now a widow.

Bonaparte's new secretary brought the bulletin just after Bonaparte and I had finished our midday meal. "It regards your sister's husband, First Consul," Méneval said.

Bonaparte scanned the bulletin, then folded it, creasing it methodically. "My poor sister," he said, standing.

Victor Leclerc, dead at thirty-six. (He was older than I thought.) "The blond Bonaparte" we called him because of his habit of adopting Bonaparte's movements, even Bonaparte's expressions—which was why he irritated Bonaparte so much, I think.

We aren't sure how to proceed, frankly. Victor's family must be notified, of course. Who is to do it? My heart goes out to his mother and father, flour merchants, so very proud of their son.


*[Undated]*
The news is even worse than we originally thought. A vast percentage of the men sent to Saint-Domingue have died of yellow fever. The numbers are stupefying: of the twenty-eight thousand who sailed, fewer than ten thousand remain. *Mon Dieu.* How is that possible?

Bonaparte is overcome. This evening I placed his coffee at his elbow, touched his hand so that he knew it was there, returned to my frame. All the while he sat motionless, his hand over his mouth.


*February 12, 1803.*
Pauline is back, her husband in a lead coffin, her beautiful black hair

shorn, entombed with Victor's body. She is enfeebled, both physically and emotionally. "They all died," she said weakly, kissing Bonaparte's hands. "Every last one of them."


*February 19, early—not yet 9:00 A.M. (and cold).*
England is refusing to honour the terms of the peace treaty. Bonaparte is not sleeping well, if at all.

"Stay, Bonaparte," I said, reaching for him in the middle of the night.

"I'll sleep when I'm dead," he said, pulling away.

I feel old in his presence—unappealing, without grace. I feel like a beggar, scrambling.


*February 28—Paris.*
"Mimi?" I found her in the wardrobe. I'd debated all morning about taking this step, was debating even as I spoke.

"I wish I could find that new lace veil, the silk one," she said, going through an open trunk. "I know I saw it here not long ago."

"Maybe it's at Malmaison. Or at Saint-Cloud." I never know where anything is anymore. I sat down on the little velvet stool in front of the chimney. "I was wondering, have you heard any rumours?"

Mimi closed the lid of the trunk. "About?"

I shrugged. "Oh, about Bonaparte and a woman."

"There are always rumours."

"For example?"

She blew out her cheeks. "Flowers are being sent upstairs of late."

"To the room above Bonaparte's cabinet?"

She screwed up her face.

"You could find out for me. You could ask Roustam, or Bonaparte's valet—or even Hugo, the cabinet guard." Even the new secretary would know, I realized with chagrin. "*Please*, Mimi."

I may be played false, but I'll be damned if I am going to be played for a fool.

*March 2, 2:30 P.M.*
"There's a young woman who comes most every afternoon around four, and . . ." Mimi put up her hands. "And that's *all* I know."


*March 3.*
"It's that actress everyone is talking about."

Mademoiselle Georges. I knew it! "The girl," I said.

"She's not a girl anymore."


*March 12—gloomy Tuileries.*
"Your powder was smudged tonight," Bonaparte said as I slipped under the covering sheet.

Of course it was—I'd been crying! Our weekly dinner for over one hundred in the Gallery of Diana had been unusually trying. Conversation kept coming around to theatre, to the "brilliance" of Mademoiselle Georges. Glances in my direction made it clear that everyone knows. "I'm miserable, Bonaparte."

Bonaparte took a candle and disappeared into the wardrobe. He looked ghostly re-emerging, the light from the candle throwing shadows over his face. "I couldn't find a handkerchief," he said, handing me a madras head scarf. "Now—what's this all about?"

I could tell from his tone that he knew the answer. "It concerns your *amourette* . . . with Mademoiselle Georges."

He sat down on the end of the bed, his nightcap askew.

"There's no use in denying it!" At the last theatrical we'd attended, Mademoiselle Georges had the audacity to wear *my* lace veil on stage.

Bonaparte crossed his arms. "Why should my amusements matter to you? I'm not going to fall in love."

"But Bonaparte, it's not right—"

"It is *my* right!"


*[Undated]*
Clari discovered me in my dressing room in tears. The gentle touch of

her hand on mine unleashed my torrent of woes. She, so sweetly comforting and wise beyond her years, advised me to be patient. "This is but a temporary affair, Madame. It will pass, time will cure."

I know, I know, I nodded—but I was raging within. Plump, aging La Grassini was one thing—this beautiful young actress is another matter altogether.

"Just ignore it, that's my advice. It's your gentle acceptance that the First Consul loves. He will return to you, in time."

Gentle acceptance? I imagine Bonaparte in the arms of that girl and I weep tears of despair! I imagine her young, supple body—so responsive and fertile—and I feel withered within. I am not a young woman, and in truth, I fear I am older than my years, for my passion is no longer of the flesh. Passion of heart I have—oh yes—and spirit in abundance. But no amount of salves, lotions and face paint can disguise the dryness of my skin, my thinning hair—my waning lust.

Oh, I know this emotion all too well, this humiliating jealousy, this *fear*. My first husband was a coxcomb, true—and he never did love me. Bonaparte does: I know that! And it is *this* that frightens me—the possible loss of his love.

## *In which Bonaparte is deceived*

*March 14, 1803—Saint-Germain-en-Laye.*
In spite of the wind and driving rain, I set out for Saint-Germain early this morning. The hastily penned note from Aunt Désirée's new husband*—sent by courier, no less—worried me: "Come quickly, your aunt is gravely ill."

Therefore I was relieved (but also, I confess, not a little surprised) to find Aunt Désirée, her husband Monsieur Pierre *and* Aunt Fanny enjoying brandy and crumpets.

"What are *you* doing here?" Aunt Désirée demanded, trying to rise from the chaise longue.

"Gentle b-b-beloved," Monsieur Pierre stuttered (for this is what he calls her!), "you have been ailing, and I thought—"

"You thought I was dying?" Aunt Désirée said in accusation.

The poor man turned crimson.

"Stop stuttering and pour my niece a brandy, Monsieur Pierre," Aunt Fanny said. "She's been out in all that fresh air. Grand Dieu, if anyone's apt to die today, it's going to be her, and then we'll all be the worse for it. She brings the First Consul good luck—everyone says so. God knows where we'd be without *her*."

"So all the more reason for the First Consul to stay *home*," Aunt Désirée said with an all-too-knowing look.

* *Not long after the Marquis's death, Désirée married the mayor of Saint-Germain-en-Laye, Pierre Danès de Montardat.*

"And not to be going out all the time to the *theatricals*," Aunt Fanny said, emptying her glass of brandy and holding it out for more.

"I'm fine, thank you," I told Monsieur Pierre, declining a glass. "You have not been well?" I asked Aunt Désirée—intentionally changing the subject. It was humiliating to discover that Bonaparte's amourette with Mademoiselle Georges was talked about even in Saint-Germain.

"Your Aunt Désirée has endocarditis," Monsieur Pierre said.

"Which rhymes with nothing," Aunt Fanny said, frowning.

"It's something to do with the heart," Aunt Désirée explained, fluttering her hands over her bosom, "with the irritation of blood passing through it. At least that's what the doctor said, but what does *he* know? I'm the picture of health, as you can see."

However, not long after Aunt Fanny departed and Monsieur Pierre excused himself to go to his club, Aunt Désirée did, in fact, become quite ill—an attack coming on suddenly and severely. I helped her to her chamber where she collapsed into her musty feather bed.

"I'm sending for a doctor," I insisted.

"No, wait," she said, gesturing me back to her bedside.

"Aunt Désirée—rest. You must not talk!"

"This is important! I speak from your mother's grave."

*Mother's* grave? But Mother isn't dead!

"Just listen! To keep a husband, a wife must be cheerful and understanding, but above all, *blind*."

I promised to heed her advice on the condition that she rest and allow me to send for the doctor. He's with her now.


5:20 P.M.

Mon Dieu, we've lost her. The doctor left with assurances that Aunt Désirée was not in danger. I was preparing the tincture he'd prescribed when she began to turn blue, struggling for breath.

"Aunt Désirée!" I cried out, overcome with alarm. She was slipping away, and there was no one to help, no one I could turn to. I ran to the door and yelled for the servants. Someone!

"Above all, be blind!" she gasped.

I was trying to calm her when she suddenly stopped breathing and died in my arms.

I persuaded a very distraught Monsieur Pierre to retire as I helped the maids lay Aunt Désirée out. I moved without tears, my heart curiously still. Gently, I closed her eyes, arranged her limbs, helped wash and dress her. We debated: should she wear stays? "She wouldn't want to be without them," I finally decided. Even in death. Even in the hereafter.

After all was done, I dismissed the servants, and sat by her side as the candles melted down. Oh, Aunt Désirée, how can *you* leave me?

*March 19, Saint Joseph's Day—Tuileries.*
I returned from Aunt Désirée's funeral in a melancholic state of mind, so it seemed only fitting to find Bonaparte sitting in a darkened room, the drapes closed against the bright spring sun. He got up, but did not pace. "I've been in meetings with the Minister of the Marine," he said, leaning against the fireplace mantel.

Decrès? "And . . . ?"

"You know how he has become so much slimmer of late? I suspected that there was a petticoat in the picture, but never in a thousand years would I have guessed whom the old dog was courting." He snorted. "My sister Pauline, the bereft widow."

I was not surprised to hear that Pauline is receiving callers. Mourning is boring, she had said when last we saw her. But *Decrès*? "I guess it's time to look for a husband for her, Bonaparte," I told him, picking a long black hair off his collar. *Above all, be blind*, I heard a familiar voice say.

*Fort de France, Martinico*
*Chère Yeyette, my beloved niece,*
*This morning Stéphanie sailed on* Le Dard *for Brest, France. She is only fifteen, so you can understand a father's concern. Have you arranged a chaperone for her? Were it not for the prospect of a proper education and a good marriage, my wife and I would have kept her near.*

*Your mother objected that the chicken coop attached to the magnificent house you bought for her in Fort de France was not sufficiently large. I ordered a larger one built, but chicken coop or no chicken coop, your mother refuses to be moved from her ramshackle country abode.*

*God bless you.*

*Your fond but aging uncle, Robert Tascher*

*April 8, Good Friday.*

I've just hired Mademoiselle Avrillion, an impoverished aristocrat of impeccable credentials: quiet, serious, virtuous. She'll help with the wardrobe for now, and when my goddaughter Stéphanie arrives from Martinico, she'll be the girl's chaperone.

*When* young Stéphanie arrives!

*April 28.*

Bonaparte is in a temper of frustration. England is flagrantly breaking the terms of the peace treaty. "Peace hasn't proved profitable for them," he said. "The perfidious British are doing everything they can to provoke war again."

*May 17.*

I've never been so upset. I don't know what to do, where to begin.

England has seized French ships near Brest. Bonaparte made sure I was sitting down before he told me, very gently and with assurances that all would eventually be well, that the ship *Le Dard* was one of those captured, and that my goddaughter had been taken captive.

I listened, I heard, but I didn't understand what he was saying. "Stéphanie has been kidnapped, you mean? By the British?"

There were tears in Bonaparte's eyes as he nodded, *yes.*

*May 22.*

The British are holding Stéphanie at Portsmouth and refuse to return her!

"Bonaparte, how can they do this? She's only a child!"

"Maudits anglais," Bonaparte cursed, pacing.

*May 25—back at Saint-Cloud.*
England has opened fire. Its navy captured one of our ships, killed ten men, wounded as many more.

No word on Stéphanie. I can't sleep.

*June 10.*
Bonaparte has received an offer from England to return Stéphanie, but along with a demand for trade concessions he felt he couldn't responsibly accept! I wept and begged and finally he agreed. We're both weak with emotion.

*June 14, 11:15 A.M.—Saint-Cloud.*
At last: Stéphanie will be returned. We are *so* relieved. "But she won't be here for a month at least," Bonaparte told me.

My breathing was coming in sharp gasps. "It's all right," he said, holding me close. "It's going to be all right."

*June 19.*
"I have to tour the north coast," Bonaparte informed me this morning. Of course, I nodded. War preparations. A fleet of flat-bottomed boats was being built, I knew—ships that could battle England's fleet, ships that could invade. "I want you to accompany me. Spare no expense. I must make a strong impression."

"Very well, Bonaparte," I told him, only too happy to oblige. "But are you prepared to pay?" Bonaparte wants me to be luxuriously attired in a new gown every evening, but he balks at paying the bills. "In advance," I persisted, suggesting an allowance not only for myself but also for Clari, the lady-in-waiting who will accompany me.

"Madame, how does one begin to dispense such a sum?" Clari asked me later in all seriousness, for Bonaparte has given her thirty thousand francs.

"Don't worry, Clari. It's really quite easy," I said, beginning a list of what I will need to take—but thinking, I confess, of what I will be leaving behind: a certain Mademoiselle Georges.

*June 23.*
We are ready, trunks packed, jewels in a velvet-lined strongbox. I've prepared for this trip as if for battle: my munitions are my gowns, my ointments, my salves.

I am forty today—an old woman, many would say, at an age when a woman has no claim on her husband's passions. I think with affection of Aunt Désirée, the seductive swish of her taffeta skirts. "Too old? Nonsense!"

"Every battle should have a definite object," Bonaparte says, and for me the object of this battle is his heart. In the north I will have Bonaparte to myself.

*June 25, I think—Amiens (overcast).*
The route to Amiens was decorated with a profusion of garlands, the streets and squares thronged with people cheering Bonaparte's arrival. In the heart of the city our carriage was forced to a halt. We heard the coachman protesting—for the people were unhitching our horses. Bonaparte looked uneasy. Crowds make him nervous, I know. Who is to say what might happen? And then a thunderous cheer went up and our carriage began to roll forward again—slowly, for we were being pulled by the people, so great was their adulation. Even Bonaparte's eyes were glistening.

*June 26—a Sunday.*
As I write this, I am deafened by the cheers of an enormous crowd at our window, crying out over and over, so fervently that the words become a heartbeat, a prayer: Long live Bonaparte! Long live Bonaparte! Long live Bonaparte!

I watch my husband, standing still as a statue. The cheers are a roar one can almost feel, a wave of rapture. What is he thinking?

"It's frightening, isn't it?" I have to raise my voice to be heard. "Who could ever have imagined *this*?"

"I did," he says, without turning, his tone strangely melancholy.

*[Undated]*

Bonaparte has succeeded in persuading most of the northern countries to close their ports to English goods. "Now if only I could stop the *exports* to England."

Russian hemp, for example, which gets sent to England to make rope for the British fleet. "Without rigging"—Bonaparte made a downward motion with his thumb—"even the invincible sink."

*July 7—Lille.*

Bonaparte threw a scented letter onto my embroidery frame. I recognized Pauline's unschooled hand. "Seems my beautiful sister has fully recovered from her devastating grief." He sat down, frowning as he counted silently on his fingers. "But she'll have to wait. It won't be a year until November."

"What won't be?" I asked, confused, trying to decipher Pauline's mis-spellings. "She's asking your permission to marry?" *Already?* Not Minister of the Marine Decrès, surely. I read on. "Prince Borghèse?"

Clari looked up from her lacework. Oh là là, her eyes said.

*Oh là là*, indeed! Prince Borghèse is the son of one of the wealthiest and most aristocratic families of Italy. I hate to think of the airs Pauline will put on if she becomes a princess.

*July 14, Bastille Day—Ghent.*

An exhausting day: audiences, visits to a public monument, two facto-ries, a dinner followed by a reception, then the theatre. Bonaparte fell asleep during the after-piece in comic verse. "I'm not made for pleasure," he said wearily, untying his neckcloth.

"Yet some forms of pleasure suit you very well." I smiled archly over my bare shoulder as I turned back the bed covers.

*August 12, 10:30 P.M.—Saint-Cloud again, at last.*
Louis, Hortense and the baby welcomed us home. Little Napoleon, big and healthy at nine months, gurgled at Bonaparte, which pleased him greatly. As we sat in the family drawing room, talking of this and that, the baby fell asleep in Bonaparte's arms—a precious portrait. Oh, how we love this child!

*August 21.*
Stéphanie has arrived! Bonaparte and I have collapsed.

She's . . . oh, how to describe her? She is tall, for one thing, a giant of a girl with the body of a woman and the restless energy of a two-year-old. "I had the best time in England," she exclaimed, smothering us in her embrace. "Getting kidnapped was so much fun!"

"When does she begin boarding school?" Bonaparte asked faintly, exhausted after only an hour of the girl's constant chatter.

In two days, I told him. In the meantime, Mademoiselle Avrillion is charged with containing this cyclone of energy. And as for Madame Campan—she's got a challenge ahead!

*October 24—Saint-Cloud, very late, long past midnight (can't sleep).*
We've survived Pauline's engagement dinner—nearly two hundred covers. There were fifteen of us at the head table: Bonaparte and I, Signora Letizia, Prince Camillo Borghèse and Pauline, Lucien, Elisa and Félix, Joseph and Julie, Louis and Hortense, Joachim and Caroline, Eugène.

Prince Camillo Borghèse is well made, surprisingly ignorant, shockingly wealthy. Pauline was already flaunting the famous Borghèse diamonds. Lucien and Joseph seemed uneasy—why? Elisa hiccupped through dinner, as usual. Joachim was more fancifully dressed than Caroline, in his pink velvet toque dripping with ostrich feathers. Eugène dutifully attended to the (constant) needs of Signora Letizia—even going so far as to fill her nostrils with snuff.

Much of the conversation was in Italian, for the benefit of Prince Borghèse, who seemed, however, not to understand what was being discussed regardless of the language. Pauline insisted on feeding him chicken morsels herself, the grease dripping onto his gold-embroidered silk vest.

"I can see why Paris is abuzz with gossip about *those* two," I told Eugène later, setting up for a game of billiards. I took the opening shot, a strong one that scattered the balls with a gratifying clatter.

Eugène shrugged, chalking his cue. By the light of the candles, he appeared to be flushed. Was it wine? No, I didn't think so. My son is moderate in his habits (at least around family). "Prince Borghèse is a good match for Pauline," he said, not meeting my eyes.

"Fortunately, they don't seem to mind waiting to marry," I said, studying the table.

"Maman . . ."

"Piffle," I said, missing my shot.

"Maman, there's something I've got to tell you. But you must promise not to tell Papa."

"You know I can't promise that, Eugène."

"Well . . ." He grimaced. "Pauline and Prince Borghèse are already married."

"They're . . . ?" *Married?*

"The first of September, Maman, at Mortefontaine—seven weeks ago. Joseph and Lucien were in on it," he went on nervously. "Julie told her dressmaker, who in turn told Hortense, who of course told—"

Hortense knew! "And she didn't tell *me*? And no one told Bonaparte?" *Mon Dieu.* I could just imagine the explosion. War with England is one thing—but to be played for a fool by his own family is another matter altogether. "Eugène, Bonaparte is going to be furious. He's just announced Pauline's engagement."

"That's why you mustn't tell him, Maman!"

*[Undated]*
"They're *what?*"

I nodded, my mouth dry. "September first," I said finally, swallowing.

"They've been married for two *months?*"

"But only a church service, not the legal one. I suppose that makes a difference?" Timidly!

"Sacrebleu! I can't believe it," Bonaparte muttered. "Who do they think I am? Some puppet they can play with—pull my strings, then put me away in a box when I get in the way?" He came to an abrupt stop, staring into the fire. "I suppose they all knew."

"I just found out myself," I said, rushing to assure him. "I debated whether or not to tell you. I know how much you have on your mind right now, and . . ." I held out my hands, palms up, a gesture of appeasement. "But in the end, I thought you would prefer to know."

"I'm leaving immediately for Boulogne on an urgent military matter," he said, sitting down at the escritoire, rummaging around for a quill, then scratching something on a scrap of paper. "Inform Pauline that I'm leaving with the express intention of *not* being present at the farce of her so-called wedding. I'll be away for two weeks."

"Bonaparte, it might be best if—"

"And furthermore!" His quill snapped, splattering droplets of ink onto his shirt. He pulled out the drawer of the secretaire with such force that it ended up in his lap, the contents strewn, sand everywhere. Quickly I scooped up a quill from the floor and handed it to him. "And furthermore," he went on, oblivious to the mess, "advise her that it would be in her best interest if she and her idiot husband departed for Rome before I return."

*November 6, Sunday—Mortefontaine.*
"Bonaparte said to send his regrets." I embraced Pauline. She was drenched in a syrupy scent that caught in my throat, made me cough. "He was called away on an urgent military matter." I made a peaceable

half-bow to Prince Borghèse (who could have used some scent).

"You don't have to lie, beloved sister." The "bride" broke into a mirthful giggle. "I guess I surprised him!"

"Yes, the First Consul was . . . *surprised*," I said, putting off informing her of Bonaparte's demand that she and her husband leave Paris immediately. Perhaps after the ceremony, I thought. But after the ceremony, Bonaparte's brother Lucien made an announcement that he himself had remarried one week before!

"I'm happy for you, Lucien," I lied, numb with shock.

Now, in the quiet of my room, I feel a sick head pain coming on, imagining Bonaparte's fury—deceived not once, but twice.


*November 10—Saint-Cloud.*
Family dinner tonight. Pauline agreed that she and Prince Borghèse will leave Paris before Bonaparte returns—on condition that she is formally "presented" at Saint-Cloud. Reluctantly I consented.


*November 13, Sunday.*
I should have guessed that *Princess* Pauline would make a theatrical event of the occasion. She and Prince Borghèse arrived at Saint-Cloud in a carriage drawn by six white horses, outriders in livery before and after carrying torches. My dame d'annonce threw open the double doors and announced (or rather, yelled), "Prince and Princess Borghèse."

Pauline entered the salon in a halo of blinding light, for she had adorned herself with virtually all the Borghèse diamonds. Her head, ears, neck and arms were loaded with a gaudy display of the priceless brilliants. Shuffling her feet to give the impression of floating, she approached me with her head bent forward in that strange position she considers regal.

"*Madame*," she said, bowing (slightly) before me, holding her hands rigid in order to avoid an unsightly bend at the wrist. Her eyes swept the crowd. *She* is a princess, and "a *real* one," she informed everyone, I'm told, coquetting with the men and loudly referring to her husband the prince as "that idiot."

They leave for Rome tomorrow.

*November 19—Saint-Cloud.*

"So!" Bonaparte yawned. "How did it go with Pauline?"

"As well as could be expected," I said cautiously, pulling the covers up over us. "They left five days ago for Rome." I didn't want to tell him about Lucien, but I knew I had to. "I have bad news, however." Quick, I thought, get it over with! "Lucien has married as well." I braced for an explosion, but there was only silence. "Madame Jouberthou, the widow of a broker." I winced before adding, "They married after the birth of their son." (But *before* they were sure that her husband was, in fact, dead. This I refrained from saying.)

"Lucien has a son?"

"Six months old now."

"I don't understand. He told me he'd consider marrying the Queen of Etruria,"* Bonaparte said, trying to comprehend. "And he was already married when he told me that?" He was silent for what seemed a long time. "Sometimes I wonder if my family even cares about me," he said finally.

"Your family loves you."

He took me in his arms. "I only have you."

We talked until dawn—of his mother, his brothers and sisters, Hortense and Eugène. We shared our enchantment with little Napoleon. Bonaparte said that although we would miss seeing the baby every day, he thought it would be good for Hortense and Louis to live in Compiègne for a time, Louis to take command of the troops stationed there. We talked of the challenges ahead, of preparing to battle England—and then, very late, Bonaparte began to talk of what was truly on his mind.

"What will happen if I die? What will become of France?" It was an outpouring of emotion, as if he had needed to unburden himself. "Who can I talk to? Who can I trust?"

I put his hand to my heart.

---

* Etruria was an independent principality along the Mediterranean coast. A family alliance would have given Napoleon control over the port of Genoa—strategically important in the war against England.

*November 24.*

"I'm tired of going out to the theatre every night," Bonaparte said last night. "Let's stay in—just the two of us." This with an amorous look.

Mimi grinned at me as she closed the door behind her. No flowers are being sent up to the little room.

## *In which once again we have reason to fear*

*January 28, 1804—Tuileries.*

I didn't know whether to be relieved or alarmed to hear Fouché announced late this evening. I knew he would not have called at such an hour without a reason.

"Ah, Senator Fouché, it's good to see you," Bonaparte said, inviting him to join us in our private suite. "A Corsican will always invite a caller to his hearth," he added, attempting to be convivial.

It was chilly in the drawing room. Bonaparte fanned the embers. "And so?" he said, turning to face his former Minister of Police, his arms crossed. "You must have something to report."

"Bonaparte!" I said, pouring our guest a glass of verjuice. "Do we not inquire, first, as to Madame Fouché, all the charming Fouché children?" I smiled at my friend as I handed him the grape drink I knew he preferred. "Everyone is well?"

"As well as can be expected," Fouché said, downing the glass. "Yes, First Consul, I thought you might be interested to know that the Royalist agent Cadoudal is back in Paris—plotting your death yet again."

Cadoudal! The Royalist agent responsible for the Christmas Eve bomb—the "infernal machine"? I looked at Bonaparte, alarmed. "But I thought Cadoudal was in England."

"It appears he has been in town for several months," Fouché said evenly, "working on behalf of the Pretender. Financed by England, no doubt."

"That's impossible!" Bonaparte exploded.

"As you so often point out, First Consul, 'impossible' is not a French word."

"Cadoudal is as big as an ox. I ask you, how could he be in this city without the police being aware of it?"

"I asked myself the same question. How *could* they have missed him? According to my informants, Georges Cadoudal was hoisted by ship cable up a 250-foot cliff close to Dieppe on the fourth of Fructidor—August twenty-first. No doubt your police know the spot: certainly it is well-known to smugglers."

"End of August? Mon Dieu, Bonaparte—that's almost five months ago."

Bonaparte faced Fouché, his hands fists. "If this is a ruse on your part to discredit the police so that you will be reinstated as minister, it won't do any good."

"I didn't expect that you would believe me, First Consul," Fouché said, handing Bonaparte a scrap of paper. "I suggest you ask your police to have a word with this man at the abode indicated. His hours are regular. He's there until 9:50 every morning. He'll tell you what you need to know. In any case, it would be prudent to double or triple the number of guards you have protecting you." In the doorway, he tipped his hat. "At your service, First Consul, as always."

"Sacrebleu! This again," Bonaparte cursed.


*February 5, Sunday—Paris.*
I was preparing to go calling this afternoon when Bonaparte appeared. He sat down in his customary armchair next to my toilette table, fiddling with the crystal stopper of a bottle of lavender water. "Where are you going?" he asked.

"Madame de Souza is receiving this afternoon." I smoothed another dab of ceruse* under my eyes. I had not been sleeping well.

"Madame de Souza, the wife of the Spanish ambassador, and a writer of romances." Bonaparte pushed out his lips, as if considering this information.

---

* Ceruse was a thick paste made with white lead—and consequently corrosive and poisonous. It was used for several centuries as a make-up base, with devastating consequences.

"It's a pre-carnival fête, she said, in lieu of a ball," I explained, leaning into the glass to see how my make-up looked, then leaning back, squinting to get the effect. "Idle chatter, ladies mostly—the type of thing you hate. I made excuses for you."

But he wasn't listening. "I'd like you to take an escort," he said, drumming his fingers.

"But Bonaparte, it's only minutes away, and I'll have the pages with me, as well as two guards." The usual parade. (Oh, for the days when I could go out alone!) "Getting an escort together would take at least thirty minutes and I'm running behind as it is."

"Josephine . . ." He paused, sitting forward, leaning his forearms on his knees. "Fouché was right. Cadoudal *is* in Paris, along with a number of other assassins, as it turns out."

"A *number*?" Bonaparte rarely showed alarm, but something in his manner—the very stillness of his expression—made me wary.

"Twenty-four, to be precise."

"In Paris!" I reached for a handkerchief, pressed it to my mouth, inhaled the calming scent of lavender.

His hand felt hot on my shoulder. "We're hiring more guards and closing the gates to the city at night."

But the assassins were *in* the city, not outside. "Bonaparte, we *need* Fouché."

"Don't worry. Unofficially Fouché will be overseeing everything."

"That's reassuring," I said, sitting back. Maybe, with Fouché watching, we will be safe.


*Shortly after 11:00 P.M.*
The city gates are to be closed from seven each evening to six the next morning. Searches have begun of all carriages and wagons, looking for evidence of Cadoudal, his accomplices.

"Just like *those* days," Clari said, meaning the Terror. Only this time, we're the ones closing the gates, we're the ones searching.

*February 8—late, almost midnight.*

"What is this about?" Signora Letizia jabbed her stiff finger at a copy of *Le Moniteur*.

"What it's about, Maman, is that England has hired a Royalist thug to murder your son," Caroline answered, lingering over the word *murder* for effect.

"Ca-doo-dahl?"

"But don't worry," I said, offering my mother-in-law the seat of honour. "The police have it well in hand." Fouché, in fact—but that I could not say. I dared not even hint that the man the clan had persuaded Bonaparte to demote had been the one to uncover the plot. Had it not been for Fouché, Bonaparte might well be dead.

"Worry? The Funds are up," Elisa said between hiccups.

"Nothing like a little crisis to stimulate the economy," Joseph responded with a satisfied look. "I've a meeting at the Bourse tomorrow morning, Maman. Would you like me to speak with the man who handles your investments?"

"Naturalmente," Signora Letizia said, her knitting needles clattering.

"Perhaps now is as good a time as any to make a family announcement." Joseph smiled uneasily. "I've word from the Islands that Jérôme has married an American girl in Baltimore."

Mon Dieu, I thought, glancing at Bonaparte. Not another one.

"That's impossible," Bonaparte said evenly. "Jérôme's only nineteen. Legally, he can't marry without permission."

"He can in America, apparently," Joseph said.

"Basta!"

First Pauline, then Lucien, and now Jérôme.


*February 10—Tuileries.*

Louis and Hortense arrived from Compiègne last night. "Did you get my letter?" I asked, embracing my daughter. She has put on weight, which pleases me. "You didn't bring the baby?"

"He's asleep in his basket," Louis said, stepping aside to let the maid in with a tray. "What's going on? We had a difficult time getting through the city gates."

"The police have uncovered another plot against Bonaparte." How much could I tell them? "Remember Cadoudal?"

Hortense looked at me, alarmed. "*He's* in Paris?"

"He is believed to be here somewhere."

"But I thought he was in England," Louis said.

"No doubt he's in the *pay* of England," I said.

We heard tuneless singing outside the door, and then a baby's squeal. Bonaparte appeared in the doorway with little Napoleon in his arms. "At least *he* likes my singing," he said with a grin.

*February 14, Shrove Tuesday—Tuileries.*
Still no sign of Cadoudal, but a Royalist in the Abbaye Prison has admitted coming to France with him. The plan, he said, was to kidnap Bonaparte. The essential coup, they called it.

"Kidnap? That's a ruse. The only way to get rid of me is to kill me," Bonaparte ranted.

Frankly, we are all shocked. According to this Royalist's confession, General *Moreau* is implicated, one of the most popular generals in the Republican armies. How can that be?

*4:35 P.M.*
Bonaparte is constantly in meetings with the Special Council. Now and again he emerges with a drawn look.

*February 15, very early.*
Bonaparte didn't sleep at all last night, tossing this way and that until the covering sheet was in a damp knot. With the first light of dawn, he sat up. "I've come to a decision."

I knew from the slump of his shoulders what it would be.

*February 16.*
The news of Moreau's arrest was made public this morning. Everyone is stunned. Even the market was silent, Mimi told me.


*March 8—Malmaison.*
I persuaded Bonaparte that we should move to Malmaison for a few weeks to escape the tension in Paris, but even here, in this beautiful season, fear robs us of repose. Couriers come and go, officials with leather portfolios and sombre expressions. Daily Bonaparte is in meetings, locked up with his advisors. Still no sign of Cadoudal.


*March 9—our eighth-year anniversary.*
Our anniversary dinner was interrupted by a caller: Fouché. "Show him in," Bonaparte said, pushing back his plate of chicken bones.

Fouché appeared in mud-splattered top boots. "Cadoudal has been found."

"Arrested?"

"One of the conspirators alerted us to a plan to move him to another hiding spot. We apprehended his cabriolet on Place St-Étienne-du-Mont, but in the struggle he managed to escape."

"Answer my question, Fouché," Bonaparte said. "*Has* Cadoudal been arrested?"

"His carriage only got as far as Place de l'Odéon, where he was cut off by two policemen. One grabbed the horse, and Cadoudal shot him dead. The second officer was shot in the hip as he attempted to hit Cadoudal with a club. Then Cadoudal jumped from the carriage—"

"Now I know you're deceiving me. Cadoudal jump? He is a big man—he finds just stepping down out of a carriage difficult."

"First Consul, I may be devious, but I never lie. As Cadoudal began to run, the wounded officer—with the help of two brave citizens, I should add—managed to grab him and hit him over the head."

"So he *is* in custody. Has he confessed?"

"Only that he came to Paris with the intention of overthrowing you. His attitude is . . . well, certainly not repentant. When informed that the policeman he'd killed was a husband and father, he suggested we send bachelors on such missions next time."

"The bastard."

"The *wealthy* bastard. His pockets were stuffed with English gold. They have paid him well."

"Give it to the officer's widow."

"We already have."

Immediately after Fouché left, Talleyrand appeared. "We have apprehended Cadoudal, First Consul," he said, bowing deeply, his voice fawning.

"I am already aware of that, Minister Talleyrand. Fouché was just here."

Talleyrand blinked slowly. Only a crease on each side of his mouth gave any indication of the displeasure he must have felt at his rival's getting the rightful credit for the arrest. "I have been studying the documents found in Cadoudal's effects." Talleyrand presented a portfolio of papers, holding it out reverently in white-gloved hands as if offering up a sacrament.

Bonaparte pulled the parchment papers out and quickly riffled through them. "Explain," he said, throwing them down.

"According to these documents, First Consul, Cadoudal and his men were waiting for someone they referred to as 'the prince' to join them before they made their move."

Bonaparte paced. "What prince?"

"Perhaps we should discuss this in your office, First Consul."

"Speak!"

"Two of Cadoudal's servants have been questioned. They each declared that every ten or twelve days a gentleman came to call on Cadoudal—a man of middle height, corpulent and balding. Cadoudal always met him at the door, so apparently he was a person of consequence. When he was in the room, nobody sat down."

"And you think this man is 'the prince.'"

"It is a logical conclusion."

"A Bourbon prince?"

"Likely."

"It doesn't sound like either the Pretender or his brother."

"But the Duke d'Enghien resides one hundred and thirty leagues from Paris, First Consul—just across the Rhine river at Ettenheim."

"Enghien fought against us in Italy," Bonaparte said, frowning.

"The last hope of the house of Bourbon, it is said. It's possible that the plan was for Enghien to come to Paris as soon as you were"—Talleyrand paused for effect—"*dispensed* with. As a Bourbon representative, so to speak, he would have held Paris until the Pretender arrived from England and mounted the throne."

"The Duke d'Enghien is slender, Minister Talleyrand, is he not?" I asked, turning. He is said to be a charming man, and handsome—certainly not corpulent and balding. It is rumoured he has secretly married Princess de Rohan-Rochefort—la belle Charlotte. "In his late twenties, I would guess, and—"

But the men were already on their way out the door. Their voices grew faint until I could hear no longer. "I believe, First Consul, that . . . a lesson to those . . . endless conspiracies . . . the shedding of royal . . ."

*The shedding of royal blood*, I believe I heard Talleyrand say.


Now, recalling that conversation, playing it over in my mind, I am more and more uneasy. Why was Talleyrand pressing Bonaparte to suspect the Duke d'Enghien—a Bourbon prince beloved by Royalists everywhere?

I don't trust Talleyrand, frankly. He reminds me of a snake—he sheds coats too easily. He expresses admiration for, even worship of, Bonaparte—but is he sincere? He is known to take bribes, to extort enormous sums in his international dealings. His "loyalty" is of the kind that is bought for money, I suspect.


*March 18—Paris.*

Before Mass this morning Bonaparte told me, his voice so low I could hardly hear him, "We've arrested the Duke d'Enghien."

At first I didn't understand. "But isn't the Duke d'Enghien in Germany?"

"What does it matter? What is important is the charge: conspiring to commit murder—*my* murder."


On the long ride out to Malmaison, I broke down, confiding to Clari that the Duke d'Enghien had been arrested.

"Arrested for what, Madame?" She burst into tears, confiding that as a girl, she had kept an etching of the Duke d'Enghien in a secret spot under her mattress.

"I believe they intend to have him tried in connection with the conspiracy."

"But *he* can't be guilty!"

"Then he will be found innocent and go free," I reassured her.

Clari's agitation was extreme. It had been a mistake to confide in her, I realized. She is young, not skilled in the art of deception. "You must not let Bonaparte know that I have told you," I cautioned her as our carriage pulled through the Malmaison gates.

"Oh no, Madame, never!"

"So you must try to stop *weeping*," I said with a smile, handing her my handkerchief.

"Yes, Madame," she sobbed.


*March 19, Saint Joseph's Day.*
"Women know nothing about such matters!"

"Bonaparte, I cannot be silent on this." My attempts to seduce my husband into listening had met with failure.

"If I don't act firmly—*now*—I will have to go on and on prosecuting conspirators, exiling this man, condemning that man, without end. Is that what you want?"

"Surely it is not so simple."

"You forget that it is the Bourbons who are the cause of the turmoil in France. *They* are the ones seeking to murder me."

"But what if the Duke d'Enghien is innocent? General Moreau was arrested over a month ago. If the Duke d'Enghien is part of the conspiracy, would he have remained at Ettenheim? Cadoudal's servants reported that the mystery prince was corpulent. The Duke d'Enghien is said to be slender."

"There is evidence!"

"But Bonaparte, even if the Duke d'Enghien is guilty, if you were to convict him"—*execute* him, I feared—"all of Europe would rise up against you." The stain of royal blood is indelible, it is said.

"Do you want me killed?" He clenched his hands. "I must show the Bourbons who they're dealing with. I must give them a taste of the terror they are trying to inflict on me. I must show them I'm not to be trifled with—and I'm not!"

*March 20, 8:00 A.M.*
Gazing out over the gardens, I saw Bonaparte walking the paths between the flower beds, his pace and gestures agitated, as if arguing with himself. How small he seemed, pacing among the roses. "Little Bonaparte" I had once thought of him—before he'd become a giant in our eyes. (Our hearts!) I know how ardently he wishes to do the right thing, and I am beginning to comprehend how hard that can be.

*9:20 P.M.*
Around noon Hortense dropped little Napoleon off for me to look after—never have I more welcomed a child's innocent prattle. "I'll see you tomorrow?" I asked, kissing my daughter goodbye.

She and Louis were joining Caroline and Joachim for dinner, she said. She was running late, the boulevards had been congested—was something going on?

I shook my head. She is newly again with child. If only I could protect her from the realities of the world! I was thankful she left quickly, before she could see Clari's reddened eyes, before she looked too closely at my own.

*March 21.*
I was going to Bonaparte's cabinet this morning to drop off the usual

petitions when I heard him yelling: "What do you mean? Didn't he get my letter?"

I paused outside the door, holding my breath. I heard a man say something, then cough. Was it Savary, Bonaparte's aide? "I saw him on the road," the man said. It *was* Savary. "He didn't get your letter until this morning." Another cough. "When it was too late."

*Too late?*

"What do you mean, this morning? I gave that letter to you last night with the instructions that it was to go directly to the Prefect of Police!"

"I gave it to his valet."

"I didn't say to give it to his valet. I ordered you to give it to the man himself! Do you realize what you've done?"

I heard footsteps approaching behind me: one of the guards. "Do you wish to speak with the First Consul, Madame Josephine?" Hugo asked, his deep voice announcing my presence.

Bonaparte came to the door. "Josephine." He looked pale. "You are dismissed," he told Savary coldly, over his shoulder. The aide hurried out the door between us. "Come in," Bonaparte said, "I have something to tell you." I lowered myself onto a wooden armchair. "The Duke d'Enghien has been executed."*

---

* Napoleon had sent the Prefect of Police a letter saying that he wished to talk to the Duke d'Enghien, but the letter wasn't delivered until after Enghien had been executed. Fouché was later to say that the Duke d'Enghien's execution was "worse than a mistake, it was a blunder."

# *In which a prophecy is fulfilled*

I found Savary in the drawing room. "General Savary, I would appreciate it if you could tell me—" Did I really want to know? "How did it happen?"

"There was a tribunal, and then . . ." Savary wiped the perspiration off his forehead with his sleeve. "And then the Duke was taken to one of the trenches outside the château."

"A moat, you mean?" I had never been to Vincennes.

He nodded. "A dry one."

A canary burst into song. "No last words?"

"Just that he didn't want a blindfold." Savary felt in his jacket pocket, withdrawing a ring, a folded handkerchief and a sheet of paper. "Earlier he asked that his wife get these. Princess de Rohan-Rochefort, he said."

*La belle Charlotte.* The letter was short and tender—*love eternal*—the ring a simple gold band with an insignia on it. "And what's this?" I asked, unfolding the handkerchief.


It is late now. I am at my escritoire. Before me is a ring, a letter, a handkerchief containing a lock of hair: the remnants of a life.

I study these artifacts, half-expecting them to speak, give me an answer. Was the Duke d'Enghien guilty of conspiring to murder my husband? Or was he innocent, and unjustly executed by him?

As I write this, Bonaparte sits in the chair by the fire, watching the flames—as if expecting to see an answer there himself.

*March 23—Paris, windy.*

"I would say that the people of Paris are *unsettled*," Fouché responded, in answer to my question. "They've been flocking out to Vincennes to view the trench, tossing in bouquets. Of course, that damn dog doesn't help."

"What dog?"

"The Duke d'Enghien's dog. It stands over its master's grave, howling day and night."

"Bring it to me."

"I suggest you reconsider. The First Consul would not care to—"

"I know someone who would very much appreciate having that dog."

*March 24.*

Princess de Rohan-Rochefort resides in Worms. I've sent the Duke d'Enghien's last effects to her in the care of Moustache, along with the trembling dog—Mohilow by name—strapped into a wicker travelling basket. Against my better judgement, I included a note of sympathy.

*March 25—Paris.*

Both Bonaparte and I were uneasy setting out for the Opéra tonight. It was our first public appearance in Paris since the Duke d'Enghien's execution. "Are you trembling?" Bonaparte asked, taking my arm. His face was pale as death.

"Just a little chilled," I lied.

Immediately on entering our box, Bonaparte went to the front, showing himself to the audience. On hearing cheers, applause, Bonaparte turned, took my hand. *Relief.*

*March 27—almost midnight.*

Fouché arrived late at the drawing room tonight. "Ironically, the support for the First Consul has, if anything, increased," he said when I told him about our experience at the Opéra. "The Revolutionaries feel that he is finally one of them—now that he has blood on his hands."

"Fouché, please, you know it's not—"

"And as for the Royalists," he droned on, "they are entirely diverted by rumours of a crown."

A *crown*. The thought made me tremble! "I understand that there was a motion in the Senate today inviting Bonaparte to make his glory immortal." What did that mean—*immortal*?

"This latest attempt on the First Consul's life has made people desperate for security," Fouché said, stroking the mottled skin on the back of his hand. "It is generally believed that some form of monarchy would bring peace—and peace, of course, would bring prosperity. If a king is required, a citizen-king crowned by the people might not be such a bad thing. That the First Consul can now be counted on not to be in league with the Bourbons makes him all the more trustworthy."

"Fouché, if I didn't know you better, I'd think that you yourself might be in favour of a monarchy."

"I made the motion."

"*You* made the motion about glory immortal?" I was momentarily speechless. "But you opposed Bonaparte being made First Consul for *Life*."

"Do you wish me back as Minister of Police?"

Oh yes!

"I want my department back. Any fool can see what's required." He smiled, a ghoulish expression on him. "If there is one thing I've learned over the years, it's that flexibility is the key to survival."


*April 5—a gorgeous day.*
Bonaparte leaned against the fireplace mantel, his arms crossed. He cleared his throat.

I put down my cup of coffee. I knew that look. Bonaparte had something to tell me—something I was not going to like.

"Josephine, my advisors are saying that a hereditary system of succession would put an end to the threats against my life."

*Hereditary.* Glory eternal. "Is that what is being proposed?" My voice betrayed my apprehension.

"Yes, that succession be hereditary in the male line, by order of primogeniture. A traditional arrangement. This is the model that is being suggested, in any case."

"And so Joseph would be your successor?" How awful!

"That is Joseph's view, unfortunately. But ideally, the heir would be my son, a child raised to the role."

I looked away, blinking. There was no heir; there would never be an heir! All the mineral waters in all the spas of Europe could not give me what I wanted more than anything in the world: Bonaparte's child.


*Very late—everyone asleep.*

"Bonaparte, there's something we should discuss."

He yawned. "Now?"

"Tomorrow, if you wish. In the morning."

He pushed back his nightcap, turned to me. "You look beautiful in the moonlight."

"You want to talk about it now?"

"I don't want to talk at all," he said, pulling me close.


"So what was it?"

"What was what?" I yawned with contentment.

"What you wanted to discuss."

"Oh . . ." I never wanted to talk about it, frankly!

"Oh *that*," he said, understanding.

I nodded against his shoulder. He was damp with perspiration, smelling sweetly of lemon.

"You should know that I'm insisting on the right to adopt," he said softly, caressing my cheek.

I pulled away. "You'd be able to *adopt* an heir?" Of course my first thought was of Eugène.

"The child would have to be a blood Bonaparte—one of my brothers' sons."

"Little Napoleon?" Smiling.

"Come back here," he said.

*April 7.*

I was surprised this morning to see our courtyard crowded with men in uniform, on horseback. "Bonaparte, why such a large escort?" And everyone in formal livery—even the pages. Perhaps I had misunderstood. "Aren't we just going to see Louis and Hortense?"

"This is an official visit," he said, pulling at the ruffle edge on his sleeve.

Hortense came down the stairs to meet us with little Napoleon in her arms. "You must not run down the stairs like that!" I admonished her (in spite of my resolve not to be overly protective). She is large for three months, already beginning to show.

"What's this about?" Hortense gave us both a quick kiss. "Is there a military review today?"

"Nonan!" little Napoleon cried out to his uncle, squirming to be let down. Bonaparte took the boy from Hortense and tipped him upside down, making him squeal.

"Careful, Bonaparte!"

"Again," the child demanded, giggling.

Hortense, tucking a lock of hair under her cap, looked out into the courtyard. "Look at all the soldiers."

"Perhaps we should have sent word first. You were painting?" I asked. A week ago she'd begun a portrait of Eugène, and was finding it challenging.

Hortense ran her long red-lacquered fingernails over her smock. "Earlier, while my sweet one was having a nap."

"No!" the boy protested, sticking his fingers in his mouth.

"Not now," Hortense reassured him with a kiss.

"Where is Louis?" Bonaparte demanded, letting the nanny take the baby from him.

"Out. He didn't tell me where, just that he wouldn't be long."

"Perhaps we might wait?" I suggested to Bonaparte.

"I'll be in the garden," Bonaparte said darkly.

"Maman, what is this all about?" Hortense led the way into her drawing room, inviting me to sit beside her on the sofa.

Hortense tended not to follow politics. I didn't know how much she knew. "Are you aware that a new constitution is being proposed?"

She nodded. "The Civil Code?"*

"The Civil Code is an important part of it, certainly, but there's more." I paused, unsure how to explain. "As you know, this last conspiracy has raised concerns once again about Bonaparte's safety—and, consequently, concerns about the stability of the nation. Our enemies know that if Bonaparte were to be assassinated, the French Republic would fall." Was she following me? I took her hand. "But if a system of hereditary succession were in place, the nation would endure."

"I thought you were against that, Maman."

"I've come to understand the reasoning. The attempts on Bonaparte's life must stop!"

"But what good is a hereditary system if you and Papa don't have have an heir?" She bit her lip, regretting her words.

"Bonaparte is going to insist on the right to adopt."

"Eugène?"

"To be legitimate, the adopted heir must be a Bonaparte." My daughter looked suddenly wary. I smiled apologetically, a pleading look. "Bonaparte would like to adopt little Napoleon as his successor."

"But he's only eighteen months old, Maman!"

"Nothing would change," I started to assure her, but was diverted by Bonaparte, standing at the door.

"I can't wait any longer," he said, beckoning me and then disappearing.

"Should I mention this to Louis?" Hortense asked, her voice thin.

"Bonaparte should be the one to say something, I think."

"Maman, if Papa suggests it, Louis will be against it on principle."


Bonaparte was seated in the carriage, impatiently tapping his sword against the floor. Soldiers on horseback were lined up behind the carriage in double file, the horses sleepy in the morning sun.

* *The Civil Code (*Code Civile des Français, *later renamed* Code Napoléon*): a combination of Roman law, existing French law and the egalitarian principles of the Revolution. It remains the basis for jurisprudence in many countries of the world today.*

"I told her," I said as the footman handed me in. "She's apprehensive, I think, but—" My train caught on the carriage door. Just as I freed it, a man on horseback came through the gate. "It's Louis." He looked alarmed by the sight of so many soldiers in his courtyard.

"Zut," Bonaparte said, annoyed at his brother for being late—late for an appointment Louis knew nothing about. Hortense was right, I thought. It would be a mistake for Bonaparte to approach Louis.

"I'll talk to him," I said, opening the carriage door.


First I had to assure Louis that nothing terrible had happened—that his son had not been murdered nor his wife abducted. "The First Consul and I came today regarding a matter of great importance to the nation," I began, "a matter that would someday bestow a very great honour on you and your son." I paused. The setting was less than ideal. We were standing in the entry, everyone watching. "We don't expect an answer, only that you consider what we are proposing."

"Which is?"

"As you know, Bonaparte must have a successor. The amendment that is being drafted to the Constitution will give him the right to adopt an heir—little Napoleon."

Louis tilted his head toward his hunched-up shoulder, cradled his weak hand. "My *son*?"

Oh dear, I thought. Louis's immediate concern was that he himself would not be the successor. "Such a fine prospect for a son might help console a father for not being named heir himself," I said, giving him an imploring look.


*April 8, Sunday.*

Hortense was just here, very upset. Caroline called on her last night: accosted her is perhaps more accurate. In an angry tone Caroline informed Hortense that she had learned of Bonaparte's proposal to adopt little Napoleon and was prepared to fight it! Little Napoleon would be the crown prince, but *her* children would be "nobodies" (her word), and she would not stand for such an injustice.

"I don't understand," Hortense said tearfully. "I thought she was my friend."

*[Undated]*
Mimi slipped me a note this morning. "It's just as you suspected," she said with a grimace.

*Mme Carolin told Louis He must not let the 1st Consul take his son. Shee told him the Old Woman wants the 1st Consul to dis-inherit all the Clan. Shee told him He wood hav to bow down to His own Son. Shee told Him that Peopl say the 1st Consul is the Father of his Child. Shee told Him that if the 1st Consul wants a Son, He must divorse the Old Woman.*

*April 9.*
Louis has sent an angry letter to Bonaparte. "He demands to know why I want to disinherit him," Bonaparte said. "He can't stand the thought that little Napoleon would be his superior. He says he'd rather die than bow his head to his son."

"He wrote that?" I asked, pretending to be surprised.

"*And* that he'd leave France and take his son with him," Bonaparte said quietly.

Pour l'amour de Dieu!

"*And* that the only solution to the problem of an heir is for me to—" Bonaparte stopped. "Listen," he said, his voice thick, "according to the new constitution, I will have the right to adopt the boy when he turns eighteen. Louis will come around, with time."

Louis, perhaps—but what about Caroline?

*April 23, evening, almost 9:00, I believe.*
Tonight Bonaparte informed me the Legislature has voted in favour of hereditary succession. "It will become law in less than a month. At that point, everything is going to have to change."

"Again?" We'd been in a constant state of change for years, it seemed.

"We're going to have to have a legitimate court, more servants—"

I sighed. We already had far more than I could manage.

"—and ritual." He made a circling motion with one hand. "And costumes."

"Livery, you mean?" We already had "costumes," as he put it.

"You'll see to it?"

"I will, King Bonaparte," I said with a teasing smile (wondering when I should break the news to him how much new liveries would cost).

"No, never king."

"No?" Hopeful!

"The title 'king' reminds people of the Bourbons. My title must be more expansive, more of antiquity. 'Emperor' harks back to the Roman Empire and the reign of Charlemagne. It alarms some people because it's vague and conveys a sense of immensity—but that's what appeals to me. What's wrong with immensity?"

"You're serious." *Emperor?*

He smiled at my puzzled expression. "Emperor Napoleon." This with theatrical flair, his hand in his vest.

*11:20 P.M.*

Yeyette, Rose, Mademoiselle Tascher, Citoyenne Beauharnais, Madame Bonaparte: *Empress.*

Grands Dieux. It's just a courtesy title, I tell myself—it doesn't give me any official standing.

I tell myself. I tell myself.

*April 26, late afternoon.*

A long meeting today with Madame Campan, who has agreed to help organize our household—our "court." (I'm so relieved.) "You must have aristocrats serving you," she said, looking over the list of those who might be invited. "Men and women of the most ancient houses of France."

The nobility of history: Chevreuse, Montmorency, Mortemart. The names alone terrify me. "Madame Campan, with respect, the men and women of those families do not even deign to speak to me. How could they possibly serve me?"

"The nobility are raised to bow, to be bowed to. They understand the power that subservience confers. It's the wife of a soldier who will balk at the notion of lowering her head, for fear of being taken for a maid. What about Countess de la Rochefoucauld?" she said, flicking the paper with her finger. "A Rochefoucauld would impress. Others would then follow."

No doubt. The Rochefoucauld name is one of the oldest—and most revered.

"She's your cousin, is she not?"

"A distant cousin," I said, "through the family of my first husband. She was at Plombières last time I went." Chastulé de la Rochefoucauld does make me laugh. A hunchback with a plain countenance, she nevertheless approaches life with humour and wit.

"It would be a victory to persuade a Rochefoucauld to be your lady of honour. It's one of the most powerful positions at court. She would manage your staff, your appointments, your budget and ledgers. Anyone who wishes to call on you must apply first to her. Such a position might interest her."

"I very much doubt that she would agree, however." Chastulé is fond of me, but blistering in her condemnation of Bonaparte—"that upstart Corsican," she is said to call him.

"I believe she might. The family is said to be seriously embarrassed."


*May 4—sunny!*
For the sum of three hundred thousand francs, *plus* an annual salary of eighty thousand (with guaranteed increases each year), *plus* a position for her husband, Countess Chastulé de la Rochefoucauld has agreed to be my lady of honour.

"Ha!" she exclaimed. "When do I start? Next month? Fine. Whoever said aristocrats had principles? Wave a little gold in front of my eyes and I'm yours, ready to serve in the house of the devil. Not that *you're* the devil." She tugged on my elbow—gestured to me to bend down so that she could kiss my cheek. "Ha! You see, Your Majesty. Everyone bows to a hunchback."

*Your Majesty,* did she say?

*May 6.*
Bonaparte insists that once the Empire is officially proclaimed, once we are named Emperor and Empress, everything we do—what we say, how we move, what we wear—must be done according to royal tradition (*legitimacy*).

I've been studying an ancient book that was found in the palace library: *The Code.* Over eight hundred articles outline what is done in any situation an emperor or empress might encounter. Even so, much is left unsaid. Consequently, I've been consulting Madame Campan. She explains how things were done in the days of kings and queens—how people were addressed, what privileges were accorded to whom. We go over the procedures, the rules and forms, considering what to keep, what to reject. Poor Clari's hand is cramped from writing down all that Madame Campan dictates—over two hundred pages already.

*May 17.*
Subject to ratification by the people, tomorrow the Republic will be formally entrusted to a hereditary emperor.

"Are you ready?" Bonaparte asked.

"I'm not sure." How did one prepare for such a thing?

Bonaparte told me what to expect: Cambacérès, Arch-Chancellor now, will come from the Senate with a delegation in order to make the official pronouncement. The officials will go first to Bonaparte, make their presentation, and then they will come to me.

Madame Campan and I have been going over the elaborate procedures. How foreign it all seems. "Look upon it as a performance," she told me, sensing my apprehension. "Look upon it as your greatest role."

*May 18.*

I was dressed long before I heard the clatter in the courtyard announcing the arrival of Arch-Chancellor *de* Cambacérès (now) and his large delegation: men from the Senate, the ministers and the councillors escorted by a regiment of cuirassiers. De Cambacérès entered my apartment with great pomp, coming to a halt six paces from me. (Why so far? I thought. Is this what it means—that from now on no one will dare come near me?) Then, dropping a full court bow—as full as he could manage with his large belly, that is—de Cambacérès spoke the one word I never wanted to hear: *Empress.*

# II

## *The Good Empress*

How unhappy a throne makes one.
—*Josephine, in a letter to Eugène*

## In which we become a "court"

*May 18, 1804—Saint-Cloud, thunder and lightning still.*
Empire. Emperor. Empress. It has been little over a day since the Empire was proclaimed, and already we have become like animals, snarling over a bone. It frightens me to see what greed can do to people.

But I jump ahead of myself.

After the proclamation, there was a formal state dinner—an *Imperial* occasion, our first. (Three footmen for each guest, and Bonaparte unhappy because Talleyrand used the aristocratic word "supper" on the invitations instead of the more plebeian "dinner.")

The family, the officials and the officers of the household assembled in the Grand Salon, awaiting Bonaparte—or rather, awaiting the *Emperor*, as we are to call him now. Of the family: Hortense and Louis, Eugène, Elisa and Félix, Caroline and Joachim, Joseph and Julie—a smaller number of Bonapartes than usual because Signora Letizia, Uncle Fesch, Lucien and Pauline are all in Italy, and young Jérôme is still in America.

Duroc—looking bandy-legged in the Imperial skin-tight knee breeches—informed everyone that Joseph and Louis are now to be addressed as Prince, their wives as Princess. Caroline cast furious glances at her husband, who was slouched in the corner in his circus finery, tossing one of the new coins in the air (Emperor Napoleon on one side, the French Republic on the other).

The *Emperor* arrived promptly at six and saluted the new princes and princesses as well as *Madame* Caroline, *Monsieur* Joachim, *Monsieur* Eugène and so forth. Caroline's expression had taken on a hard aspect.

Just then a violent thunderstorm broke outside. A flash of lightning followed by a roll of thunder sent the pugs scurrying.

Duroc announced that we were to proceed to the table, and both Louis and Joseph claimed the honour of following Bonaparte. "I am the eldest," I heard Joseph hiss, urging his wife to step ahead of Hortense. Caroline grabbed her husband's arm and strutted by. I glanced back at Eugène—he was standing by the fireplace with a bored expression, quite content to be at the end of the line.

Bonaparte placed me on his right, inviting "Princess" Hortense to sit on his left. Caroline choked gulping down a glass of water, so great was her distress.


*May 19—Saint-Cloud, beginning to clear.*
Caroline and Joachim arrived early for the family dinner. Caroline, her smile fixed and bright, was dressed in a gown of ruffled green silk, her bosom adorned with a string of paste gems. Battle gear, I thought. (For once she outshone her husband.) It was a more informal occasion than the imperial dinner the night before—but consequently became somewhat raucous. Fortunately, Hortense and Julie were not present.

Caroline was conspicuously silent throughout the meal. Bonaparte—in an effort to be obliging, I am sure—did not complete in his usual fourteen minutes, but lingered, encouraging us to finish each course. After desserts (Caroline helped herself to a generous slice of the almond cheesecake, eight figs and virtually all the Gruyère), I suggested that we retire to the drawing room for coffee. Bonaparte bolted from his chair as if the doors to his prison cell had been opened. I purposely allowed Caroline to proceed ahead of me out of the room.

When everyone was settled, the butler brought in the coffee service on a tray. "I'll have a barley water," Caroline demanded.

"Are you not well?" Bonaparte asked his sister.

"What do you care about my health?" she said with such violence that the butler very nearly upended his tray. And then it came out: why were his own sisters to be condemned to obscurity, while strangers were loaded with honours?

"That's right," Elisa chimed in, setting down her coffee.

"Joseph's wife and Louis's wife are not strangers," Bonaparte observed with admirable calm (his thigh muscle twitching, I noticed).

"Julie and Hortense are not Bonapartes and yet *they* are princesses, while your own flesh-and-blood sisters are nobodies!"

"I distribute honours as I deem right for the nation," Bonaparte said, "not to fulfill *your* personal vanity."

"You think it's baubles I seek? I'm concerned with posterity, my *children's* future," Caroline said bitterly.

"Your children are not in the—"

Not in the line of succession, Bonaparte was going to say, but before he could finish, Caroline broke in. "They are your nephews and nieces—your *blood* relatives. They will be commoners! Is that what you want?"

I got up and closed the windows. It wouldn't do for this quarrel to be reported in the journals.

"One would think I had deprived you of the crown of our father, the late king," Bonaparte said sarcastically.

"You expect me to bow down before Hortense?" Caroline shrieked.

"Or Julie?" Elisa added, scowling.

"You dishonour your own flesh and blood!" And with that, Caroline placed the back of her hand to her brow and sank to the floor, her voluminous silks billowing out all around her.

"Caroline?" Joachim looked down at his wife, puzzled to see her stretched out at his feet.

The pugs, delighted to have someone at their level, started licking her face. When she didn't respond, I realized that she wasn't acting. "Juste ciel, Bonaparte!" I sent the butler for smelling salts. Bonaparte knelt beside Caroline and shook her shoulder, trying to get her to rise. "Hold some spirits under her nose," I suggested, but there was no need, for her eyelids began to flutter.

Bonaparte sat back on his heels, shaken. "Look," he said, addressing his family. "I'll give it some thought."

"And what about my husband?" Caroline demanded, sitting up.


*June 2—Malmaison for the day.*
"*Princess* Caroline? All of Paris is laughing!" Thérèse reported, fluttering

her neroli-scented fan. "She parades through the streets as if she really *were* royalty. But people love *you*—it's said you seem born to the role."

Born to it? Hardly!

*June 12—Saint-Cloud.*
Bonaparte has been in a meeting with the Special Council for three hours. The men come and go. Now and again I hear the word "coronation."

*[Undated]*
There *is* to be a coronation: the date has been set for July 14, Bastille Day. Only one month from now!

*[Undated]*
I'm so relieved. The coronation date has been put forward to November 9 (18 Brumaire*).

*June 16.*
An exhausting day reviewing the proposed staff list with Madame Campan. Here is what my household will look like, so far:

First almoner: Prince Ferdinand, often in his cups, but Bonaparte insists because he's cousin to the Duke d'Enghien. ("Fusion," Bonaparte decrees.)

First equerry: Monsieur d'Harville, the most powerful person in my household. Count Etiquette, I've named him, for that will be his task—to make sure everything is done properly. Not an easy job.

Five chamberlains: the first chamberlain will be General Nansouty, a wonderful cavalry officer, according to Eugène.

Introducer of the ambassadors: Monsieur de Beaumont, with his comical high voice.

* *18 Brumaire: date of the coup in 1799 which overthrew the government of France and instituted Napoleon as First Consul.*

Intendant of the household: Monsieur Hainguerlot.

Lady of honour: little Chastulé.

Ladies-in-waiting: I'm going to hold it to twelve, although Madame Campan insists I will need twice that number. Clari will be first lady-in-waiting.

Mistress of the wardrobe: Mademoiselle Avrillion.

Chambermaids (four, at present).

Dames d'annonce: Madame Campan says I'll need at least four more.

Pages: six charming boys, very proud of their uniforms.

Valets de chambre (six).

Ushers (four).

Footmen (eight).

Coachmen (three).

Errand-runner: quick little Benoist.


No wonder I'm having trouble sleeping. It's a terrifying list, and Bonaparte's staff is three times as many. I think with longing of my life of eight years ago—my staff of four.


*June 19.*

The Empire unfolds in lists: the staff announcements will be made tomorrow, the swearing-in ceremony in two weeks, everyone to begin shortly after. Et voilà: *court.*


*July 1—Paris.*

"Court" officially opened this morning—it was not a perfect debut.

My newly sworn-in aristocratic ladies-in-waiting regarded the comings and goings in a daze. They are happy to be back in the familiar milieu of a palace—except for the pace we keep here, which is so . . . well, *wrong.* Bonaparte insists that every step of every royal ritual be performed—but everyone must hurry it up, he hasn't got all day, he has work to do! So we go through the ancient genuflections in double time, as if to the beat of a drum.

Fouché, who joined us for dinner, observed the commotion with a hint of a smile. "I suppose I have this to look forward to," he said, as the cook's maid crashed into the footman coming through the door, a china dish of quails spilling onto the carpet.

"Oh?" I inquired, ordering three bottles of our best champagne brought up from the cellar. Bonaparte had just made the announcement that Fouché was going to be reinstated as Minister of Police—a celebration was called for.

"Fouché is the new owner of Grosbois," Bonaparte explained, tearing off the end of a loaf of bread.

"General Moreau's château?" I was astonished. I know the château of Grosbois well (too well)—"the house of traitors" I've come to think of it as.*

"General Moreau was happy to sell it to me for half a million," Fouché said, dragging his lace cuffs through the soup. Even in extravagant finery he looked slovenly, his smell sour, his buttons mismatched.

"Next I suppose you'll be wanting a title, *Citoyen*," Bonaparte teased, reaching over to tweak Fouché's ear.

*July 2, 4:45 P.M.*
After dictation this morning, Madame Campan and I walked through the rooms of the Apartment of Honour, reviewing the staff, their roles, the procedures. The porter at the door of the antechamber stood disdainfully, halberd in hand. "You must strike it on the floor at Her Majesty's approach," Madame Campan told him. "And the lackeys?" She looked over the crowd of pages and footmen to the men in green coats with red waistcoats and black breeches. They jumped to attention, clattering their swords against the furniture. "As soon as Her Majesty is announced, you must unroll a carpet." Patiently, I waited.

In this manner we made our way through the antechamber to the first drawing room (nodding to the pages, the citizens awaiting an audience,

* Before General Moreau—who was exiled to America after being found guilty of involvement in the Cadoudal conspiracy—the ancient château had been owned by Josephine and Napoleon's friend Paul Barras, who had conspired with the Royalists and was overthrown by Napoleon.

the officers not on duty), the second drawing room (everyone jumping up and bowing: the aides-de-camp, officers and their wives, the usher, chamberlain, equerry), until we reached my drawing room—or rather, the room in which I receive the most honoured of my guests.

"*Both* doors are opened for the Emperor and Empress," Madame Campan instructed the ushers, who positioned the chairs and stools appropriately: armchairs for Bonaparte, his mother and me, chairs for the princesses, stools for everyone else. "Your Majesty," Madame Campan hissed, when she saw me about to wearily lower myself onto a stool close at hand. "An *empress* must never . . . "

Must never, must never, must never . . .


*July 4—very hot.*

Who would have imagined that the life of an empress could be so complex? Walking, for instance: simply strolling from one room to another must be done in concert with two pages (becurled and beribboned): one six steps in front, one behind, carrying my train. "Ready?" I whisper to them, for I must catch their attention before I make a step, lest I move too quickly, lest we end up in a jumble.


*July 5.*

Monsieur Despréaux, the dance master, is beside himself with frustration. Bonaparte expects him to transform us into true-blood aristocrats in a matter of weeks. "Easier said than done," Monsieur Despréaux laments.

Everyone complains. They ache from the drills, the constant exercises—all just to learn how to walk, how to enter a room, doff a hat, *bow*.

"And is the Emperor not to . . . ?" Monsieur Despréaux mentioned hesitantly.

Bonaparte scoffed at the notion that *he* should take lessons from the dance master. "I create myself," he said, not untruthfully. However, I've noticed that he is frequently closeted with Talma, of late, and is moving with a bit more grace (not much). Now and again I catch him observing himself in my looking glass, checking his position.

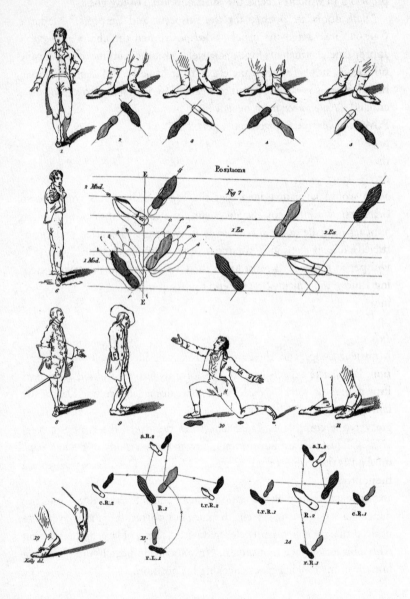

Positions

*Fig 7*

2 Mod.
1 Mod.
1 Es
2 Es

Kelly del.

a.R.2    a.L.2
c.R.2    R.1    t.r.R.2    t.r.R.1    R.2    c.R.1
r.L.1    r.R.1

*July 9.*
Dress rehearsal in three days. Everyone at court is to be presented, execute a proper bow. "We are not ready," Monsieur Despréaux gasped, pressing his neatly folded handkerchief to the corner of each eye.


*July 12, late afternoon.*
Oh, mon Dieu, what an entertainment. Bonaparte sat on his throne, I sat on mine. (They are cushioned, fortunately.) The Princesses—Hortense, Julie, Elisa, Caroline, Pauline—sat on tabourets. Prince Joseph, Prince Louis and the officers stood at attention on either side. Then the procession began: my ladies-in-waiting, the marshals and generals with their wives (some trembling), the officials and ministers—all in court dress. First the ladies came to the throne and curtsied, and then the gentlemen, who bowed. All the while Monsieur Despréaux stood to one side hissing: *Shoulders back, elbow up, chin forward! Relax!*

It was all I could do not to laugh—and all Bonaparte could do to sit still, for it took a *very* long time. After an hour, he signalled to Monsieur Despréaux to hurry things up—he didn't have all day!—and the pace increased so much that the men were racing to the throne, jackknifing into a deep court bow, and then racing backwards, very nearly tripping up the next in line.


*July 17.*
Princess Dolgorouki, who attended the drawing room at the Tuileries two nights ago, is going around Paris saying that "it" undoubtedly is a great power, but certainly *not* a court.

"Not a court? What does it take!" Bonaparte fumed. "Your attendants must all be countesses," he said, and at a stroke of his pen, countesses they all become. They smile disdainfully behind their fans: *parvenu*. (But accept the titles, nonetheless.)


*[Undated]*
"Your Majesty, the Emperor has asked me to" —Dr. Corvisart shuffled

uneasily through the stack of papers in his hand— "address the problem of your . . ."

My infertility, he meant. I looked away, downcast in my spirits.

"You've been to Plombières a number of times, Your Majesty," Dr. Corvisart said, squaring the papers and setting them neatly in front of him on the writing-table. "Perhaps a change is in order. I recommend the waters at Aix-la-Chapelle."

"The spa near Brussels?"

"The waters there are said to be good for . . ." He shrugged. "It's worth a try."

A futile try, we both knew. We are all of us pretending.


*July 19.*

Cannon signalled Bonaparte's departure for his northern tour. I'm staying in Paris for a few days before departing for Aix-la-Chapelle—staying behind in the palace, alone.

Well, alone except for a staff of hundreds. I'm at a loss, I confess. The household has become like some large beast, impossible to tame. "That's *my* job, Your Majesty," Monsieur d'Harville (Count Etiquette) assured me, handing me my schedule for the day. My marching orders.


*July 21—Saint-Cloud, early afternoon.*

I've been deceived. Count Etiquette is not my servant, he's my jailer! He is present at each audience, standing behind my chair. With every move I make, his hand is out—to help, which is kind, but according to etiquette, *his* is the hand I must wait patiently for, regardless of the number of helping hands present, for *he* is the highest officer of my household. "It's an honour to serve you, Your Majesty," he reminds me officiously.

This morning, preparing to leave for Aix-la-Chapelle, I remembered that I'd forgotten to ask that my new cashmere shawl be edged. I crossed two halls to find Agathe, whose handiwork I know to be precise. I was shortly informed by Count Etiquette that all orders to servants must be given through him, and him alone—that to do otherwise would, in his words, "compromise the dignity of the throne."

"I may not speak to my own maid?" Agathe has been with me for over a decade!

"It would be contrary to the Code to suggest that your Imperial Majesty may not speak to a person, even to a servant," the count informed me, his voice unctuous, "but I would not be doing my duty if I did not inform Your Majesty that there are formalities to be observed."

Grands Dieux! I can't get used to being "Empress"—I detest it, frankly. If I drop so much as a fan, I may not stoop to pick it up. The most "honoured" lady-in-waiting present must first retrieve it, then hand it to Count Etiquette, who then hands it to me.

I wasn't raised for such a confining role. How I long for the delicious freedom of being a simple citizen, just to stroll along the Champs-Elysées on a sunny afternoon and go to Frascati for an ice. I informed Count Etiquette—with a smile and carefree air that I hoped would temper my words—that although such etiquette was entirely suitable to one born into a world of restraint, it was not always perfectly suitable for me, and that, therefore, on occasion, I would continue to give my orders directly.

I've since repented this burst of "rebellion." I am fortunate that Count Etiquette has accepted this position—and a difficult one it is, tutoring us parvenus on royal procedures. Somehow, I must find the patience to be an empress.


*[Undated]*

We are crawling through Europe, my four ladies-in-waiting, two chamberlains, two chambermaids (one ill), an equerry, master of the horse, private secretary, butler, two ushers and ten footmen in addition to an army of coachmen and kitchen staff . . . *and* a financial controller, who is tearing out his hair at the expense. At each relay we require over seventy horses and twenty postillions. To move this group in concert is a monumental task—and all just to escort *me* to a spa.

I am reminded of an incident in my childhood: when a swarm of bees surrounded us, Mimi courageously reached for the queen bee and carried her to an open field, the swarm following.

I am the queen bee, and this is my swarm.

*July 30—Aix-la-Chapelle, about 8:00 in the evening.*
We've arrived, at last, in Aix-la-Chapelle, a sordid little town—"wretched," my ladies say (a word I hear often from them), in spite of its glorious history, its monumental cathedral, its treasure: the body of Charlemagne, Emperor of the West.

*September 3.*
Bonaparte has arrived and suddenly this sleepy town awakes. Banners are flying everywhere. Even the nags roped to crude carts sport ribbons.

*September 7.*
After a Te Deum in the Cathedral of Aix, Bonaparte was given the talisman Charlemagne wore on his collar when going into battle. Tonight Bonaparte returned to the talisman again and again, holding it in his hand, studying it, turning it. "Charlemagne was crowned by the Pope," he said, "and I will be as well."

"You will go to Rome?"

"Pope Pius VII will come to me."

I smiled, but perhaps it had the appearance of a scoff, for Bonaparte tugged my ear. "You don't believe me?"

*August 19, 1804, Paris*
*Chère Maman,*

*How is the treatment going? What do the doctors say? I enjoyed your account of turning down the bone from Charlemagne's arm. Everyone thinks your response clever.\**

*Don't worry so much about me! Louis will be returning from Plombières next month. Until then I am quite busy organizing the layette. I feel enormous, but the midwife assures me I am just as I should be at seven months.*

*It is terribly hot here in Paris. Little Napoleon, the charm of my days, is*

---

\* *Josephine refused the bone fragment, saying that she had for her own support an arm as strong as Charlemagne's.*

talking more and more. His favourite word is "no," however!

*Your loving daughter, Hortense*

Note—I have just this moment had news that Pauline's son died of a fever in Rome. How terribly sad—Dermide was such a dear child. Poor Pauline—first Victor and now their son. I don't know how one could survive the death of a child.


September 12, 1804, Saint-Leu
Chère Maman,

Louis returned to Paris on the eighth, and immediately we set off to Saint-Leu. Our new country château is beautiful! We wanted to have some time here before returning to Paris for my confinement in one month.

The château requires repairs, but even so, our sojourn here has been restful. Health permitting, Louis and his beloved water spaniel roam the hills and fields as I busy myself in domestic pleasures. I was in the kitchen all this morning, helping put up some delicious fruit preserves. Yesterday we made soap and next week it will be candles. Little Napoleon "helps," of course. He is much happier now that his papa is home.

His poor papa, whose health was not improved by this last spa treatment. Dr. Corvisart is of the belief that Louis suffers from chronic rheumatism, as you suspected. He's been taking spirit vapour-baths every evening along with regular doses of extract of smartweed in addition to the anuric tablets Dr. Corvisart prescribed. These do seem to help temper the pain. He's been told to avoid mutton, goose and pork—all of which he is sorely fond of. It's no wonder his spirits suffer now and again.

Whatever you do, Maman, don't worry: I'm well cared for. I'm enclosing a "drawing" little Napoleon made for you. That big scribble in the lower right corner is me!

*Your loving daughter, Hortense*


October 7, Sunday—Saint-Cloud.

I returned to Paris ahead of Bonaparte in order to be with Hortense during her confinement—only to discover that she and Louis are *still* at their country estate. She's due any day now!

*October 9.*

"What took you so long? You should have been here weeks ago," I scolded my daughter (embracing her). "Look at you!" For she is *huge* with child and carrying quite low. "You shouldn't be travelling over rough roads."

"Maman, don't worry! The midwife assured me I have lots of time. The countryside was healing."

Yet she seemed uneasy. "Is that a sentry box in the garden?" I asked, looking out her bedchamber window. The guard was standing directly below. "And the garden walls are new, are they not?" The stone walls had been built up so high that a good part of the kitchen garden was now in shadow. The place had the feeling of a prison.

"For security," Hortense said, weaving a white ribbon through the lace edge of an infant cap.

"Because of a follower?" Since the Empire had been proclaimed, both Hortense and I had been plagued by strange men—harmless simpletons, for the most part.

"No," she assured me (but colouring—why?).

I gave her the bag of bulbs I'd brought from my travels and was explaining how they should be planted when little Napoleon ran into the room and bounded into my arms. "Oh, you are so big!" With a studious expression he pried open two fingers. "I know," I said with a smile, kissing him. Our beautiful Prince—our *heir*. "Tomorrow you will be two." I gave him one of the (many) gifts I'd brought: a small wooden sword from his Uncle Napoleon.

"From Nonan the soldier?" The child clasped the gift to his breast with such earnest sincerity that both Hortense and I laughed.

"Your Majesty?" The governess curtsied. "May I . . . ?" Little Napoleon's cap had come off.

"No!" The boy squirmed as his governess tried to put it back on.

"Your Uncle Napoleon wears one just like it," I told him, which changed his outlook immediately. He settled happily into my lap, clutching his new toy.

Soon Louis arrived with an aide-de-camp, Monsieur Flahaut. "I didn't know you were expected," Louis said. He limped coming in and seemed to walk with difficulty. One would take him for a man of fifty instead of the young man of twenty-six that he is.

"How good to see you, Louis—and *you*, Monsieur Flahaut," I added, dipping my head to the aide-de-camp, my friend Madame de Souza's son.

"Your Majesty," Flahaut answered with a graceful bow. A pretty man with elegant manners; it is easy to see why the women fuss over him. (Indeed, it is rumoured Caroline fancies him.)

Louis stooped to kiss Hortense on the cheek. "You are well, my precious love?"

"Oh yes, perfectly well, darling," she said with a bright smile.

What a lovely portrait, I thought: the young, happy mother, the doting father.


*October 11—quite late now (exhausted).*

It was still dark when Mimi woke me, whispering, "Your daughter's footman is here. Her confinement has begun!"

Bonaparte was asleep, dead to the world. I slipped out of bed, following Mimi into the adjoining room. "What time is it?" I asked, wrapping a cashmere scarf about my head.

"Twenty after three," she said, checking a yawn.

"Are the horses harnessed?"

"Slow down, Your Majesty." Mimi smiled, handing me a mug of hot chocolate. "You can't go out like that. What will Count Etiquette say? The baby will take its imperial time and you should, too."

But I felt there was a fire under me; I could not be idle imagining my daughter's discomfort. I quickly slipped on the gown Mimi brought from the wardrobe and left. Empress or not, my daughter was having a baby.


Louis met me at the door, en déshabillé. "Oh," he said, as if surprised to see me. "I thought you were the accoucheur."

I removed my cape and gave it to a butler in livery (thankful that Mimi had persuaded me to dress respectably). "But the midwife is here? How is Hortense?" I asked, trying to get my hat ribbons untied, for in my haste I had knotted them. "Has the Arch-Chancellor been sent for?" Impatiently I pulled the hat off my head, tearing one of the ribbons.

Louis gave me a puzzled look. "De Cambacérès?"

"There must be a witness at Imperial family births, remember? According to the new protocol."* This *had* been discussed, had it not? The amended Constitution decreed that an official witness must be present at the birth of any child in the line of succession.

"Pour l'amour de Dieu," Louis muttered, and headed up the stairs.


The accoucheur didn't arrive until just before noon. Shortly after, Arch-Chancellor de Cambacérès arrived in a carriage drawn by six horses and accompanied by six pages, a footman and a chamberlain. The servants kept the Arch-Chancellor content at the dining table with dishes of bloated herring à la Dublin, mutton kidneys and several glasses of an excellent Madeira. (De Cambacérès related all this to me later in detail.)

The baby was born at half-past two. Another boy! "A good specimen," the midwife pronounced. De Cambacérès saw enough through his silver-rimmed lorgnette to fulfill his duty as a royal witness (but not so much as to upset his stomach). Louis examined the baby thoroughly before he was swaddled by the nursemaid.

"What a blessing: two sons," I told him. "He looks like you."

"Do you think?" Louis said.

My daughter pressed my hand against her cheek. "Isn't he beautiful, Maman?" she said, the colour rising in her cheeks.

"*You're* beautiful," I said. How brave she had been.

---

* Queen Marie Antoinette and queens before her had been required to give birth in a room crowded with gawking witnesses.

## *In which I am offered a crown*

*October 15, 1804—Saint-Cloud.*

"The Pope has finally answered," Bonaparte informed me as I came in the door. "It's not official yet, but he's agreed: he'll come to Paris."*

"To crown you?" I asked absently, putting down my basket. I'd been with Hortense all morning and was sick with concern. The new baby—Petit we're calling him—is thriving, but Hortense herself is still not strong, not eating well, if at all.

"Call the architects, set up a meeting for later this afternoon. I'm free at five. The Pope will stay in the Pavillon de Flore. We'll need to renovate." He paused at the door. "What's the matter? You don't think it will suit?"

"Bonaparte, I'm sorry. I guess I wasn't . . . Did you say the *Pope* is coming? You're serious? You're not jesting?"

"I told you before."

"It's just that . . . How does one do that—receive the Pope?"

Bonaparte let out a little laugh. "What's the problem? *I'm* the Emperor."

*October 16.*

Hortense has milk fever. She's in terrible pain, her breasts hard and

* *The Pope was initially reluctant to crown "the murderer of the Duke d'Enghien." He only agreed after promises of concessions to the Church—though these were never fulfilled.*

inflamed. A bread-and-milk poultice has done little to relieve her distress. The doctor will consider bleeding her if she does not improve by the morning.

*[Undated]*
Fifty-six rooms are going to be redecorated to house Pope Pius VII and his entourage.

Fifty-six rooms: imagine! I remember, not long ago, when a new bedstead was too great an expense.

Between tending Hortense and preparing for the coronation, I'm run ragged.

*October 17—Saint-Cloud.*
Busy! This morning I met with fashion designer Leroy and artists Jacques-Louis David and Isabey about the new court dress. I finally succeeded in persuading them that it would be brutal to resume the hoop. French women simply won't tolerate such a medieval construction! What we have decided on is simple but elegant: a dress very much like the gowns worn today, but with the addition of a long mantle and a ruff. Although impractical, a ruff is, no doubt, becoming. Leroy has suggested one with long points, made of tulle embroidered with gold or silver. It attaches at the shoulders and comes up high behind the head, as in the portraits of Catherine de Medici. My ladies are in ecstasies.

*October 19—a beautiful fall evening.*
"I've got it—*finally*." The poet Chénier was euphoric.

"Got what?" I asked.

"The subject for the tragedy the Emperor has asked me to write in commemoration of the coronation."

"Ha! It should be a comedy, the way things have been going around here," Chastulé said.

"All the poets in the Empire have been asked to create a piece to celebrate the coronation, Your Majesty," Clari explained.

"Aren't you going to ask about my subject, Your Majesty?" The poet scratched his head.

"Oh, yes, of course, Monsieur Chénier. Forgive me. What is the subject you've decided on?"

"The Emperor Cyrus!" Talma's voice boomed behind us, making us jump. "Played by guess who?" The actor struck a heroic pose, looking for all the world like a Roman statue in spite of the curious costume he was wearing.

"I was going to tell her," Chénier complained.

"Talma! What on earth are you wearing?" The tight breeches did not flatter his figure. The vain actor usually took pains to disguise his bowed legs.

"You don't know, Your Majesty?" Talma twirled. "*This* is the new court dress."

"Are you serious?" I frowned in disbelief. It was an ensemble in the style of the Renaissance, an embroidered satin doublet with a ruff and *puffed* pantaloons over skin-tight breeches, silk stockings and white high-heeled shoes with rosettes.

"The Emperor approved it this afternoon, but we can't decide what to call it. What do you think? Spanish?" With a twirl. "À la Henri IV?" Another twirl. "The Troubadour? That's what *I* suggested." Three twirls, the short cape flying. "But who am I to say? I was merely" —he threw the velvet cape across his shoulder and strutted across the drawing room— "the *model*."

"Bonaparte is going to wear that?"

Talma threw the black hat festooned with ostrich feathers into the air. "Apparently." He caught it and positioned it back on his head. The plumes bobbed comically. "Or at least something like it. What His Majesty actually said was" —and here he imitated Bonaparte's voice and movements exactly— "'Enough. That's it. Don't bother me anymore about it! I have better things to do than to decide about lace. Do whatever you think. Just get out of here.'" At which the actor flung himself into the air as if propelled by some invisible force and landed on his backside.

"Talma," I gasped. "Are you all right?"

The famous actor stood, brushed himself off, and before our very eyes *transformed*, as if by magic, into a Roman figure once again.

*October 20, 6:00 P.M. or so.*

"Please, darling, just try a little," I coaxed my daughter, trying to tempt her with a crumb of the rhubarb cake she had loved as a child. "Show little Napoleon." I smiled down at my grandson, who studied his mother with a grave expression.

"Make it like a horse," he said, showing me the trick his Uncle Napoleon uses to get food into *him*.

Obligingly, I made it like a horse, and my daughter fainted dead away.

I'm so worried! Afterwards, perplexed and concerned, I dropped in to see Eugène, who was himself frantic. His mare had rejected her foal and he was spending days and nights in the stable trying to save the little thing. On top of all that, he was going crazy with the renovations being done to his house.* I helped with some decisions about wallcoverings and drapes—and then we talked about Hortense. "She *is* getting better, Maman," he assured me, for he calls on her every day.

He will make some young woman a wonderful husband—in time—but for now I get the feeling that he'd rather be with his horses.


*October 25.*

Hortense has been relieved of her milk, which has been causing her such terrible pain.


*10:20 P.M.—Saint-Cloud.*

The coronation was to be held in two weeks—but this evening Bonaparte learned that the Holy Father hasn't even left Rome yet! Consequently the coronation has been put forward to December 2. Frankly, I'm relieved. There is *so* much to do.


*October 26, late, after 2:00 in the morning—can't sleep.*

Tonight, after Bonaparte returned to his cabinet to work, Eugène

---

* *Napoleon had given Eugène the use of Hôtel Villeroy, 78 Rue de Lille. It is now the German embassy.*

suggested a game of billiards. He played well, though with too much force—I won the first game, he won the second, but not without a struggle. By the third we were laughing and talking: of his newest mount, of finding a good (quiet) riding horse for me, of Hortense—who is sitting up and eating—and her beautiful boys. Then we talked of my growing staff, my need to hire yet more ladies-in-waiting (as Madame Campan had long ago predicted).

"Madame Duchâtel would be good," Eugène blurted out.

"Adèle Duchâtel?"

"She asked if I could help her get a position." Flushing.

Aha, I thought—winsome Adèle Duchâtel had caught my son's fancy. Certainly she is a beauty: slender, with an abundance of golden hair, blue eyes, good teeth. On the other hand, she is tall, and her nose is a bit beaky. I find her manners cold, but perhaps she is simply shy. "I think Madame Duchâtel would be a lovely addition to my staff, Eugène, but I'm not sure she's qualified." Adèle Duchâtel is married to an elderly, disagreeable man, a councillor of state. His status doesn't merit a position for his wife at court, regardless of her personal charm.

"*Please*, Maman."

I took up my cue and circled the table, assessing the shots. Thinking: it is time my son started dreaming of something other than horses. Thinking: Adèle Duchâtel has a husband, so marriage wouldn't be a possibility. That is good. The choice of a wife for Eugène will have to be dictated by political concerns—he understands that, understands that it is one of the sacrifices demanded by our position. "I'll see what I can do," I said, sinking two balls.

"Promise you won't tell Hortense or Papa?"

"I promise," I said, ruffling his hair. My boy.


*October 27.*
Madame Duchâtel begins tonight, at our ball. I've sent a note to Eugène.


*Past midnight.*
It was painful to observe Eugène courting Adèle Duchâtel, painful to see

his confusion, for she refused his invitation to the contredanse.

Eugène slouched against the wall all night with a despondent air. "Come to my drawing room tomorrow evening," I suggested.

*October 30.*
Bonaparte lingers in the drawing room each evening of late. Tonight he cautioned Madame Duchâtel against taking a green olive. "An olive in the evening will upset your stomach," he said, and the girl lowered her eyes.

"And we wouldn't want *that*," Caroline said, putting her arm around Adèle's shoulders.

"Perhaps a brandied cherry?" Eugène offered, ever hopeful.

*[Undated]*
Bonaparte is being gallant. I'm suspicious.

*October 31, Décadi—Tuileries.*
This morning a model of the interior of the cathedral of Notre-Dame was set up on a table in the Yellow Salon. Cardboard figures of the people in the procession were lined up in order.

"Where is yours, Maman?" Eugène asked, studying the layout before we joined the clan for dinner. I pointed to the figure that represented me, standing on the mantel. "Why isn't it on the table with the others?" he asked, perplexed.

"Because they haven't decided where to put me yet."

"They?" He tilted his head in the direction of the room where the Bonapartes were assembled.

"*They* argue that I'm not to be part of the ceremony, that I'm to be merely a witness," I whispered, taking his arm as we entered the room, the family all rising to bow.

*November 3—Saint-Cloud.*
I've ruined everything! This evening at around seven, Bonaparte left the

drawing room. A short time later, Madame Duchâtel got up from her embroidery frame and left as well. I waited for her return: five minutes, ten minutes, twenty.

Finally I could stand it no longer. I called Clari over to a window recess and told her that if anyone asked where I was, to say that I had been summoned by the Emperor. "Where are you going?" she asked, her tone apprehensive.

"I've got to find out if something is going on." I slipped away before she could protest.

I proceeded in the direction of Bonaparte's cabinet. I told myself he was working, as he often did in the evening. No doubt Madame Duchâtel was simply indisposed and had retired. There were any number of explanations.

These were the thoughts going through my mind. But what would I say to Bonaparte? I wondered, stopping outside the door to his cabinet. I would ask him if he wished to play a game of chess. No, he would know that I would not venture through the cold, dark corridors to ask such a thing. I decided to tell him that I needed a private moment to talk with him regarding my concerns about Hortense, her health.

The antechamber to Bonaparte's cabinet was dark. The moonlight illuminated the sleeping form of a guard. Stools had been positioned around the perimeter of the room, a room at rest. I tapped lightly on the door to the cabinet. No answer. The guard stirred, but did not wake. Was the door locked? I lifted the iron latch and the door swung open. The room was empty. I slipped up the stairs behind the bookcase, the stairs that led to the private suite of rooms above. Bonaparte had recently had the rooms redecorated.

At the top, I heard voices—Bonaparte's, and that of a young woman: Adèle Duchâtel.

Foolishly, I knocked on the door. (Why? What possessed me?) I heard scurrying about, then the door opened: Bonaparte, shirtless. "What are *you* doing here?" he demanded. Behind him, in the shadows, I could see the frightened girl.

I knew from the tone of his voice that I should not speak, yet heedlessly I cried out, "This is wrong, Bonaparte!"

Enraged, he picked up a stool and brought it down with force against the stone hearth. The girl let out a squeal. "Get out!" he yelled. "Get out of my sight!"

I tumbled down the stairs, letting the pewter candle holder clatter onto the stones. I heard the door slam shut, the bolt slide into place and I was plunged into darkness.

Trembling, I hurried back to the salon. With others present, I would be safe—at least this is what I told myself. In truth, I was not myself. I'd never seen Bonaparte in such a rage, and it frightened me—frightened and angered me.

Four of my ladies were still around the game table by the fire. Clari was at her frame. They all stood when I entered, bowed. "Please, be seated, continue," I told them, taking my place behind my embroidery frame. I took up my needle. I'd been working on the stem of a vine, in cross-stitch. I made a stitch, but it was unruly.

The only sounds in the room were the crackling of the fire, the shuffling of cards and an occasional groan or murmur from the players. Thoughts of Bonaparte's infidelity, his rage kept coming back to me. "Clari," I called out, my voice shaky—and louder than I'd intended. She jerked her head up, regarding me with a look of caution. "I'm . . . retiring for the evening. Please attend me." Good, I thought, standing, at least I'm not trembling.

I looked about my bedchamber as if I'd never seen it before. "Your Majesty?" Clari inquired from the door.

"I . . ." But no sooner had I opened my mouth than tears spilled. "I discovered them," I managed to say. "Bonaparte and Madame Duchâtel." My hands felt like ice, yet my heart was racing. "He's furious! Soon he will come here, and . . ."

"*Please*, Your Majesty, permit me to go! His Majesty would be furious were he to think that you confided in me. It will be best if he finds you alone."

I sat down at my toilette table, fussing without thinking over my baubles. I put a pearl ornament in my hair, then took it out. It was sharp—it might inflict harm.

Shortly after, the door flew open: Bonaparte, in stocking feet. He came into my room, snorting like a bull about to charge. "How dare you spy on me!" he yelled. "I will not put up with it!"

It humiliates me now even to think of it, for I cowered like an animal. I crouched trembling but dry-eyed as he destroyed what he could, throwing bottles and gems against the looking glass (glass shattering everywhere), splintering the leg of my Jacob toilette chair, tearing the lace bed-curtains.

"You're to move out immediately." He sneezed, overwhelmed by the jasmine scent that filled the air. "We'll work out the details of the divorce proceedings next week," he said, holding a handkerchief over his mouth and nose.

And then the door slammed shut.


The floor was strewn with debris. A clock chimed eight bells. Only eight? I stood and, stepping carefully, reached for the servants' bell rope. A chambermaid came to the door. "Please tell Madame Clari that I'd like to speak with her," I told her, my voice surprisingly calm. "I believe she is in the Yellow Salon."

The girl took a long, gaping look at the floor, and stifling a nervous giggle, hurried off down the hall.


Clari found me at my toilette table, looking into my shattered image. "Oh, Your Majesty!" she exclaimed, dismayed by the state of my room. "Are you all right?"

"Yes," I said dreamily. "You are going to Paris tonight?"

"Our coach has been called for nine," she said, stooping to pick up a broken crystal decanter, and then another, putting these on a side table. "Oh là là! Perhaps you'd prefer if I stayed."

"Others can attend to it. I'd like you to go to Paris and call on my son. Tell him . . ." I leaned my chin on my hand.

"Your Majesty?" Clari asked, retrieving a powder puff from under the bed.

"Tell him the Emperor and I have had a . . . disagreement," I said. "Tell him the Emperor has demanded a divorce." And then I broke down.

"Maman?" Eugène called to me from the door of my bedchamber. The light from the lantern he was carrying made him look like an angel—which he is, to me. "Are you awake?" he asked softly, glancing around the room. The glass had been swept up and the bed-curtains and vanity quickly replaced, but even so, he must have sensed that something was different.

"Come in," I said, sitting up, pulling on my bed jacket. "I was just lying here." Cursing. Praying. *Repenting.* "Do you know what happened? Have you talked to Bonaparte?" I wasn't crying any more.

He nodded, putting the lantern down on the little table beside my bed. "He's upset," he said, lowering himself onto a stool.

I wondered how much Bonaparte had told him. "Did he tell you he wants a divorce?" My voice quavered in spite of myself. "Did he tell you I discovered him with a woman?" I wondered if Eugène knew *who* it was I had found Bonaparte with.

My son nodded in a matter-of-fact way. (Good, I thought. He doesn't know it was Adèle Duchâtel.) "I told Papa I would follow you into exile—"

*Exile!* Was I to be banished?

"—even if it meant going back to Martinico with you." He smiled sweetly, so full of love.

*November 4, late morning—just rising.*
"I suppose you've heard?" I asked Mimi as she handed me a dish of morning chocolate. My hands were unsteady; I had to be careful not to spill any.

"Gontier and Agathe told me," Mimi said, slipping a note under my pillow.

*This Evinng Princes Carolin told her Husband that her Plan workd. The Emperor bedded the girl & the jelos Old Woman found Him with Her naked. Now the Emperor will Divors the Old Woman & they will have Everything.*

Mimi gave me an orange-blossom infusion, to calm. "I told you she's a witch," she said.

*November 5.*

"How was the family dinner last night?" I asked Hortense (peeking at the sleeping baby in the bassinet, blowing him a kiss). The weekly clan dinner had been held at the home of Bonaparte's mother. I had not been invited, of course.

"I was too ill to go," Hortense said, sitting forward so that the maid could plump the big feather pillows. "*Fortunately,*" she hissed, as the maid closed the door behind her.

"Oh?" I asked, placing a pretty box of comfits on her bedside table. Although still confined to bed, Hortense seems better. There is spirit in her voice.

"The Bonapartes have been . . . how should I put it?" She reached for a comfit. "Rather openly pleased, one might say, over recent *developments.*"

"I'm not surprised."

"But they're gloating so openly over what they see as their 'victory,' they've managed to annoy Papa. I gather he had a big fight with them last night."

"Bonaparte?" *That* surprised me. "Was Eugène there?"

"No, I wasn't invited," said a voice at the door.

"Eugène!" I jumped up to embrace my son. "What a surprise." He smelled of winter chill.

"Maman and I were just talking . . . about *Papa,*" Hortense said self-consciously.

"Oh?" Eugène said, leaning against the windowsill and crossing his arms.

Hortense widened her eyes at her brother.

I glanced from one to another. Something was up. This "encounter" had been planned. "Oh?" I echoed.

"Maman, Eugène and I have been thinking," Hortense said finally.

"About?"

Eugène shrugged sheepishly. "You and Papa."

"Oh." I inhaled sharply. *That.*

"It's just that Papa is a young man, Maman," Hortense said, flushing.

Eugène cleared his throat. "It's natural for a man to . . . you know."

I sat forward, my hands on my knees. "Are you taking *Bonaparte's* side?" They didn't understand!

"We don't think you need to feel jealous, that's all," Eugène said. "Papa loves you."

Hortense nodded, her eyes filling. "And we love him."


*November 6, 7:00 P.M.*

Thérèse was shocked, and not a little reprimanding. "You did what?" she exclaimed, very much flurried. "You walked in on them—*intentionally?* Are you crazy? After all I've told you? And what about your dear departed Aunt Désirée? I thought you promised her to 'be blind'—on her deathbed! I know, I know—it's hard not to notice when it's right under your nose, but where else is an emperor supposed to go? It's not as if he can wander the streets like an ordinary soldier. No wonder he's provoked! Oh, forgive me, I'm sorry. It's cruel to harangue, but trust me, my dear, *dear* friend—you don't want to be divorced. It's hell!"


*November 7.*

I knocked on Bonaparte's cabinet door. It was early; I knew he would be working. "Entrez."

Courage, I told myself, and pushed open the door.

"Josephine!" Bonaparte stood, taken aback. For a moment I thought he looked happy to see me, but then his expression changed, growing severe. "I've a meeting in fifteen minutes with Talleyrand."

"It will only take a moment, but I can return later," I said. "Whenever you wish."

He paused before motioning me in, slouching back down in his chair. "What do you want?"

"I want . . ." What did I want? I wanted Bonaparte at my side—I wanted my husband, my "spirit-friend." I wanted our quiet moments together, our rides in the park, our early morning walks in the garden. I wanted our consoling moments of tenderness. "I want peace between us," I said finally.

"I don't see how that's possible."

"You mistake me, Bonaparte. You believe I am motivated by jealousy. It is more than that. What you call innocent dalliances are damaging your image with the people."

"You spy on me in the interests of policy? Josephine, you are not a good liar."

He was right. I *was* lying—to him, as well as to myself. What *was* the truth? "I will own that my preference is for fidelity, Bonaparte, but I believe I can learn to live without it if I must—so long as I have your love."

"I do love you," he said angrily. "This . . . *business* means nothing to me. It is merely an amusement."

"Yet you become harsh toward me."

"Because you wish to control me—and I will not be controlled!"

"Very well then, I see a solution. I will raise no objection, and you will not be harsh." I opened my hands.

"I may do as I please?"

"With my blessing," I lied.


*This Evinng Princes Carolin told Prince Joseph that the Emperor is a Fool. Shee say the Emperor must divors the Old Woman. Shee & Prince Joseph will talk to Him tomorrow Evinng at 8 hours.*


*November 10, Décadi.*

"Good evening, dear sister." Joseph kissed me on both cheeks. "You look especially lovely tonight. Doesn't she, Caroline?"

"Indeed," Caroline said. "That gown must have cost a million francs."

"Thank you both so much." We were all lying—smiling from the teeth out, as Bonaparte says. "You are so very kind." Like a rabid fox. "I understand you have a meeting with the Emperor at eight," I said, glancing at the clock.

*Shortly before midnight.*

Bonaparte tore off his jacket in angry frustration. "What is it?" I asked, helping him with his vest.

"Do you know why Joseph does not want you crowned? Because it would be against his interests. *His* interests—it has nothing to do with policy, with what might benefit the Empire."

"I don't understand." I'm to be *crowned*? I thought they had met to persuade Bonaparte to divorce me.

"Because if *you* are crowned, then Louis's children will stand above his, Joseph said, because then *Louis's* children will be the grandsons of an empress. Bah," he growled, struggling to get his nightshirt on, his head finally popping through. "Do you know what it takes to make a tyrant out of me?" He threw back the bed-curtain with such violence that one tie tore free. "My family, *that's* what it takes. All they have to do is speak, and I become a monster. Sacrebleu! You're going to be crowned all right, even if it takes two hundred thousand soldiers."

"You're serious?"

"Of course I'm serious. I'm always serious."

I felt breathless with anxiety. Me—*crowned*? "I don't know if that's such a good idea." A crown would elevate my status. I'd have courtiers aplenty—as well as enemies. "Is it even customary?" I'd never heard of a woman being crowned.

"Not in the least."

"But then why?"

"To spite them!"

"Bonaparte, that's not a good reason," I said with a teasing smile.

"You're right. It is a mistake to jest. However, I *am* perfectly serious. I will crown you. You married me when I was nobody. I want you beside me." Taking my hand, pulling me toward the bed.

"Bonaparte—I'm going to have to consider."

"You'd turn down a crown?"

Easily! "I need to think about it." And talk to my children.

*November 11, evening, late.*

"Oh, that's frightening, Maman." Hortense (standing, *walking*) covered her cheeks with her hands.

"I know!" I didn't want a crown; I didn't even want Bonaparte crowned.

"Papa suggested this?" Eugène asked. "What would it mean, exactly? You're already Empress. How would being crowned change that?"

"From what I can make out, I would become more of a symbol of the Empire, so that wherever I went, whatever I did, I would have to be shown the respect due the crown."

Hortense rolled her eyes. "*They* won't like it."

The clan, she meant. "Not in the least."

"Because it will strengthen your position," Eugène observed.

Strengthen my tie to Bonaparte. "Frankly, that's the only argument in favour," I said.

"And a good one, Maman," Hortense said.

*[Undated]*

Yes, no, yes, no.

Yes.

No.

Yes?

Oh, if only I could sleep!

*November 12, 10:20 A.M.*

I went early this morning to Bonaparte's cabinet. He looked up from his big desk, which was covered with plans and drawings and memoranda regarding the coronation. "I've decided to accept your offer," I told him.

"What offer?"

Had he changed his mind? "To be crowned."

"Ah!" He stood and came around to me, pulling me into his arms.

## In which I am crowned

*November 15, 1804—Saint-Cloud.*

"Mon Dieu, Maman, you should see how crowded Paris has become," Eugène said, his cloak thrown back. "The population has doubled, I swear, people everywhere! And now, with all the troops that have been ordered in, it's crazy."

He said that already people are desperate to get tickets to the coronation, that one family has paid three hundred francs for a second-floor window just so they can watch the procession. Tickets are even being sold to see the preparations that are being made inside Notre-Dame. Yesterday, one man got knocked senseless by a stone that came loose from all the hammering. "I've never seen anything like it, Maman. All the masons in Paris are occupied, even the carpenters. How am I to get the work completed on my house?"

"Would you like me to ask Messieurs Percier and Fontaine?" I suggested, but immediately regretted it. Our Imperial architects are overwhelmed with the task of transforming Notre-Dame and renovating both the Tuileries and Fontainebleau palaces in anticipation of the Pope's arrival. "I'll be meeting with them in . . ." I glanced at the clock. That late already? "In ten minutes."

"No, Maman." Eugène put up his hands. "They're too expensive. And besides, I don't want a Roman temple, or even a Greek one. I just want it to be a comfortable house . . . with a *splendid* ballroom," he added with a grin.

"Eugène, does this mean that you're giving a ball? Oh, your sister is going to be so pleased. Surely, you'll need my help. I could—"

"No, Maman, I want to do it myself!" He turned at the door. "One thing, though. Do you mind if I hire your musicians?"

"Of course not." Eugène is an enthusiastic dancer—music-mad, as Hortense says.

He grinned, twirling his hat on his index finger (or trying to). "I happen to know that one of your ladies-in-waiting is very fond of them."

Adèle Duchâtel. I started to say something, to warn my son—but I couldn't bring myself to tell him about Bonaparte and . . .

Bonaparte and Adèle.

"Above all, be blind," dear Aunt Désirée told me on her deathbed. If only it were easy! I promised Bonaparte that I would no longer object to what he calls his "amusements." I appear calm and accepting, but inside I feel a whirlwind of emotion: jealousy, fear—anger—but also, curiously, a feeling of peace, for I do know that Bonaparte loves me. Loves me, and what's more: needs me.

Last night he woke me as he so often does, wanting me to come walk with him in the moonlight. The gardens were dusted with an early frost, giving the landscape an eerie glow. We walked and talked until the chill set in, then we tiptoed back to the warmth of our bed, whispering like naughty schoolchildren.


*November 17.*
Bonaparte was in a Special Council meeting all afternoon. I wondered what such an important gathering might concern—war? peace?—and was rather disconcerted to discover that it had to do with who is to carry my train during the coronation. Joseph has lodged a formal protest on behalf of the female Bonapartes: they flatly refuse.


*November 18, early evening.*
A compromise has been struck. Caroline, Pauline and Elisa have finally consented to carry my train—or rather (as it must now be worded), to "hold up the mantle," which is to be viewed as "an attribute of sovereignty."

"But on condition that the princesses' trains are in turn carried by their chamberlains," I explained to Jacques-Louis David, who is co-ordinating the procession.

"That's ridiculous," he complained. "You're going to look like a centipede!"

*November 19.*
"We'll need the crown jewels for our meeting with the jewellers," Bonaparte told me at breakfast, and suddenly we were all of us in a flurry. We had to get down the Code to see how it was done. To obtain the jewels, the Emperor (Bonaparte) must instruct the Grand Chamberlain (Talleyrand) to give a written order on behalf of the Treasurer-general (Monsieur Estève) to the Master of the Wardrobe (Clari's husband) for those pertaining to the Emperor (Bonaparte), and to the Lady of Honour (Chastulé) for those pertaining to the Empress (me). It has taken us all morning to work this out.

*November 20, early afternoon.*
Bonaparte's mother will not make it to Paris in time for the coronation. She lingered too long visiting her beloved son Lucien in Milan. "Sacre-bleu," Bonaparte said, but softly, with a melancholy air.

*November 21.*
Tomorrow we go to Fontainebleau in anticipation of the Holy Father's arrival. I doubt that I'll sleep.

*November 25, Sunday—Fontainebleau.*
Pope Pius VII arrived at noon along with Bonaparte's Uncle Fesch (now a Cardinal), and all the members of a fairly large papal entourage: sixteen cardinals and bishops and well over a hundred clerics (*all* of them excitable—oh, it's noisy here).

Everyone in the château lined up to welcome His Holiness at the door. He stooped coming in, perhaps out of habit, for he is very tall—

he towers over Bonaparte. He was dressed entirely in white, shivering in a long cape draped in the manner of a Roman statue. (I've ordered his fireplaces stoked hot—I'm concerned that the chill might harm his health, which is not robust and considerably weakened by the strenuous winter journey.) Even his shoes—unfortunately thin for this climate—were white, although muddy from alighting to meet Bonaparte at Croix de Saint-Hérem. He's grave, dignified, a simple man, more like a man of fifty than the sixty-two years he is, in fact. Perhaps it is his coal-black hair (does he colour it, I wonder?), so striking against his white robes, his peasant's sheepskin cap, his slender hands and long fingernails. His voice is curious: high and somewhat nasal. He speaks excellent French, but with an Italian accent, pronouncing *u* as *ou*. A man of gentle manners—unlike his entourage of rough and noisy priests (spitting everywhere!). He has a pallid complexion, although this may be due to a cup of sour broth he mentioned taking at a posting house this morning.

After a brief reception, Talleyrand escorted the Pope to his apartment, where he is resting now. How, I do not know, for the palace resounds with the voices of his entourage, yelling boisterously in Italian. "The Holy Father may be gentle and mannerly, but it is evident that his people are not," Clari observed primly, taking up her needlework.


*Late evening.*

After his rest, His Holiness met with Bonaparte for about a half-hour. Then Bonaparte conducted him to the Hall of the Great Officers where we had an informal dinner of only six covers: the Holy Father and his secretary, Bonaparte and me, Eugène (who remembered not to break bread before grace) and Louis (who did not). The Pope ate and drank with enthusiasm. He *loved* the turkey stuffed with truffles and the sauté of lark fillets.

Before he retired, His Holiness presented me with a ring. It is an amethyst encircled with diamonds, simply cut, simply set, exceptionally clear. And blessed by the Pope. "Thank you," I said, looking into his benevolent eyes.

"Daughter," he said.

I must gather the courage to speak, make my confession—soon. Tomorrow?


*November 26.*
The Pope was taken aback when I confessed that Bonaparte and I had not been married by the Church. "I was not aware."

"Forgive me," I said. "I have spoken without the Emperor's knowledge, Your Holiness." Much less his consent!


*Early afternoon.*
Bonaparte entered my dressing room scowling. "There seems to be a problem," he said, taking a chair by the side of my toilette table. "We have to be married by the Church, otherwise the coronation is off; the Pope refuses."

I feigned an expression of consternation.

"Zut." Bonaparte snapped one of my combs in frustration.


*November 27—back in Paris.*
This morning the terrace resounded with the sound of people crying out for the Pope, kneeling to receive his benediction. He brought only a few rosaries and medallions to give out and already they are gone. "I was told that the French are not religious," he said, his voice plaintive. He blesses whatever objects are brought to him: eyeglasses, inkpots, even a pair of scissors. Both Royalists and Revolutionaries come for his blessing, even Jacques-Louis David, an atheist. The Holy Father has captured our spirits, our hearts.


*November 28, 7:30 P.M.*
"And the oil I'm to anoint you with?" the Pope inquired this afternoon, at our daily meeting working out all the (endless) details. "I understand that there is a flask of holy oil that has been used since Clovis was

anointed in 496." The Holy Father is an amateur historian, and proud of his knowledge.

Bonaparte frowned, puzzled.

"It was destroyed, Sire," Bonaparte's secretary spoke up. "During the Revolution."

"We will begin a new tradition," Bonaparte said, commanding his secretary to have a suitable flask made.

I flushed: the ancient flask had been destroyed after my first husband proposed (and I quote, for I remember it well) "that the baubles of tyranny and superstition be burned on the altar of the Fatherland."


*[Undated]*
Chaos! The hundred and forty Spanish horses purchased for the coronation procession have all been delivered at once.


*November 29—Tuileries, not yet noon.*
We had a tour of the work being done on the cathedral this morning. Amazing. Two of the side altars and the choir screen have been removed and tiers of seats installed on either side of the nave. "Painted cardboard will give it a Greco-Egyptian style," Jacques-Louis David explained.

"Not Roman?" I asked.

"That, too," he said, pointing out that the bare stone walls will be entirely covered over with flags, tapestries and velvet hangings.

"What a stage," Talma exclaimed, throwing out his hands, his voice echoing in the huge vault.


*4:45 P.M.*
A terrible rehearsal. We're *still* tripping all over ourselves.

"I'm to carry some bit of bone?" Joachim protested on being assigned the relic of Charlemagne. Eugène, after all, is to carry the coronation ring.

As a result Bonaparte decreed that Joachim will carry my crown, which of course infuriates Caroline.

*9:00 P.M.—shortly after.*

Is there to be no end to it? Now Jacques-Louis David is beside himself. The master of ceremonies assigned him to a seat in the stands at the coronation and he very nearly had a fit, threatening a duel. He'd been promised a box so that he could set up his impedimenta, work on his drawings undisturbed. I was called upon to settle the matter: yes, he absolutely did require a box directly above and in front of the altar in order to set up his easels and make sketches, and no, a duel would absolutely *not* be permitted.

A duel! I confess I almost laughed at the thought of this ardent Revolutionary settling a rather minor conflict in such an aristocratic manner. We are all going mad.


*November 30—only two more days.*

This morning, first thing, Bonaparte came to me at my toilette, hiding something behind his back. "What are you up to now, Bonaparte?" I asked, for he had that playful look.

"I want you to try something on." He brought a glittering ornament out from behind his back and twirled it in the air as if it were a trinket. He caught it neatly and held it out with one hand, holding it by the gold cross perched on top.

My crown! "Bonaparte, isn't it heavy?"

"Exceedingly. Take it!"

"I've never seen anything quite so beautiful," I said, a lump rising in my throat. Or so frightening.

"Try it on." He reminded me of an eager boy.

The crown sat snug on my head. The jeweller had devised a padded velvet band around the inside, but even so, I felt a head pain threatening. "It's perfect," I said.


*December 1—only one more day.*

It is one-thirty, a cold winter afternoon. I'm in my dressing room, awaiting my entourage. We will have one last rehearsal in preparation for tomorrow. Outside in the courtyard I hear César yelling. Thirty carriages to make ready, a hundred and forty horses to groom. No wonder he is raving.

The fervour, frankly, is unnerving. Two of my ladies are planning to rise at two in the morning just to have their hair dressed. It seems that everyone in Paris is going mad with last-minute preparations. Three orchestras—four hundred and fifty musicians in all—have been rehearsing. Scribes have been busy copying out over seventeen *thousand* pages of music for the choir of four hundred. And every tailor in Paris, it seems, is sleepless from making uniforms for how many soldiers? Eighty thousand, I think Bonaparte said, just to guard the route.

I'm not frantic, but nervous, yes: tomorrow I will be crowned Empress in the Cathedral of Notre-Dame. In all this, I keep forgetting that Bonaparte and I are to be married tonight.

*1:20 A.M.*
At midnight, between salvos of cannon and thunder, Bonaparte and I were married before God by his jolly uncle, Cardinal Fesch, in front of a makeshift altar set up in Bonaparte's cabinet. It was done quickly, without fuss, much like our first, civil, ceremony.

"I am your wife, forever and ever," I told Bonaparte. A truth. He clasped my hands and pressed them to his chest.

*December 2 (or rather December 3).*
It is almost two in the morning. Bonaparte sleeps. It is snowing lightly again. I am wrapped in a fur, sitting at the little escritoire by the fire—embers now. My crown is set carelessly on my toilette table, next to my diamond tiara. I start for a moment, considering the danger, the temptation to thieves, and then remind myself that Roustam is asleep outside our door, recall the great number of guards who watch over us as we rest: Bonaparte and me, man and wife, Emperor and Empress.

It has been a very long day. I was woken by gun salutes at six this morning, followed by a deafening tumult of bells. "Well, Your Majesty?" Mimi said with a grin, handing me a cup of hot chocolate. "This is your big day. Too bad your mother couldn't be here to see it." She laughed. "Your mother in her mended socks."

My mother, who is convinced I've married an ogre. I felt Bonaparte's side of the bed. He'd risen? Already?

"The Emperor is in his cabinet," Mimi said, clearing a spot for a plate of rolls.

"He's working?" I don't know why I was surprised.

"You know what I was thinking of, Yeyette? Remember the fortune the obeah woman told you back home on Martinico? You were only thirteen."

"Fourteen," I said, biting into the hot roll. How could I forget? *You will be Queen.* And then I recalled the words: *But not for very long.* Did the voodoo priestess really say that? I couldn't remember. It all seemed a dream to me: a bad dream.

"I told you she was never wrong. Did you sleep?"

"Thanks to you." Mimi and her box of magic herbs. "Is that *rain*?" It had been snowing when Bonaparte and I had gone to bed.

"It's miserable out," Mimi said, pulling back the drapes. "The streets are a mess."

Reluctantly I swung my feet out from under the warm covers. "That's a shame," I said, thinking of the crowds huddled in the cold. Thinking of the freezing cathedral. Concerned about the Pope, his frail health.

I looked out into the courtyard. Already it was thronged with people, shivering in the slush, the soaked banners and flags hanging from the balconies.


The morning unfolded like a fairy tale. Chastulé brought in my diamonds: the diadem, belt, necklace and earrings. Clari and Mademoiselle Avrillion staggered under the weight of my white satin gown, heavy with gold and silver embroidery. Chastulé assessed me up and down, her hands on her hips. "Ha! We begin with the chemise."

After I was clothed, Isabey was announced with his big wooden box of paints and powders, to "create" (his word) my face. I sat before my looking glass, fingering the ring the Pope had given me, watching as I was slowly transformed: my bosom and face whitened with ceruse ("Venetian—the finest, mixed with egg white, much preferred over powdered pig bone," Isabey said in all seriousness), veins lightly delineated with blue liner, cheeks rouged with Spanish Red, eyebrows defined with black lead.

"A little belladonna?" Isabey suggested, lining my eyes with a hint of kohl.

"The poison?" I asked, alarmed.

"To give a wide-eyed *sensual* look."* He opened his eyes wide, to demonstrate.

"I prefer to see!" And live.

Then Monsieur Duplan, my wonderful hairdresser, began, powdering my hair with gold dust before dressing it. "Oh, that's *beautiful*, Your Majesty," Clari said, watching every new development with great interest.

"Ha, you look not a day older than twenty-five," Chastulé said.

Perhaps if one didn't look too closely, I thought. "You're magicians," I told Isabey and Duplan, who hovered like proud parents.

"But remember, Your Majesty, no laughing—and certainly no weeping," Isabey cautioned. "We don't want you to flake."

And then came time to put on my gown and my jewels. Chastulé stood on a stool to position the diamond diadem. She breathed heavily with the exertion as she fastened the necklace, my earrings and belt. Then she pulled me over to the big looking glass.

I regarded the image. *You will be Queen.* Feeling a little faint, I sat down. It was only half-past seven. I felt I'd been up for days . . . for a lifetime.

"She's in here," I heard a woman's yell from the other room, followed by a hiccup. Elisa? Soon Pauline and Elisa appeared, and behind them Caroline, huffing and complaining about the weight of her train, her tight stays.

"Is it supposed to stand up like this?" Pauline asked, fussing with her ruff.

Following the three princesses were Joachim (in a pink-lined cape), Joseph and Julie, Louis and Hortense . . . and, breaking free of his nursemaid, little Napoleon. I held my arms open and he came bounding into my arms. "Careful," the nursemaid cried out.

I kissed the boy, and stood him up so that I could admire his uniform. "He looks so handsome," I told Hortense (who is healthier now, but still wan, still thin), wiping a smudge of rouge from the boy's

---

* *Belladonna, or deadly nightshade, dilated the pupils, imparting a languorous look of desire.*

cheek. "Sit here, near your grandmaman," I whispered, pulling out the little upholstered armchair I had had made especially for his visits.

He climbed up onto it and sat watching us, sucking two fingers. Bonaparte entered the room in a purple velvet tunic and plumed black velvet toque. "I feel like a stuffed monkey," he said.

I hid my smile behind my hand.

Little Napoleon let out a delighted squeal. "Nonan the monkey?"

We laughed as Bonaparte chased his nephew around the room making monkey noises, his silly cape flying. The Emperor!

And then all my lovely ladies arrived, looking so beautiful in their white silk gowns, their long sleeves embroidered in gold. They paraded for our benefit, protesting as the pugs stepped on their trains.

Bonaparte stood before the glass with his brothers Joseph and Louis. "If only our father could see us now," he said. I knew what he was thinking: if only his mother could be here, too. And *mine*, so far away in Martinico, I thought, tears rising, checking to make sure that my earrings were secure.

It was still raining when we were summoned to our carriages. Bonaparte and I were escorted to the Imperial coach—a glittering conveyance ornamented all over with stars and laurel leaves, Bonaparte's bee emblems. I thought I might be transported to some magical place were I to set foot in it. I recalled the soiled trundle that had taken me to prison in the dead of night—how long ago? A decade?

I looked up at the coach driver, so high up on the box. César tipped his green-and-white feathered hat and grinned, pleased, no doubt, to be looking so fine in gold-embroidered silk stockings, his wide green coat trimmed with gold lace. The eight rather impatient grey horses pawed at the cobblestones, tossing their white head-plumes.

I got in first so that I might be seated on Bonaparte's right, followed by Joseph (who was irked: he'd expected to be awarded the seat of honour next to Bonaparte, I suspect) and Louis (his cloak covering his enfeebled arm). Bonaparte drummed his fingers on his knee, examining the white velvet upholstery embroidered in gold, the golden lightning bolts on the ceiling, the golden N crowned with laurels. Trying (still) to loosen his itchy lace cravat, pulling down on his toque with its eight rows of diamonds, picking at the bees embroidered on his cape. Impatient! Finally, cannon and a salvo of artillery announced our departure. I was relieved to be moving—although *moving* is perhaps not the right word. Crawling would have been faster.

We were hours, it seemed, traversing the short distance from the Tuileries to Notre-Dame. It was so cold! (There was no foot-warmer in the coach—only a bearskin underfoot.) I smiled and nodded to the crowd along Rue Saint-Honoré as the three brothers talked: of the ceremony planned for the fifth of December on the Champ-de-Mars, Chénier's new tragedy opening this coming weekend, the fête the city of Paris was planning, the cost of the renovations that had been made to the Hôtel Brienne in anticipation of Signora Letizia's arrival—whenever *that* might be.

Soldiers were lined three deep along the route. From somewhere I could hear kettledrums and trumpets. Hawkers were selling sausages and rolls. (Suddenly I was so hungry.) All around our carriage the Imperial Guard rode, the bravest of the brave, Bonaparte called them, his "old moustaches"—revolutionaries who had fought beside him in Italy and Egypt, following now in great state to see their "little corporal" (as they called him) crowned Emperor. Eugène was with them, proudly riding Pegasus.

"You look beautiful, Maman," he mouthed and then grinned, that look of bedazzlement that was becoming so familiar. I wondered if he thought of the crowds he'd seen on these streets as a boy, thronging to watch the tumbrel carrying prisoners to the guillotine. I wondered if he remembered—as he regarded his mother in her golden carriage—catching a glimpse of her through the window of her prison. I wondered if he remembered crying for bread, going to sleep hungry. I wondered if he thought of his father.

Yes, I thought then, looking out over the cheering throng, nodding and waving, nodding and waving (just like a queen), I believe my son does think of such things. Perhaps we were all of us recalling those days. Perhaps it was the memory of that terrible time that was at the heart of the wild joy that seemed to fill our beautiful city, in spite of the cold and the damp. *Long live the Emperor!* Long live the man who has saved us, I thought, giving my (impatient) husband an appreciative look. *Long live Napoleon!*

It was eleven by the time we arrived at the west entrance of Notre-Dame. Cannons went off, bells pealed and the crowd cheered. As we stepped out of the carriage, the sun came out. "Ah," Bonaparte said, as if he'd been expecting it.


It was warm, at least, inside the archbishop's palace next to the cathedral, the fires blazing brightly. All the running to and fro made it seem like backstage at a theatre. It took four valets to help Bonaparte into his Imperial robes. "Well?" Bonaparte said, turning to face me. *Emperor!* (Although, in truth, he looked more like the king of diamonds on a deck of cards, dwarfed by his enormous ermine mantle.) His expression was vaguely distressed—perhaps because of the weight. My own mantle was so heavy I could hardly move, even with the reluctant princesses helping to carry it.

Then, at last, we began the procession into the cathedral. Ahead of me were the heralds, the pages, the Master of Ceremony (looking distractedly around to make sure we were all in order), a glowering Joachim with my beautiful crown on a crimson cushion, the chamberlains and equerries, each ten paces apart. "Now?" I asked Count Etiquette. I looked back to make sure that the Princesses (Elisa, Caroline, Pauline, Hortense and Julie) were ready to bear the weight of my long train—and that *their* chamberlains were positioned, in turn, to carry theirs.

On a signal from Count Etiquette, we all began to move—very, *very* slowly. A centipede, indeed! Just before I entered the doors of the cathedral, I glanced behind me, smiled at my daughter. Behind her I could see Bonaparte motioning to Joseph, Louis, de Cambacérès and Lebrun to hurry up, pick up his mantle. And behind *him*, after the marshals, I spotted the face of my cheerful son, waiting so patiently. I searched the crowd for little Napoleon and his governess, finally spotting them near the door of the cathedral. I kissed the air and little Napoleon grinned, opening and closing his hand: bye-bye, Grandmaman. Bye-bye.

I don't believe I will ever forget that moment, entering Notre-Dame. The audience lost its dignity and burst into applause as the four orchestras played a triumphal march. The light streaming in the brightly coloured windows, the enormous tapestries, the painted backdrops, pigeons swooping high above the glittering crowd, the hat plumes bobbing, gems sparkling, all made it appear like a scene out of the *Arabian Nights*.

I'm told it was after one o'clock when we reached the altar. I can believe it, for we proceeded at a snail's pace. Pope Pius VII, who had been waiting in the cold for hours, was seated near the Grand Altar in his simple white robe. *My daughter*, his eyes said as we approached.

As the angelic choir sang Paisiello's *Coronation Mass,* Bonaparte and I climbed the steps to the thrones in front of the altar. I was relieved to have something to sit on. Bonaparte looked calm, as if he were crowned every day.

Then the ceremony began. The Pope, intoning Mass in his high nasal voice, blessed the Imperial emblems: the ring, the sword, the mantle, the sceptre. (Twice I saw Bonaparte stifle a yawn.) Then, after *Veni Creator*, Bonaparte and I knelt on the big velvet cushions and the Holy Father took up the (new) flask of holy oil, anointing first Bonaparte and then me with the triple unction, intoning, *Diffuse, O Lord, by my hands, the treasures of your grace and benediction on your servant.* Bonaparte was listening with a pious expression, but I suspected that he didn't like having the oil on his hands and was wondering what to do about it, whether or not he could wipe it off somehow.

Then the Pope took Bonaparte's crown from its cushion on the altar and Bonaparte, removing his golden wreath, took it from him and, turning to the crowd, placed it on his head himself. (Everyone gasped!) Just then a loose pebble fell from the ceiling and hit his shoulder but he did not flinch. His face shone with a radiance I'd never seen in it before. He looked . . . *heroic*—that is the only word I can think to describe it. I moved toward the altar and knelt before my husband, my hands clasped in prayer.

I'd never experienced such silence; surely it was the silence of heaven. As I knelt there, waiting, my life welled up before me. I thought of my beloved father; how I wished he could see me. Tears spilled onto my gloves as Bonaparte approached. Trying hard not to weep, I studied the embroidered bees on his white satin slippers. I felt him fussing with my hair, felt the weight of the crown—and then felt him lift it off. I raised my eyes, a little concerned: was there a problem? Was my tiara in the way? He was looking down at me with my crown in his hands and the hint of a smile in his eyes, as if to say: Maybe I will, and maybe I won't. As if to say: Don't be so sure. As if to say: This is my gift to you, this is *our* moment. As if to say: I love you with all my heart, and I want the world to know it.

Only Bonaparte would have the audacity to tease at such a moment. I held my breath; it wouldn't do to laugh! And then I felt him place the crown firmly on my head and a murmur went through the crowd, a reverent hush. A calm feeling of courage filled me and I stood, my knees steady. I was there by the grace of God.

But *not*, certainly, by the grace of Bonaparte's sisters, for as I started to climb the steps up toward the altar, I was yanked back and very nearly toppled.* I heard Bonaparte hiss something sharply and I was freed.

The rest of the ceremony went by as if in a dream. The chorus sang, "May the Emperor live forever." The heralds proclaimed in full (and wonderfully sonorous) voice, "The most glorious and most august Napoleon, Emperor of the French people, is anointed, crowned and enthroned!"

"Vive l'Empereur!"

"Vive l'Empereur!"

"Vive l'Empereur!"

The thick stone walls of the ancient cathedral shook as hundreds of cannon were fired outside and the great bell of Notre-Dame began to ring. As we emerged into the bright winter sun, fire-rockets flared. Already the dancing had begun.

* *A member of the assembly wrote: "Nothing could have been more comical than the way the Bonaparte sisters acted. One sulked, another held smelling salts under her nose, and the third let the mantle drop."*

## In which Bonaparte honours my son

The Emperor and I dined alone, infused by the glow of glory. (And with relief that it was over.) "Leave it on," Bonaparte said, as Chastulé was about to remove my crown. "It becomes you." Over a simple meal of roast chicken with crayfish butter, hashed apples and a vanilla soufflé (which Bonaparte ate first), we talked, chattering like children. He'd not even noticed the stone that had hit his shoulder, and yes, he'd barked at his unruly sisters. "Imagine if I had fallen over backwards!" I said, both of us laughing now that it was over.

After, we joined everyone in the Yellow Salon: family, officials and household staff. Over the booming of cannon and the hiss and cackle of the fire-rockets outside, we shared story after story. My ladies demonstrated how, on the way to the cathedral, they'd had to pick their way through the slush in their silk slippers, shivering in the icy wind. There had been one uncomfortable moment when the crowd near the market had laughed at the Pope's prelate in his broad-brimmed hat, riding a white mule and carrying a huge cross. Uncle "Cardinal" Fesch, flushed with fine wine, told how his nephew—the Emperor—had poked him in the backside with the Imperial sceptre.

Bonaparte grinned. "It got you moving, didn't it, Uncle?" (Little Napoleon giggled, half-asleep in my arms.)

"And were those *stones* that fell from the vault?" Hortense asked, taking the baby Petit from his nursemaid.

"It was the birds I worried about."

"With reason," Eugène said with a laugh.

"And what happened at the altar, Your Majesty?" Chastulé asked. "It looked as if you were going to fall over. That mantle must be heavy."

"It *was* heavy," I said, glancing at the Bonaparte sisters. "Ask the princesses," I suggested with an innocent air.

"And were you weeping, Your Majesty, when the Emperor put the crown on your head?" Clari asked.

"I couldn't help it," I told Isabey, who looked mortified at the damage to his handiwork. "I tried not to."

And then everyone began to chatter at once:

"Sire, did His Holiness know that you were going to put the crown on yourself?"

"Ah, so it was planned that way."*

"It was glorious, just glorious."

"A day I will never, ever, ever, ever, *ever* forget."

I sat and listened, taking it all in, caressing my sweet little Napoleon, now asleep in my arms. I caught Bonaparte's eye and smiled. Our day. Over at last.

*December 18, late afternoon—Paris.*

Madame Mère (as she is to be called now) has finally arrived back in Paris—none too happy, and certainly not the least bit apologetic about having missed the most important event of her amazing son's life. She regards the magnificence Bonaparte has bestowed upon the family and the nation with something akin to contempt. "So long as it lasts," she said sceptically, ferreting coins away.

She was too ill to come to the last family gathering—sick with chagrin, her daughters reported, over having to buy a length of expensive silk for a gown. She has rationed her cooks to one dishcloth, one apron, one towel a day, and refuses to buy more than three half-pound loaves of bread at a time. "We have to bring bread when we dine there," Caroline complained to Bonaparte.

"You must *spend* the money I give you," Bonaparte later instructed his

---

* *In crowning himself, Napoleon was following a ceremony Charlemagne had ordered when his son was crowned.*

mother. "You must entertain, keep an open house, be generous with your staff. It is the aristocratic way."

*January 6, 1805, morning—Sunday and Kings' Day (cold).*
Fouché, looking uncharacteristically dapper in a fur-lined cloak, sidled up to me at last night's ball in my honour. "Why are you smiling?" I asked. "It makes me uneasy."

"I thought you might be interested in two items in the latest police report." He blinked his eyes slowly. "Concerning members of your family."

"Perhaps." Of course I wanted to know!

"One concerns the Emperor's youngest brother."

"Jérôme?" The scamp.

"He and his bride are apparently on the frigate *La Didon*, returning to France—to the welcoming arms of his brother the Emperor."

"Welcoming?" I rolled my eyes. It was doubtful that Bonaparte would agree even to see Jérôme. "And the second item in the report?"

"Concerns your son."

*Eugène?* In a police report! "It doesn't have anything to do with Adèle Duchâtel, does it?"

"Ah, the devious Madame Duchâtel—that's another matter altogether. No, the report divulged rumours of a possible marriage between your son and Princess Auguste-Amélie of Bavaria—the most beautiful princess in Europe, it is said." Fouché studied my reaction. "The Princess's family is one of the most ancient and distinguished in all of Europe."

*Indeed.* Princess Auguste's family has ruled Bavaria for eight centuries—the blood of Charlemagne flows in her veins. "The rumours are unfounded. Princess Auguste is betrothed to Prince Charles of the House of Baden." Unfortunately!

*January 18.*
Tired, a troubled sleep. Eugène's ball in his newly renovated town house last night was a success, especially with the young. The revelry went on until dawn—or so I'm told, for Bonaparte and I left early, shortly after

Caroline and Hortense's duet. (Caroline braying, trying to compete with Hortense, the crowd crying out for an encore from my daughter—painful.)

"Your fête is a big success," I told Eugène, on taking my leave.

"I suppose," he said, uncharacteristically morose.

I've since learned the reason for my son's dejection. Caroline had cruelly informed him that the woman he courted had been "taken" by his stepfather.

*January 19, Décadi—close to midnight.*
A blizzard howls both outside and in—Bonaparte is in a foul temper.

*January 21.*
Eugène called on me at my morning toilette, his hat damp from melted snow. "Papa has ordered me to leave with my regiment."

Leave? For where?

"For Milan."*

"*Now*, Eugène?" The storm was severe. It was difficult to ride across town, much less over the Alps.

"Within twenty-four hours," Eugène said, handing me the order. "I don't understand, unless . . ."

Unless Bonaparte wanted Eugène out of Paris. "Eugène, may I ask you something?" Something I had no business knowing. "Have you done anything that might have angered Bonaparte?" His evasive look gave the answer. "Something to do with Adèle Duchâtel, perhaps?"

And then Eugène confessed: he'd been upset, he said. He'd called Adèle a coquette (and worse, I suspect). "I told her I'd tell her husband about . . . you know." He tapped the tip of his riding whip against the toe of his boot.

About Adèle and Bonaparte. What was I to say? It was such a complex web. "And so?"

---

* *Napoleon was sending troops to Milan in order to protect Italy from invasion by Austria, which tended to view northern Italy as its domain.*

He hunched his shoulders. "And so she said she would tell the Emperor about *me*."

He seemed so much a boy still, all fluster and freckles, hardly equal to this bedchamber duel with his Emperor stepfather. "And what might there be to tell, Eugène?"

"Maman, she'd have to lie," he said, blushing angrily. "I got nowhere!"

*January 22.*
This morning my obedient, loyal son headed off into the storm at the head of nine hundred chasseurs and grenadiers. I am struggling with my conscience. I promised Eugène I wouldn't say anything to Bonaparte.

*[Undated]*
"Zut," Bonaparte said under his breath, pacing. "So Adèle lied to me about Eugène. That was devious on her part—devious and manipulative. I'm afraid you're going to have to let her go."

"You want *me* to dismiss your mistress, Bonaparte?"

The thought gives me pleasure, I confess.

*February 1.*
Today Bonaparte made an announcement to the Senate, naming Eugène Prince and Vice-Arch-Chancellor.

*February 24—noisy: carnival parade starting outside.*
I should have guessed that this would happen. An enraged (and hiccupping) Elisa descended upon Bonaparte: "Eugène is a prince now, even Joachim is a prince—so why not Félix? What about *my* husband?"

*This* is a problem. Elisa's husband is lazy and inept and alienates everyone with his haughty rudeness. "I must get them out of Paris," Bonaparte said, scratching his head.

*March 19, Saint Joseph's Day.*

Bonaparte has found a solution to his sister's complaints: he is awarding Elisa and Félix the little kingdom of Piombino in northern Italy.

"How charming," Caroline commented with biting sarcasm. "My sister is to rule an army of four soldiers."

"Better than ruling only one soldier," Elisa said evenly—meaning Caroline's husband Joachim.


*March 21—Saint-Cloud.*

I've been busy getting everything ready for the baby's baptism on the weekend—by the Pope no less. (He has wisely decided to linger in Paris, waiting for the passage over the Alps to clear.) Bonaparte insists that Hortense and Louis's second son be baptized exactly as a Dauphin would have been baptized during the Ancien Régime. Complex! The Holy Father has confided that he's never performed a baptism before, much less an Imperial one.


*March 22.*

Caroline has had her baby, another girl. "Bad timing," Bonaparte said during our evening ride. "She expects the infant to be baptized along with Hortense and Louis's boy next week."

"But wouldn't that mean two entirely different ceremonies?" Caroline's children are not in the line of succession—the ceremony would not be the same.

"Exactly. I'll tell her it would take too long," he said.


*[Undated]*

Caroline's in a rage!


*March 24, Sunday, 4:00 P.M.—Saint-Cloud.*

And so it has been done: Hortense and Louis's baby Petit was baptized by the Pope (with Uncle Fesch prompting): Napoleon-Louis, he has been named. The five-month-old obliged us by crying the entire time. Bonaparte, the proud godfather, held the squalling child at the font. Madame Mère, as godmother, stood beside Bonaparte, scowling in her expensive new gown. The baby finally quieted, sucking on Bonaparte's finger.

And now, that behind us, we rush to get ready to leave for Milan in one week—one more coronation to get through. Bonaparte is to be crowned King of Italy—unless he can succeed in persuading one of his brothers to take his place, that is (to avoid alarming the Royalist nations).

*March 28.*
Monsieur Rémusat left this morning for Italy—escorted by a sizeable guard. He carried with him the Imperial insignia and Crown jewels. Clari is in tears at the thought of her husband having to endure the "wretched Savoy roads and their ignorant postillions." And the bandits! Bandits just waiting to murder her husband in order to get their hands on his treasure. But most of all she is in a fret over the Mont Cenis pass, "with its steep descents and no wall at all on the outer edge!" In spite of my assurances that I myself have crossed two times over "that fatal" Mont Cenis, she continues to be convinced that her husband will perish. In comforting her, in assuring her that there is no danger, I begin to conquer my own fear. I try to think only of the pleasure of seeing Eugène in Milan, try not to think of the mountains that must be crossed to get to him.

*March 30—snow!*
I'm "in a state of perturbation" (as Clari puts it)—but it's not only me. *Everyone*, it seems, is in a fluster, getting ready to depart in two days. The servants can't figure out who to take orders from, whom to give orders *to*.

And then excitement beyond measure: the new Imperial travelling coach was delivered and everyone went out in the snow-covered courtyard to gawk at the enormous berline. The outside is plain—intentionally, so as not to attract bandits. The only indication that it is an Imperial coach is a small coat of arms on the door.

Inside, the coach is remarkable, for it is divided into two compartments. In the one at the front are two deep seats, separated by an armrest. Opposite is a bank of drawers, equipped with toilet articles and a table service, as well as a desk. In the back compartment is a bed that can be made into a sofa.

I let the children of the household climb inside—they scrambled from one compartment to another. "*My* seat," little Napoleon said, climbing into the leather chair opposite the desk—Bonaparte's chair.

"He'll make a fine emperor someday," I heard a maid say.

"Our Crown Prince."

Our *heir*.


*April 1—Fontainebleau.*
The coach is remarkably comfortable: the big body swings on wide leather straps attached to heavy springs. "Time to try out that bed," Bonaparte said meaningfully as soon as we had passed the Paris gate. He pulled the blinds and took my hand. And so our first Imperial expedition is off to an excellent start, the Emperor (*and* Empress) content.


*April 22—Palazzo Stupinigi, near Turin.*
We crossed the Alps without incident. In fact, the weather was glorious, the vistas stimulating to the imagination, bringing back memories of youth. A decade ago I crossed the Alps into Italy to join my new husband on his first campaign. I remember my fear then, the wonder of a journey into an unknown world. If I had known then what an amazing journey it would, in fact, turn out to be . . .

Eugène, so bronzed from the sun he looks like a peasant, met us at this regal lodge not far from Turin. He and Bonaparte immediately set off on a hunt. I've bathed, changed into an evening toilette. The intoxicating scent of spring is in the air.


*April 24—still at Palazzo Stupinigi.*
We've had word that Bonaparte's young brother Jérôme is in Turin! He's

sailed from America to Portugal and come on horseback into Italy, seeking his Emperor brother's favour—and approval of his marriage. Eugène has just left with the unhappy message that Bonaparte refuses to receive his youngest sibling, refuses to recognize "that girl" as his wife.

"*Forgive* him?" Bonaparte ranted when Eugène and I pleaded for him to reconcile with Jérôme. "He's lucky I haven't court-martialled him for desertion!"

*1:20 A.M.*
On hearing a horse trot into the courtyard, I crept down the stairs in my dressing gown and cap, shielding the candle flame against the warm breeze that billowed the curtains. "Oh, Maman, it really is a little sad," Eugène said, unbuckling his spurs. "He does care for her."

"It's a matter of policy, Eugène." *Policy* has nothing to do with love and individual happiness. Policy has to do with peace and prosperity. Policy has to do with the well-being of a people, of a nation.

Eugène threw down his hat. "That's what I told him. I explained that with power came responsibilities, that the Imperial family must set the example and that an illegal marriage could not be condoned." All this in the mock voice of Bonaparte.

"And he accepted?"

"Not until I told him Papa would find him a buxom princess to marry."

"You didn't!" Both of us laughing.

*A balmy evening, May 6—Alessandria.*
Jérôme and Bonaparte embraced. With promises of a princess and a crown someday soon, Jérôme has agreed to have his "marriage" declared null and void.

The young man set off this morning, waving his hat from the high road. "That scamp," Bonaparte said, shaking his head, his eyes misty.

*May 8—Milan.*
We're in Milan, in the royal palace facing the cathedral. How noisy it is!
The thick stone walls shake (I swear) every time the bells ring, which is
often. We've a water closet, but the arrangement of the rooms is
awkward, our bedchamber uncomfortably small. Bonaparte is already
pacing it off, deciding how it's to be renovated.

*May 24, close to 11:00 A.M.*
Yesterday a mounted detachment was sent to Monza to bring back the
Iron Crown. It's a simple band of gold (not iron) about three inches
high, decorated with a few irregular gems. Rather crude for a crown, I
thought, but Bonaparte held it as if it were made of diamonds. "Charlemagne wore this crown," he said reverently, placing it on his head to see
if it would fit (it's a little small).

"Is it decided?" I asked, shifting it forward on his head. "You're to be
King of Italy?" Certainly that's what the Italians want, but England and
the other Royalist nations won't like it, that much is clear. Any indication that France is growing in power and prosperity alarms them.

"I tried to talk one of my brothers into it, but . . ." He made a gesture
of futility. His brothers don't want to give up their place in the line of
succession for the French crown.

"So you will be King, but you'll appoint someone to rule?" I asked,
emboldened by the moment.

"Curious to know who that might be?" he teased, tugging my ear. And
then, his countenance suddenly serious, he added, "Joachim was the
obvious choice. He speaks the language and has commanded troops
here."

"You say he *was* the obvious choice." Not any longer?

"Prince Bully-Boy is none too popular here, it would appear. He's
made a number of enemies."

*May 26—a superb day.*
Yet another coronation behind us. Bonaparte shocked everyone by walking in carrying Charlemagne's crown under his arm, like a hat.

Now everyone awaits the big announcement: whom will he name Viceroy?

*June 7.*

"You appointed *Eugène*?"

"I thought this was what you wanted," Bonaparte said, perplexed.

"Oh yes!" I said, but overcome by the realization that my son would no longer be living in Paris, or even in France; overcome knowing, suddenly, how very, very much I was going to miss him.

*[Undated]*

"Maman, I can't sleep for worrying," Eugène confessed. "I'm only twenty-three."

"You have the best of teachers. Bonaparte has so much confidence in you."

"I'm going to miss you and Hortense—and what about her boys? Little Napoleon will forget me."

"We'll just have to find you a wife," I teased. *Soon.*

*July 6—Genoa.*

As feared, England has joined with Austria and Russia to wage war against us—yet another Royalist coalition determined to put an end to the French Republic.*

"I must leave for Paris immediately," Bonaparte said, ordering the travel carriage. I begged to return with him. "There will be no stops," he warned. "I'm going to travel night and day."

Yes, I nodded, ringing for a maid to pack my trunks. Now I am ready; *he* is not.

---

* *England was involved financially, paying Russia and Austria to send troops against France.*

*July 11—Fontainebleau.*

We arrived at Fontainebleau before anyone expected us. The flustered cooks managed to find some tough mutton for us to eat.

Immediately I fell into bed (my feet swollen) and slept for hours, waking dazed. People can't believe that we travelled from Genoa in eighty-five hours—a *record*—and this with a three-hour delay on Mont Cenis due to a storm. "This comet called Bonaparte," Hortense once said. This comet indeed! Sometimes I feel I'm hanging on for dear life.


*Milan*

*Chère Maman,*

*You will be pleased to know that I'm following up on your suggestion to establish a nursery-garden in order to supply trees to all my kingdom. Fruit trees are unknown here. Any recommendations?*

*I've also been thinking of creating a museum to display the fine works of art hidden away in the cellars of the monasteries and churches. I have so many dreams: of a library, a museum of natural history, a medical museum (don't laugh). I think a school of design might do well here, too.*

*I get daily letters from Papa. I'm learning so much from him.**

---

* Napoleon's instructions to Eugène on how to rule Italy included these guidelines: "We live in an age where one cannot underestimate the perversity of the human heart. I cannot empha-sise enough the importance of circumspection and prudence. Italians are naturally more deceit-ful than the French. The way to earn their respect is not to trust anyone. Dissimulation is natural at a certain age; for you, it must be a matter of principle. When you have spoken openly, tell yourself that you have made a mistake, and resolve not to do it again.

"There will come a time when you will understand that there is little difference between one nationality and another. The goal of your administration is the well-being of my Italian subjects. You must sacrifice the things you care most about, and embrace customs which you dislike. In Italy, you must forget the glory of being French. You must persuade Italians that you love them. They know that there is no love without respect. Learn their language, social-ize, take part in their festivities. Approve of what they approve of, and love what they love.

"Speak as little as possible. You do not have enough training, and your education is insuffi-cient for you to take part freely in discussions. Although Viceroy, you are only twenty-three. People may flatter you, but everyone will realize how little you know. You will earn more respect by virtue of your potential than by what you are today.

"Do not imitate me; you must be more reserved.

"Rarely preside over Council of State. You do not have enough knowledge to do so with

*A million kisses. I miss you and Hortense terribly. Kiss my nephews for me, remind them of their lonely uncle.*

*Your Prince Eugène, Viceroy of Italy*
*Note—You'll be happy to know that my efforts to reduce the violence in the city have already had results.*


*July 19—Paris.*

Caroline flashed a smile. "Joachim and I wish to convey sincere congratulations on your son's appointment as Viceroy of Italy," she said, her fingertips pressed together. "Don't we, Joachim?"

"The Emperor is flawless in his wisdom." Joachim doffed his pink hat and bowed, straightening with difficulty.

"What's wrong with your leg?" Bonaparte demanded. "Better get in shape. We'll be riding out soon." Riding out to war again.

"Oh, it's nothing!" Caroline said, answering for her husband—but I've since discovered the cause of Joachim's leg injury. On learning of Eugène's promotion, he broke his sword over his knee in a rage.

*success. When you do preside, do not speak. They will listen to you, but they will soon see that you are not competent. One cannot measure the strength of a prince who remains silent.*

*"Do not be overly friendly to foreigners—there is little to be gained from them. An ambassador will never speak well of you because it is his job to speak poorly. The foreign ambassadors are, in a manner of speaking, official spies. Preferably, surround yourself with young Italian men; the old ones are useless."*

*In which my son falls truly in love*

*September 2, 1805, late afternoon—Malmaison.*
It has been some time since I opened these pages. Anger impels me to pick up a quill once again. Anger and fear, I confess. This afternoon Caroline called to announce in a tone of victory that Joachim has been named Bonaparte's second-in-command in the coming campaign. "How surprising that Louis was not chosen, or even Eugène," she said, purring like a cat with her claws out.

"Eugène is quite busy governing Italy." And doing so well!

"It must be difficult without a wife," she said, helping herself to a fistful of aromatic pastilles. "*Speaking* of which, I heard the most astonishing rumour. It's being said that Eugène is going to marry Princess Auguste of Bavaria."

"Princess Auguste is betrothed to Prince Charles," I said evenly.

I was so relieved when she left! Whatever marriage negotiations are undertaken, the last person I would want to know about them is Caroline.


*September 9.*
Austria has invaded Bavaria. "They must be stopped," Bonaparte said, closeting himself with the Minister of War. Soon, I know, he will announce that we're leaving. I've already sent silver, linen and furniture on ahead to Strasbourg.

*September 23, the first day of the Republican New Year.*
We leave in the morning, before dawn. The carriages, *fifty* of them, are lined up. I've been reviewing the lists. Bonaparte has just told me to make sure the telescope and compass have been packed. Which reminds me: dentifrice powder (for me) and wart paste (for Bonaparte).

I must make sure that the cooks prepare dishes we can take with us. Bonaparte doesn't believe in stopping for something as unnecessary as eating, much less answering a call of nature.

*September 26, I think.*
We're in Strasbourg, another flying trip. Keeping up with Bonaparte will be the death of me! We left at four in the morning and travelled without stopping for two days. At each posting house, the wheels had to be cooled with buckets of water. But no, I will *not* complain, lest Bonaparte command I stay behind.

And as to staying behind—the carriage carrying all the kitchen utensils broke down en route. Of the fifty carriages (the dust was terrible), only five were able to keep up.

Already Bonaparte is at work, organizing an attack on the Austrians. "Speed is my weapon."*

*October 1—Strasbourg.*
Bonaparte left this morning. "A kiss—for luck," he said, pulling on his battered hat. It has been five years since he rode to battle. He was anxious, I knew, and eager.

"I will be thinking of you." Praying for him. (This I did not say.) "I put barley water in the berline—in the top right-hand cabinet." That and a number of other remedies that helped "keep the balance," as he put it.

"We won't be long," he called out as the carriage pulled forward. "I promise you."

---

* *The Austrians believed Napoleon and his army were still on the Channel coast. It was an understandable assumption: never in history had so large an army been moved so quickly.*

*12 Vendémiaire, 11:00 P.M., Munich*
*The enemy has been beaten, lost its head, and everyone is telling me that it*
*was the happiest campaign, the shortest and the most brilliant ever made.*
*The weather is terrible. I change clothes twice a day because of the rain. I love*
*and embrace you. N.*

*October 23—Strasbourg.*
Great Patience, Little Patience, Windmill. Every night I lay out the
cards, praying for victory, fearing defeat. Tonight I won all three games:
"They are victorious," I announced to my ladies. A short time later a
breathless courier was announced: Victory! I gave him my pearl ring, so
great was my joy.

*27 Vendémiaire, Elchingen*
*I did what I intended. I destroyed the Austrian army. Now I'm going after*
*the Russians. They are lost. Adieu, a thousand kisses everywhere. N.*

*Yesterday I made thirty-three thousand men put down their arms. I took*
*sixty or seventy thousand prisoners, more than ninety flags and two hundred*
*cannon. Never in the annals of military history has there been such a cata-*
*strophe. I have a bit of a cold. N.*

*October 27—Strasbourg.*
The wife of Bonaparte's chamberlain stood with her hands clasped in
front of her. "I have a message from the Emperor, Your Majesty," she
told me.

   She had just come from Munich. I'd been expecting to hear something—something too delicate to entrust to a military courier. Something to do with the spoils of war. Something to do with the hand of a
princess.

   "The Emperor asked me to tell you that he has discussed a certain
matter with King Maximilian of Bavaria."

"Indeed?" I said, opening my fan. No doubt King Maximilian was grateful to Bonaparte for liberating his country from the Austrians: but *how* grateful? "And did he say King Maximilian was amenable?"

"Everything has been arranged, Your Majesty," she said with a bow.

I'm to travel to Munich, she said, giving me Bonaparte's detailed instructions itemizing exactly how much I'm to spend on gifts, whose carriage is to precede my own and whose is to follow. I'm to be heralded in every town by the ringing of bells, cannonading, drumming and trumpeting. I'm to accept the homage as my due. I am the wife of the victor.

*November 21, 1805, Paris*
*Chère Maman,*

*Paris has been dispirited without you and the Emperor. Louis is with his regiment on the north coast, in case England invades. I am alone with my angels right now, but not for long. My dear friend Mademoiselle Adèle Auguié has agreed to be my lady's maid—she'll be starting next week. You can imagine how happy this makes me.*

*We read* Le Moniteur *for the names of the injured. Louis will want information pertaining to his aide-de-camp, Monsieur Flahaut. He was wounded at Lambach. Do you know anything?*

*Little Napoleon sends his love. He is sweet with Petit, who has just begun to crawl. They both suffered a bit of an ague that was going around, but are recovering well. My own health is improving with each day. I've been taking your tonics—don't worry.*

*Your loving daughter, Princess Hortense*
*Note—I enclose an account of the disaster in Spain: twenty ships captured!* *Fortunately the Emperor's victories in Germany help to console us for the loss. It is said all our luck is with him. It is also said that you are his luck, Maman.*

*December 4—a posting house somewhere en route to Munich.*
Karlsruhe, Stuttgart, Ulm, Augsburg. Everywhere I go, I cast out gifts—

---

* *On October 21, 1805, the French-Spanish fleet was defeated by England off Cape Trafalgar, on the southwest coast of Spain.*

ebony snuffboxes, enamel miniatures, gems of every size and hue. I feel like a fairy godmother. (And I love it.)

*December 5, Munich—snow, very cold.*

I'm in Munich finally, at the royal palace—called the Residenz. This is a gay country, although curious. The women pile flowers on top of their heads with feathers and bits of chiffon tucked in, using an enormous number of little pins with diamond heads on them. And no face paint, no Spanish Red, and many wearing stays and awkward hoops. Their carriages, much like our old mail coaches, are unusually wide just so that the ladies in their hoops can fit in. (Even then it isn't easy.) Sad-looking nags are harnessed to the carriages with rope. Turning a corner is, of course, difficult.

The Residenz itself is more like a city than a palace. How many court-yards—seven? There are eight galleries and even a museum, I'm told. It's a maze, each apartment suite decorated in a different era: Renaissance, baroque. Mine is luxurious rococo. We have been greeted like royalty.

Well, we *are* royalty, I remind myself. However, walking these ancient halls hung with the portraits of illustrious ancestors dating back centuries makes me feel very much what I am, in fact: *a parvenue.*

Tomorrow the receptions begin. I'm anxious to meet King Maximilian, Princess Auguste's father.

*December 6—Munich.*

"Please, call me Max," King Maximilian said in flawless French. "Everyone else does, even my servants." He laughed gaily.

What a charming man! Tall, handsome, a noble face (in spite of a ruddy complexion), robust for his age, which I take to be about fifty.

He was guarded, however, on the subject of his daughter. "She will agree, I am quite sure."

"She has *not* agreed?"

King Max threw up his hands. "I can't force her."

I've since made inquiries and discovered that Princess Auguste has refused to break her engagement to Prince Charles. She is encouraged in this by her stepmother. As well, the Princess's governess and an aunt are said to be opposed to marriage with Eugène.

All this has me terribly worried. Tomorrow I've been invited to dine with King Max and his family. I've laid out my gifts, sent for a jeweller.

Chastulé will accompany me: the Rochefoucauld name will inspire respect. I've instructed her that she is to entertain our hosts with stories of what a good horseman my handsome Eugène is, how he excels at the hunt, what a fine ruler he is. (I'd prefer to tell them how much Eugène loves children, how gentle and kind-hearted he is, but I'm not sure that they would approve.) Chastulé will praise my son and I will modestly protest. My battle plan.

*December 8.*

Oh, my goodness, she *is* lovely. Tall (I made sure to mention how very tall Eugène is), and *so* beautiful, but in an entirely natural, unstudied way. Seventeen years old with a sylphlike figure—she reminds me of Hortense. A lovely complexion, big dark eyes—*soft* eyes. Shy, gracious— I saw my grandchildren in her lovely arms.

But she is, as well, loyal. She is fond of her pudgy cousin and refuses to break her engagement to him. And headstrong, too, for she resists her father's will.

*[Undated]*

"Ha. It's the three women we must first convince, Your Majesty," Chastulé said.

*The three women*: the stepmother ("Madame Hard-face," Chastulé calls her), the governess ("Madame Fat-face") and the aunt ("Madame Old-face").

"Chastulé, you're cruel," I protested, laughing.

*14 Frimaire, Austerlitz*

*I've concluded a truce. The Battle of Austerlitz is the best I have ever fought. Forty-five flags, more than one hundred and fifty cannon and thirty thousand prisoners—plus twenty thousand killed, a horrible spectacle.*

*Tsar Alexandre is in despair. He showed neither talent nor bravery.** 

*Finally peace has returned to the continent. One can only hope that peace will now come to the world.*

*Adieu, my good friend. I very much long to embrace you. N.*

*December 19—Munich.*

Caroline has arrived. We kissed and pretended to be happy to see one another. I'm in dread of her finding out about the delicate negotiations going on right now.

*[Undated]*

Auguste is holding firm. "What do you think it will take?" I asked Chastulé, discouraged.

"To get the Princess to consent?" Chastulé made herself comfortable in one of the enormous armchairs, swinging her feet back and forth like a child. "Well, for one thing, the Three Faces object because there's no crown," she said. "Ha. Yes, a crown *always* helps."

The crown of Italy. "Of course," I said, shrugging, "but—"

"Or if your son were to be named *heir* to the crown. Even King Max objects that Eugène is 'merely' a French gentleman."

"I thought King Max favoured this match."

"He has consented to it, Your Majesty, but that does not mean he favours it."

"But Eugène is a prince, Chastulé. How can King Max say he's 'merely' a gentleman?"

"Prince-*parvenu*, and not even the Emperor's son."

---

* *The Russian Tsar Alexandre wrote to a French general after the battle of Austerlitz: "Tell your master that I am going away. Tell him that he performed miracles yesterday, that the battle has increased my admiration for him, that he is a man predestined by Heaven, that it will take a hundred years for my army to equal his."*

"So if Bonaparte were to formally adopt Eugène as his son and declare him heir to the crown of Italy . . . ?"

"That would help."

I paused, smiling slowly. "If that's what it takes, Chastulé, then perhaps that's what the Princess should demand."

*December 21.*

"Ha. The Three Faces are very long this morning, Your Majesty."

My heart jumped. "The Princess has accepted?"

"Not quite, but she *has* agreed to consider breaking off her engagement to Prince Charles."

"In order to marry Eugène?"

"Not quite. I'm told there are *conditions*." Chastulé grinned.

*December 23—Munich.*

"Is Princess Auguste betrothed?" Caroline asked as we dined tonight.

"Yes," I said, lying with conviction. "To Prince Charles."

*December 31, early—not yet 9:00 A.M.*

Bonaparte arrived just before midnight last night—chilled, weary and *furious* that the wedding contract has not yet been signed. "But she hasn't agreed to it, Bonaparte!"

*4:20 P.M.*

"I'm sending for Eugène," Bonaparte announced.

"She agreed?" *Finally!*

"But on two conditions: one, that I adopt Eugène, and two, that he be made heir to the throne of Italy."

"And so . . . ?"

Bonaparte shrugged. "And so I said yes," he replied with a sheepish smile.

*January 1, 1806, New Year's Day—a Wednesday (not Primidi—hurrah! No more Republican calendar).* *

Caroline has had a nervous fit and taken to her bed. "I wouldn't go to too much trouble, Your Majesty," Chastulé said as I was preparing a basket of healing tinctures and salves to take to her. "It's said Princess Caroline is indisposed because of Prince Eugène's engagement, because now your son's children will take precedence over her little monsters. It's even said she tried to convince the Emperor that he should divorce you and marry Princess Auguste himself."

Mon Dieu, that girl . . .


*January 6, Kings' Day—Monday.*

Now Auguste is ill. The wedding will have to be postponed, we've been told. Bonaparte sent Dr. Corvisart over to "help."

"I could find nothing amiss," the doctor reported back.

"The girl is dissembling," Bonaparte said, smiling at her nerve.

I'm praying that Eugène will get here soon. Until the vows are spoken, I won't be able to sleep.


*January 7, Munich—snowing again.*

Auguste has "miraculously" recovered, but is now claiming a sprained ankle. The wedding will have to be postponed, we were told yet again—until after the Emperor leaves for Paris, her stepmother said.

"They're stalling," Chastulé said. "Once the Emperor is out of Munich, they'll back out."

Bonaparte gave his "assurance" that he'll stay in Munich until the young couple is wed, *whenever* that may be.

Checkmate.


*[Undated]*

Now *I* am ill.

---

* *As of this date, the French Empire officially returned to the Gregorian calendar.*

*January 10, Friday morning.*

I was woken by my husband. "I have a surprise for you," he said, grinning mischievously. I *screeched*! In the door I saw Eugène. "Grand Dieu, at *last* you've arrived." I clasped his hands, kissed him. "You look as if you've been on a horse for a week." He hadn't shaved and his hair was uncombed. "You've grown a moustache?" It looks horrible on him!

"You don't like it?" he asked, pulling on one point.

"Sweetheart, you are the handsomest prince in all of Europe, but that moustache will have to go. Bonaparte, send someone for the barber. We'll have to get Eugène cleaned up before we introduce him to Princess Auguste," I said, squeezing my son's hand, my heart in a flutter.

Eugène looked at Bonaparte and then back at me.

"What does that look mean?" Slowly it dawned on me. "Bonaparte, you didn't!"

"It was fine, Maman, truly."

"Bonaparte, you took Eugène to meet Princess Auguste—*already*? Without telling me?" I was furious with them both.

"You haven't been well, Josephine. I didn't want to wake you."

"Well, now I'm really sick." All our plans were ruined—and all because of an ugly moustache! "How *could* you? Just look at him. He's a *mess*."

Eugène handed me a handkerchief. "It's all right, Maman," he said, laughing.

"Your son arrived at ten this morning, precisely when he said he would." Bonaparte gave Eugène an approving nod. "I took him directly to King Max—nothing formal, just a family affair, or so I had to assure him."

"I *was* a bit nervous, I admit."

"Actually, I had to pull him along." Bonaparte rocked on his heels in front of the fire.

"And so . . . ? How did it go? What happened!"

"King Max commanded his daughter to enter," Bonaparte explained. "She did, but just stood staring at the floor. I think she was even trembling."

"Auguste didn't expect to be introduced like that, without any warning," Eugène said.

"Go on, Bonaparte," I said slowly. There was something in my son's voice . . . a manly gentleness, a protective caring. *Auguste*, he said.

"That's pretty much it. We parents left the room so that they could be alone together."

"And?" My hands over my mouth like a child.

"She was upset, Maman. She told me she'd only agreed to marry me for the sake of her father."

Oh no! So it hadn't gone well.

"I told her that if she really was against the marriage, I would do everything in my power to prevent it."

"Eugène, you didn't!" I looked at Bonaparte, alarmed. Had my son no idea how important this was?

Bonaparte grinned. "I don't think we need to worry, Josephine. When Eugène and the Princess came out of the room, they were holding hands."

"She's . . . *pleased* with you, Eugène?"

My son smiled shyly. "I think we're in love, Maman."

Bonaparte reached over and tugged a lock of Eugène's hair. "The charmer."


*January 12, a beautiful Sunday.*
This afternoon, in a quiet ceremony, Bonaparte adopted Eugène as his son and designated him heir to the throne of Italy. He embraced Eugène with love in his eyes. The look in Caroline's eyes was of another sort.


*Monday.*
"Caroline is too ill to come," Joachim told Bonaparte, his chin buried in a ruff of artificial pink lace. "She sends her regrets."

Bonaparte looked up from cleaning his fingernails with a coral toothpick. "Ill with bile, I venture."

"Ill with good reason."

I glanced from Joachim to Bonaparte, not a little concerned. Now was not the time for a brouhaha. In two hours the contract was to be signed, followed by the civil wedding ceremony.

Bonaparte frowned, methodically tucking the toothpick into its gold case. "And what might that *good* reason be?"

"These royal fops scorn us." Joachim spat into a spittoon.

"What do I care what they think? You are jealous, face it. Eugène's children will have the blood of Charlemagne in their veins. They are not even born and their future is writ large on the pages of history. And you say this is a bad thing? I see it as a great victory—equal to the victory at Austerlitz."

In fury, Joachim knocked a vase over with his sword on his way out. "You see, Josephine?" Bonaparte said, picking up the book he had been reading. "Our people don't even know how to walk properly."


*January 14.*

At seven this evening in the Royal Chapel, Eugène was married to Princess Auguste-Amélie of Bavaria. The young couple could not take their eyes off each other. We bask in the glow of this miraculous love.

As is the royal custom (we've learned), Bonaparte and I saw the newly-wed couple to the door of their suite. "So," said Bonaparte, clearing his throat. "I guess this is it." He grasped Eugène's hand and gave it a mighty shake.

I embraced my new daughter-in-law. "I can't tell you how happy I am." *Truly.*

Auguste looked up at Eugène and slipped her hand into his. "Well, I guess this is it," Eugène said, repeating Bonaparte's words.

I kissed them both (a blessing) and took Bonaparte's arm, tugging him away. We meandered down the wide marble halls arm in arm, the portraits of centuries looking down upon us.

## In which we are devastated

*January 27, 1806—Paris, at last.*
Tears sprang into my eyes when I saw Hortense. "Are you not eating?" I exclaimed, embracing her. She is so gaunt.

"I am fine, Maman," she assured me. "Now, tell me *everything*."

With pleasure I described how wonderful Auguste is, Eugène's happiness, how much in love they are. "If only I could have been there," Hortense said wistfully. "Louis would not allow me to go."

"No doubt he was concerned about the rough roads, especially in this season." Especially considering her health.

We talked for a time of this and of that—of the boys, Louis's latest (bizarre) treatments,* a song she was composing. I described the curious fashions worn in Munich, the elaborate royal rituals we'd observed there. I told her that the new furniture Messieurs Fontaine and Percier had designed for my suite at the Tuileries was hideous, but that I was pleased with the chambermaid my hairdresser Duplan had recommended. Hortense had been using Duplan herself, she said—did I mind if he dressed her hair on Wednesday?

"Are you and Louis planning to go see Talma play Manlius that night?" I asked.

But before she could answer, we were diverted by the sound of the

---

* *Believing that skin eruptions would draw the "morbid humours" out of Louis's body, Dr. Corvisart was intentionally exposing Louis to scabies by having him wear the unwashed linens of a diseased man. Another treatment involved "bathing" in steaming entrails.*

children outside the open door. Little Napoleon ran into my arms. "I can count, Grandmaman."

"That's wonderful," I said, covering his cheeks with kisses, counting with each one.

The baby staggered toward me and then fell onto the carpet. I held my breath, waiting for a howl. Instead he scampered at a crawl to my feet and, grasping my gown, pulled himself up. I hoisted him onto my lap, little Napoleon close beside me. "Oh, what treasures you have given us," I told my daughter, my heart overflowing.

*Wednesday, January 29.*
We didn't get to the theatre until the end of the first scene. Seeing Bonaparte, the audience cheered with such passion that the actors decided to begin the play again. We stayed to the end. Talma got a standing ovation—even the critic Geoffroy was observed to applaud.

Caroline and Joachim were there with an entourage, including a comely maid in a daring ensemble, Caroline's new reader—whom Caroline took special pains to introduce to Bonaparte, I noticed. I'm watchful.

*March 2, Sunday.*
Bonaparte made a number of announcements to the family tonight: in addition to naming Joseph King of Naples, he will add Lucca to Elisa's domain, and will name Joachim and Caroline Duke and Duchess of Berg.

Caroline looked as if she'd eaten something sour. "Berg isn't even a kingdom," I heard her hiss to Joachim.

"But maybe it comes with the droit de cuissage,"* he said, guffawing.

*March 5.*
Bonaparte has just returned from the Murats' country estate—where he

---

* *Droit de cuissage: the feudal right of a lord to sleep with the bride of a subject on their wedding night.*

went to hunt, he told me cheerfully, taking me into his arms. I pretended to believe his lie. He smelt of a boudoir, not a stable.

*Princes Carolin builtt a litle House for her Readr. This day the Emperor was 2 hours with the Readr in it.*

*[Undated]*
Oh, I *do* find this difficult. How do other women manage to be so accepting of a husband's mistress? I may pretend to "be blind," but I rage within!

*April 10.*
"The Kingdom of Holland has formally requested a sovereign from us," Bonaparte informed me at dinner tonight.

This had been rumoured. Caroline expected that the crown of Holland would go to her husband.

"I'm considering Louis." Bonaparte opened his snuff tin, but closed it without taking a pinch. "Hortense would be Queen, of course."

"Oh?" I said, dissembling my surprise. Louis didn't seem to have the energy to walk, much less to rule a nation. And as for Hortense . . . "Do you think Louis would want such a position?"

"What he *wants* has nothing to do with it. We do what we do because we must, because it is the will of destiny."

I nodded, but thinking, I confess, that we do what we do because it is Bonaparte's will.

*June 1, Sunday—Saint-Cloud, a glorious day.*
At the Bonaparte family dinner tonight, Bonaparte made the announcement that at the request of Holland, Louis will be their King, Hortense their Queen.

Now both Hortense and Caroline are miserable. Caroline wants a crown; Hortense does not.

*June 12, Thursday.*

Bonaparte and I bade farewell to Louis and Hortense this morning (King and Queen!), farewell to little Napoleon and Petit. "Bye-bye, Grandmaman," little Napoleon said solemnly. "Bye-bye, Nonan the Soldier." Giving his beloved uncle a salute.

"Take care of your brother," Bonaparte said, tugging little Napoleon's ear. (Little Napoleon, his heir—Bonaparte is uneasy about letting the child out of France, I know.)

"*And* your mother," I said, eyes stinging. God knows when we will see them again.

*June 15.*

"I wish I didn't have to give this to you," Mimi whispered, slipping a scrap of paper into my hand.

*Princes Carolins Readr is 3 Months With Child—by the Emperor, Shee says.*

*July 14, Bastille Day—Saint-Cloud.*

I've been ill for over a month, in bed with a fever.

*Tuesday, August 19—Rambouillet.*

We're at Rambouillet, a dank and cheerless hunting abode. Caroline arrived with a full suite to attend her, including her reader, clearly with child. Bonaparte has been gay.

As I write this, the court makes merry dancing to fiddlers. Fifteen wolves were bagged today.

*August 26, 1806, Milan*
*Chère Maman,*

*I have the most wonderful news: my lovely Auguste is with child. Don't worry—we are taking the utmost care.*

*The news of the Prussian advance is disturbing. I'm putting the Army of Italy on a war footing in case we are needed.*

*Auguste sends her love.*

*Your loving and happy son, Eugène*

*Note—I'm not in the least bit surprised to learn that Pauline and her prince have separated.*


*[Undated]*

"Auguste will have a girl," Bonaparte predicted.

"Why do you say that?"

"Charlemagne's son Pépin—the one he sent to rule Italy—had daughters. Five daughters and one son. Eugène will have the same."

"Excuse me for being confused, Bonaparte," I said with a smile, "but I thought you were the embodiment of Alexandre the Great." He'd once told me as much!

"Charlemagne's reign is, in fact, closer to mine," he said in all seriousness.

This curious comment sent me into the library for information on the ancient Emperor of the West. The similarities are striking: Charlemagne was not tall, but he was strong, with a thick neck. He dressed simply. He was temperate in his eating and drinking and, like Bonaparte, remedied illness by fasting. Also like Bonaparte, he was in the habit of rising several times during the night to work. Charlemagne crossed the Alps into Italy and he was crowned Emperor by the Pope.

I was amused by the parallels until I read that Charlemagne repudiated his first wife, by whom he had no children, and married a woman of high birth, by whom he did have children.


*September 6, Saturday, 7:10 P.M.—Paris.*

It was a hot afternoon for a military review: Bonaparte sweltered in his black beaver hat and greatcoat. In spite of the marching bands, the stirring spectacle of bayonets glittering, flags waving, the heart-stopping cavalry charge—in spite of all this, the crowds seemed curiously silent. They watched sombrely as the soldiers marched by.

"Funds down," Mimi said.

There is a sense of departure in the air, a sense of something ending. Our men will soon be marching out to war.

*September 24.*
Bonaparte is humming "Malbrough." Tomorrow he leaves on campaign.

*Gera, October 13, 2:00 A.M.*
*I am at Gera today, ma bonne amie. Things are going very well. The Queen of Prussia is at Erfurt. If she wishes to see a battle, she will have that cruel pleasure. I am well. I've gained weight since I saw you. All thine, N.*

*October 16, Weimar*
*Everything has gone as I calculated. Never has an army been so beaten and so completely lost. The fatigue, the bivouacs and the watches have fattened me. Adieu, ma bonne amie. All thine, N.*

*November 2, Berlin*
*We have taken Stettin. Everything is going as well as possible and I'm very satisfied. I miss the pleasure of seeing you, but I hope that it will not be long. Adieu, mon amie. All thine, N.*

*December 3, Posen, 6:00 in the evening*
*You must calm yourself. I wrote you you could come when winter had passed; thus you must wait. The greater one is, the less one can do as one pleases. One depends on events and circumstances. As for myself, I am a slave, and my master is the nature of things. N.*

*New Year's Day, 1807.*
Caroline's reader has given birth to a boy.

*January 16, 1807*
*My dear, your unhappiness pains me. Why the tears? Have you no courage? I*
*will see you soon. Show character and strength of spirit. Adieu, I love you. N.*

*January 18, 1807, Warsaw*
*I'm told that you always cry. Fie! That's terrible! Be worthy of me and have*
*more character. I love you very much, but if you cry all the time, I will think*
*you are without courage. I do not like cowards. An empress must have heart,*
*even down to the small cousins. Speaking of which, I kiss them. They must*
*be low, because you are always sad. Adieu, mon amie, I kiss you. N.*

*Tuesday, February 10—Paris.*
The carnival season is gay; I am not. I'm trying to be the empress that
Bonaparte wishes me to be, one with spirit and character. As it is, I'm an
empress with a head pain. They've been coming frequently again.

*Mon amie, your letter grieved me—it was too sad. Your heart is excellent,*
*but your powers of reasoning are weak. You experience things wonderfully,*
*but you think poorly. There, enough quarrelling. I want you to be happy*
*with your lot—not grumbling and crying, but cheerful and gay. The nights*
*are long. N.*

*February 9, 3:00 in the morning*
*Mon amie, we had a big battle yesterday. Victory was with me, but I lost*
*many men. The enemy's loss, which was considerably greater, does not console*
*me. I love you. All thine, N.*

*February 14, 1807*
*Mon amie, I'm still at Eylau. This country is strewn with the dead and the wounded. It is not the prettiest part of war. One suffers and the soul is oppressed to see so many victims. However, I did what I wanted and repulsed the enemy. Calm yourself, and be gay. All thine, N.*

*[Undated]*
Publicly we celebrate victory; privately we mourn. Daily couriers arrive with lists of the dead, the wounded, the missing. I'm mortified how close Bonaparte himself came to death, how he exposes himself to danger.

*March 15, 1807, Milan*
*Chère Maman,*

*Wonderful news! At 6:47 last night, Auguste gave birth to a beautiful baby girl. I hope you and Papa aren't disappointed. I'm going to write to him now, to tell him we'd be delighted if he chose a name for her.*

*My Auguste was as brave as any soldier, Maman. She is remarkably well, and the baby is sucking strongly. How is it possible for one's heart to be so full?*

*Thank you for the bulletins you sent on the Eylau victory. It's excellent news, but oh, the losses! I understand that you are upset the Emperor exposed himself to danger. You must have faith, Mama—Papa is blessed by Lady Luck. Did you know that the soldiers are convinced that* you *are his Lady Luck?*

*A million kisses,*

*Your son, a father! Eugène*

*April 28, La Hague*
*Chère Maman,*

*Little Napoleon is very sick with measles. I have been up for two nights. Pray for our dear little prince, Maman.*

*Your devoted (and worried) daughter, Hortense*

*Chère Maman,*

*This is just a quickly scribbled note to let you know that our prayers have been answered: little Napoleon has recovered.*

*Your devoted (and very much relieved) daughter, Hortense*


*May 5, Tuesday.*

I was awoken before dawn by Mimi. "There's a courier downstairs. He rode all the way from La Hague without stopping." She handed me a cap. "He insists on speaking to you."

The mud-splattered courier had a message from King Louis of Holland, he said. Prince Napoleon's condition had worsened. The child had developed a congestion in the chest and was having difficulty breathing. King Louis wished me to send Dr. Corvisart.

"Order the Master of the Horse to have our travelling carriage harnessed to our fastest horses," I commanded a sleepy chamberlain. "Have the cook put together a basket of provisions. Have the controller provide a purse of coins, both French francs and Dutch florins. Dr. Corvisart will be leaving immediately for Holland."

"Immediately?"

"Immediately!"


*[Undated]*

I feel like a sleepwalker, not of this earth. A light drizzle, the dank smell of the gardens, a pale early morning light envelop me. I know that when I wake from this dream, life will never again be the same. The fabric of our happiness has been forever rent.

Little Napoleon is dead.


*May 6, 1807*

*Aunt Josephine:*

*I'm leaving tonight for Holland. My brother King Louis will need me. I've instructed Arch-Chancellor de Cambacérès to organize everything for your journey. I suggest you meet your daughter at the Château de Laëken near Brussels.*

*Princess Caroline*

*May 15—Château de Laëken, Brussels.*
Hortense endured my embrace with patience. "Good afternoon, Maman," she said—but without any emotion.

"Oh, darling!" Her manner confused me.

"Hortense," Louis said, "your hat."

"Thank you," she said, slowly reaching out her hand, dreamlike. "He liked the flowers on it. He wouldn't want me to lose it." And then, to Clari, "He is dead, you know."

Petit tugged his father's hand. "Brother?" Louis motioned to the child to be silent.

"It doesn't matter what the boy says," Caroline said, gesturing to the servants to move the trunks out of her way. "She's not listening."

We followed Hortense into the great hall. She stood looking around at the entryway, the walls covered with tapestries. There was a chill about her; she seemed of another world. "*He* was here with me not long ago. I held him on my knees—there." She pointed to an upholstered chair. And then she fell silent and would not speak.

*Early evening, 6:20, I think—awaiting dinner.*
Louis and I sat on a musty sofa in the château library, Dr. Corvisart on a cracked leather armchair opposite us. I gave Louis a look of sympathy. "You are being admirably strong." It was true.

"At heart I weep," Louis said with feeling. And then he recounted how it had happened: little Napoleon had recovered, but then suddenly his face turned blue and he began to have difficulty breathing. They summoned the best doctors in Holland—

"Well-respected medical practitioners, Your Majesty," Dr. Corvisart assured me. "Your grandson had the best treatment available anywhere."

The doctors administered leeches and a course of blistering, but they were unable to check the disease's progress. "At that point I sent for Dr. Corvisart," Louis said, his voice tremulous. In desperation they even tried English Powder, a quack remedy. "It was a miracle," Louis said. "Little Napoleon sat up in bed and asked to play Go Fish."

I smiled through my tears. I had taught him how to play that game.

"And then he relapsed." We waited in silence as Louis struggled to continue. "Hortense leaned over to kiss him. He said, *Bonjour, Maman*, and closed his eyes." Louis looked at me, his cheeks glistening. "And that was it."

I put my trembling hands to my lips in a gesture of prayer. How were we ever going to bear it?

"Hortense fell to the floor in a swoon. Her eyes were open, but she was not responding. She . . ." Louis stopped, overcome.

"Your Majesty, your daughter was in a state of paralysis for over six hours," Dr. Corvisart said.

"In the morning she was able to speak, but"—Louis clasped his hands together to still the trembling—"she has yet to shed a single tear."

"You must understand, Your Majesty, your daughter is not herself," Dr. Corvisart said gently. "One must be patient. It's as if she is in a walking coma."

He recommended a voyage, a stay at a spa—to which Louis readily agreed. "Would you look after Petit?" he asked.

Oh, *yes*.


*[Undated]*
This morning Caroline offered Petit a little cake and, without realizing what I was doing, I grabbed the sweet out of his hand. The confused child bawled.

Caroline stood looking at me steadily. "I'm . . . I'm sorry," I stammered, and gave the cake back to Petit.

"Would you like one, Aunt Josephine?" Caroline asked with a baby-faced smile.

Now, on reflection, I realize that I don't trust Caroline around Petit, don't trust her not to try to harm the child in some way. What an evil thought! Caroline is not the monster: I am.

*Sunday, May 17—Château de Laëken, Brussels.*

This morning after Mass Hortense and I walked in silence down to the pond at the end of the park. "He threw pebbles in the water here," she said.

I burst into sobs. "I'm sorry, it's just that—" But I couldn't explain, couldn't tell her that I grieved not only for little Napoleon, but for my daughter, too.

"I am fortunate," she said with a smile that chilled me, "for I feel nothing. Otherwise I would suffer."


*Thursday, May 21—Château de Laëken, Brussels.*

Tears, *finally*—but oh, how painful.

Hortense and I were on our afternoon walk. I'd stopped to have a word with a neighbour. Hortense wandered off, but shortly after a cry of anguish set me running. I found her seated on a bench, writhing. "Maman, I can't bear it!" she wept, falling into my arms. My heart was breaking for her, for the pain of her despair, yet it was with dismay that I saw that glazed look come over her once again. She pulled herself free and sat up. "Ah, that's better," she said. "I can't feel anything now."

## In which we must be gay

May 14, 1807, Finckenstein
I understand your sorrow over the death of poor little Napoleon. You can imagine what I feel. I wish I were near you. You have had the good fortune never to have lost a child, but it is one of the painful realities of life. Take care of yourself and trust in my feelings for you. N.

May 22, 1807, Milan
Chère Maman,

Poor, poor Hortense, poor Louis: how they must suffer! Auguste and I clasp our little one close—our beautiful little Josephine she has been named. (At Papa's request, Maman.) If only we could keep her from harm, forever and ever. How hard it is, becoming a parent.

Your faithful son, Eugène

June 7, 1807, Paris
Darling,

I weep for you! There is nothing more devastating than the death of a child—and such a child. If a visit would help console, please allow me the honour.

Your loyal friend, Thérèse

I broke down the moment I saw Thérèse, upsetting sweet Petit. Thérèse cheered him with a gift of a tin shovel set. "So you can play in the mud—although perhaps princes are not allowed?" she added with a worried look.

"May I, Grandmaman?" Petit asked, his big eyes filled with hope.

"Of course," I said, stroking his fine curls. He's been delicate since the tragic loss of his big brother, not eating well and waking often in the night. He misses his mother and father, I know. Daily we send his "letters" (scribbles) to their spa in the Pyrenees, so very far away. Far from the devastating pain of grief, I pray.

"You and Mimi," I added, gesturing to Mimi to take the child. "Grandmaman Josephine allows mud play," I explained to Thérèse, leading the way out the double-sash doors to the garden, "but *Maman* Hortense does not." And then I started to weep again, remembering how little Napoleon had loved to play in the puddles. Thérèse didn't say a word, just took my arm. We walked in the garden thus while I blubbered like a fool. "Forgive me!"

Thérèse led me to a bench by the pond where we sat for a moment in silence, watching the two black swans glide over the surface of the water. In the distance we could see the gazelles grazing in a meadow, the baby gazelle bounding about. "And how is the Emperor taking it?" Thérèse asked.

"He writes me to have courage, but I'm told he weeps." Poor Bonaparte. He rarely broke down, especially in front of his men. "He loved that child so much."

"Little Napoleon was his chosen heir."

"That's just it! But it feels wrong to think about *that*—about the political consequences, the personal consequences."

"Yet how can you not?" Thérèse asked, giving me her handkerchief.

"It's true. Since little Napoleon's death, it seems that everyone is obsessed with one thought: what would happen if Bonaparte were to die? Who would be the heir? Heir! If I hear that word one more time, I will scream. I'm sorry," I said, taking hold. "The concerns are just. If Bonaparte *were* to die without an heir, chaos would reign. There would be civil war, no doubt, over who would take his place."

"Princess Caroline is saying her husband should be the one."

"To rule?" A look gave away my thoughts.

"Joachim would make a good queen," Thérèse said, letting out a throaty laugh.

"And Caroline a good king, for that matter," I said ruefully, drying my cheeks, my eyes.

"That girl *really* wants a crown."

"I don't know why anyone would."

"Oh, my poor sad Empress," Thérèse said, squeezing my hand.

"But Empress for how long, Thérèse?" I told her about Caroline's reader, about the boy she had given birth to—Bonaparte's child. "Now that Bonaparte knows he can father a child, what's to keep him from divorcing me and marrying a woman who can give him a son? Especially *now*—with everyone so desperate for an heir."

Thérèse smiled. "I just happened to have heard something that may be a cure for the vapours."

What she told me astonishes me yet: that Joachim had been heard to brag that Caroline's reader had been bored by the Emperor's attentions, but had been very pleased with *his*. "Joachim may be the child's father?" And not Bonaparte?

"Murat would seem to have it so."

"Does Caroline know he was 'visiting' her reader, do you think?"

"My guess is she not only knew about it, she set it up."

"Why would she do that?"

"Think about it: they wanted the girl to get in a certain way."

Of course: it made perfect diabolical sense. "So Joachim seduced the girl in order to make her pregnant?" In order to fool Bonaparte into thinking *he* could father a child. In order to induce Bonaparte to divorce *me*.

"I'd make sure the Emperor learned of this, if I were you," Thérèse said.

"Of course," I said, overwhelmed with sensation: relief certainly, but indignation, too, for Bonaparte's sake, at having been so ill-used.

*Mon amie, by the time you read this letter, peace will have been signed and Jérôme will be King of Westphalia. I love you and hope to learn that you are happy and gay. N.*

*July 12, Sunday.*
"*Jérôme* is going to be a king?" Caroline could not conceal her rage.

"*Is* a king," I corrected her, going through the papers on my escritoire. I didn't have time for one of Caroline's tantrums, frankly. Bonaparte had written with instructions that the celebrations of the peace were to be lavish, "a show of Oriental splendour." Even Chastulé had taken to her bed, overcome with all that had to be attended to: the celebrations of the peace, Jérôme and Princess Catherine of Württemberg's wedding, to be followed by two months of festivities at Fontainebleau. Every sovereign of Europe would be attending. Where were we going to put them all?

Caroline stomped her foot. "Jérôme has a crown, Napoleon has a crown, Joseph has a crown, Louis has a crown. Even Elisa has a stupid little crown. Everyone has a crown but *me*!"


*Saturday, July 25, morning, very hot.*
"Ah, crowns," Fouché said, "it seems that there can never be enough."

Oh, I am weary, so weary of conflict, of intrigue and doubt. If only Bonaparte would return. Last night I sprinkled my covering sheet with the lemon scent he uses. It has been ten months.


*July 27, Monday.*
At five this morning I was awoken by a commotion in the courtyard. Mimi came rushing in. "It's the *Emperor*!"

Oh, mon Dieu. I jumped out of bed. "Mimi, hurry, fetch my best nightdress," I said, splashing water on my face. "And my new lace bonnet." I sat down at my toilette table. I looked old. There wasn't time (nor enough light) to apply a proper face.

"Is this the one you meant?" Mimi said, panting, for the wardrobe is in the attic and the stairs are steep. She held out a lovely nightdress and cap.

"Oh no. I mean, it's gorgeous—but it's English muslin. Don't worry," I assured her, taking the bonnet and slipping it over my dishevelled hair. "I'll wrap myself in a shawl." I dusted my nose with rice flour. "The one I wore last night—the rose one." A good colour in the morning light.

"I saw it in the antechamber," Mimi said, running out the door and almost immediately returning with it. I dabbed on the lavender water Bonaparte favoured (lightly—not too much), threw the shawl around my shoulders, took one last anxious look in the long glass (not too bad: the effect was rumpled but slightly erotic), slipped into my slippers (a new gold-embroidered pair—perfect) and rushed out the door.

I stood at the entry, taking in the scene: five Imperial carriages thick with dust, grooms and postillions unharnessing the steaming horses, servants struggling under the weight of huge trunks. Jérôme, Joachim, Duroc . . . everyone—but where was Bonaparte? And then I heard a man yell, "I already told you. I do not repeat myself."

Was it Bonaparte? It sounded like him, yet the voice was harsh.

"Ah, there you are," he said, appearing behind the Imperial coach. I saw old Gontier hobbling toward the stable with a miserable look on his face.

"Oh, Bonaparte." I said, embracing him. Tears welled up, in spite of myself. It had been a very difficult ten months without him, and now that it was over, I felt my courage weakening.

"Why are you crying?" he said, standing back.

"I'm so happy to see you." I was confused, in truth. Bonaparte's voice was different, as was his manner. This man was neither husband nor friend nor lover. "*Sire*," I added, with an apologetic smile. It is often difficult after a long separation, I reminded myself. It takes time to get to know one another once again.

"Your Majesty?" Clari's husband, Monsieur Rémusat, was accompanied by four pages. In spite of the hour they were all in full livery. "I am informed that you wish to speak to me." He and the four pages bowed in unison, their plumed hats crushed against their hearts. (Clearly, they'd been rehearsing.)

"Yes, fire that old man. I don't want to see his face again." And with that Bonaparte marched into the château, leaving me on the steps.

Monsieur Rémusat offered me his arm. "Don't worry, Your Majesty," he whispered. "According to the Code, first the Emperor returns, and *then*, a few days later, the husband."

"Of course," I said, smiling at his gentle humour. Strangely, I felt even lonelier than before, now that Bonaparte was back. "But don't fire Gontier," I told him as we followed Bonaparte into the château. "Or rather," I added quickly, seeing the look of consternation on Monsieur Rémusat's face, "assure Monsieur Gontier that he will be reinstated—when the *husband* returns, that is."


*Wednesday.*

Not long ago the Governor of Paris stormed out of Bonaparte's cabinet, and, shortly after, Joachim was announced.

Clari leaned forward over her embroidery hoop. "Do you suppose the Emperor has found out about Governor Junot and . . . ?"

Junot and *Caroline*, she meant.

"I wonder if the Emperor also knows about all those other men his sister has been receiving," Chastulé whispered.

"What other men?"

"You don't know, Your Majesty?" Clari asked. "Princess Caroline lured the Austrian ambassador into her bedchamber, which she'd strewn with rose petals I've been told."

Rose petals! Caroline had come out to Malmaison not long ago asking me for sacks of them—for a tincture she was making, she'd told me. (Some tincture.)

"Ha! As well as Talleyrand—"

"That's impossible," Clari objected, flushing. (I suspect she's sweet on the dour Minister of Foreign Affairs.)

"—*and* the Minister of Police," Chastulé went on.

Fouché? "Now *that's* impossible," I said.

"Everyone's calling Prince Murat Prince Cuckold," Mademoiselle Avrillion joined in, looking up from mending one of my petticoats.

"But it doesn't seem to bother him. I was hoping for a duel, at least," Chastulé said.

"That's because Princess Caroline told him that she does it for *him*," Clari confided.

"That's a good one," Chastulé said. "I'll remember it the next time my husband catches a lover in my bed."

"To seek advantage, she told him."

"Caroline told Joachim that?" I could understand the advantages Fouché, Talleyrand and the Austrian ambassador might have to offer—but Junot? "I don't understand how the Governor of Paris could—"

"He commands the troops in the city, doesn't he?" Mademoiselle Avrillion asked.

"Ha! You never know when a cannon or two might come in handy."

*August 15—Saint Napoleon's Day.*
As I write this, fire-rockets flare, lighting up the night. Paris has given itself over to revelry: tournaments, plays, concerts, illuminations and ballets. Everywhere there is some kind of festivity in celebration of Saint Napoleon's Day—in celebration of Napoleon, Emperor and peacemaker.

Bonaparte and I watched the celebrations from the Tuileries balcony. The crowd cheered to see their hero, Napoleon the Great.

Napoleon the Unapproachable. He takes everything in with a frown. He is not a happy man—and I, certainly, am *not* a happy woman. It's just as well I'm so desperately busy preparing for Jérôme's wedding festivities, the arrival of a royal bride.

*Sunday, August 23—Tuileries.*
This morning Jérôme and (buxom) Princess Catherine were married in the Gallery of Diana in the presence of the entire court (eight hundred now). Jérôme looked dazzling in his suit of white satin embroidered in gold. We are in a frenzy of forced gaiety.

*August 27, 11:20 P.M.—the family drawing room, Saint-Cloud.*
Mimi came to fetch me during the second act of *Cinna*. She signalled me from the door. "I'm wanted about something," I whispered to Bonaparte, and slipped away.

"Hortense is back," Mimi said, her hands crossed over her heart.

"Here? Now!" I followed Mimi out of the theatre and through the orangerie to the château.

Hortense laid her head on my shoulder as if weary, as if she needed a mother's shoulder to rest on. "I'm better, Maman," she said.

"I can see that," I said—and it *was* true. She spoke from her heart.

"Have I interrupted something?" she asked, looking out at the court-yard, crowded with equipages.

"*Cinna* is being performed. I'll send for Bonaparte."

"No, wait, Maman. That's Papa's favourite play. There will be plenty of time."

"Shall I go get Petit?" Mimi suggested with a grin.

"He's up?" Hortense sounded hopeful.

"I'll wake him," Mimi said. "He's been talking about his maman every day."

"His maman who is looking well," I told my daughter.

"It was a good trip," she said, caressing my cheek—as if I were *her* child. "I've been writing songs." She paused, raising her eyes. "For *him*."

*Him.* Little Napoleon. As if his spirit hovered. "Petit has been wonderful. I have so many stories to tell you. He's the sweetest child." But frail and fearful of late, often waking in the night. "Ah, he's up," I said, on hearing the child's sleepy chatter.

Mimi appeared with the boy in her arms. "Oh, Petit!" Hortense said, her voice tremulous. I knew what she was thinking, that he looked so very like little Napoleon. And yet so different.

The child stared at his mother and then hid his face in Mimi's neck.

"Three months is a lifetime to a child," I said, fearing a problem. "Remember how you felt, darling, when I got out of prison? You didn't even recognize me."

"I don't remember," Hortense said, leaning down to catch her boy's eyes. She covered her face with her hands and surprised him with a peek-a-boo. Petit studied his mother sombrely, his thumb in his mouth, a hint of a smile in his eyes. She did another peek-a-boo for him, eliciting a tiny giggle. Then she opened her hands and he dove into her arms. She pressed him against her heart, tears streaming onto his fair curls, cooing, "Oh, my Petit, my sweet Petit." Mimi and I stood sniffing, our hearts full of love and sorrow.

"Ah, there you are." It was Bonaparte, standing in the door.

"Papa! *Sire*." Hortense made a respectful dip, balancing her child in her arms. She swiped one eye with the back of her free hand.

"*Still* weeping?" he said reproachfully. "You've cried enough over your son. You're not the only woman to have suffered a loss. Other women are braver than you, especially considering that you have a child who needs you. Now that you are back, smile and be gay—and not one tear!" And with that he left.

Hortense lowered herself onto the little bench by the door. "How can Papa reproach me like that?" she asked, her breath coming in sharp gasps.

"Try to understand, Hortense," I said, motioning to Mimi to take Petit. "Bonaparte is just as upset as we are, but he believes we make it worse by weeping." Sorrow unnerved him, made him uncomfortable.

"Doesn't he understand how a mother feels?"

"He believes being stern will help you." I put my arm around her thin shoulders. "He loves you."

It is true. Bonaparte has a great, *great* heart. If only I could find it.


*Sunday morning at Malmaison, lovely—not too hot yet.*
I've just talked with the housekeeper and the head cook about the family dinner tonight: Madame Mère, Julie,* Louis and Hortense, Pauline, Caroline and Joachim, Jérôme and Princess Catherine, Stéphanie and Émilie, Bonaparte and me. Is that everyone? Table for thirteen. And all the children, of course: Petit, Julie's girls (Zenaïde and Charlotte), Caroline's four (Achille, Letizia, Lucien and Louise). Mimi is organizing a picnic for them out under the oak trees.


*10:10 P.M.*
The dinner went fairly well—for a Bonaparte gathering, that is. Joachim was so transparently obsequious toward Bonaparte—offering him his snuffbox, bowing not only in greeting, but with *every* sentence—it annoyed both Louis and Jérôme, who addressed him as "Prince Bully-Boy," much to Joachim's annoyance. Caroline, as well,

---

* *Although Joseph had moved to Naples to reign as king, his wife Julie and their two daughters continued to live in Paris. In Naples Joseph lived openly with the Duchess d'Atri.*

seemed in a temper—this business of crowns, no doubt. But worst of all, Pauline—who was carried in on a tasselled silk litter by four Negroes dressed as Mamelukes—berated Hortense for wearing black: "Your son was only five when he died. You're not supposed to wear mourning."

My god-daughter Stéphanie was a little giddy, but otherwise restrained, thanks to Madame Campan's stern tutelage. Hortense only pretended to eat, I noticed. Then, as the desserts were being brought out, she abruptly excused herself from the table.

I found her in the water closet with a china bowl in her lap, Louis beside her. Her face was flushed, beaded with perspiration. "It's all right, Maman," she said, seeing the concern in my eyes. She looked at Louis. "Should I tell her?"

"Hortense is with child again," Louis said.

Caroline flushed on hearing the news—her heated complexion visible even through a thick layer of ceruse. She gave Joachim "a look," a very slight widening of her kohl-lined eyes. "How wonderful," she said with a bright smile, methodically tapping a beauty patch stuck on her chin. "What a surprise."

At the close of the evening, Louis proposed a toast. He and Hortense would be returning to their kingdom, he said, and so consequently, they must bid everyone adieu.

"Cin-cin! Cin-cin!" Jérôme called out, spilling wine on his new (and doting) wife.

"Blood is everything," Madame Mère said.

"No, Maman: you're supposed to say salúte."

"Salúte."

"Salúte!"

"Santé," I echoed faintly, weak with concern.

*[Undated]*

Alarming news: Hortense is consumptive. "Does that mean she has consumption?" I asked Dr. Corvisart. People die of that disease!

"It's more of a tendency in that direction," he told me. "No doubt she will recover, but I'm concerned that the climate of Holland might be too . . ." He made a grimace. "A damp climate might—"

"Harm her health?"

"Especially in her delicate condition." He cleared his throat. "And I've concern about the child, as well. He is sickly, and one doesn't want to take any risks."

*Dieu nous en garde!*


*September 19.*
Louis has returned to Holland alone—without his wife, without his son. "But he left *furious* at me, Maman," Hortense sobbed.

"Dr. Corvisart explained it to him, didn't he? About the dangers?"

"I don't know. Louis wouldn't even speak to me!"


*Sunday morning.*
Caroline's ball last night was shocking in its splendour: tightrope walkers and acrobats, a miniature village in the garden. As Caroline and Joachim (tipsy) escorted Jérôme's bride to a replica of her summer chalet, a choir dressed in peasant costumes appeared, singing the traditional songs of her country.

It was a triumph, of course. Caroline made sure Bonaparte was aware of all that she had done to further his glory. She also made sure, I later discovered, that a rumour was circulated that Hortense is with child by a man named Monsieur Decazes.


*4:45 P.M.*
"I believe I've discovered the reason for Louis's temper," I told my daughter. "Do you know Monsieur Decazes?"

"He was at the spa, mourning the death of his wife."

"It seems that there is a rumour going around that he is the father of the child you are carrying."

"Monsieur Decazes?" Hortense wrinkled her nose. "That's . . . that's crazy, Maman."

"I agree! I was outraged. But it might help explain why Louis was so angry. Perhaps if you were to—"

"It explains nothing! How could Louis believe something like that about me?"

"Well . . ." I understood what it was like to be consumed by jealousy, knew how it could make a person act.

"All a man has to do is look at me and Louis is convinced of my infidelity. I will never forgive him!"

"But Hortense, don't you think maybe—"

"Never!" she cried, bolting for the door.

I put my arm out to prevent her from running out of the room.

"Let me out!" she demanded.

"I want the truth, Hortense."

"I'll tell you the truth!" she said, her voice tremulous. "But it won't be what you expect. The truth is something you don't want to hear. The truth is that Louis torments me! He *hires* people to spy on me. He has me followed. *Every* outing I make he assumes has a romantic purpose—even to visit a relative's deathbed! He listens at my door at night, he opens my mail. I might as well live in a convent. Do you know how he begins each day? With a search of my closets. Is that how a man is supposed to regard his wife?"

I listened in stunned silence as she sobbed out years of torment. I could not believe what she was saying, yet suddenly it all made sense—the high wall Louis had had built around their house, the sentry posted below Hortense's bedchamber window. "I'm so sorry, Hortense," was all I could say. If only I had known! If only she had told me! But perhaps it was true, what she said: perhaps I hadn't wanted to hear.

"You know what he tells me, Maman, about *you*? He says you're a harlot. He says you're not my mother, that Madame Mère is my mother now—and she detests me! He says any love I show you is a stab against him! He's in a constant rage. I cannot even speak to a man without Louis threatening to run him through. I've *never* been untrue to him, Maman, yet he treats me like a criminal," she sobbed. "Every time I try to please him, he finds something in me to hate, something to doubt. He loves his dog more than he loves me! I can't bear it any longer. Please, *please* don't make me go back to him. I fear it will be the death of me!"

And then she gave way to a convulsive fit of coughing that frightened me terribly. I took her in my arms, rocking her like a baby. Slowly the coughing eased. "Forgive me, Hortense—I've been blind." And worse—wilfully so. "But now I know."

And now, I vow, things will be different.

## *In which I am betrayed*

*September 22, 1807—Fontainebleau.*

At last we are settled at Fontainebleau for a month of hunting and festivities—*all* of us. (Moving a court is not easy.) Settled, but in chaos still, everyone rushing about trying to find trunks, getting lost in the vast corridors, frazzled from lack of sleep. Even the actors and actresses are in hysterics. They are to perform Corneille's *Horace* in less than two hours, "and our props haven't even arrived," Talma exclaimed, the back of his hand to his forehead.

*Thursday, September 24, 4:45 P.M.*

Duroc addressed the assembled court this morning. Here are the rules:

One evening a week the Emperor will receive. On that evening there will be music followed by cards.

On another evening I'm to hold a reception at which cards will be played. (But not for money: Bonaparte insists.)

Two evenings a week there will be a tragedy performed. (No comedies: Bonaparte considers them a waste of time.)

As well, the Princes and the Ministers are required to give dinners, inviting all the members of the court. Duroc, as Grand Marshal, and Chastulé, as lady of honour, are required to do the same, laying covers for twenty-five. A table will be provided for any who have not received an invitation to dine elsewhere.

"I want to dine at *that* table," Hortense whispered.

"And finally," Duroc said, raising his voice, "only the Emperor and Empress will have the liberty of dining alone—*should* they choose to do so."

There was a rustle of fine silks, a tinkling of gold pendants, a murmur—of envy, I realized, over the privilege of privacy. Fortunately the assembly was diverted by Duroc's announcement that for the deer hunt, the gentlemen were required to wear a green coat with gold or silver lace, white cashmere breeches and riding boots without flaps. The shooting costume was to be "a simple green coat without any ornament but white buttons," Duroc said, looking expressly at Joachim, who was known to embellish even his nightcap. "But on those buttons, some characteristic of the species being hunted is to be engraved."

"The prick," Joachim guffawed.

Duroc ignored him, and continued by saying that hunting costumes would be required as well for the ladies and their households, and for this purpose the designer Leroy had been engaged. At this point Monsieur Leroy, flustered but clearly enjoying the acclaim, was called upon to display his creation: a tunic, rather like a short redingote, over a gown of embroidered white satin. I applauded, which signalled to the assembly that they could do likewise.

So on this pretty note court was adjourned. The first hunt is to be held in four days at eight in the morning. Tardiness is forbidden. The Emperor has spoken.

*September 27, Sunday—Fontainebleau.*

"We must be a court!" Bonaparte exploded, hitting the table with the flat of his hands. "A *real* court, with dancing and gaiety. I will it!"

*I will it.* If only it were as easy as that! Bonaparte has everyone terrified. It is impossible to be gay. My ladies are so fearful of being publicly reprimanded that they don't dare speak, much less *enjoy* themselves.

"Zut. I've brought hundreds of people to Fontainebleau to amuse themselves. I've arranged *every* sort of entertainment for them and yet they just sit with long faces."

"Pleasure cannot be summoned by the beat of the drum, Your Majesty," Talleyrand observed in his expressionless manner.

"How long are we here for?" Hortense asked plaintively, later.

Six weeks. Six *long* weeks.


*Wednesday.*

The first "crowns" (as Chastulé calls them) have arrived from Germany—the brothers Prince Mecklenburg and Prince Mecklenburg-Schwerin, charming young men with old-fashioned manners. Prince Mecklenburg-Schwerin, recently widowed (his wife was the Russian Tsar's sister), hovered at the edge of my drawing room last night. Understandably he refrained from joining us at the whist table, but sat to one side, watching how I played my cards with apparent interest. Later, when ices were served, he confided that he has not been well. I offered him condolences but immediately regretted it, for he seemed suddenly close to tears. "Forgive me, Your Majesty. It was a mistake to come to Fontainebleau," he said, touching a lace-edged handkerchief to the corner of each eye. "I only came because I wished to persuade the Emperor to withdraw his troops from my country."

"Have you discussed this with the Emperor?"

"Yes, this afternoon, but . . ." He looked discouraged.

"Give it time," I suggested, tendering an invitation to both him and his brother to join us in our box for the theatrical performance tomorrow evening.


*[Undated]*

"I see you've made a conquest," Bonaparte said. "It's a good thing I'm not a jealous husband."

"Hardly," I said, but with an edge of regret. There was a time when Bonaparte *had* been a jealous husband. "Prince Mecklenburg-Schwerin's wife died not long ago. He talks to me of his grief." I paused, considering how best to proceed. "He's very impressed by you."

"That I doubt. He is disappointed in me. He wants me to withdraw my troops. That's out of the question. These princes seem to think I should come in with my soldiers, liberate their country and then, job done, just leave. They live in another world."

"So there's *no* chance that our troops will be withdrawn . . . someday?" I took his hand in mine.

"I take it the Prince has recruited you to advance his cause," he said, tweaking my ear—hard.


*La Pagerie, Martinico*
*Madame Bonaparte,*
   *I regret to inform you that your mother has been taken by the Lord. She changed worlds at 3:47 P.M. on the eighth of July, at La Pagerie. I was the only person in attendance, not counting the slaves. I will notify you if there is anything left of value once the estate debts have been paid.*
                    *In the service of the Eternal Lord, Father Droppet*


*Fort de France, Martinico*
*Chère Yeyette, my beloved niece,*
   *Our profound condolences on the passing of your dear mother. You did what you could to make her last years comfortable.*
   *Stéphanie writes that she may be wed soon—and to a prince? Is this possible? Surely she is jesting.*
   *God bless you,*

                    *Your aging uncle, Robert Tascher*
*Note—Father Droppet is going to send you the accounts of the estate, such as they are. Be sure to check his numbers. He is known to be "imaginative."*


*Saturday evening.*
"I understand how you feel," Prince Mecklenburg-Schwerin said. "Grief sets one apart."

"Yes," I said, clutching my handkerchief.

"There will be a period of mourning?"

I shook my head. Bonaparte didn't want the news of my mother's death made public. A period of official mourning would put an end to the festivities. I understood, but a part of me rebelled. Was no one to mourn her? I felt so alone in my grief. "The timing is . . ." I waved my soggy handkerchief through the air.

"Inconvenient?"

"It makes me sad, nonetheless. Hortense and I are the only mourners in all of France."

He slipped a narrow black silk ribbon off his queue and threaded it through a buttonhole on his jacket, tying it in a tidy bow. "There," he said. "I wager you thought I wouldn't know how to tie a bow."

"I admit it crossed my mind," I said with a smile.

"A bit unusual as a mourning ensemble, but I believe the Almighty will understand."


*October 4, Sunday.*
Mimi, Hortense, Chastulé, Clari and even Monsieur Etiquette are now all sporting a little black ribbon. I feel strengthened beyond measure.


*October 5—Fontainebleau, 2:00 P.M.*
Caroline joined the hunt this morning wearing a little black ribbon tied to a buttonhole. "It's the fashion," she informed everyone. "Haven't you noticed?"


*Thursday, October 8, very late, possibly 2:00 A.M.*
Every evening before dinner, Bonaparte and I go for a ride through the woods. He drives and I try not to ask him to slow down. It's a welcome hour, for me, a chance to be alone with Bonaparte (if one doesn't count the mounted escort riding fore and aft).

Often we ride in silence—that comfortable silence of the long-married—but tonight Bonaparte was cheerful (unusual for him these days) and we talked amiably of this and that: of Jérôme's latest mischief, the foreign princes. And then, as if it were inconsequential, he informed me that he was having an amourette with my reader. "Your spies will inform you in any case," he said, glancing at me to gauge my reaction.

"Madame Gazzani?" How could I not have known? "I appreciate how discreet you've been. And Madame Gazzani, as well."

"You're not angry?"

"Bonaparte, there are only two things I wish for. One, your happiness. And two . . ." I paused, feeling the calming lull of the even clip-clop of the horses' hoofs. I'd given up even wishing for a child, I realized sadly.

"And two . . . ?" He turned the horses in the direction of the palace.

"And two, I wish for your love."

He pulled in the reins, bringing the horses to a halt. "Don't you know how much I love you?"

"I do know that, Bonaparte," I said. "That's what makes it so hard."


*Saturday afternoon.*

Carlotta put a vase of roses on my escritoire. "Thank you, Carlotta."

She curtsied. "It is my pleasure to serve you, Your Majesty."

I believed her. "I would like you to join us tonight, Carlotta, in the drawing room." The girl was no doubt bored to tears, relegated to her small attic room.

"But Your Majesty, I'm merely a . . ."

Merely a reader, she started to say. Readers are not granted drawing room privileges; my ladies would no doubt object.

"It would please the Emperor, Carlotta," I said with a knowing smile.


And now—at long last—I believe I have finally begun to understand. Carlotta has become my gift to Bonaparte, like some succulent fruit I place before my husband. In loving her, he must love me. In loving her, he must feel beholden.


*October 25, Sunday.*

This morning, returning from Mass, Fouché (lurking in a window recess) pulled me aside. "I have a matter of grave importance to discuss with you, Your Majesty," he said, clearing his throat. He glanced toward the door, where a guard was stationed.

"Oh," I said, not a little concerned. His manner was uneasy. And when had he ever addressed me as "Your Majesty"?

He pulled a tightly rolled paper out of his inside coat pocket and handed it to me. Sunlight caught the diamond in the ring on his little finger.

Warily I slipped off the silk cord and unrolled the scroll. The script—Fouché's—was tiny, difficult to make out. "I'm afraid I don't have my reading spectacles with me."

"Read it later, Your Majesty. I'd like you to . . . *reflect* on the contents."

"And what is it, may I ask?" Why were we being so polite with each other?

"It's a draft of a letter I suggest you send to the Senate."

"You think *I* should write a letter to the Senate?" *Why?*

"You are no doubt aware of the public fears that as the Emperor ages, he will follow in the traces of Sardanapalus."

I wasn't sure what he was talking about, but I thought it sounded like something concerning Bonaparte's health.

"Even the general public, so deserving of peace and security, is crying out. As devoted as they are to you, Your Majesty, they are even more devoted to the Emperor and the Empire he has created—an Empire which they know will crumble upon his death."

Did Bonaparte have a life-threatening disease? Was there something I did not know? "Fouché, is the Emperor—?"

"The Emperor suffers, Your Majesty," Fouché said, taking out an ivory snuffbox adorned with precious gems, "for he has reached the painful conclusion that a compelling political necessity, however abhorrent to him personally, must be undertaken for reasons of state. Yet, as brave as he is on the battlefield, he lacks the courage to speak to you on this matter."

My hands became cold, and my heart began to skitter. A nervous apprehension filled my veins. This had nothing to do with Bonaparte's health. "And what matter might this be?"

Fouché sniffed a pinch of snuff, then dusted off the tip of his nose. "Why, the matter of a divorce, Your Majesty."

"You're suggesting that I—?"

"I'm suggesting that you write to the Senate, informing them that you are willing to make this sacrifice for the good of the nation. I know how devoted you are to the Emperor, and I believe your love for him is such that you would sacrifice your life, if it meant that *his* would be spared."

I leaned against the wall. This is it, I thought. Bonaparte doesn't have the courage to speak to me, and so he has arranged to have Fouché speak on his behalf. The coward!

"Our soldiers are willing to sacrifice their lives for their country," Fouché said, grasping my elbow. "It is rare for a woman to have an opportunity to prove her devotion, her—"

"I must know one thing," I said abruptly. I felt on the edge of a precipice. I feared I might lose control, but I had to know. "Minister Fouché, did the Emperor *ask* you to speak to me about this?"

"Although I know the Emperor's thoughts on this matter, I had no order from him," Fouché said evenly, examining a timepiece which hung from his breeches on a heavy gold chain. "I regret to say that I must bring an end to this melancholy interview, Your Majesty, for I have an urgent appointment."

And without even so much as a bow, he left. Hortense found me shortly after, standing near the window recess clutching the drapes.


*[Undated]*

I went to Bonaparte's room early this morning, just after seven. I thought it best to talk to him before his work began, so I was surprised to find him dressed in a hunting coat, with his valet helping him on with his Hessian boots. "You're not going on the hunt, Josephine?" He pulled on his left boot and stood to embrace me. "Not feeling well?"

"No, I'm not—not going on the hunt, that is." I'd forgotten entirely. "Bonaparte, I need to talk to you." It was hot in the room; a fire was roaring.

"Fine," Bonaparte said, sitting down and sticking out his right foot.

"Privately," I said, clasping Fouché's letter, which I'd rolled into a tight tube and secured with a yellow ribbon, the colour of betrayal.

Bonaparte stood and stomped his foot. "That's good," he told Constant, dismissing him. He led me to one of the chairs by the fire.

"You're pale. You must be cold." He kicked the burning log, sending embers flying, and then sat down, watching the flames.

"I always imagine that you're thinking of camp when you look at a fire like that," I said, fumbling to untie the ribbon, which had become knotted.

"Josephine, I'm willing to talk, but I can't take all morning. The Austrian ambassador is expecting me. What's the problem?"

"It's . . . complex," I said, finally succeeding in sliding the ribbon off and handing him the rolled-up letter.

"This is for me?" He tried to get it to lie flat on his thigh. "Who wrote it?" Squinting.

"Your Minister of Police."

"Fouché wrote this?" He held the paper close to his face and then back, at arm's length. "My eyes are getting so weak," he complained. "Haven't those spectacles been delivered yet?"

How could Bonaparte be thinking of such details? Our life was falling apart and all he could think about were his new spectacles. "Yes, *Fouché*," I said, making an effort to sound calm. "He gave it to me yesterday, after Mass. He . . . he suggests that I write such a letter to the Senate."

"Basta," Bonaparte exclaimed, reading. He threw the document into the flames.

"You knew nothing about this?"

"Of course not. Fouché has no business in our bed."

I pulled a handkerchief from my bodice. (I'd thought to bring several.) It was difficult to gauge Bonaparte's reaction. Was he pretending to be innocent? "I was so afraid that you might have asked Fouché to do this terrible thing," I said, my voice breaking.

"Josephine, I am quite capable of bringing up such a matter myself. I have no need to get Fouché to talk to you on my behalf." There fell an uncomfortable silence. Bonaparte cleared his throat. "And so, since we *are* speaking of it, I will ask you: What do you think?"

"I think you should dismiss him," I said, knowing perfectly well that that was not what Bonaparte meant.

"Fouché?" Bonaparte scoffed. "His crime, if anything, is an excess of zeal. He acted out of devotion, to me and to the Empire."

*Devotion*. It was the same word Fouché had used. "Devotion to *his* self-interest," I said heatedly. "You are surrounded by flatterers, Bonaparte. They delude you into thinking that by divorcing me and marrying a young and fertile princess, you would be rendering a great service to your country."

"Josephine, you must not—"

"You asked me what I think and I will tell you!" I persisted, twisting my handkerchief into a rope—a rope to hang myself with. "If I believed for even a moment that by our divorcing peace would come and the Empire would prosper—*if* I thought that, I would do it! But I *don't* think that." My brave speech broke down in stupid female whimpers. "I will be honest, Bonaparte, since we must speak of this. I do fear for myself, for I love you. I don't care about my crown, or my rank. All I care about is you."

"Josephine—"

"I *beg* you to listen to me! I believe they are wrong. I fear that they are pushing you down a path that will lead to your downfall, and the downfall of the Empire with you. *They* don't care about your happiness—they only care about their own. They are greedy and fearful and do not understand you as I do."

Bonaparte watched me, his big grey eyes glistening. "I have one more thing to say," I said, "and then I will go. You and I have travelled a very great distance together. Indeed, in many ways I believe that our . . . our *destiny* is so extraordinary that it must be directed by Providence." I paused, afraid of saying what I truly feared might be true—that in some mysterious way, Bonaparte's extraordinary luck was linked to *me*, to our union. "We've talked of this before," I said instead, my heart pounding. He nodded, very slightly, but an acknowledgement nonetheless. "You put me on a throne, Bonaparte. It would not be right for me to step down from it. If you ask me to, I will. I want you to know that. But you will have to be the one to say so."

"I couldn't, Josephine," he said, his voice a whisper. I fell into his arms. The valet found us thus, weeping and embracing.


*November 20—back in Paris.*

"I was tempted to burn this one," Mimi said, handing me a scrap of paper.

*Princes Carolin & her Husband were with Min. Fouchay last Evinng. Min.*
*Fouchay say Everything wood be easyer if the Empress wood die.*


[Undated]

It is late, two in the morning; everyone is asleep. Bonaparte is on the way to Italy. I am alone in the palace—alone with my fear. My ring of keys sits on the desktop before me. They sprawl, a long-legged insect—an insect with the insidious power to open locked doors.

One of the keys—a heavy, slightly rusted one—is the key to Bonaparte's cabinet. I could, if I dared, open that door, look into his files. I know where to look, know where Fouché's police reports are kept. I can see that leather portfolio as if it were lying in front of me now: black cowhide, thick and unbending, secured with a grosgrain white ribbon, stained from having been tied and untied by men with snuff on their fingers.

I could go—*now*. Discover exactly what is being said behind my back, know once and for all who my enemies truly are. The secretary is not here, nor is the valet; Roustam is not asleep outside the bedchamber door. They are all with Bonaparte in Italy, with Bonaparte always. But what of the others, the night watchmen, the guards?

No, I will go in the morning, early. I will tell Hugo, the cabinet guard, that I need to get something out of the Emperor's files—something he wished to have sent to him. I will bring Hugo a coffee laced with cognac, to cheer and distract.


Police Report of November 17: *People were astonished not to see the Empress on Tuesday at the performance of* Trajan. *It was said that she was upset. Most spoke of the dissolution of the Imperial marriage. This news is the talk of all classes, and the truth is that there is not one who does not view it as a guarantee of peace.*


Police report of November 19: *At court, in the homes of the princes, in all the salons, people are talking of the dissolution of the marriage. The people who are in the confidence of the Empress share the opinion that the Emperor would not resort to this rupture. They say that the Empress is adored in France; that her popularity is useful to the Emperor as well as to the Empire; that the good fortune of both the one and the other depends on the duration of this union; that the Empress is the Emperor's talisman; that their separation would be the end of their good fortune.*

*The other part of the court—the part which regards the dissolution as necessary to the establishment of the dynasty—try to prepare her for this event, giving her advice that they judge appropriate to the situation.*

*In the Imperial family, there is one opinion only: they are all unanimously in favour of a divorce.*

*December 2—Malmaison.*

I became suddenly ill last night after the fête for the ambassadors. Mimi insisted I empty my stomach, making me take mustard mixed with warm water and tickling the back of my throat with a goose feather. Then she sent for Dr. Corvisart, who pronounced my symptoms "puzzling."

"And if I were being poisoned," I asked him weakly, "what would my symptoms be?"

"Your Majesty, who would do such a thing?" he said gently—but not answering my question.

*[Undated]*

I'm still quite ill . . . and frightened. There are some, I know, who wish me dead.

*January 2, 1808—Tuileries.*

"Josephine?" I heard a man say as I slept. The voice was soft, caressing: Bonaparte's voice. Was I dreaming? I opened my eyes, swollen shut with fever. It *was* Bonaparte, standing at the side of the bed with a New Year's gift in his hand—a box of pink, white and blue sugared almonds. He put the box down and took my hand. "They told me you were ill, but . . ." His eyes filled.

"I had a bad reaction to a purge," I reassured him weakly. So Dr. Corvisart insisted—nothing more. "I'm getting better."

"You *must*," he said, clasping my hand so hard it hurt.

*January 12—Paris.*
Stronger today. I spent an hour this afternoon making the final plans for Stéphanie's wedding next month to Prince d'Aremberg.

*Fort de France, Martinico*
*Chère Yeyette, my beloved niece,*

*My wife and I are grateful for the part you have played in making the arrangements for Stéphanie's marriage. It is hard to imagine that our little girl will be a princess. Remind her not to let her stockings sag and to cover her mouth when she burps.*

*God bless you,*

*Your aging uncle, Robert Tascher*

*February 1—Tuileries.*
Preparing to go to Hortense's for Stéphanie's wedding, I was startled by a pounding on the door. It was Bonaparte's valet. "Your Majesty, come quickly—the Emperor is terribly sick. I think it's one of his episodes!"*

I scooped up my train and rushed up the dark stone staircase after Constant, my heart's blood pounding. "It happened just as the Emperor got out of his bath, Your Majesty," Constant said, trying to hold the light so that I might see better. "He forbids me to summon Dr. Corvisart. He said he had need only of you."

We stumbled into Bonaparte's suite. The roaring fire and a candle on a table afforded little light. Constant raised his lantern in the direction of the bed where Bonaparte was buried under the covers. His face was grey. "Speak to me, Bonaparte!"

Wordlessly Bonaparte grasped my arm and, in spite of my finery,

---

* Napoleon had occasional seizures of an epileptic nature.

pulled me into the bed. A tremor seemed to go through him. Was it the falling sickness? "Constant, get the vial." The valet looked confused. "The nitrite of amyl—in the Emperor's travelling case."

"Josephine!" Bonaparte blurted out finally.

Constant reappeared. "Two or three drops on a handkerchief," I told him.

"Oh dear, oh dear," the flustered valet murmured, pulling out a handkerchief, dosing it and handing it to me.

"Breathe," I said, holding the cloth to his nose.

"Josephine, I can't *live* without you," he said finally, gasping.

*Mon Dieu*, I thought. "Bonaparte, we can't go on like this," I heard myself say, holding him to my heart, stroking his fine hair, as if he were an infant I was soothing.


*Saturday, April 2—sad.*

Bonaparte just left for the south—very quickly. (As quickly and as secretly as an entourage of thirty-six carriages can leave, that is.) Officially it's being said that he's making an inspection tour of Bordeaux, but in truth he intends to study the situation in Spain.

"Don't be long," he said, holding me in his arms. I'm to join him in a few days.


*April 6—Saint-Cloud.*

I've just returned from seeing Hortense, bidding her farewell and Godspeed, for I leave in the morning to join Bonaparte in the south. I leave with a worried heart.

I took her a number of pretty items to add to her layette—as well as a copy of Madame de Souza's new novel, *Eugène de Rothelin**—and promised to return in time for her confinement in six weeks. As I was folding a tiny flannel waistcoat and putting it on the table next to the

---

* *Madame de Souza's son, Charles Flahaut, was in love with Hortense. The novel's main character, Eugène de Rothelin, is believed to be based on Flahaut and the character Athénais on Hortense.*

cradle, I saw something black at the bottom of a travelling basket of embroidered muslin.

"What is this?" I asked Hortense—for it looked like a shroud.

"Oh nothing," she said uneasily. "Just a length of fabric the dress-maker left here."

She wept when I left. She is a young woman alone now; no husband to plague her, but no husband to care for her, either.

As I was getting into my carriage, I saw Hortense's friend Mademoiselle Adèle Auguié—now her lady's maid—returning with Petit. I called out to them.

"I'm . . ." I am concerned about Hortense, I wanted to tell Adèle. "I regret having to leave at this time."

"Don't worry, Your Majesty. We'll look after your daughter," Adèle said, smiling down at the boy. "Won't we?"

I wanted to ask her about that length of black cloth, but dared not. "I know you will," I said.


*April 10—Palais de Bordeaux.*
Bonaparte welcomed me with open arms. He was relieved to see me, much in need of my help with a demanding (and sensitive) social calendar. I'm exhausted from the journey, but will nonetheless attend a reception tonight.


*April 24, 1808, Paris*
*Your Majesty,*
*You will be relieved to know that Queen Hortense has been delivered of a boy—almost a month early! Both mother and son are safely out of danger.*

*On the twentieth of April, a Wednesday, Princess Caroline invited your daughter and Petit to a fête. In spite of Queen Hortense's delicate health, she decided to attend (travelling lying down in the carriage). It was to be a fête for children, with a number of nursemaids and nannies and parents and even important officials standing about watching Princess Caroline's children swing from the lamps and terrorize the guests. In short, the usual circus; and a circus it was, complete with clowns and tightrope dancers performing above* the children's heads! Every time one of them slipped (which was often), Queen Hortense clutched my hand. We were both terrified that one of the performers would fall onto the children—and, in particular, onto our sweet Petit. (It is my contention that Queen Hortense's alarm precipitated the contractions.)

Arch-Chancellor de Cambacérès was standing beside us and, claiming to feel ill, begged your daughter's permission to leave in order to return to his home and have leeches applied.

Queen Hortense assured him she would not be needing him—that she would not go into confinement that night—but as if Providence were reminding us all who was in charge, within an hour of the Arch-Chancellor's departure, her first pain came. Quickly the contractions became violent, and it was with great difficulty that we managed to get her back home, where the midwife and Arch-Chancellor de Cambacérès soon joined us, the poor Arch-Chancellor with three leeches still stuck to his back. (This story has been the cause of much merriment in Paris!)

The baby was born nearly lifeless and terribly, terribly small. You can imagine our fear! Bathed in wine and wrapped in cotton, he revived, but then we began to have concerns for Queen Hortense, for her pulse had become irregular.

She is delicate yet, Your Majesty, but three days have gone by and the doctor assures us that your daughter is out of danger. Queen Hortense specifically asked me to tell you that you are not to return to Paris. The Emperor has need of you, and believe me, your daughter is well looked after. Petit, especially, is tender in his care of both his mother and new brother.

As you suggested, Dr. Jean-Louis Baudelocque was awarded a gift of ten thousand francs in a gold box adorned with diamonds, and Madame Frangeau a handsome ring.

Please forgive the mess this quill has made.

Your humble servant,

Mademoiselle Adèle Auguié

Note—I've notified King Louis.
And another—Unfortunately, the early arrival of this child has led to all manner of rumours, in spite of the accoucheur's declaration that the baby was a month premature.

*[Undated]*

Bonaparte discovered me weeping over Adèle's letter. "Your daughter has had another son. Is that not cause for celebration?"

"I wasn't beside her!"

He comforted me tenderly. We walked hand in hand through the gardens.

*April 27, Wednesday, I think—Château Marrac (not far from Bayonne).*
How wonderful to be close to the sea again. I can smell it in the air.

By the morning light I see that this room has been decorated in soft violet and yellow silks. Our bed (which we share here), of a beautiful cherrywood, is topped by a crown. The drawing room has been made to look like a tent with the sides looped up—a blue satin tent braided with violet and yellow. A sofa (not very comfortable), armchairs and a footstool are covered in a striped blue silk trimmed with yellow. There's even a bathing chamber with a wooden tub in it—which is being filled for me now.

A tall Basque maid in rope-soled shoes has just brought me a dish of chocolate and marzipan. "A gift from the Emperor," she said—or rather, that's what I *think* she said, for they speak a curious language here. (Euskara?) "He say to say he *love* you," she added in French, enunciating the words proudly.

*May 5.*
The King of Spain has ceded to France. Bonaparte has persuaded Joseph to give up Naples and take the crown of Spain. "Not Joachim?" I asked, relieved but surprised. Caroline had made it clear that the Spanish crown was to go to her husband.

"Bah!" Bonaparte muttered. "Joachim has bungled things here. I'll give him Naples. That should make Caroline happy. She'll have a crown at last."

But not the crown she wanted. Not a *big* crown.

*Friday afternoon.*

There is something in this salty, bracing breeze that enlarges our spirits. The melancholy cries of the gulls sing "home" to us both. How alike Bonaparte and I are, both born and raised on islands, the sea ever before us.

If only we could live like this forever, far from the intrigues of Paris. We talked late last night, whispering in the dark: "When we're old and grey, we'll have a little château by the sea," he said sleepily. "You'll tend the flowers and I'll tend the vegetables."


*[Undated]*

Bonaparte and I arrived back at the château giddy this afternoon. My maids shook their heads in wonderment at my wind-tousled hair, my bare feet. "The Emperor took my shoes and hid them," I explained, and then burst into laughter at their puzzled faces. A maid is preparing a bath for me now, for I've sand in my hair, my ears.

The day was glorious. We set off at a fast pace in one of the new light carriages and soon were within sight of the ocean. "Ah," said Bonaparte, inhaling, taking my hand. The sun sparkled off the water.

As soon as we came to a deserted beach, Bonaparte ordered our driver to stop. "Too wild, do you think?" he asked, examining the rocky cove.

"It's perfect," I said, tying my hat ribbons.

At the sand's edge I kicked off my shoes and tucked up my skirt. I heard Bonaparte call out behind me, and I bolted into a run. He caught me, the foaming wave swirling around our feet. We were laughing and out of breath. He tried to push me into the water, but I twisted away, escaping his reach.

We were how long thus, playing like children? Hours. An eternity.

I wonder what our guards thought, watching their Emperor and Empress running back and forth along the shore, watching as we fell laughing onto the sand, watching as we walked hand in hand—watching as we embraced.

Perhaps they thought we were very much in love.

## In which we return to the camp of the enemy

*August 15, 1808, Bonaparte's thirty-ninth birthday—Saint-Cloud.*
Bonaparte and I were both rumpled and weary as our carriage pulled into Saint-Cloud. We'd slept in the coach the night before, but even so, there was no time to bathe—only time for a change of clothes and a quick repast.

I'm writing this now in the drawing room off the garden, the doors open wide, waiting for Bonaparte to emerge from his cabinet on the other side of the courtyard. In a few minutes we're to receive the Senate, then go to Mass and a Te Deum in honour of "Saint Napoleon."

I'm anxious to see Hortense, Petit, the new baby, but it will have to wait. (Wretched duty!) It's hard to believe that we've been away for over four months—four *wonderful* months.

*Late afternoon.*
"He's a good baby," Hortense said fondly, handing the infant to me.

"Oh, Hortense, he's . . ." In fact, I was alarmed. The baby seems small, with the exception of his head, which is big. "He's beautiful," I said, and with truth. He has the ancient beauty of a new soul.

"His name is Oui-Oui," sweet Petit said, standing beside me, his dimpled hand on my knee. I bent forward to give the boy a noisy kiss. "Tickles," he said, but then added, "Again?"

"*Later* we'll have a rumpus," I said. "But right now, I think you might want to have a look at"—I nodded in the direction of the door and dropped my voice to a stage whisper—"something I brought you." His eyes widened. "Did the coachman bring it in?" I asked Adèle.

"The coachman *and* the butler," she said. "It's heavy!"

"Maman, *what* have you brought?" Hortense asked, stretching out on the chaise longue.

"Yes, Grandmaman, *what* have you brought?" Petit echoed as the sound of great clattering on the parquet floors was heard in the hall. The butler appeared, pulling a model of a warship on wheels (and trying, in spite of it, to appear dignified).

Petit turned to me, a look of wonderment on his face. "Yes, for *you*," I said, rocking the infant, who had started to fuss.

"Say, Thank you, Grandmaman," Hortense called out as Petit ran to the wondrous object.

"Thank you, thank you, thank you, Grandmaman!" the child sang.


*Monday morning, August 22.*
A ball last night. "I'm the one who won Spain," I heard Joachim boast, well in his cups. "I'm the one who should have gotten that crown, not Joseph. He can't even ride a horse. And what do I get as thanks? Naples! But maybe at least Joseph will leave the Duchess d'Atri behind for me." Guffaw, guffaw.

He's gone, at last. He left for Naples this morning. That poor kingdom.


*August 28, Sunday.*
A family gathering at Malmaison: Madame Mère, Pauline, Julie Bonaparte and her girls, Hortense and sweet Petit. The children loved the orangutan, dressed comically in a gown. Its antics had them screaming with laughter. Then Bonaparte pretended to be a bear, much to the delight of the children *and* the pugs.


*September 10, 1808, Milan*
*Chère Maman,*
*Little Josephine is walking. You should see her—she is so charming! My*

*lovely Auguste is exceptionally well, considering her condition (three more months). Please tell Papa that I have taken his advice to spend more time at home with the family—no more working until midnight.*

    *A million kisses,*

Your loving son, Eugène

*Note—I am hopeful that Papa will be able to come to an understanding with Tsar Alexandre at the upcoming conference in Erfurt. If he can get Russia to agree to support a blockade against England, England will be forced to negotiate for peace.*

*September 16, Friday.*

It seems that everyone—our best actors and actresses, my cooks, even Dr. Corvisart—is going to Erfurt in Saxony . . . for the peace talks, it is said, but what is whispered is that Bonaparte will be meeting with Tsar Alexandre to discuss marriage to the Tsar's sister.

"Nonsense," Bonaparte told me tonight when I teased him about this rumour. "Talleyrand, explain to my wife that my meetings with the Tsar will be strictly political."

"Your Majesty, the meetings will be strictly political."

"And royal marriages are not political?"

As a result of this "innocent" banter, I could not sleep last night and have been in bed all day. Every hour or so, Bonaparte pops his head through the bed-curtains. "You worry too much," he said, suspecting the cause of my malaise. "You shouldn't listen to the gossips."

*September 22—Saint-Cloud.*

Bonaparte left for Erfurt at five this morning. He embraced me farewell, kissed me with feeling. "I'll be back in a month. Promise you won't worry?"

"I promise," I lied.

*September 26, Monday—Malmaison.*

Thérèse's hat was even more fanciful than usual: an exotic confection of birds and flowers. "What is there to worry about?" she asked, getting right to the point. "Has the Emperor ever made a woman pregnant? No! He's not about to divorce you and marry some young thing only to make a public fool of himself."

"That's the one thing that consoles me," I confessed—and that makes me sadder still.


*October 19.*
Bonaparte arrived back from the peace talks laden with magnificent Russian furs. "Why the disguise?" I asked, for he was dressed as an advocate in a black wool cape.

"I had need of speed. Spain is in trouble."

"You're *returning* to Spain?"

"Joseph has abandoned Madrid, fled without even a struggle! King Pepe Coxo, the Spaniards call him—vice-ridden incompetent. With family like mine, I have no need of enemies."

"Will there be no end to war?"

"Do you think I seek it?" he asked sadly.


*Saturday, October 29—Rambouillet.*
Bonaparte refuses to allow me to accompany him to Spain. "It's too dangerous," he insisted. "The Spaniards are unpredictable."

Murderous, he meant. I pressed my cheek against his heart. If he only knew how much I worried! My attention was drawn to something under his vest. "What's this?" It felt like a soft, small sachet, about an inch in circumference. Bonaparte pulled away. "What is it?" I persisted. His hands were cold.

"Josephine, you wouldn't want me to be . . ."

I closed my eyes. It was poison, I realized, in case of capture.


*November 13—Paris, the awful Tuileries.*
I've moved back into the Tuileries: the dark, dank palace—now garishly renovated, alas. I'm too ill to care, frankly, too upset about the Spanish

campaign, trembling every time I think of that terrible, impossible war. Bonaparte wouldn't even be there had he not been advised that the Spaniards were eager for "liberation." And now, once in, how does one withdraw? Certainly not Bonaparte. *Le feu sacré*. He'd be the last to admit defeat—especially to England.

*December 4, Sunday.*
The most astonishing news—the most *disturbing* news. Talleyrand invited Fouché to his home on Rue de Varenne. They were seen to walk arm in arm through the rooms. "But Fouché and Talleyrand detest one another," I said.

"When enemies unite, there is bound to be trouble," Chastulé said.

*December 22, 1808, Milan*
*Chère Maman,*
*I have succeeded in intercepting a letter that Governor Junot sent to Queen Caroline in Naples. As you suspected, Talleyrand and Fouché are in league to put Joachim on the throne of the French Empire—should the Emperor be killed in battle, they will have it, but the scheme looks suspect in my view. Caroline has even set up a communication system between Paris and Naples so that her husband can quickly be summoned. Junot guaranteed her military "protection"—you know what that means.*

*I've alerted the Emperor, who will no doubt return to Paris immediately. The enemy are not in Spain—they are at home, and in the intimacy of his family circle.*

*My lovely Auguste is well. The midwife says "any day."** *
*Your ever loyal son, Eugène*

*Tuesday—Malmaison.*
"So *that's* what Caroline was up to," Thérèse said. "She's been planning this little coup for some time. I have to say, I admire the little vixen. She

---

* *A daughter, Eugénie, was born the following day, on December 23.*

figured she needed Fouché on her side so she honeyed him. Junot, as Governor of Paris, controls the militia, and so she dragged him into her bed. And—of course—an intimate relationship with the Austrian Ambassador *would* prove to be helpful were she to become Queen of France. What a terrifying thought! You alerted the Emperor?"

"Eugène did."

"Let's pray he gets back soon."


*January 23, 1809—Tuileries.*
Bonaparte is back from Spain, roaring at everyone. Talleyrand has been demoted,* but Fouché, alas, is still Minister of Police. The man who knows everything knows too much, it would appear. "It's safer to keep him near," Bonaparte said.

And what of his sister Caroline? I dared not ask. *Blood is everything.*


*April 12—Saint-Cloud, 10:00 P.M.*
An hour ago, as we were dining, a message came announcing that Austria has invaded Munich—*again*. Between war in the southwest and war in the northeast, Bonaparte is run ragged.


*Saturday, April 15—Strasbourg.*
Nothing in Bonaparte's manner warned me: no loud and tuneless humming of "Malbrough," no rush of last-minute preparations. After a late dinner he returned to his cabinet to work—as usual. I played whist with my ladies until one and then retired. I think it was shortly after three that I was awoken by the sound of a horse's whinny. I sat up, puzzled. Wagon wheels? I went to the window, drew back the drapes: there, in the courtyard below, was Bonaparte's travelling carriage. Servants, grooms and aides were rushing about with flambeaux . . . and there was *Bonaparte*, pulling on his hat. The footman opened the carriage door and let down the step.

* *Talleyrand went directly to the Austrians, offering "services" in exchange for one million francs.*

He was leaving—without even a good-luck kiss? I groped through the dark rooms to the entry, knocking over a table. I flew down the steps and into the carriage.

"Josephine?" Bonaparte was startled to see me.

"You can't leave without telling me, Bonaparte!"

"I was afraid you would insist on going, and—"

"Well, you were right."

"But you can't just—"

"Sire, we're ready to set out." Duroc glanced at me, puzzled. What was the Empress doing in the coach in her nightdress and cap?

"That's fine," I said, with an attempt at authority.

"But Josephine, you're not even dressed."

"I'm serious," I growled, which made Bonaparte laugh.

"Order the Empress's trunks sent on to Strasbourg," he told Duroc, draping his greatcoat over my shoulders. "Ah, Josephine, whatever am I going to do with you?" he sighed as we passed through the Paris gates and onto the cobbled avenue.


*Sunday morning—Strasbourg.*
We've only just arrived in Strasbourg and already Bonaparte is leaving to join his army—yet another hurried departure, another tearful leave-taking, another quick good-luck kiss. I've set out the candles, the cards: keeping vigil yet again.


*May 6, noon*
*Mon amie, the cannonball that touched me caused no wound—it barely grazed the Achilles tendon. My health is excellent. Don't be anxious. Things are going very well here. All thine, N.*


*Schönbrunn, May 12, 1809*
*I am master of Vienna. Everything is going perfectly. My health is very good. N.*

*May 27*
*Eugène has joined me with his army. He has achieved the mission I assigned him, almost entirely destroying the enemy army in front of him. I am very well. All thine, N.*


*[Undated]*
News from headquarters: the Emperor is victorious.

Rumours from headquarters: the Emperor is often in the company of a young Polish countess.

Go back home, Bonaparte writes. Don't join me here.

I am packing, returning with regret.


*September 20—Malmaison.*
"It's the Minister of Foreign Affairs, Your Majesty, Monsieur Maret, or rather"—Clari stuck her nose in the air in imitation of a haughty demeanour—"the *Duke* de Bassano."

"Are you sure, Clari?" I thought Hugues Maret was in Germany, with Bonaparte.

But it was, indeed, the Minister of Foreign Affairs—Citoyen Maret, as I think of him. (After all, I've known him since before the Revolution.) "Forgive my surprise, Minister Maret. I thought you were with the Emperor."

"I was, Your Majesty," he said, sticking his nose in the air, just as Clari had demonstrated. "I've a message from him."

"A letter?"

"No, Your Majesty. A verbal communication."

"Would you care to walk in the garden, Minister Maret?"

Two of the pugs got lazily to their feet and sniffed the Minister's boots. He smiled down at them, showing false teeth. "That would be delightful," he said, taking two steps back.

The day was crisp and bright. "And how is the Emperor?" I asked, picking a decayed leaf off a potted auricula. The Emperor my husband; the Emperor in the arms of his Polish mistress. My husband whom I missed very, very much, nonetheless.

"The Emperor is exceptionally well, Your Majesty," Minister Maret said, jumping to open the grille-work gate for me.

I stopped on the path to inhale the scent of a bloom. *Rosa Longifolia, Rosa Pulila, Rosa Orbessanea*, I recited silently in my mind. "You said you had a message for me." I broke off a bloom long past its prime; the petals scattered on the stones. "From the Emperor."

"I do," he said, and fell silent.

"Then perhaps you might tell me what it is?" I suggested gently.

"Your Majesty, perhaps we . . . That is, perhaps you . . ." He waved his arm over a bench.

He wanted me to sit. Wary, I sat down, gathering my shawl around my shoulders.

"Your Majesty, the Emperor has a proposal to make to you, one which he wishes you to know arises out of the deep well of his love for you." Minister Maret licked his thin lips. "It's respecting a woman, Your Majesty, Countess Walewska. I am given to understand that you are aware that she and the Emperor . . . ?"

"Yes, Minister Maret, I am aware."

"The young lady is confirmed to be with child, Your Majesty."

*Rosa Longifolia, Rosa Pulila, Rosa Orbessanea.* "The Emperor's child?"

Minister Maret nodded, not meeting my eyes.

"And there can be no doubt?"

Minister Maret coughed into his fist. "It is early yet, Your Majesty, so it's possible that *things* may not develop, but as to the parentage, there is no doubt whatsoever."

A child—after so many years. *His* child. It must seem a miracle to him. "The Emperor must be very happy," I said, a lump rising in my throat. "But surely this is not why you have come all the way back to Paris, Minister Maret."

"Indeed, Your Majesty, I have come with a highly confidential and delicate proposition. The Emperor wishes to know if you might consider . . . *adopting* this child."

Bonaparte's child? Oh, yes! "I might."

"And more, the Emperor wishes to know if you would be willing to feign a pregnancy—so that the child would appear to be your own."

"You may tell the Emperor that I will do *anything*."

*[Undated]*

So. A young Polish countess is with child by Bonaparte. I'm told she is shy, gentle, sincere in her love for my husband. I am told she is called his "Polish wife." Oh, my murderous thoughts! She is my undoing—*his* undoing. Is that *gentle*? Is that *sincere*?


*October 1, 1809, Schönbrunn Palace*
*Your Majesty,*

*The Emperor, who is in Raab, has charged me with letting you know that Dr. Corvisart regretfully demurred not so much on account of his considerable integrity as a physician, but because of his conviction that the undertaking would be eventually discovered with disastrous results. He has persuaded the Emperor not to pursue this course of action.*

*Burn this letter.*

*Your devoted servant, Hugues Maret,*
*Minister of Foreign Affairs*


*October 14, 1809, Schönbrunn*
*Your Majesty,*

*You mistake me. I am in full sympathy with your plea. I understand the importance of this issue, both to the Emperor and yourself, and especially to the Empire. However, as a physician, I appreciate the risks involved. When the eyes of the world are upon one, even the truest action will appear false. I warned the Emperor, and I now caution you against a folly which, however well intended, would lead to the Emperor's disgrace.*

*The Emperor's health is excellent. The delirious joy we have all felt since the signing of the peace accord has been darkened by the attempt on his life. The Emperor would like to pardon the overzealous student who attempted to pull a knife on him, but the young man foolishly insists on declaring his guilt. That the lad very nearly succeeded has us all somewhat shaken, as you can imagine. I wish to assure you that the Emperor was not hurt in any way. This is not being made public as it would no doubt inflame concerns about the future of the Empire.*

*Your most humble servant, Dr. Corvisart*

*October 26, Thursday.*

Moustache came cantering through the gate. "Your Majesty," he yelled to me in the rose garden. "The Emperor is in Fontainebleau!"

"But . . ." Bonaparte wasn't expected back until late tomorrow, at the earliest.

"May I make a suggestion, Your Majesty?" Moustache pulled at one end of his massive appendage. "*Hurry.*"

It was almost six by the time I got to Fontainebleau. I found Bonaparte alone, sitting at a table in the drawing room. "It's about time," he said, looking up briefly, then lowering his eyes.

"Bonaparte, *please* don't be cross."

"Is it too much to ask my wife to be here to greet me after an absence of over six months?"

"Sire," I said, using the formal salutation, "if I may be allowed the impertinence of reminding you, you wrote that you would not be arriving until tomorrow night, at the earliest. My ladies and I were planning to arrive tomorrow morning, in order to be in readiness."

"I suppose it would have *inconvenienced* you to have come a few days early?"

"In all our years together, Bonaparte, this is the first time I've been late to meet you. Just once! We've been apart for half a year, and this is how you welcome me?"

He pressed his hands against his chest, as if he'd been wounded.

*Saturday, October 28—Fontainebleau.*

Once again, we are required to be gay. Three nights a week for theatre, the rest of the week for receptions, one evening at the Emperor's salon, perhaps a ball. When nothing is planned, Chastulé sets up game tables in her drawing room.

Daily Bonaparte hunts, and with a frightening energy, galloping as far as twenty leagues. When not hunting, he is shooting with falcons.

In the evening, at dinner, theatre, receptions and balls, we are careful around each other, our speech and movements studied. Now and again

I see him watching me with a melancholy expression. I know what he is thinking: should he divorce me, or should he not?

*October 29, Sunday—raining.*
Bonaparte's sister Pauline arrived three days ago with a blue-eyed, lascivious lady-in-waiting. Smiling mysteriously, Mademoiselle Christine follows Bonaparte's every move, all the while swinging a huge gold cross on a velvet ribbon, as if trying to entrance him.

*[Undated]*
The light from Pauline's windows is bright: it illuminates the courtyard, the guards standing by the fountain. A door onto the balcony opens and suddenly I hear the sound of violins, merriment. I hear Bonaparte's voice, Mademoiselle Christine's shrill giggle.

*[Undated]*
"I think you should just smile and pretend not to notice, Your Majesty," Clari said.

"I would take a lover," Chastulé said. "The Prince of Mecklenburg-Schwerin will be arriving soon, will he not?"

"That's what *they* would like me to do," I said. What the Bonaparte clan wanted me to do, certainly—in the hope that I would make a fatal error. "I think Bonaparte is intentionally trying to make himself unlovable—"

"Ha! And succeeding."

"—for a reason." My reader adjusted the shawl around my shoulders. I gave Carlotta a sympathetic look. We had both of us been rejected. "I know Bonaparte. He is acting a part. He wants me to look upon . . ." I stopped. I could not speak the word "divorce." "He wants me to look upon a separation as a desirable thing."

"Maman," Hortense interjected, her voice wistful and sad, "perhaps he is right. Perhaps it would be a desirable thing."

I looked down at my needlework, tears blurring the stitches.

*Wednesday, November 8.*

I'm writing this in a golden room. I'm adorned with diamonds, my finest gown, a hat. Damn him!

Oh forgive me, for I am frightened. For my own weak soul, yes, but also for Bonaparte, my exasperating husband, the *Emperor*. This man who is capable of being so heroic—so saintly—but who is also capable of being base and destructive.

Yes, I am frightened, for myself, for Bonaparte, for my children, but also for all the people of this nation who have honoured me with such devotion. I concede: I have lost the battle, and the battle was over Bonaparte's heart.

*You will be Queen,* a voodoo fortune-teller once told me. How clearly I remember those terrible words. *But not for very long.*

I don't care! I don't want to be Queen, Monarch, Empress. I don't want to sit on a throne. The crown has only made me miserable. But I have the misfortune to want very much to sit beside the man on the throne. It is not the Emperor I love, but the *man*. And who else loves *him?* Nobody.


*November 13.*

A fearful slaughter. I'm ill.

For days Bonaparte has been talking about a boar hunt. Today the Emperor got his way: *Je le veux.*

We drove out to where a huge pen had been built in a clearing: the ladies in their hunting finery, their plumes and velvet jackets over gowns of white satin. We climbed up onto a high stand, trembling with nervousness. The men were all standing on a huge platform that had been built in the centre of a pen, loading their guns. Soon we heard fearful sounds, a savage grunting and snorting as over eighty wild boars, stampeded into the pen. Then Bonaparte and the men proceeded to kill them all. The squeals of fear filled the air with a sound I cannot forget. The ladies tittered at first, and then paled.

It has become torture here. Tomorrow, thank God, we return to Paris.

*November 14.*

Paris: city of whispers. I enter a room, and suddenly there is silence, embarrassed smiles. Isabey, making up my face each morning, says nothing about my red-rimmed eyes. "Perhaps a little ceruse?" he suggests, applying the thick white base. I look in the mirror and my face is a mask. "But no crying, Your Majesty," he scolds me tenderly, and tears fill my eyes once again.

*November 15.*

"Monsieur Calumet?" The man who had been my legal advisor years ago had aged. Why was I surprised?

"Madame Bonaparte," he said, rising with difficulty. He hesitated to extend his bare hand. "*Empress,* Your Majesty. Forgive me."

"How are you, kind sir?" I asked, taking a seat. Monsieur Calumet had been witness to my civil marriage to Bonaparte. How things have changed. Now diamonds adorn my headdress and tears my heart.

"Oh," he said, his voice quavering, "your husband has been good to us all. Long live the Emperor!"

This with a burst of emotion that quite took me aback. "I'm afraid I've come about a . . . delicate matter, Monsieur," I began, my hands on my knees, like a schoolgirl. "I wish to consult with you regarding the legitimacy of my marriage—at least in the eyes of the Church. Have you had a chance to consider the document I had sent to you?"

"The Catholic certificate of marriage?" He withdrew it from a drawer and placed it carefully before him. "Your Majesty, forgive me for being the one to tell you, but I'm afraid that there is a problem."

"Oh?" I said, my heart sinking. This was my last hope.

"According to Church law, the requisite witnesses were not present."

"*What* requisite witnesses?"

"The priest of your district, for one. Your Majesty, I do not wish to . . ." He cleared his throat, his hand to his chest.

"Monsieur Calumet, I have come to you because I know I can count on you to tell me the truth. Honesty is rare when one sits on a throne."

He looked away. "Your Majesty, the truth is that this document is worth nothing."

*Nothing?* The word burned! I am your wife forever, I told Bonaparte that night. Is that nothing?

I returned to the palace in a daze. I stood before the fire in my bedchamber for a time, this "worthless" document in my hand. Twice, I started to throw it into the flames . . . and twice I held back. In the end I sent Mimi for the oak strongbox. I've locked it back in there, along with my old journals, along with Bonaparte's fiery letters of love.

It is true: documents are worth nothing. What binds is the heart—the heart's true story. I love Bonaparte and Bonaparte loves me. We *are* man and wife. Come what may, come what will.


*December 1, Friday.*
Bonaparte has spoken.

I wore a wide-brimmed hat to dinner, to hide my eyes. We ate in silence, our attendants standing like statues behind us. Our plates were put on the table, then taken away, the food untouched.

"What time is it?" Bonaparte asked one of the kitchen officers, mechanically hitting his knife against the side of his glass.

"Five to seven, Your Majesty."

Bonaparte stood and headed into the drawing room. I followed, a lap cloth pressed against my mouth. I felt I was moving through deep water, that every step I made required all my concentration. We eat, Bonaparte stands, I follow him. We've been through this ritual for all the days of our life together, but suddenly, it seemed foreign.

The drawing room was stifling hot. The butler entered with the usual tray, standing before me so that I might have the honour of pouring the Emperor's coffee. I reached for the silver jug, but Bonaparte was there before me. Watching me steadily, *defiantly*, he poured his own coffee, spooned in the sugar, and drank. He put the empty cup on the tray and made a dismissive motion, closing the door behind the flustered attendant.

"Josephine," he said, turning to face me, "we must divorce."

He wanted me to see reason. The security of the Empire required this sacrifice. He relied on my devotion to give my consent. "This is a great and noble sacrifice we must make," he said firmly.

"You are wrong, Bonaparte. This would be a mistake! We would live to regret it."

There is no solidity to his dynasty without an heir, he repeated. He'd come to see the absolute necessity of it. The Empire must endure more than a day; it must endure for all eternity.

"Name Eugène heir," I argued. "You've trained him well. He's loyal and devoted to you. He understands your aims, your vision. You *know* the nation would benefit." The Empire would flourish! "You can *trust* him. Under Eugène, your legacy would endure."

"He is not a Bonaparte."

*Blood is everything.* "Then what about your nephews? What about Petit?"

"It's not the same as a son, born to the purple, raised in a palace. I *must* have a child of my own, Josephine. It's cruel of you to deprive me!"

And then I began to weep. "You don't know the pain we will suffer." I felt crazed, beyond reason.

"I will always love you. I will come to visit you—often."

"Don't you understand? It will not be the same!" He was deluding himself. This man who prided himself on his clear vision did not know his own heart.

"I *promise* you," he went on, as if words would heal. "You will keep your title. I will give you five million a year. You may have Malmaison. I'll buy you a country château—anything! I'll make you Queen of Rome. You will have your own domain."

"Bonaparte, no! Whatever you do, *please*—don't send me away." I envisioned myself alone and unloved. I fell on the carpet, giving way to pitiful sobbing.

I remember very little of what followed. I was carried down the narrow passage to my room and Dr. Corvisart was summoned. "You've suffered a violent attack of nerves, Your Majesty."

Hortense appeared before me through a laudanum blur. "Eugène and I will follow you," she told me. "Together we'll lead a quiet life. It will be peaceful. We will know true happiness."

I wrapped my arms around her thin shoulders. Mother and daughter, we were both alone in the world. It is perhaps best that she does not know what lies ahead, I thought. I felt like a Cassandra, calling out futile warnings of impending doom. Destiny has been crossed; the downward slide will now begin.

## *In which we must part*

At eight, as is her custom, my maid of the wardrobe entered my bedchamber with a selection of gowns. "Come in, Mademoiselle Avrillion," I said, parting the bed-curtains. "I have something to tell you, but first, make sure that the door is closed." I fell back against the pillows. I still felt weak, but calmer.

Mademoiselle Avrillion put down her basket and smoothed her skirt, her expression apprehensive. We'd all been expecting the worst, waiting for the sky to fall—knowing that it would, but not knowing when. Not knowing how life would go on after.

But life does go on. I took a breath and began. "The Emperor informed me that he has decided to—" In telling her, I was again overcome. I struggled to finish. "He has decided to pronounce a divorce." Mademoiselle Avrillion clapped her hands over her mouth, let out a cry. "However, everything must appear normal for the time being."

"That's cruel of him, Your Majesty." Her look was defiant—loyal.

"The Emperor suffers," I told her firmly. "He does what he must."

And so, by the bright winter light, my new life begins. I look ravaged, yet I will play the part, assume the costume of the Empress, recall her calm and charitable heart. After the celebration of the peace, Bonaparte will make a public announcement. As for this moment, I'm suffering an indisposition, that's all.

Brave words, but as soon as Mademoiselle Avrillion left, I gave in to despair. How can I do this? I've a reception at Malmaison tomorrow, and the day after is the big celebration, a ball. And then more balls and fêtes, and fêtes and balls, all in a spirit of gaiety. How will I find the courage, the strength?

*Saturday, December 2—Malmaison.*
It is late. I'm writing this at the little mahogany writing table in Bonaparte's bedchamber at Malmaison. I'm in my nightgown, warmed by the bearskin I've pulled off the bed.

The sovereigns have all departed, even Bonaparte, who decided to return to the Tuileries in preparation for the morrow—in spite of the snow and freezing rain. "This is your lucky day," I told him, on leaving. He looked puzzled. "The second of December." The anniversary of the coronation: how could he forget?

"Oh," he said, shrugging, as if luck no longer mattered.

It is a relief to be alone now. The hardest part was receiving the family. Queen Caroline and King Joachim, newly arrived back from Naples, watched me closely. They suspect, I know. And what will they do, I wonder, when they learn that they have won the day, won the battle, won the war? They will proclaim a victory, no doubt. They will have the Emperor to themselves, at last—all his power and all his riches. And all his heart, they will assume—not knowing his heart, not realizing that this sacrifice will harden him.

It is now almost two, I suspect. The fire has burnt down; I begin to feel the winter chill. My portrait by the bed is in shadow—Bonaparte's favourite, though not mine.

Five years ago today Bonaparte crowned me Empress. Oh, it was the most glorious day! I accepted that crown as if it were a betrothal ring, thinking that it would bind me to my husband. And now . . . *now* I see that it is the one thing that has pushed me away from him. Without issue, I have no right to that throne—no right, indeed, to the Emperor's Imperial bed. As Empress, there was only one thing I was required to do: provide the link to the past and to the future, secure the Emperor's place in history. In the womb of an Empress, the future unfolds. She is the past, she is the present, she is the future. And I? I was never an Empress. Only Yeyette, Rose, Josephine—an ordinary woman from Martinico. An ordinary woman who loves her husband.

How much does it matter, in the end, my love for Bonaparte? Not much, truly, when balanced against the needs of a nation. Indeed, it *is* a sacrifice we are making, Bonaparte and I—a noble sacrifice. I only pray that it will not be made in vain, that my fears are unfounded. "Superstitious nonsense," as Bonaparte would say, "womanish imaginings." (Pretending not to be superstitious himself.)

Oh, Bonaparte—how hard it is for me to comprehend the changes that lie before us. I feel you in this room with me now—your light lemon scent lingers. Your spirit is everywhere. A half-empty crystal champagne glass engraved with your monogram is on the table beside a stack of journals, a snuffbox. A small, battered medal catches my eye: Charlemagne's talisman, carelessly tossed in among the pocket clutter. A book you were reading—*History of the Revolutions of the Roman Empire*—is facedown on a chair beside the bed, the spine cracked, the pages dog-eared. Your vest is thrown over the arm of the black leather chair. A crumpled news-sheet litters the carpet.

The clock has just chimed two. I don't want to leave this room, this moment so full of memory, but I've a difficult day tomorrow, I know. I will lock the door when I leave, forbid entry. It will always be here for me.

*Sunday.*

First, a Te Deum at Notre-Dame. I was not to go there in the Emperor's coach, was not to sit beside him, Duroc explained, his manner officious, as if I were a servant he was instructing. Rather, I was to sit with Caroline and Jérôme's wife, Catherine. "The Emperor wishes the people to begin to be prepared," Duroc said. "He wishes it to be conjectured."

*Conjectured.* Of course. Rumours would be circulated, hints given, predictions printed in the popular journals. And perhaps it is for the best. Perhaps in this way I, too, will begin to be "prepared."

"Does anyone in the household know?" I asked.

"Only the Imperial family, Madame."

Madame. Not *Your Majesty*—just *Madame*. Well, so be it, I thought, swallowing hard.


"Madame Bonaparte," Caroline said with a bright (smug) smile. "How lovely you look this afternoon."

"How kind of you to say so," I replied with a bright (false) smile. "*Queen* Caroline." (How trivial it all seemed to me, in truth, catching a glimpse of the tomb of little Napoleon tucked into a corner of that vast cathedral.)

After Mass, the Imperial cortège drove to the Legislature, where Bonaparte was received with thunderous cheers. My heavy heart gladdened to the sound of "Hail to the Peacemaker! Long live the Emperor!" From habit and affection, Bonaparte glanced over his shoulder at me, sharing the moment.

At five the cortège returned to the Tuileries, where we received the foreign ambassadors before proceeding into the Gallery of Diana for the Imperial banquet. (My last, thank God—how I hate them.) King Joseph was seated on my left, Madame Mère on my right. King Louis, newly arrived from Holland, sat next to his mother (with whom he is staying). Bonaparte sat directly across from me, with the King of Saxony on his right. Hortense was on his left. I avoided my daughter's eyes, for fear I might weep.

And then, of course, all the others: the King of Württemberg, King Jérôme and his wife Catherine, a conspicuously gay Princess Pauline, King Joachim in pink silk embroidered with gold stars—and, of course, an exultant Queen Caroline, ordering the servants about as if she were in charge, as if *she* were the hostess.

Bonaparte seemed anxious, motioning to the chamberlain for no purpose, wiping his mouth even when he wasn't eating, creating a growing pile of soiled napkins behind him.*

We ate without speaking, each silently attended by three footmen, the

---

* *After a napkin was used once, it was thrown behind the diner's chair and a new one was supplied.*

only voices those of the carvers, passing the trays to the footmen. I don't believe I was ever so glad to see Bonaparte rise. Immediately everyone stood, turned, advanced one pace toward the line of butlers, who offered trays. With trembling hands I squeezed lemon into the white bowl, cleansed my mouth and swished the tips of my fingers in the blue bowl. To think I've finally mastered this little ritual, I thought, tossing my napkin into Caroline's pile.

*December 4, Monday—Paris.*
My demise—my loss of a throne, a crown, a husband—begins to be "conjectured." At the military review this morning, a market woman placed flowers at my feet, as if I had died.

The review was followed by a fête given by the city of Paris, with the court of the Hôtel de Ville transformed into an enormous ballroom. I'd been instructed to go alone. My ladies would be there to meet me, I was told, but when I entered, I found the foyer empty, the small drawing room beside the grand staircase where the attendants waited deserted. Where were my ladies, my entourage? The head butler came running down the marble stairs. "Your attendants have been seated," he said, out of breath.

"I'm to enter alone?"

"It is the Emperor's wish."

*I will it.* Bien. Drums sounded my entry into the Grand Salon. I could hear the hushed whispers as I made my way to the dais: an Empress without an Emperor. As I approached the throne, my knees began to give way. Quickly I was handed into the velvet-cushioned throne. I sat back, faced the crowd.

The drums beat again, and Bonaparte entered with Caroline on his arm, Jérôme following behind.

Caroline caught my eye, glowing with the triumph of victory.

*December 5—Paris, shortly before dinner.*
A message from Eugène—he'll be here in a few days.

*Thursday.*

I was at my toilette when Hortense appeared at the door, her cheeks flushed and her eyes glistening. "Eugène is here!"

I pressed my hands to my heart. I hadn't seen my son since he and Auguste had married—almost four years ago now.

"He's with the Emperor," she said, touching her cheek to mine. "Are you sure you're all right?"

"I'm . . . *fine.*" I reached for the vial of herbal essence Dr. Corvisart had prescribed, for nerves. I put a drop on my finger and held it to my nose, inhaled slowly. I had not been sleeping, and already this morning I'd had one of my "tropical storms"—a torrent of tears that seemed to come upon me unexpectedly and without warning. I inhaled again and sat back. "I'm all right," I repeated (but with tears welling up). "I've been—"

I was interrupted by the thundering sound of footsteps in the private passage. "Come in," I called out at the sound of Bonaparte's characteristic *rap-rap.* How I've missed that sound!

Bonaparte stumbled into the room, blinking against the light. "Hortense *is* here," he said over his shoulder.

And then close behind him appeared a tall, good-looking young man with broad shoulders and honest, smiling eyes: Eugène! I stood to embrace my beloved son. "Oh, mon Dieu, Eugène, you look so old!" So handsome—so manly.

He swung me playfully in his embrace, crooning, "Oh Maman, Maman, Maman . . ."

"And you've grown sideburns." And a kingdom. And two daughters. "You look wonderful," I said, blinking back tears. "Doesn't he?" I said, turning to Bonaparte—*Papa.* "Doesn't he?" Turning to Hortense.

"Oh Maman, *don't,*" Eugène said, his eyes brimming. He pulled me against his chest, patting my back, stilling my sudden sobs.

"Hold her, Eugène." Hortense saw my knees beginning to buckle.

Supported by them both, I regained my strength. "Forgive me. I'm sorry." I glanced up. Bonaparte was staring at the three of us, his cheeks wet with tears.

"Oh, Papa," Hortense whispered, pulling him into the circle of our embrace.

*December 8.*

As we married, so we must divorce: with ceremony.

We begin with specifics: who, what, when, where. The date has been set for a week from today, next Friday. Evening, court attire. Reception in the throne room, the ceremony itself in Bonaparte's cabinet. In the presence of family and a few officials, Bonaparte will make a statement, I will follow, and then the legal document will be signed. Arch-Chancellor de Cambacérès will see to the legalities. His secretary will send out the invitations.

"As you wish," I said, my mouth dry.

*[Undated]*

"Your Majesty, did I understand you correctly? There is to be no lace, no embroidery, no pearls—*nothing*?"

"The gown must be plain, Monsieur Leroy," I said, "like one a nun would wear."

*[Undated]*

Arch-Chancellor de Cambacérès has given me a draft of a divorce statement he thinks would be appropriate. I cannot speak his words. I will write it myself.

*[Undated]*

I tried to write my divorce statement this morning—gave up in tears.

*No longer having any hope of conceiving children, I give my beloved husband proof of my devotion by . . .*

By divorcing him.

Oh, mon Dieu—this is not the right thing to do, Bonaparte!

*December 13, Wednesday evening.*

An exhausting day attending to my charities, my wardrobe.* To bed. Tomorrow there is a formal reception followed by dinner in the Gallery of Diana. I've begged permission not to attend, but I'm told I must. It will be my last appearance as Empress.

*I declare that, no longer having any hope of conceiving children, I am willing to give my husband proof of my devotion by . . .*

*December 14.*

The reception and dinner were difficult. At least it is over. "It always gives me a head pain anyway," I told Chastulé as she took my crown away.

*I declare that, no longer having any hope of conceiving children, which would satisfy the interests of France, I am willing to give the greatest proof of my love and devotion by . . .*

*December 15, Friday.*

Leroy has delivered my gown. "I finally understand, Your Majesty," he said. "You wish to adorn yourself in precious gems. The simplicity of the gown will be what designers call a counterpoint."

"No, Monsieur Leroy, I intend not to wear a single gem." Only my wedding ring, which I will wear to my grave.

He looked at me as if I'd gone mad—and perhaps he is right.

Mademoiselle Avrillion came for me shortly before nine. "Your Majesty, are you ready? The Emperor is expecting you in his cabinet."

* *Josephine doubled her usual contribution to charity and, as well, gave away 72 pieces of lace, 380 gowns, 17 shawls, 146 bonnets and hats, 39 lengths of cloth, and 785 pairs of boots and slippers—virtually every pair she owned.*

"I am ready."

She burst into tears. "You should see them all."

"They've arrived?" Already?

"They're in the throne room, Your Majesty. I've never seen Caroline and Pauline looking so grand. Even Madame Mère is wearing a fuchsia-and-yellow brocade—and rubies! One would think it was carnival. I will be honest, now that we are leaving. I think that they're beastly individuals and I detest them!"

At the landing, I sent Mademoiselle Avrillion away. "I'll be all right," I assured her, proceeding through the antechamber, the waiting room, the drawing room, nodding to the guards, the maids. Hugo, his chin puckered in misery, threw open the door to Bonaparte's cabinet. "The Emperor is expecting you, Your Majesty." Bowing deeply.

Bonaparte was seated on the chaise by the fireplace, his back to the door. "Josephine!" He jumped to his feet. He was wearing a blue velvet suit richly embroidered in gold. He wiped his hands on his breeches and came to me, hands extended, as if I were a guest he'd been expecting. But stopped short. "The family will be shown in soon. I thought you would sit here, by the writing table." He pulled out the antique chair.

Slowly, I sat down. The chair needed to be reupholstered, I noticed—the silk piping was beginning to fray. The fabric was an unusual shade of green kersey. It would be difficult to match. I vaguely recalled that a length of it had been stored in the attic wardrobe. I should let Bonaparte's chamberlain know.

"Josephine, are you . . . ?" Bonaparte patted my shoulder, very lightly—as if afraid to touch me.

I nodded, swallowing, my eyes stinging. A gold quill stand had been placed on the table before me in readiness, a parchment beside it. I put my own parchment down, smoothing it out so that it lay flat. *I declare that . . .*

Bonaparte took up a matching chair and placed it in front of the fire. "And I will sit here. Everyone else can sit on the stools—but for my mother, of course. I thought perhaps she might sit on the chaise. What do you think?"

"Your mother doesn't care to sit too close to a fire."

"She doesn't?"

Nor too far. "Perhaps if the chaise were placed against the wall," I suggested.

"Good idea," he said, shoving the chaise into place and then tugging at the corner of the carpet to straighten it.

The big pendulum clock began to sound the hour.

*One.*

*Two.*

*Three.*

At the fourth chime the door creaked open. "Your Majesty, it is time," Christophe Duroc informed Bonaparte (without glancing at me). He was wearing the grandest of his Grand Marshal ensembles: an enormous cape with a batwing collar made stiff with bone.

*Five.*

*Six.*

*Seven.* Bonaparte and I looked at each other for what seemed a very long moment.

*Eight.* Let's leave, I felt like crying out. Let's escape to some island, frolic in the surf, grow flowers and vegetables. Let's grow old together, fumbling and fond.

*Nine.*

"Send them in," Bonaparte said, looking away.

I could hear Caroline's voice, and then Pauline's shrill giggle. I pulled out a fresh handkerchief, took a deep breath.


Duroc announced everyone in order of status. First Madame Mère (smiling), then Louis—leaning heavily on two walking sticks, his expression hooded—followed at a distance by Hortense, Jérôme and his wife, Caroline and Joachim (snickering), Julie (Joseph is in Spain), Eugène and, at the last, a giggling Pauline.

Hortense reached for the back of my chair as Eugène strode across the room to stand beside Bonaparte. My son crossed his arms on his chest and stared at the carpet, paler than I'd ever seen him.

I touched my daughter's hand and looked up at her. Her red-rimmed eyes glistening, her face streaked by tears—that sensitive face so full of intelligence, so full of grace. No wonder the Bonaparte sisters loathe her, I thought. Hortense is everything they are not.

Arch-Chancellor de Cambacérès came in, his cape pulled back to better display the medals and ribbons that covered his vest, followed by dignified Count Regnault, the clan lawyer. We lapsed into the uncomfortable fifteen minutes of silence required by the Code, broken only by Hortense's sniffs, one muffled occurrence of flatulence (Joachim, I suspect), Pauline's and Caroline's whispers. I caught Bonaparte's eye. He smiled wanly and looked away. My throat tightened and a wave of tears rose up within me. I took a deep breath, tracing a circle on the head of the gilt-bronze gryphon that ornamented the arm of my chair. *I declare that* . . .

Bonaparte broke the silence. "You have been summoned here," he began, "to witness the declaration the Empress and I are obliged to make." He cleared his throat. "We are divorcing."

Eugène reached out for the mantel. He was trembling, I realized with alarm. Hortense stifled a sob. I caressed her fingers, my eyes fixed on my husband.

He read quickly at first, as if racing to get the ordeal over with. Then he paused. "She has adorned fifteen years of my life. The memory of those years will be forever inscribed on my heart," he read haltingly, finishing with difficulty.

I felt Hortense squeeze my shoulder. It was my turn.

The parchment shook in my hands. "I declare that . . ." I began to read, but at the words, *Everything I have comes from his kindness*, I broke down, and handed the paper to Count Regnault. Leaning one elbow on the table, I listened as he read my words, so true and so heartfelt: *The dissolution of my marriage will make no change in the feelings of my heart. The Emperor will always find in me his truest friend.*

Count Regnault put the paper on the table and pulled out a handkerchief to wipe his eyes.

Bonaparte sat motionless. Through a blur of tears, I saw my son's stricken face. Cambacérès indicated to Bonaparte that the time had come to sign the official document. Bonaparte stood and scratched out his signature—that messy scrawl I knew so well.

"Josephine?" he said then, with a sweet-sad smile, handing me the quill.

4:30 A.M.
The night sky is lightening. I don't believe I've slept at all.

It was close to midnight when I gave way to my heart. En déshabille, I fumbled up the connecting passage, lighting my way with a single candle. The guard woke with a start when I rapped on Bonaparte's door. He looked at me, confused, his hand on the pommel of his sword. "It's just me, the Empress Josephine." Fortunately, Bonaparte's valet opened the door.

"Your Majesty," he said, astonished as much by my unexpected call as by my disordered appearance.

"Who is it, Constant?" I heard Bonaparte call out. I stepped into the room. By the light of a lantern on the washstand, I saw that Bonaparte was in bed, under a pile of comforters.

"Bonaparte, I just wanted to—" I began calmly, but my voice suddenly went high, like that of a child in pain. "I don't know if I have the strength to do this," I gasped.

Bonaparte sat up, his nightcap slipping off. I fell sobbing into his arms. "Courage," he said, tender and caressing. I touched his cheek, now wet with tears. "Oh, Josephine, how am I ever going to manage without you?" he whispered, holding me close.

Saturday, almost 2:00 P.M.
I will be leaving soon, leaving the palace, never to return, leaving my place beside Bonaparte. Soon another empress—young, royal, fertile—will sit at this desk. I have no illusions. Bonaparte will come to love her; that is her right. She will be the mother of his children.

And I, who will I be? I will be "the other one," growing old alone.

I've sprinkled the room with my light lavender scent. He will never, ever forget me.

"Ready, Maman?" Hortense touched my shoulder, a gentle motion that gave me strength.

"What about the pups?" I asked, slipping a veil over my head to hide my tear-streaked cheeks. Two days ago, one of the pugs had given birth to a litter.

"Don't worry, they're in Mademoiselle Avrillion's carriage," Hortense said, taking my hand. "Along with the canaries," she added with a smile.

All the servants were lined up in the entry. As soon as they saw me, saw that the moment had come, a terrible wail rose up, a heart-rending lamentation that echoed off the marble surfaces. I was blinded by tears; Hortense pulled me forward.

"Oh dear," I heard her say, once we were out the door. There was a crowd in the courtyard, standing in the cold winter rain. "It's the good Empress Josephine!" I heard a woman call out. Hortense hurried me into the carriage. As the horses pulled forward at a fast pace, Hortense reached to close the leather curtains. I did not look back.

# III

## *The Other One*

If he is happy, I will have no regrets.
—*Josephine*

## *In which a king is born*

*Sunday, December 17, 1809—Malmaison.*
I woke this morning to the sound of Mimi humming a familiar créole song. "*He's* here," she said, poking her head through the bed-curtains.

"Bonaparte?" I sat up, my heart jumping.


"The Emperor awaits you in the garden," an aide I didn't recognize informed me, neither addressing me as Empress nor bowing, merely ducking his head.

"In the rain?" I asked. It was more of a drizzle now, but damp nonetheless. I sent Mimi for boots and an umbrella—not the English one—a cape and a hat.

The aides followed like an unwelcome shadow to the rose garden gate. Bonaparte, pacing at the far end in his familiar grey coat, turned to face me. He touched the brim of his tricorne hat, as if in salute.

The aides lined up like sentries along the fence—close enough to watch, I realized. Bonaparte stepped back as I drew near. I understood: we were not to embrace.

"I didn't expect to see you so soon." I took a shaky breath, another. Tears would upset him, I knew.

"I needed to know how you were doing." He looked grim—his eyes red-rimmed.

I dared not answer, for fear of speaking truly.

"Let's walk, Josephine," he said gently, offering his arm.

*December 17, 8:00 P.M.*

*Mon amie, I found you weaker today than you should be. You must not surrender to such a devastating melancholy. You must find happiness, and above all, you must care for your health, which is so precious to me.*

*Never doubt my constant and tender feelings. You do not understand me if you think I can be happy if you are not at peace.*

*Adieu, sleep well. N.*


*December 21—Malmaison.*

Thérèse burst into tears when she saw me. "I told you never to get divorced!" she said angrily. "I told you it was hell." And then she embraced me, held me tight. "Forgive me!" she cried, enveloping me in a cloud of her familiar neroli oil scent. "You *love* the brute—and he loves you. That makes it even worse."


*Sunday.*

Bonaparte removed his hat, held it over his heart. "I'd like you, Hortense and Eugène to join me for dinner tomorrow. Christmas dinner," he added, as if I did not know.


*Monday, Christmas Day.*

"That was the most miserable meal I've ever experienced," Hortense exclaimed on our return.

I stroked one of the pugs' ears. The dog looked up at me with sorrowful eyes, as if she knew my thoughts. It *had* been miserable. Bonaparte had sat silently throughout the entire meal, now and then wiping his eyes.

One sweet note: the tender welcome of Bonaparte's staff. "The Emperor misses you terribly, Your Majesty," Constant whispered to me. "We all do."

It seems lonelier here now at Malmaison. I see him still, walking in the garden, working at his desk.

Oh, Bonaparte . . . how hard this is!

*January 1, 1810—Malmaison, almost dinnertime.*

What a terrible way to begin the year.

The ordeal began after the noonday meal. The servants of the household were instructed to enter the music room one by one. I was to give them a New Year's gift, and they in turn were to declare themselves: tell me if they would be staying with me or seeking employment elsewhere.

"Chastulé, perhaps you could record what everyone says," I suggested.

"Ha! But who will write down *my* declaration?"

"You wish to declare yourself now?"

"Why wait?"

"Countess d'Arberg, could you? Would you mind?" My tall, elegant lady-in-waiting did her best to squeeze into Chastulé's little chair and desk.

"Don't I get my gift first?" Chastulé demanded. "It's the one on the right, with the scarlet bow." Countess d'Arberg checked the tag and handed it to her. "My husband insists I stay with the court," Chastulé said, pinning the diamond brooch to her bodice. "I have my family to think of, and you won't be needing a lady of honour any more since you won't be entertaining and holding drawing rooms or suppers." She glanced at what Countess d'Arberg had written. "I said *suppers*, not dinners."

"You're leaving me, Chastulé?" I felt her words as a blow.

"I've already written to the Emperor, Madame," she said, edging toward the door.

"Just send in Carlotta, if you would, Countess de la Rochefoucauld," Countess d'Arberg said coolly.

The door slammed shut behind Chastulé. The silence was oppressive. Even the canaries were still. "Would you care to be my lady of honour?" I asked Countess d'Arberg weakly.

"I've coveted the position ever since I joined your household, Your Majesty," she said, efficiently blotting the ledger book and turning the page.

I was surprised. Countess d'Arberg is a Belgian aristocrat of German extraction, allied to the ruling houses of Germany. I had assumed that she would want to stay with the court.

The door creaked open. "Your Majesty, you summoned me?" Carlotta's dark eyes widened seeing Countess d'Arberg seated at Chastulé's little escritoire.

"You were," I said, guarded. Carlotta would leave me, too, no doubt. "Today everyone is to make a declaration, as you know."

Carlotta coloured as she said, "I want to serve you, Your Majesty—that is, if you will have me. Forgive me—have I said something wrong?" she asked, puzzled by my reaction.

"I assure you, Madame Gazzani, you have not," Countess d'Arberg said, giving my reader her gift.

"And this, as well, Carlotta," I said, taking a ring off my finger, pressing it into her hand.

And so, throughout the afternoon, there were many, many tears. A significant number of the servants will be leaving—understandable, I tell myself. A few will retire with a pension. (Agathe is one, alas. She is betrothed to the groundskeeper at Fontainebleau.) Clari would have liked to stay, she assured me, but for health reasons begged to be allowed to retire. I will miss her.

It's a smaller household now, but a good one. Mademoiselle Avrillion will stay, as mistress of the wardrobe. Mimi will stay, of course, and old Gontier. "I'll see you to your grave, Your Majesty," he declared, leaning on a cane, one hand pressed to his heart.


*February 6, almost midnight.*
Eugène pulled on a pug's tail and growled playfully. "Sorry I'm late, Maman."

"And?" I put down my needlework. He had set out late this afternoon for the Austrian Embassy to deliver Bonaparte's formal request for the hand of Archduchess Marie-Louise.* "How did the Austrian ambassador respond?" The offer had been made on condition that an answer be given within a day. The seventeen-year-old Archduchess would not even be consulted.

---

* It was important for Josephine and her children to show public support for the new marriage. Indeed, both Eugène and Hortense (as well as Josephine) were involved in the discussions as to which royal princess should be chosen.

"The contract will be signed tomorrow at noon."

"I suppose this is cause for celebration."

"I suppose," he echoed, embracing me.


*February 14.*
Eugène has left to return to Milan. "I'll be back soon," he promised, "with Auguste." For Bonaparte's wedding, he did not say.


*Saturday noon.*
*Le Moniteur* is full of news about the preparations that are being made for "the wedding of the century," all the fêtes and spectacles that are being planned.

"Your Majesty, perhaps it would be best not to read the news-sheets," Countess d'Arberg said gently, bringing me a cup of tea (and slipping the journal away).


*Monday, February 19—a bit of a drizzle.*
"Uncle doesn't like his dance lessons," Oui-Oui told me this afternoon.

Bonaparte is taking dance lessons?

"Aunt Caroline said he must learn," Petit explained.

"Well, of course," I said, dissembling. How many times had I tried to persuade Bonaparte to learn to dance only to be told no, impossible, don't even mention it! And *now*—now that he will have a young wife—he has decided to learn.

"*And* he has a new shiny suit with a high collar." Petit demonstrated how high with his fingers.

"But it's too tight," Oui-Oui said with a giggle.


*February 20, Tuesday.*
My hairdresser was miserable this morning—and now I am, too. "I'm sorry, Your Majesty, but—"

"Monsieur Duplan, you've been dressing my hair for over a decade."

"Queen Caroline is helping the Emperor set up the new household and insists that—"

Insists that from now on, Duplan—*my* Duplan—is to be hairdresser to one woman and one woman only: the soon-to-be-Empress Marie-Louise. "I understand," I said, but fuming, I confess. It is one thing to lose a husband and a crown, quite another to lose a hairdresser.


*[Undated]*

"Not you, too, Monsieur Leroy." How was I to manage without my dress designer? I'd discovered Leroy! I'd been his patroness. Together we'd created a new fashion.

"Your Majesty, you know I would far prefer to make gowns for you," he said tearfully, his manicured hands pressed to his rouged cheeks. "But—"


*[Undated]*

"Dr. Corvisart, please don't tell me that you won't be able to attend me any more."

"Now, now," Dr. Corvisart said thoughtfully, taking my pulse. He sat down across from me, his thumb on his chin—preparing to tell me I was dying, no doubt. "Your Majesty, your eyesight has become quite weak," he observed. "Do you weep often?"

"No," I said, weeping.

He smiled. "I will be honest. Your nerves have suffered quite seriously *and*, dare I say, your heart."

I pressed my hands to my chest. I *was* dying; I knew it! "What's wrong with my heart?" Dr. Corvisart is a heart specialist—he has written a medical text on the subject.

"I believe it is broken," he said gently, handing me a cambric handkerchief. "The waters of Aix-les-Bains are excellent for nerves." Tapping the end of his pencil against his cheek. "June would be a good time to go—not too hot and not too cold," he said, marking it on his calendar.

"But Dr. Corvisart, I've never been to that spa." Aix-les-Bains was southeast, in the mountains bordering Italy.

"Exactly," he said. "No memories."

*Friday night, March 9, quite late.*
Fire-rockets brighten the night sky. Another fête, no doubt, to celebrate the coming wedding—another fête to which I haven't been invited.

Fourteen years ago today, Bonaparte and I married.


*March 12*
*Mon amie, I hope you will be happy with the Château de Navarre. You will see in it another proof of my wish to please. It's not far from the village of Évreux, about thirteen posting houses from Paris—twenty-eight leagues, to be exact. Joachim, who arranged for the purchase, informs me that the château was designed by Mansart, the architect of Versailles, and that it is famed for its gardens. You could go on March 25 and spend the month of April there. Adieu, N.*


*March 12, Monday—Malmaison.*
"Why March 25?" Countess d'Arberg asked, examining the calendar. "Oh," she said, and fell silent.

March 25: two days before Archduchess Marie-Louise is expected to arrive in France.


*March 20.*
Hortense has just left in a flutter. Every king and queen in Europe is coming to the wedding. "Where are all these sovereigns going to stay?" she demanded. Jérôme and Catherine alone had arrived with a suite of over thirty servants. "And all requiring a bed, Maman—impossible!"

I remembered the problems Chastulé and I had had in December, trying to find suitable accommodation for everyone during the peace celebrations. One can't put kings and queens in just any establishment. "Chastulé should be able to help," I suggested.

"You don't know, Maman? Papa sent her packing. He was furious that she refused to stay with you."

Countess d'Arberg caught my eye and smiled.

*March 24.*
Eugène and his lovely Auguste arrived (exhausted). Soon they'll leave to join Bonaparte at Compiègne to join the party that welcomes the young bride to France.

"Aren't you going to the country, Maman?" Eugène asked anxiously. "Didn't Papa buy you a château? Shouldn't you be there now?"

Don't worry, I assured him. "I'm leaving in the morning." I won't be around when *she* comes to Paris.

Don't worry, don't worry, don't worry. The old Empress will be long gone.

*March 29, Thursday—Château de Navarre.*
My château—my "gift" from Bonaparte.

My curse, I fear. The people of Évreux have named it "the saucepan." The ugly cube structure is topped by a bizarre dome, intended at one time to support an enormous statue. One enters into a dark circular hall—the only light from slits two stories up. And all around, opening onto this hall, are strange triangular rooms.

The chair I'm sitting on, like all the furniture here, is ancient and uncomfortable. I had a splintered oak table moved close to the (smoking) fireplace because it is so very cold. None of the windows both opens and closes. Some cannot be opened, but most, unfortunately, cannot be closed, so swollen is the wood from the damp.

Mademoiselle Avrillion is with me now, huddled by the fire. The bedchambers are small, cold, *dismal*. Each day we burn fifteen cartloads of wood and seven sacks of coal, and even so, we shiver.

"The grounds are lovely," Mademoiselle Avrillion said quietly, as if reading my thoughts.

Yes, I agreed: were it not for the bogs and the stagnant pools.

*[Undated]*
Four servants left today, two yesterday . . . and who can blame them?

*[Undated]*
Three cartloads of furniture arrived from Paris this afternoon. The servants descended on them like starving men attacking a banquet table. A distressing melee ensued, the servants fighting over stools and bed frames while the driver cried out for them to stop. (Futile.)


*April 1, April Fish Day—Château de Navarre.*
As I write this, Bonaparte and Marie-Louise are being joined in marriage.

We have made some progress clearing the swamp. Very cold still, bitter. My health suffers.


*April 5, Thursday.*
In spite of my resolve, I have read the accounts of the wedding in the journals. The crowds along the Champs-Élysées were so thick the troops had difficulty restraining them. Eight thousand were in attendance at the ceremony. (Who carried the bride's train? I wonder.) The usual concerts, fire-rockets and fountains gushing with wine. Food was distributed as prizes in a lottery.* (No banquets?) At one signal from the palace, the entire city was illuminated—I would like to have seen *that*.

It's only eight, but I'm going to bed. We've sealed the window cracks with wax, which helps. I wonder if Uncle Fesch remembered to bless their bed.


*April 18—Château de Navarre.*
I could not believe my eyes, for who should be announced this evening as I was playing trictrac with the Bishop of Évreux but my son! I jumped to my feet and threw my arms around him, forgetting all sense of propriety. "Why have you come?" I demanded, suddenly alarmed. Was Hortense all right? Her boys! And what about Bonaparte? Was he . . . ?

Eugène held up his hands. "Everyone's fine. Papa got your letter. He

---

* *The prizes: 4,800 pâtés, 1,200 tongues, 3,000 sausages, 140 turkeys, 360 capons, 360 chickens, and 1,000 legs and 1,000 shoulders of mutton.*

sent me to tell you that he'll give you the money you need for repairs."

"But no letter from him?"

"He said to tell you he would write soon. He wanted me to have a look, see how you're doing." Eugène frowned at the rotting windowsill. "Well," he said, his hands on his hips. "I see the problem."

"It's really much improved." In my joy to see my son, my complaints had vanished. "And the fishing here is excellent, I'm told. Isn't it, Bishop? Oh, forgive me, I've neglected civilities. Prince Eugène, Viceroy of Italy, may I have the honour of introducing you to the Bishop of Évreux. The king of trictrac, we call him."

"A defeated king, alas," the old man said, struggling to rise.

"Please, stay seated," my son insisted, lowering himself onto the (hard) sofa.

"No, no, I only care to get trounced once in an evening," the Bishop said, taking his leave. "Tomorrow evening, Your Majesty, as usual?"

"A charming man," Eugène said, after he'd left.

"He has saved my life here," I said, sitting beside my son and taking his hand. "And how *is* Bonaparte?" How is the *Empress*? I wanted to ask, but dared not. Not yet.

"Papa is well," he said, after a moment's hesitation. "Although—" He grinned. "Although he has had to make a few *adjustments*."

I frowned. Bonaparte did not care for "adjustments."

"She calls him Popo, for one thing."

Emperor Popo?

"She likes her bedroom icy cold."

Bonaparte could not tolerate the cold!

"She becomes *vexed* if rushed."

"Oh-oh."

"And she *refuses* to watch tragedies." Eugène sighed. "Consequently the court is required to sit through a burlesque every single night, while the—"

"Bonaparte as well?" I couldn't imagine him sitting through a comedy.

"—while the Emperor sleeps in his chair."

"And does he . . . ?" I tilted my head, smiled, my finger on my chin—as if posing a light, almost fanciful question. "Does he *love* her, do you think?"

Eugène looked down at the worn carpet. "It's different, Maman."


*Thursday, early afternoon—Château de Navarre.*

A lovely morning with my son. I showed him the new herb bed, my roses and lilacs, the pretty cascades and pools, the charming vistas. "Already you've created a paradise here," he said.

"It's peaceful." Isolated, in truth: but I didn't want him to worry. "And just think: no intrigues."

"No *clan*, you mean," he said, for even the new Empress has been made to suffer. "Even Auguste," he confided.*


*June 10, Sunday—Malmaison.*

I'm back at Malmaison again, at last. It is quiet except for the distant crack and fizz of the fire-rockets. Most of my staff are in Paris at the fêtes in honour of the Emperor and Empress. The servants will return drunken and gay. I plan to be asleep.


*Mon amie, I'd like very much to see you. I need to know that you are happy and well. Never doubt the sincerity of my feelings for you. They shall last until I die. N.*


*June 13.*

Bonaparte arrived this morning precisely at ten. A startled maid directed him to the garden, where I was tending roses. I hurried toward him, then stopped short. (We were being watched.) I *would* not weep!

We sat side by side on a curved stone bench for over an hour—talking

---

* *Eugène's wife Auguste wrote her brother regarding the Bonaparte family: "When one has known them at close quarters one can only despise them. I could never have conceived anything so abominable as their ill-breeding. It is torture to have to go about with such people."*

and talking, as if nothing has changed between us. "I understand Prince Mecklenburg-Schwerin made you a proposal," he said.

"Who told you that?" I'd been touched (and surprised) by the offer, but had not given it more than a moment's thought.

"So it's true? I think you should accept."

"He's young. It wouldn't be fair to him." And in my heart I was still married, still very much in love with my husband.

At my urging, Bonaparte talked to me about Marie-Louise, his difficulties and concerns. (She's not pregnant yet, which worries me.) "And unfortunately she's exceedingly jealous of you," he said. "She was upset to learn that you are back at Malmaison. I had to use the utmost secrecy to come see you today."

"Perhaps if I met her." I want Marie-Louise to regard me as an older sister, as someone she can confide in, learn from. I could help her. I could tell her what pleased the Emperor—and what did not. I could tell her how to tend to his delicate health, how to calm his easily ruffled temper.

"Impossible! She's a child in many ways." Bonaparte stood, paced. "And perhaps she is right, perhaps she has good reason to be jealous. It's likely for the best that you will be going to Aix-les-Bains to take the waters soon."

For the best that I go away—and stay away.


*June 18—Aix-les-Bains.*
I've arrived at the spa, exhausted from days and nights of travel. Already I long for home.


*July 6, 1810*
*Chère Maman,*
   *I've just received shocking news: I don't know what to make of it. In what Papa calls an "act of madness," Louis has abdicated the throne of Holland, disappearing with his beloved dog.**

---

* *The water spaniel jumped out the open window of Louis's carriage at a posting house. It fell under the wheels and was crushed to death.*

*So I am no longer a queen, Maman. I am not unhappy, I confess. I have no ambition but to lead a quiet life with my boys.*

*I hope the spa treatment at Aix-les-Bains is proving beneficial for your nerves. Is it true that Madame de Souza and her son Charles are both there? Perhaps I will visit.*

*Your loving and dutiful daughter, Hortense*

*Note—I spoke with Madame Clari Rémusat at Talleyrand's salon. She looks remarkably well.*

*And another—Empress Marie-Louise is suspected to be with child.*


*September 14, Saint-Cloud*

*Mon amie, the Empress has been with child for four months. She is well. Do not doubt the interest I take in you, the feelings I have for you. N.*


*November 11—Malmaison.*

I am back at Malmaison, but for only a few weeks. I've had a fever, but I'm better today. Dr. Corvisart has ordered rest. The Château de Navarre won't be ready until the end of next week, in any case.


*6:15 P.M.*

Countess d'Arberg has just informed me that an Imperial baptism was held yesterday. Bonaparte and Marie-Louise baptized a number of infants—sons and daughters of the grandees of the Empire. Every baby girl brought to the font was named Josephine, unfortunately. This will only inflame Marie-Louise's jealousy of me. I had hoped it would be different. I don't want to go to damp, cold Navarre right now, but I know I must.


*December 9, 1810, Milan*

*Chère Maman,*

*I'm now the father of a big, healthy son. The labour was difficult, but my lovely Auguste seems to be out of danger. Don't worry—we'll do exactly as the midwife says.*

*My girls are thrilled to have a brother. Augustus Karl Eugen Napoleon he will be named—Augustus, for short. Do you like it? Little Josephine asked me to send you this drawing she made of him. You can see that he has a healthy crop of black hair. Eugénie has decided that Augustus is her doll—she will be two on Christmas Eve. It's hard to believe. Where does the time go?*

*I think your decision to go to Navarre until after the birth is wise, Maman.*

*I must be off—I hear the baby crying!*

*Your very proud and happy son, Eugène*


*March 19, 1811—Château de Navarre, Évreux.*
The villagers of Évreux came in carts harnessed to field nags, reciting verses that they'd written in my honour. They presented me with a bust they'd had made of me, decorated with a crown of wilting spring flowers.


*March 20—Château de Navarre.*
I was resting, nursing a head pain, when I heard the bells begin to ring in town. "The child is born!" I heard someone call out. A gun salute was followed by another a minute later, and then another, and then another. The silence after the twenty-first salute seemed an eternity. And then . . . one more. *Twenty-two* guns: a boy!*

Thank God! My sacrifice has not been in vain. The Empire has an heir.

---

* *Twenty-one guns announced the birth of a girl, a hundred and one a boy. In Paris, on hearing the decisive twenty-second shot, the* Gazette de France *reported: "One single cry, one alone rose in Paris and made the walls of that old palace where the hero's son had just been born tremble, and round which the crowd was so thick that there was not room even for a fly. Flags waved in the air, handkerchiefs fluttered—people ran hither and thither, embracing one another, announcing the news with laughter and tears of joy."*

## In which all is for naught

Eugène embraced me at the door, sweeping me off my feet. "Our prayers have been answered."

"Bonaparte must be overjoyed!"

"He commanded me to come to you immediately," he said, leaning against the wall so that a servant could pull off his muddy boots. "He's going to write to you tonight, he said. He can't take his eyes off the baby."

"Coffee and breakfast cakes," I told a maid. "And a bottle of champagne," I called out to her. "Come," I said, taking my son's hand, pulling him into the drawing room. "I want to hear *all* about it."

And I did. Grands Dieux—the young Empress had very nearly died. "Oh, the poor girl."

"It was awful, Maman. They had to pull the baby out by the feet. Marie-Louise fainted dead away, mercifully. The accoucheur was in a frightful state. *Imagine.* At one point he told Papa that he was going to have to choose between the life of the child and the life of the Empress. Papa never hesitated—he told the doctor to save Marie-Louise."

"But she's all right?"

"It's early yet, of course. She seems well—fatigued, of course."

"And the baby?" King of Rome.

"A big boy."

Mon Dieu—and feet first.

"They thought he was dead, but he revived. A lusty crier," he said, grinning broadly.

"Bonaparte loves children so much." A child, at last—and a *son*. "And so, no doubt, there is much celebrating in Paris?"

"Except on the part of the *sisters*," Eugène said, imitating their long faces. "All they could think of was that their influence would be lessened, that *their* children would lose rank."

"Why does that not surprise me?" I said as the maid came in with a collation. "A toast," I said, handing my son a glass of champagne. "To the King of Rome. To *peace*."

"To the Emperor!"

"*And* to his wife," I said, raising my glass. I sacrificed my marriage for this baby, but young Marie-Louise had very nearly sacrificed her life.

*March 22, Paris*
*Mon amie, I received your letter. Thank you. My son is big and very well. He has my chest, my mouth and my eyes. I hope that he will accomplish his destiny. N.*

*April 2—Malmaison, at last.*
How beautiful Malmaison is, the air sweet, the flowers blooming. I've been all morning with my gardeners. Yet even so my thoughts pull ever toward Paris, toward *them*.

*May 18, Saturday.*
My daughter appeared like a fairy angel, her cheeks pink under a lime green velvet hat with a high feathered crown. She has gained weight, which is encouraging. I suspect she's in love (at last), for she blushed when I inquired about aide-de-camp Charles Flahaut.

She stayed only an hour, telling me all about the new baby. "He's big and handsome—although he does take after *her*," she said, wrinkling her nose.

"But people say the Empress Marie-Louise is pretty."

"Big jaw, Maman." (We giggled, I confess.)

She told me Marie-Louise is childlike in her attachment to the

Emperor, that she weeps to be separated from him for even a minute, but also does not care to travel. "That makes it difficult," I said, concerned. "An emperor must travel." Especially Bonaparte.

"Especially now," Hortense said, filling me in. Russia is refusing to enforce the blockade against England.

"I don't understand. Tsar Alexandre agreed. He gave Bonaparte his word."

"And now there is even talk of war," she said with a grimace.

With Russia? What a terrible thought! "Does it look serious?"

Hortense started to answer when her boys came running; they wanted to ride the pony, they said. "I'm afraid we must go," Hortense told them, tying her hat-strings. "I have an engagement in town."

I persuaded her to leave the children with me for a few days. We waved until her coach was out of sight and then I rang for cakes while the pony was being tacked up. All the while we chattered, chattered, chattered. Petit and Oui-Oui are so sweetly excited about the new baby in the family—"Little King," they call him.

Petit is mature for a six-year-old, I think, but Oui-Oui is still very much a baby. He seems a bit anxious about being three now. "Uncle says I am grown," he told me solemnly. Their Uncle Napoleon, who insists on their company at his midday meal, who supervises their lessons, who is tending a rose garden at Saint-Cloud.

"Himself?" I asked, incredulous.

"He's going to be a gardener when he grows up," Oui-Oui told me.

"Yes, I think so." Oh Bonaparte! "And what about the Empress? Do you see her often?"

Petit shrugged. "I don't think she likes us. We're wiggly, she says."

"But Grandmaman does!" Oui-Oui sang, diving into my arms.


*[Undated]*

Petit, to Mimi: "Maman spoils me when I'm good, but Grandmaman spoils me all the time."

And this afternoon, in the woods, Oui-Oui threw his cap in the air, exclaiming, "Oh, how I love nature!"

How I love *them*.

*[Undated]*

Hortense came for the boys this morning. She looked distressed about something, so I lured her into the rose garden to talk. At last she confessed: Caroline, who is supposed to stand as godmother at the baptism, can't leave Naples. She has asked Hortense to take her place.

"That's quite an honour," I said.

"But the ceremony will be held in Notre-Dame, Maman."

Then I understood. Little Napoleon's tomb is there. "You haven't been in since . . . ?"

She shook her head. "I'm so afraid I'll break down!"


*June 9, Sunday.*

Little King was baptized today. The procession schedule was posted in the market: at two o'clock the Imperial coaches would arrive at Notre-Dame.

I'd planned a number of activities to keep my mind occupied, but with the gun salutes and church bells ringing, it was impossible. At noon I told Mimi: "We're going." She looked alarmed. "Incognito," I assured her. I would wear a broad-brimmed hat and a mask. "I *have* to see." Had to see the Empress, the *baby*. "We'll take the landau." It is a plain vehicle, without insignia, used for riding in the park when the weather is good. "If we leave now, we can get there in time."

I hadn't reckoned on the crowds, however. It was well after three by the time the coach driver had fought his way into the heart of the city. I asked Antoine to let us down a few blocks from the route. "We'll walk."

The streets were thronged. It was all the troops could do to hold people back. Festive banners had been hung from the rooftops and everywhere I looked I saw garlands of flowers. "Let's wait here," I told Mimi, ducking into a recess. Stone steps leading up to the door of a boot-maker's shop afforded a view over the heads of the crowd.

And wait we did: four, four-thirty, five. The crowd began to thin, the hungry citizens reluctantly returning home. Mimi and I edged our way closer to the street. By luck, we found a spot that gave us a clear view. At five-thirty, at last, guns sounded and bells rang.

"What do you suppose that means?" a woman standing beside us asked.

"That the Emperor and Empress have just left the palace," I told her.

"It won't be long now," someone behind us said. My heart thrilled to the distant sound of drums, a marching band.

"They're coming!" a man behind us yelled.

I looked at Mimi and grinned. "It's exciting on the street."

"I see it," a child straddling a man's shoulders cried out as the glittering coronation coach pulled into view, drawn by eight white horses, just like out of a fairy tale. "Where's the baby?" the boy demanded.

Bonaparte, in purple velvet and gold, looked out over the crowd. He's thinking of his work, I thought. He's wondering how long this ceremony is going to take. He's gauging the enthusiasm of the people. He's thinking how uncomfortable his jacket is.

"Empress Marie-Louise is prettier than I expected her to be," Mimi said, covering her face with her shawl.

Marie-Louise. Big lower lip, strong jaw, plump. I thought she'd be more attractive. And she seemed bored—disdainful even. "She's younger than I expected." Only a girl. She was dressed—not very elegantly—in white satin, wearing a diadem of brilliants. *My* diadem.

"The other one used to smile," the woman beside us said. "This one never does."

"I see the baby!" the boy cried out behind us. "He's in the next carriage. He's dressed in white with red ribbons."

Everyone craned to see as the second carriage pulled into view. The King of Rome was held by Madame de Montesquiou, his nanny. The fat, complacent baby was sucking his thumb. I blew him a kiss, my blessing.


*Monday, June 10, 4:30 or so—Malmaison.*

Hortense was full of stories about the Imperial baptism. "I'm so relieved that it's over." She'd gone to Notre-Dame the night before and persuaded the guards to let her in. In the empty cathedral she'd fallen to her knees before little Napoleon's tomb and wept. "It was a good thing," she assured me, seeing my stricken look. "The next day I was able to get through the ceremony without a tear."

Now that the baptism is over, she would like to take the waters, she said. Could I look after the boys? (Gladly!) On leaving, she embraced me somewhat stiffly, and with reserve. Something about the way she walks makes me think of a woman with child. No—*surely* she would tell me.

*Lake Maggiore, September 2, 1811*
*Chère Maman,*
*I must stay away longer than I expected. My health is a little frail.*

*I am sending some trinkets for Petit and Oui-Oui. How I miss them! Embrace them for me. Speak to them often of their maman. I hope to be back in October. Will they even remember me after four months?*

*How are your eyes? (No weeping, remember!) Are you applying the salve I sent you?*

*I smiled, I confess, on learning that you are trying to make "economies." Your heart is too good, maman. Your hand is always open.*

*Ah, my tender, gentle maman—the trials of this world do weigh upon me. We are punished for our pleasures; if only we were rewarded for our pain.*

*Your loving and dutiful daughter, Hortense*

*October 11—Malmaison.*
Hortense returned in time for Petit's seventh-year birthday fête. She is thinner, and has an air of melancholy. I suspect, but will not ask; know, but cannot say.

*[Undated]*
Bonaparte came to see me today. He seemed gloomy—it was clear that there is much on his mind. "Tsar Alexandre refuses to enforce the blockade against England," he said, his hands on his knees. "And he promised! He's shipping hemp to England—he *knows* it's used to make rigging for their Navy. A continental blockade is the only way to get England to the peace table."

I watched Bonaparte go out the gate with a heavy heart. There will be war again soon, I fear. I saw it in his eyes. *Le feu sacré.*

*February 11, 1812, Shrove Tuesday—Malmaison.*

Carnival. Tonight there is a costume ball at the Tuileries—a ball to which I have not been invited, of course. Hortense will be performing a quadrille. She was here yesterday, showing me her intricate choreography, the lovely costumes. "Please come, Maman. I want you to see it! Nobody would know. You'd be in costume."

I told her it was too risky, but that was only a partial truth. I cannot bear the thought of seeing Bonaparte attend to his young wife while I stand alone in the shadows.


*February 12, Ash Wednesday.*

"Your daughter's quadrille was *brilliant*," Mademoiselle Avrillion told me. "You should have heard the cheers! Men were standing on their chairs to see her perform. What a talent she has, every move so precise, so light, so . . ." She made a floating motion with her hand. "So *elegant*. And her troupe of dancers—they were absolutely magical. It brought tears to my eyes to see them. Queen Caroline looked as if she was going to have a fit, she was so angry. Oh, everyone clapped for her dance certainly, but only out of politeness. All that dreadful clumping! And the Emperor? He loved your daughter's quadrille, it was easy enough to see, but otherwise . . . ? Three times I saw him yawn and pull out his timepiece. And when he and the Empress stood to take their leave, you know what I heard him hiss at her? 'Try to be graceful.'"

"Oh, the poor girl."

"Your Majesty, she didn't smile, not even once."


*Monday, early afternoon at Malmaison, March 9.*

Bonaparte stood at a distance, in full view of his aides. It had been months since we'd seen one another, but I had been expecting him. It was, after all, our sixteenth wedding anniversary.

"You've gained weight," he said with a smile.

"So have you." Even so, he looked unhealthy. "How are you, Bonaparte?"

"Well enough." He needed to get back in shape, he said, for the coming campaign. He'd been hunting every day in the Bois de

Boulogne, to toughen himself. He'd managed to "disappear" this morning, in order to visit me.

"You can stay a few minutes?" I invited him to join me on the stone bench under the tulip tree. "I want to hear all about your son." He would have his first birthday in two days.

"He's a big, healthy boy—a bit of a temper, though."

Like his father, I thought fondly. "Petit and Oui-Oui tell me so many stories about him. I think it's wonderful, the time you take with the children."

"Marie-Louise thinks it unnatural."

I'd heard that Marie-Louise rarely saw her baby, that weeks went by without her sending for him. "Certainly it's unusual for a man to enjoy the company of children the way you do." To *dote* on them. "I'd love to see your son, Bonaparte."

"I've been thinking about that," he said. "It will have to be arranged carefully, so that Marie-Louise does not find out."


*[Undated]*
Baron de Canisy, first equerry to the Little King, has let me know that Madame de Montesquiou will be taking the child to the park of Bagatelle next Sunday. I am to wait for her in the little château there.


*Sunday, a beautiful spring day, bright and crisp.*
I rode to Bagatelle, as arranged.* As soon as I saw the Imperial carriage approaching, I went to the little room at the back. Soon the matronly figure of Madame de Montesquiou appeared with the baby in her arms. I stood, bowed: the King of Rome.

"What a *surprise* to see you, Your Majesty," Madame de Montesquiou

---

* Madame de Montesquiou has left the following account: "I arranged with Baron de Canisy that I would tell him as I got into the carriage that I left him the choice where we would go. A little time later, I would call out to him that if the baby needed to stop, we would go to Bagatelle. In effect, we arrived there. In entering the courtyard, Baron de Canisy announced, with a show of surprise, that the Empress Josephine was there. I responded that it was too late to turn back—it would be improper."

said in carrying tones. (This was the fiction we'd arranged.) "I'm going to rest with the baby here for a moment," she told her attendants in the other room.

She sat down beside me, gently prying open the baby's grip on her hat ribbon. "You see what a good baby he is? Watch." She bounced him on her knees to make him laugh.

Big forehead, heavy jaw. "He takes after the Empress," I said, catching the baby's eye, making a funny face at him. He gazed at me for a long moment and then jammed his fist into his mouth. Lively eyes—Bonaparte's eyes.

"But his spirit is that of his father," the nanny said with a laugh, struggling to hold onto the baby as he squirmed to climb down. "Quite *wilful*."

I reached into my basket and brought out a wooden doughnut with brightly coloured objects attached to it, dangled it in front of him. He reached for it, missed, and then reached for it again, closing his fingers around the ring.

"Do you think he'd mind?" I asked, patting my knees.

"He's become particular," she said, "but we could try. He doesn't even let his mother hold him." She shifted the baby onto my lap.

He was quiet, absorbed in the toy. In a reverie of emotion, I inhaled his sweet baby scent, and something else, a hint of lemon. "He smells like the Emperor," I said, grinning (eyes stinging).

"He was with his papa just before we came. His papa who said to send you his regards." She looked at me tenderly. "His papa who still misses you very much, Your Majesty," she added quietly.


*April 17, late afternoon.*
Bonaparte leaned forward, his forearms on his knees. We were sitting, as had become our custom, on the curved stone bench in the rose garden, under the tulip tree. "I've sent for Eugène," he told me. "I'm giving him command of the 4th Corps: eighty thousand men. He should be pleased."

"Then it's true, what everyone is saying, that there is going to be war?" Bonaparte's silence gave me the answer. "Who will act as Regent while you are away?"

"I'm not sure who I can trust."

*April 22—Malmaison.*

Eugène has arrived. First he called on Hortense, who lent him a carriage to take to Saint-Cloud. "So you've already been to see Bonaparte?" I asked.

"He was in meetings. He said to come back for dinner." Eugène looked at the clock on the mantel. "Maybe I have time to go fishing."

I laughed. "What you have time for is a talk with your mother. I want to hear all about the children." Josephine, five; Eugénie, three; Augustus, one (already).

"And Auguste is due again in only three months," Eugène said, proudly showing me the chain of miniature portraits he carried with him, one for each child. "I promised her the war would be over by then."

The *war*. "She's going to miss you." And worry.

"I already miss *her*, Maman." He started when the pendulum clock began to strike the hour. "Papa's waiting!"

*9:15 P.M., a balmy evening.*

"Well?" I demanded, meeting Eugène at the door. I'd been anxiously waiting for him to return.

"I got to hold the baby—Little King, as the boys call him. But only for a moment. He was fussing—teething, his nurse said. Twelve teeth at thirteen months bodes well, don't you think?"

"And your meeting with Bonaparte?"

He took off his hat and ran his fingers through his hair. "He asked me to act as Regent while he's on campaign."

"That's wonderful!" I said, pretending to be surprised.

"I refused, Maman."

I put my hand to my chest. Refused?

"It's a great honour, I know, but how could I sit at a desk in Paris while my men were fighting?"

So much more was at stake than a battle or two! Didn't he see that? "What did Bonaparte say?" I asked, disheartened.

"He said he'd have felt the same."

*April 30.*
Every able man in the Empire, it seems, has rushed to join La Grande
Armée.* I am guarded by sixteen disabled soldiers, who sadly must stay
behind. All of my good horses have been drafted.


*May 2, Saturday, late afternoon.*
Bands blaring, bells pealing, Eugène and his men left for Poland this
morning, their muskets decorated with flowers, people hanging out the
windows cheering: our glorious Grande Armée.


*Friday, May 8, storm threatening.*
"I've come to say goodbye," Bonaparte said, his eyes solemn.
   "It has been a long time since you left on campaign."
   "I had hoped it wouldn't come to this."
   Yes, certainly. The marriage to Marie-Louise, the birth of an heir—all
this should have secured a lasting peace.
   "At least I leave knowing that if anything should happen to me, the
Empire will endure in my son."
   "You will miss him."
   We were both of us uncomfortable, both aware that this was the first time
he'd be going into battle without a "good luck" embrace. He looked at me
for a long moment, and then his footman opened the carriage door. I
watched the carriage pull through the gates, not even daring to blow a kiss.

* The Grande Armée (Grand Army) was the largest army of all time. It was made up of
200,000 men from France, 150,000 from Germany, 80,000 from Italy, 60,000 from Poland and
110,000 volunteers from other countries.

## *In which we are defeated*

*November 18, 1812—Malmaison.*
We've been months without news, rumours only. We wait and we worry. We worry and we pray.


*November 30, Monday.*
A young woman, not more than twenty, accompanied by an elderly maid, came out to Malmaison today. Mademoiselle Aurélie de Beaumont, she introduced herself, turning her straw hat in her white-gloved hands. Her father, Monsieur de Beaumont, was the bosom friend of Monsieur Bataille.

Auguste Bataille? "Monsieur Bataille is one of my son's aides."

She nodded, withdrawing some folded papers from the crown of her hat. "He has been sending my father letters."

"Of the campaign?" My heart jumped. News—*true* news, is rare. The official bulletins sent to Paris cannot be trusted, I know.

"My father suggested that I copy the letters out for you. He thought you might desire to have news of your son, Your Majesty."

"Yes," I said, almost breathless.

"This is one of the originals." Aurélie showed me a scrap of paper. The writing was minuscule, crossed.* "Sometimes I have to use a glass to make it out." She promised to return when the next letter came.

---

* *A letter was said to be "crossed" when the letter-writer filled a sheet of paper, then turned the page sideways and continued writing across the filled-in sheet.*

*Plock. Mon ami, we've been in this Polish town for almost two weeks, await-*
*ing orders from the Emperor. It feels as if we're in the middle of nowhere. A*
*number of us have fallen ill. The Prince Eugène's baggage and horses have*
*finally arrived so he will be able to tour his regiments. Salut et amitiés,*
*Bataille.*

*Thorn. Mon ami, we're expecting the Emperor any day. I've been busy trying*
*to find food for the troops and hay for the horses. We were allotted some corn,*
*three hundred bulls and thirty thousand bushels of oats, but the corn was*
*green and the horses got colic, and many of the soldiers have dysentery from*
*the sour black bread. Salut, Bataille.*

*Soldau. Mon ami, from Thorn we marched to Soldau. The villages are*
*wretched. Prince Eugène sleeps in a tent, in spite of the cold. We have eighty*
*thousand men to feed and only a few sacks of corn. Amitiés pour toujours,*
*Bataille.*

*Late evening.*
Plock, Thorn, Soldau. I've found a map in Bonaparte's cabinet and am
tracing the route. They are so very far away.

*Mon ami, we are in Russia now, looking for an army to fight. It's a dull*
*landscape—nothing but trees (a few birches) and sand. It's after ten P.M. but*
*so bright I am writing this without a candle. The sun wakes us at two in the*
*morning. Toujours, Bataille.*

*Vitebsk. Mon ami, how can we go on? By day we boil; by night we freeze.*
*We've over three hundred sick soldiers—our men are dying of sunstroke.*
*Thousands of horses have perished. The Emperor arrived last night. He insists*
*on pressing on to Smolensk. Ten more days, if we survive. Adieu, Bataille.*

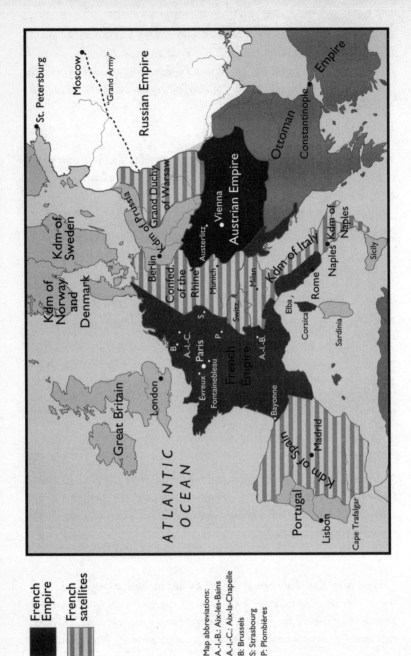

French Empire

French satellites

Map abbreviations:
A.-l.-B.: Aix-les-Bains
A.-l.-C.: Aix-la-Chapelle
B: Brussels
S: Strasbourg
P: Plombières

*December 3—Malmaison.*
I'm ill with concern. Bataille's letters both reassure and dismay. I worked all morning in the hothouse with the gardeners, but my thoughts turn always toward the northeast, toward Russia, that barren land.

*Mon ami, we've made it to Smolensk, a heap of smoking ruins. Moscow is "only" two hundred miles more, the Emperor tells us—but one mile more will kill us. The farther we chase after the enemy, the farther we are from home, the farther from food and shelter. Amitiés, Bataille.*

*Mon ami, the Russian army has come to a stop—at last we will see battle. Some Cossacks were taken prisoner—savages with bandy legs. They gulped down tumblers of brandy as if it were water, holding their empty glasses out for more. Their horses are stumpy and have long tails. They're much impressed by King Murat, his plumes and glitter. They have asked to have him as their "hetman." They're welcome to him! Salut, Bataille.*

*Mon ami, it was bloody. Prince Eugène was rallying his troops when thousands of Cossacks fell on his reserve. He galloped back to face them head-to-head. A victory, yes, but hard won. Adieu, excéllent ami, Bataille.*

*Mon ami, as we crested a hill and caught sight of the city, the soldiers broke into a run crying out, "Moscow! Moscow!" The spires and onion-shaped domes glittered in the sun like a mirage—and a mirage it is, for the Russians, a barbarous race devoid of all honour, have set fire to it, the most magnificent ancient city in all of Europe. As I write this, flames light up the sky. We are sheltered in a small wooden house outside the city. The landscape is dreary: cabbage fields and more cabbage fields. Amitiés, Bataille.*

*December 14—Malmaison, cold, but bright.*
I was honoured this afternoon by a visit from Countess Walewska and her child: "the Polish wife" and her son by Bonaparte. (He looks *just* like Bonaparte—I was so moved.) It has taken numerous entreaties to persuade the young Countess to call on me, but now that she has, she will return, I hope. We are uniquely united by our prayers for a singular man. She turned pale and very nearly swooned after I showed her the letters from Bataille.

*Mon ami, the Tsar has not responded to the Emperor's request for peace. King Murat has persuaded the Emperor that the Russians are in disarray and that the Cossacks are ready to quit. Therefore, we press on. Amitiés, Bataille.*

*Mon ami, King Murat was defeated by the Cossacks so we're on the move again, heading for home, if we can make it. We're a sorry spectacle, soldiers pushing wheelbarrows of looted treasure, a rabble of prostitutes following after. The cannon keep getting stuck in the mud. À toi pour toujours, Bataille.*

*Mon ami, Prince Eugène had a glorious battle, worthy of every honour, but we've suffered heavy casualties, and now a frost has lamed hundreds of our horses overnight. In consequence, the Emperor ordered all the carts emptied into a lake. We watched as priceless works of art sank through the ice. The enormous cross of Ivan the Terrible was the last to disappear, like some dreadful omen of doom. Cossacks harass us. They encircle us, whooping like wild beasts. We march in a freezing fog. We are at the end of the world. Bataille.*

[Undated]
"Your Majesty, would you prefer it if I did not bring you the letters?" Mademoiselle Aurélie asked, clutching her straw hat.

"No! Please, you *must* bring them," I said, giving her two of my rings.

• 314 •

*Mon ami, what was left of the Grande Armée was destroyed on the icy marshes. Those who escaped drowning were set upon by Cossacks. Prince Eugène managed to save what was left of his troops. Luck stays with him, such as it is. Two horses have been shot from under him. Bataille.*

*December 17, Thursday, chilly.*
A stunned despair hangs over Paris. The extent of our losses in Russia—the death of so many of our men—has finally been revealed in *Le Moniteur*. Every heart is filled with the terrible apprehension that a loved one will likely not return. I am sick with fear for Eugène, Bonaparte.

*December 19, Saturday—Malmaison.*
The familiar sight of Bonaparte's courier cantering up the drive stopped my heart. I pushed the window open, leaned out. "Monsieur Moustache! What's happened?"

"The Emperor is at the palace," he yelled up.

"Bonaparte? He's in *Paris*?" How was that possible?

Moustache nodded, catching his breath. "He sent me to tell you. And to let you know that your son is well."

That's the last I remember, for I fainted.

*Sunday.*
Bonaparte looked like a Cossack in his bear coat and hat. His face was dark, burnt from the sun. "I can't stay long." He took my hand, did not let it go. "Come outside."

We sat on the cold stone bench under the tulip tree, its branches bare, the winter garden grey and featureless. I listened to his account with tears in my heart. He'd hastened back to calm the populace, he said. He feared people would panic on learning the extent of the losses. The campaign would have been glorious if the Russian winter had not come early, and had not been so severe. All he needed was to raise another army.

I could not speak. *Another* army? Where will the soldiers come from?

Did he not see that we are a nation of women—a nation of women in mourning? The only men left are either old or crippled.

Four hundred thousand is all it would take, he said.


*February 28, 1813.*
Carnival season opens as the wounded return, yet even so the fêtes and the balls go on—"the balls for wooden legs," people call them now.

Every day, it seems, we learn of some new tragedy. One of Carlotta's brothers has died in Russia. Mademoiselle Avrillion's aunt has lost two sons, and the third son who did return lost his hands due to frost.


*March 6.*
We've been working all week making lint bandages for the wounded. My drawing room looks like a hospital.


*Wednesday, April 14—Malmaison.*
Bonaparte and I sat for two hours this morning under our tulip tree. He told me charming stories about his son, now two and temperamental, and complained of his young wife (she wipes her mouth after he kisses her). Then he began to speak of the war, the coming campaign, his conviction that he will be victorious this time, that a peace will be signed. "But not a dishonourable peace. Not a peace at any price."

I want to believe him—and why should I not? Has he not wrought miracles?

He touched my hand before he left, promising to give Eugène my love. "My prayers are always with you."

"I was happy here," he said, looking out over the gardens.


*April 26, Mansfeld*
*Chère Maman,*
   *Forgive my penmanship: I've developed a bit of rheumatism.*

*My army is on the move again, riding out to join the Emperor. I'm confident that this new campaign will be over quickly and that soon there will be peace. Both sides long for it.*

*Take care, lovely Maman, and give my love to my sister and her boys. We sing her songs often—they give us courage.*

*Your loving son, Eugène*

*May 5.*
Bonaparte has had a victory! "Funds up to 76.90," Mimi said.

*Friday, May 7.*
*Another* victory! Cannons have been booming all morning.

*May 12, 1813, Lützen*
*Chère Maman,*
*The big battle has been won. The Emperor is allowing me to return to Milan—to my beautiful Auguste and our children. I'm to raise and train another army.*

*I bade the Emperor Godspeed about an hour ago. He looked worn. We are all weary. I've been at war for a year.*

*Your devoted son, Eugène*

*June 11, a glorious day.*
At last, an armistice has been signed. Dare we believe we shall have peace?

*August 23, Monday, early evening.*
The Emperor of Austria has denounced the armistice, declared war on France. Mon Dieu—Marie-Louise's *father*. How could he turn on us—turn on his own *daughter*?

*October 30—Malmaison.*
Disaster at Leipzig. I wept when I read the words: *The French army has lost.* Reduced to only forty thousand men!

I've locked myself in my room—to pace, pray, weep. Against all better judgement, I've written Bonaparte.*

*November 9.*
Bonaparte is back, at the head of his defeated army. He returned without fanfare, without cannon or marching bands.

*December 2.*
On this, the anniversary of the coronation, on Bonaparte's "lucky" day, I received a distressed letter from Milan—from my lovely Auguste. Her father, jolly King Max of Bavaria, has joined the enemy! Furthermore, he tried to persuade Eugène to do so as well.

Of course Eugène refused. "God gave me an angel as a husband," Auguste wrote. And God gave an angel to him.

*January 3, 1814, Monday.*
Hortense's cheeks were flushed. "Maman, terrible news! An army of over one hundred thousand Cossacks has crossed the Rhine and is headed for Paris. I've never seen the Empress Marie-Louise so upset. Do you know what she told me? That she takes bad luck with her wherever she goes, that everyone who comes near her is made to suffer."

"And what did Bonaparte say?"

"He told her that's superstitious nonsense."

"No—I mean about the Cossacks!"

"He said not to worry—he has a plan."

---

* *Josephine wrote: "Sire, I saw in the bulletin that you suffered a great loss and I wept. Your sorrows are mine, they will always be in my heart. I am writing you because I am not able to resist the need to tell you this, in the same way that I am unable to stop loving you with all my heart."*

*January 14.*

A call has been sounded: soldiers needed.

"I'm going to volunteer," Oui-Oui told me in all seriousness.

"Me, too," Petit echoed.

I explained that there were age requirements.

"Uncle said he wanted us."

"Everyone," Oui-Oui explained gravely. "Even *old* men."

Even old men, indeed: dear old Gontier just informed me that he was going to enlist. "Gontier, you mustn't!" He is over sixty, I am sure.

But nothing I could do or say would dissuade him. I gave him a good pony, one of the few I have left, so many have been drafted.


*Saturday, January 22.*

Bonaparte stood by his carriage as he told me that he was leaving for battle in the morning. In three months he would be either victorious or dead.

*Le feu sacré.* "I didn't come to make you weep," he said, perplexed by my response.

I tried to dissemble my fear. All of Europe has joined forces against him. He has only fifty thousand men. Victory is impossible!

But "impossible" is not a French word, I reminded myself. "May I—" Kiss you, I almost said. "I would like to wish you good luck." Dropping a curtsey.

Bonaparte looked at me for a long moment. "Remember me, Josephine," he said, stepping back, tipping his hat.


*February 4.*

Terrible rumours—it's being said that Bonaparte's troops have been repulsed, forced to retreat onto French soil. I don't know what to believe. I sent Mimi into Paris to find out what she could. She returned with a worried look: prayers are being said at Notre-Dame and the Louvre's collections are being packed.

*February 18, 1814, Milan*
*Chère Maman,*

*I fear this will distress you terribly, but you must know. Caroline and Joachim have joined the enemy and this morning Joachim made an open declaration of war against the Army of Italy—against me. I do not need to tell you the degree of my disgust—nor the depth of my sympathy for the Emperor. Such a "family" he must suffer.*

*Your loyal son, Eugène*

*March 28.*
People are coming into Paris in droves, fleeing in advance of the enemy.

"Bonaparte will save us," I assured Hortense, rolling lint bandages, stacking them up. "He calculates everything so carefully, taking into account every possible outcome. Surprise has always been his strategy. No doubt this is part of his plan."

*[Undated]*
A cobbler from town just came to warn me that he has met wounded soldiers on the road. They've told him the enemy is near. What does that mean: *near?*

*Tuileries. Maman, we've learned that the enemy is approaching from the south. Empress Marie-Louise intends to flee Paris in the morning with the baby. You must go to Navarre—immediately. Take every precaution. Don't worry about me and the boys. I'll get word to you. Hortense.*

*March 29—Mantes, 7:20 P.M.*
Hortense's note came after midnight, in the dead of night. I woke everyone, gave the order that we would be leaving Malmaison in the morning, taking as much as we could with us. We've decided to leave the farm

animals, the orangutan and the birds in the care of the groundskeeper, but to take the pugs and the horses.

Mimi and I stayed up stitching my gems into the lining of a wadded skirt. The remaining jewellery we put into strongboxes, along with the oak box of Bonaparte's letters—my true treasure. It was almost three in the morning when we finished. We would be leaving early, at seven—there was not much time for sleep. I bade Mimi goodnight and got into bed. I lay there for some time, listening to the spring rain, thinking of Empress Marie-Louise all alone in that big ormolu bed in the Tuileries Palace. Was she sleeping? Or, like me, was she tormented with fear and doubt—and *guilt*, surely, at fleeing Paris.

I got out of bed. Taking the night candle, I slipped down the stairs and walked through the château. Would my beloved Malmaison be ravaged by Cossacks, my treasures carried off? I ran my fingers over the harp strings—the light, rippling sound brought back the memory of summer evenings. What a magical place Malmaison has been—what a magical *life* I've had here.

I went into the study—the room Bonaparte had worked in, built an empire in. I spun the globe. Where is he?

I returned to bed with a heavy heart. At dawn I woke sweating. It was grey and raining, a cold spring drizzle that made me shiver. No point lighting a fire, I told Mimi, slipping into my wadded gown.

We didn't reach Mantes until nightfall. It was slow going with all the horses in the pouring rain.

This inn is full of people escaping Paris. I am Madame Mercier, I tell them. Nothing is known; everything whispered. I am dead with exhaustion, but rest eludes me. Where is Hortense as I write this? Where is Bonaparte? What is happening in Paris?

## In which I entertain the enemy

*April 1, 1814—Navarre.*

It was the sound of boys' voices in the cavernous entry that brought me to my feet. I very nearly collided with Hortense at the door. "Mon Dieu, it *is* you!" I threw my arms around her, pressed her to my heart. "Forgive me, we've been tormented not knowing."

The servants crowded into the room. Hortense paused before announcing, "We've capitulated."

There was a moment of incomprehension, followed by cries of disbelief.

"Where is the Emperor?" I demanded.

"Maman, I don't know! All I know is that a treaty of surrender has been signed and that the Empress and the baby are in the southwest, at Blois."

*Saturday, April 2.*

"The army wouldn't take me," old Gontier said sheepishly. He returned to Malmaison on my sturdy little pony only to be told that we'd fled to the north. He's been three days travelling to reach us.

He left Paris on Wednesday, he said. In the morning he heard cannon in the direction of Saint-Chaumont. As he headed out, he saw Russian soldiers on the road. "Well-behaved lads wearing caps with green leaves stuck in them." There had been no sign of plunder or violence, he said, which is a great relief to us all. (Though hard to believe.)

*Sunday.*

As Hortense slept, I took the boys to Mass at the cathedral in Évreux. The town was quiet—there was little to indicate that France had fallen. The Imperial sign over the posting house had been taken down, but nothing put up in its place.

"Are you sad, Grandmaman?" Petit asked. He is tall for a boy of nine; his name no longer suits him.

"Very."

"I am, too," Oui-Oui said, snuggling into me for warmth. The weather was bright, but brisk. "I had to leave my rocking horse behind," he told me, his lip quivering.

"I will get you a new one," I promised.

"No, Grandmaman," Petit solemnly informed me. "Maman says we must suffer like everyone, that we are nobodies now."


*April 4, Monday—Château de Navarre.*

At last, a note from my groundskeeper: Russian guards have been assigned to protect Malmaison. He included a copy of *Le Moniteur*, but all that it contained was Tsar Alexandre's proclamation.

Where is Bonaparte? What is happening?


*April 7.*

Shattering news. The Pretender is to take back the throne.


*Later . . .*

Worse news yet. *Talleyrand* is at the head of the new provisional government, in league with the enemy.

Chameleon! Opportunist! That he should prove a traitor does not surprise me in the least. Indeed, I am calmed by the revelation of his true colours. But what dismays me beyond measure is the story that it was *Clari* who helped him, that it was she who opened the gates of Paris to the enemy.

We've received journals from Paris. I'm filled with disgust, a bitter taste. Is there no honour? No loyalty? Bonaparte's marshals—men he favoured and raised to glory—have rushed to publicly proclaim themselves in favour of the Pretender. These men—*soldiers*—swore fidelity and allegiance to Bonaparte, and now they attack him, portray him as an ogre.

Disillusion has weakened my heart. Defeat at the hands of the enemy is nothing compared to this corruption from within. I weep for Bonaparte, for us all.

*April 8.*
Mimi woke me in the night, tugging gently on my toes. "There's someone downstairs who would like to see you, Yeyette—Monsieur de Maussion. The bookkeeper," she reminded me, lighting a lamp. "He has news of the Emperor, he said."

"Of Bonaparte?" I sat up, my heart pounding.

Monsieur de Maussion stood by the dying fire in the drawing room. He was wearing a short green hunting coat. A small travelling pistol hung from his broad belt. "Your Majesty," he said, bowing stiffly from the waist. "I beg forgiveness for disturbing your repose."

"I am told you have news of the Emperor," I said, taking a seat, neglecting civilities in my anxiety. I gestured to him to sit down in the chair opposite, but he stood ramrod-stiff, as if at attention.

"The Emperor is at Fontainebleau," he announced. "He has abdicated and will be sent into exile. I've been—"

"Exile?" I was alarmed, but relieved, as well. At least Bonaparte was not to be executed.

"To Elba, Your Majesty. I've been—"

"Where is Elba?"

"Elba is a small island in the Mediterranean, Your Majesty, separated from the Italian mainland by the Strait of Piombino. I've been—"

"A very *small* island, is it not, Monsieur?"

"Between one and three-and-a-half leagues in width, Your Majesty, six leagues in length. I've been—"

"But that's smaller than the park at Malmaison!"

"I do not recall the dimensions of the park at Malmaison, Your Majesty. I've been—"

"Have you *seen* the Emperor, Monsieur de Maussion? Have you talked to him?"

"I have seen him, Your Majesty, but no, I have not spoken with him. I've been—"

"*Please* tell me: how did he look to you?"

Monsieur de Maussion frowned. "Like the Emperor, Your Majesty."

I pressed my fist against my mouth. If only I could see Bonaparte! I would know in a glance how he was feeling. I would know if he was sleeping, if he was eating, if his stomach—oh, his sensitive stomach!—was upsetting him. I would know by the abruptness of his movements if a falling fit might be threatening. "Yes, of course," I said weakly, remembering myself. "Did he look . . . *well*, did you think?" I asked, using the cuff of my sleeve to dry my eyes. It wasn't fair, I knew, to ask this man to see with the eyes of a wife.

"Yes, Your Majesty. I've been asked by the French Ambassador to Russia, the Duke de Vicenza, to—"

"De Caulaincourt?"

Monsieur de Maussion nodded. "Yes, he asked me to—"

"De Caulaincourt is with the Emperor?" Gentle, aristocratic Armand de Caulaincourt. It would comfort me to know that he was with Bonaparte.

"Yes, Your Majesty. He sent me expressly to tell you to do what you can." This last in a rush of words for fear I would yet again interrupt.

"What does that mean?" *Do what you can.*

"It means that you try to seek favour for yourself and your children at the court of the enemy, Your Majesty."


*April 13.*

A note from Armand de Caulaincourt. He urges me to return to Paris—it's in my best interest, he said. It behooves me to show myself, press my case with the Tsar. It is the Emperor's wish. *Je le veux.*

And then, a note at the bottom, in the secretary's tidy script: *Your Majesty, it is urgent that they be persuaded to be charitable with respect to the Emperor.*

I'm packing.

*4:45 P.M.*

"Very well," Hortense said, but in a tone that suggested she did not approve.

"You don't think I should go," I said.

"Do what you want, Maman," she said, "but I won't be going with you."

"You'll stay here?" I was relieved, frankly. She and the boys would be safer at Navarre.

"I've decided I must go to Blois, to see the Empress."

"But Hortense, that's risky!" A show of allegiance to the Empress would be held against her. "You must think of your future, and that of your boys."

"It's my duty, Maman," she insisted. "Marie-Louise is young and very much alone. Imagine the torment she must feel! You have raised me to do what is honourable."

"I understand," I said, turning away, both furious and proud.

*April 15, Friday—Malmaison.*

It was disconcerting to see Russian guards at the gates to Malmaison. I tried to explain who I was, but it wasn't until my groundskeeper came hobbling that I was allowed in. "What happened?" I asked, alarmed, for he had bandages on his head and one arm was in a sling.

"Cossacks. I tried to stop them, Your Majesty, but—" He shrugged, a movement that made him wince. "They broke the leg off the table in the entryway, but that was all. It was the orangutan that scared them away."

And so it was with a sense of disbelief that I walked back into my home of priceless treasures to find it all untouched. But for the Russians at my gate, one would not know that the nation had fallen.

*[Undated]*

Oh, the stories: that the theatres in Paris closed for only one day—the day Paris capitulated—that the actors carried on even as cannon boomed. That it was Joseph Bonaparte who gave the order to raise the white flag of surrender and then disappeared, not even handing over command. (Just as he had in Madrid—the coward!) That everyone in Paris is wearing a Bourbon white rosette, that Bourbon banners are everywhere. (Ingrates!) That the Pretender's brother, the Count d'Artois, has arrived, that he wears a powdered wig topped by a silly hat. That his servants wear strange Gothic tunics with enormous crosses hanging from the buttonholes. That Cossacks sleep with their boots on. That shopkeepers are doing a brisk trade. That in the Tuileries Palace they have simply pasted Bourbon fleur-de-lis over the Imperial bees. That Talma played for the Tsar and was forced by the crowd to proclaim, "Long live King Louis XVIII," but left the stage in tears. (Poor man.) That Empress Marie-Louise's father, the Emperor of Austria, paraded down the Champs-Élysées in full daylight, not even trying to hide the fact that he had profited from his daughter's misfortune. That the people were falling over themselves to bow before the new regime, claiming that they'd detested "that monster" Napoleon. That even his family has deserted him.

How devastating all this is.

*Almost midnight (can't sleep).*

Clari looked like a matron in her bonnet, clutching a wicker basket. "I was afraid you would not receive me," she said, fingering the gold cross that hung from a yellow velvet ribbon around her neck.

"It is not in my nature to hold a grudge," I said, feeling vindictive nonetheless. She had betrayed Bonaparte, the nation, *me*. "Speak your business." And go.

"The Tsar Alexandre begs permission to call on you."

"I take it you are his servant, then?"

"I help out where I can." Her sharp nose in the air.

"I understand you helped the enemy enter Paris." Clari and Talleyrand. "Such helpfulness is well rewarded, I expect."

"I did not intend to hurt *you*."

"I think you should go."

"Will you consent to receive the Tsar? It would be to Napoleon's advantage for you to do so."

"How dare you speak his name!" A vase fell to the floor, shattered.

"He murdered the Duke d'Enghien!"

"You're a fool. If anyone can be held responsible for the death of the Duke d'Enghien, it is your friend Talleyrand. He's the one who persuaded Bonaparte to arrest the Duke."

"He told me you would say that."

I took two steps toward her, trembling.

"Forgive me, Your Majesty," she whispered, backing out through the door.


*April 16, Saturday.*

Tsar Alexandre arrived attended by only a few guards. "I am honoured," he said, bowing before me. He is attractive, a man of middle years—thirty-five? thirty-six?—imposingly tall, with golden curls, pale blue eyes.

I was surprised (and reassured) by his show of respect. I am the ex-wife of an ex-emperor. He is the victor, ruler of one of the most powerful countries on earth. "Your Majesty," I answered with self-loathing, "the honour is all mine." As I spoke, he stooped close, and I recalled that he was slightly deaf. "The honour is all mine," I repeated, raising my voice, flushing (knowing the servants could hear).

I took him on the usual tour of Malmaison—through the gallery, the music room, the theatre, the rose garden, the hothouse—and even through the dairy (my Swiss cows interested him). I found him easy to talk to, for his French is excellent and his mind of an inquiring nature. (So like Bonaparte in that respect.) He wanted to know about the grafting technique my gardeners had been using with success on evergreen shrubs, how much sun was advisable on tulip beds, what proportion of cow-dung was added to the compost used for the auriculas, how much milk my cows yielded.

We paused in front of the hothouses, talking of theatre: he'd been to see Talma in *Iphigénie en Aulide* at the Théâtre Français and had been tremendously moved. "Although," he said, "there was an incident after-ward that was painful to witness, I confess."

"I have heard of it." Poor Talma—I was beginning to fear his mind had turned. He'd physically attacked Geoffroy for having written a critical review.

"The actor remains attached to the Emperor. His feelings are honourable and should be respected."

"We *all* remain attached to the Emperor," I said with more heat than was wise.

"I understand," the Tsar said with feeling.

But it is you who have destroyed him! my heart cried out.

It was then that we were—fortunately perhaps—diverted by the sound of children's voices: Petit and Oui-Oui! They raced down the path, stopping short when they saw the tall and imposing stranger beside me. "Come, come," I said, stooping to embrace them. Why were they at Malmaison? Hortense had taken the boys with her to Blois, to see the Empress Marie-Louise. "I'd like to introduce you to Tsar Alexandre of Russia."

Petit looked concerned. "It's all right," I whispered. "Make your best bow."

The Tsar smiled and bowed in turn.

"Where is your mother?" I asked anxiously.

"She's coming *slowly*. She has to stop to admire *everything*," Oui-Oui said, dramatically rolling his eyes.

"We didn't stay long at Blois," Petit informed us, pulling at a ringlet. (Oh dear, I thought. Now the Tsar will know that Hortense went to see Empress Marie-Louise.)

"We've been in a carriage for *days*," Oui-Oui said, rolling his eyes yet again.

Hortense had stopped beside one of the rose beds. I waved to catch her eye. She smiled—*There* you are!—then frowned, twirling her percale sun umbrella, taking in the figure beside me.

"We're over here, Maman," Petit said.

"With a Cossack," Oui-Oui cried out, throwing up his cap.

"Shush," Petit said, frowning at his younger brother.

Tsar Alexandre laughed. (I was relieved.)

"I'm so happy to see you," I said, embracing my daughter.

"Malmaison looks fine. Nothing was taken?"

"Thanks to the Tsar Alexandre," I said, introducing my daughter.

"Honoured," she said coolly, with only a slight dip of her head.

"Can I offer you both an ice and tea?" Hortense wasn't helping!

"Cossacks drink vodka," Oui-Oui said.

"Pardon?" Hortense said with a reproving look.

"I'd be delighted," the Tsar said. "And yes, if you had vodka . . ."
Pulling the brim of the child's cap down over his eyes.


"He impresses me," I told Hortense after the Tsar had left. "He seems sincere in his desire to put an end to the conflicts."

Hortense shrugged.

"You disapprove of my receiving him, don't you?"

"We discussed this at Navarre, Maman. I understand your reasoning perfectly."

"Then why . . . ?"

"It was disconcerting, I admit, seeing *you* entertaining the enemy."

"Hortense, Tsar Alexandre has the power to help you and your children." As well as the power to ruin them.

"There is nothing we need."

"Now is not the time for idealism! Do you want to be exiled from France, never to return? It might be wise to be civil, at least for the sake of your boys. And, need I remind you, for Eugène's sake, *my* sake—*Bonaparte's* sake. Who do you think must make the decision about Bonaparte's future? The Tsar—that man you treated so rudely."

We both burst into tears. "Oh, forgive me, Maman! I've had such a terrible two days."

And then it all came out: how after Hortense's long and arduous trip to Blois, the Empress Marie-Louise had kept her waiting, how when she'd finally received Hortense, she'd told her that it would be best, perhaps, if Hortense left, because her father, the Emperor of Austria, was coming to get her, and how the one thing that *really* worried her was that her father might force her to follow Bonaparte into exile.

I sat for a moment in stunned silence. "But I thought Marie-Louise was sincerely attached to Bonaparte. I thought you said she couldn't stand to be separated from him even for one day."

"I thought so, too, Maman."

Poor Bonaparte! Everyone is deserting him, even his wife. "And the boy?" The son he loves so much.

Hortense smiled sadly. "He was so happy to see Petit and Oui-Oui. You know what he told them? That he knows he's not a king any more because he doesn't have any pages. Madame de Montesquiou told me he cries for his papa."

I stood and went to the fireplace, holding my hands out over the embers. "I'd go to Bonaparte in a minute if I could."

Hortense came up behind me, held me in her arms. "I know you would, Maman."


*Early evening.*

The sight of the horse cantering up the laneway puzzled me. The rider looked familiar, yet I could not place him. I went to the garden gate, my basket full of cut roses. "Moustache?" But I wasn't sure. "What's happened to your . . . ?" I pointed to my upper lip.

"I cut it off and gave it to the Emperor," he said, handing a letter to me. "I told him he already has my heart; he might as well have my namesake."

How touching, I wanted to say, but could not speak. The letter was from Bonaparte.


*Fontainebleau*

*I wrote you on the eighth of this month (it was Friday), but perhaps you never received my letter. The fighting was still going on so it may have been intercepted.*

*I won't repeat what I said—I complained then about my situation. Today I am better. I've had an enormous weight lifted from me.*

*So many things have not been told. So many have a false opinion! I loaded benefits on thousands of poor wretches. What did they do for me? They betrayed me—yes, all of them. With the exception of good Eugène, so worthy of you and me.*

*Adieu, my dear Josephine. Resign yourself as I have. I will never forget you.*
*N.*

"Thank you," I told Moustache, slipping a diamond ring off my hand. He'd aged during his years as Bonaparte's courier; his face was lined with furrows. "How is he?"

"The Emperor?"

I leaned toward him. "Yes." Tell me.

"He's . . . not well, Your Majesty." His voice had a pleading quality.

I nodded. And?

He looked away. "I'm told he tried to poison himself."

There was a century of silence, heavy and ponderous and dangerous. "*Tried?*"

"Apparently it was not strong enough."

"Thank you, Moustache," I said weakly, turning away.

Grand Dieu. I *must* get to him.

*Very late, past 2:00 A.M., I think.*
Perhaps I'm going mad. My emotions rage within me. Oh, Bonaparte! I feel so helpless—

*Monday.*
Shortly after dinner I called for my carriage. "Fontainebleau," I told the driver.

"But Your Majesty . . ." It would take hours and the roads were not safe, Antoine said. "And what about an escort?" The men were just sitting down to eat.

"I won't be needing them," I informed him. "I'll be travelling incognito." Alone.

The leather mask was curiously reassuring. I was of the world, but not part of it. Lulled by the sway of the coach, I watched the sun set, the moon rise, the outline of the hills become liquid and dark. I sat as if in a trance, without thinking.

Nearing Fontainebleau, we stopped at a posting house to refresh the horses. "Where in Fontainebleau?" Antoine asked.

"The château."

"But . . ." The Emperor was inside the château. It would be heavily under guard.

"I am expected," I said, and even believed it to be true.

As we neared the sentry hut by the main gate, I perceived my foolishness. There were Russian guards everywhere.

I thumped the ceiling of the carriage roof with my fist: stop, please! I had to reconsider. "Your Majesty?" my driver called down.

"Wait a moment, Antoine." A few lights were visible in the château: Bonaparte's suite. A light went out, then flickered.

Out, on, out, on—as if someone were pacing back and forth, back and forth. "Pull over to the side of the roadway," I said, my eyes on that light. On. Out. On. Out. And then on.

I waited, listening to the frogs croaking—so very like Martinico, I thought, but for the wind, which carried no scent of the sea. "Home now," I said, tears streaming.

## *In which my heart is with my husband*

*April 19, 1814, Tuesday—Malmaison.*
"The French ambassador to Russia wishes to speak to you, Your Majesty."

Armand de Caulaincourt! At last. "Thank you for coming so promptly," I told him, once civilities had been exchanged, once we'd made what has become a ritual acknowledgment that the world has changed, and that we are all rather deceitfully playing new roles.

"I've been intending to call in any case, Your Majesty." His blue eyes looked sad, resigned.

"About the Emperor?"

There was a moment of embarrassed hesitation. Which emperor? "About the Tsar Alexandre," he said apologetically.

"But you've seen Bonaparte? You've been to Fontainebleau?"

"Yes, Your Majesty. I've been with him throughout his . . . this terrible ordeal."

Ah! I thought, as if I had come upon a treasure. "I've been so anxious for news of him, Armand," I said, dropping all formality. "I've been told terrible things." I toyed with my handkerchief, already damp. "I've heard—" How did one ask such a thing? "Is it true, did the Emperor try to . . . ?"

"I'm afraid so, Your Majesty." Armand sat forward. "I don't know if you are aware, but before the last Spanish campaign, the Emperor had taken to wearing a small sachet suspended from a ribbon around his neck."

The sachet!

"It contained a deadly mix of belladonna and white hellebore, in case of capture in battle. He did consume it, but it was old, no longer potent." He smiled ruefully. "You can imagine the Emperor's frustration."

"But it must have made him terribly sick." I felt ill at the thought. Bonaparte is so sensitive. The least thing causes him terrible pain.

"Very." Constant stuck his finger down Bonaparte's throat, to make him retch, he told me. "Then I forced him to drink milk. We thought he was dying," Armand said, his voice thick. "And *he* thought so, too. At the time he asked me to tell you that you'd been very much on his mind."

The sound of a canary singing broke the poignant silence. Oh, Bonaparte! "When will he be leaving for Elba, Armand?"

"Tomorrow."

Oh, mon Dieu, so soon! "I *must* see him." One last time. *Please.*

Armand shook his head, not meeting my eyes. "I'm sorry, but it just isn't possible. The Emperor hopes to be reunited with his wife and child. Anything that might jeopardize that reunion must not—" He stopped. It pained him to have to explain.

"I understand," I lied, thinking with bitterness of Marie-Louise's reluctance. "I would never do anything that might cause the Emperor more pain than he has already had to endure."

A maid entered with a tray of refreshments. I took the opportunity to recover my composure. "You said you wished to speak to me about the Tsar Alexandre," I said, lifting my cup of tea, testing the steadiness of my hand. I took a careful sip. "He paid me a call several days ago. I found him to be respectful and courteous."

"As ambassador to Russia, I've come to know Tsar Alexandre well. Certainly he honours me with his confidence. The last time I saw him, he appeared dejected. He confided to me that your daughter had received him coldly."

"Hortense and I had a talk after he left," I told Armand, chagrined. "These are *difficult* times. Hortense is fierce in her loyalty. However, I believe she now understands the importance of diplomacy."

"He would very much like to call again, Your Majesty, and has asked if this coming Friday might suit you, for supper."

"Of course." One did not refuse such a request.

"You are wise. The Emperor likely would have been executed had it not been for the Tsar's intervention."

Before he left, I gave Armand a small parcel of things to give to Bonaparte, things he would be able to take with him into exile: a miniature of myself (from the first year of our marriage), Hortense's book of songs, some bulbs—including an asphodel lily, so helpful for his sensitive digestion. "And *this*," I said, enclosing the talisman Charlemagne had worn, heading into battle. "Tell him . . ." I turned away. Tell him I'll be waiting.


*April 20, Wednesday.*
In bed all day. I hardly have the strength to walk. I can't bear the thought of Bonaparte's isolation.

I imagine him saying farewell to his men, riding captive in a carriage, surrounded by Russian guards. They will likely take the road to Lyons, but this time there will be no triumphal arches, no cheering crowds. This time it will be different.

I see him so clearly! He sits motionless (for once), watching but unseeing. What are his thoughts?

He will travel incognito, no doubt, but even so people will line the road to watch him pass—their "little corporal," this man they once worshipped as if he were God. Oh, such glory! Will the world ever see the like of it again? It's like a dream now.

And, as in a dream, I see the people standing in silent witness, watching his carriage as it trundles by. They lower their heads, as if for a funeral procession. The veterans with their wooden legs—are they there? Yes, I see them with tears in their eyes.

He did not want it so.

Adieu, Bonaparte. My spirit-friend.


*[Undated]*
I have given away almost half of my wardrobe to the servants. They are

overjoyed. Tomorrow I will go through my papers. I've a ringing in my ears that prevents me from sleeping. I've so little strength. Where is he now?


*April 22, Friday.*
Tsar Alexandre came to dinner tonight. He played with the boys—Hortense was gracious and even charming. I watched as if from a distance, thinking of Bonaparte.


*May 3.*
A gloomy day. The Pretender—King Louis XVIII now—has entered Paris. I'm told that the crowd was large, but unenthusiastic. "He's boring," Carlotta reported, as if this were an evil thing. I listen with indifference, my thoughts elsewhere.


*May 8.*
Eugène has arrived from Milan. He held me in his arms, telling me not to worry so, telling me that he'd been to the palace to see the King.

"Already?"

"It went better than I thought it would."

If my children are taken care of, then I can rest, I thought. "I've been sorting through my things. I have something I'd like to give Auguste." Eugène looked at my diamonds in astonishment. "Don't worry, I'm giving quite a few to Hortense, as well. And I've a crate of things I'm putting aside for you."

He looked at me for a long moment, his eyes filling. "Aren't you going to need them, Maman?"


*[Undated]*
Hortense, Eugène, the Tsar Alexandre: young, ardent, idealistic. How ironic that they have formed a friendship. I sit by the fire and make polite

conversation, but my heart is far, far away, on a small Mediterranean island. *Elba*. He should be there by now. The sea.


*May 12, Thursday.*

"But Maman, you *must* come," Hortense begged. She's invited Tsar Alexandre to her country château at Saint-Leu and now she is anxious. "After all, aren't *you* the one who insisted I entertain him? It won't be the same without you."

"I know," I protested, "but—" The ringing in my ears has become constant, making sleep impossible. I've been having spells of dizziness and malaise. And melancholy—oh, melancholy.

"But you'll come?"

"Of course, darling." I smiled.


*May 14—Saint-Leu.*

I managed the journey to Saint-Leu well enough, but shortly after I arrived yet another of my spells came on. How they frighten me! I'm in the guestroom, recovering. Mademoiselle Avrillion has brought me an infusion of lemon water and orange flowers. The weather is cold and damp—it was foolish of me to have gone for a ride in Hortense's open calèche. I can hear Tsar Alexandre's and Eugène's voices downstairs, Hortense's musical laugh.

I must gather strength for the dinner hour. "Restore the balance," Bonaparte used to say. Oh, Bonaparte!


*May 15—Saint-Leu still.*

The carriage is being prepared for my return to Malmaison. I'm still not well. While I have the energy, I want to record my conversation with the Tsar last night.

Before dinner, I sent word that I wished to see him. He came immediately to my room. "Your Majesty," he said, "I fear we have tired you. Don't stand," he insisted, asking leave to take the chair closest to me.

"Tsar Alexandre, I am—"

"Your Majesty, I implore you—please call me Alex. I command it," he said with a smile.

"Very well, then, *Alex*."

"I have a confession to make." He placed his right hand over his heart. "I love your family." I searched for a dry handkerchief, weakening again. "Oh, you see, I *have* wearied you."

"Tsar—*Alex*, I mean, I must speak frankly. I am anxious about what is to become of Hortense and Eugène. I won't be able to sleep until their futures are settled."

"I will see to it immediately," he said, kissing my hand.

If only I could believe him. Bonaparte trusted him, and was betrayed.


*May 16, Monday—Malmaison.*
Home again, but still *so* ill. A devastating weakness has come over me, an unbearable sorrow. Dr. Horeau prescribed an emetic, which has not helped.


*May 23.*
Eugène escorted me to my bedchamber after dinner tonight with guests.

"I'm fine," I insisted.

He put his hand on my forehead. "You must rest, Maman."

"I *will* rest, Eugène—once it's determined how you and Hortense are to be looked after."

"Maman, Maman, Maman."

Hortense came to my room shortly after. "Eugène said you aren't well."

"I'm just a little tired."

"I'm calling the doctor."


*Tuesday.*
"Dr. Horeau is right, you should not receive guests," Mimi said. "You should be in bed."

"Did Dr. Horeau tell you to say that?"

Mimi reached her hand out to feel my forehead but I ducked away. I had a fever, I knew, but it was slight. "Send the cook up," I insisted. The Tsar and the Russian Grand Dukes would be coming for dinner. The menu had to be carefully considered. Any day now, they—"the Powers," Mimi calls them—will make a decision about Hortense and Eugène.

*May 26.*
Slight fever, light-headed. I'm writing this in bed, covered with a terrible rash. Hortense wants to summon her doctor, but that would upset Dr. Horeau, I know. "I will do whatever you tell me," I told him. Now I've a disgusting plaster on my throat.

Still no word from "the Powers."

*[Undated]*
Hortense looked puzzled when I told her I needed her to fetch a box hidden behind my hats. "Please—get it down for me," I told her.

"Why don't I get a manservant to help?"

"No," I said, falling back against the damp pillows.

The oak strongbox *was* heavy, to judge by Hortense's pink cheeks, the beads of perspiration along her hairline. She plunked it down on the bedside table. "No, on the bed," I said, struggling to sit. "The key is in the upper left drawer of my escritoire—under the box of calling cards."

The metal felt cold in my hands. I fiddled with the lock and eventually got it to open. And there it all was: my old journals, the Church marriage certificate, Bonaparte's letters tied up in a scarlet ribbon. These I took out, carefully. Mere scraps of paper—yet such passion, such burning love. "I'd like you to put these in a safe spot," I told Hortense. She leaned forward to reach for them. "But not yet," I said, pulling back. I wasn't ready to let them go. "And these," I said, indicating the old journals. "I'd like you to burn them . . . when the time comes." Hortense looked confused. "Can I trust you?" She made a tiny nod, her expression wary. "And one other thing: you must not read them."

"Maman, why are you doing this?"

"Just *promise*."

She exhaled with exasperation. "Yes, Maman," she said, like a dutiful schoolgirl.

I smiled. "Do you know how much I love you?"

Her eyes filled. "Yes, Maman." A sniff. Two. She pulled a handkerchief out of her bodice. "And I love you!"

I opened my arms and she fell into bed beside me, as if she were a girl again, not the woman she'd become. I held her close until her breathing steadied. The pendulum clock rang four gongs. And then, in the heavy silence that followed, I asked, very quietly, "Hortense, is there anything you want to tell me?"

"No, Maman, why do you ask?" she said, sitting up and wiping her cheeks with the backs of her hands.

"It doesn't matter." *Remember that.*


*[Undated]*

I can't talk, but I can write. My throat! The children are so very dear. I see the distress in their eyes—the *fear*. I love them so much! At least they have each other.

Oh, Bonaparte, if only . . .

# *Postscript*

*Sire, Emperor (Papa),*

*I am writing to you now with tears in my heart. Your beloved Josephine passed away suddenly. We still cannot comprehend that she is no longer with us. Our distress is made more bearable knowing that she lived a full life, a life full of love. She loved us. She loved you—profoundly.*

*She got chilled riding in the Montmorency woods and developed a fatal infection in her throat. However, it would seem to have begun earlier, for after your exile, her constitution steadily weakened. Mademoiselle Avrillion tells us that she was subject to episodes of a devouring melancholy—so very unlike her, as you know.*

*It didn't help that she insisted on rising, insisted on entertaining. She was anxious about me and Hortense, how our futures would be decided. We have just now learned that we will not be exiled, that we may keep our properties and the titles that go with them. So perhaps she rests in peace.*

*But at what a cost! On the return from Saint-Leu, her doctor-in-ordinary advised a small dose of ipecacuanha as a corrective. Although suffering, she seemed better, well enough even to breakfast with guests. That night she tried to join us in a game of prison-bars on the lawn, but had to sit down. After the guests left, she attempted to take her customary stroll through the rose gardens, but became so weak she could not walk and had to be helped back to the château. It was at this point that we began to be alarmed. A few days in retirement revived her once again, but on reading in the news-sheets that little Napoleon's body was to be exhumed, she* *relapsed.\** Even so, she persevered in her efforts to persuade the Austrian and Russian rulers on our behalf.

Had I known how ill she was, I would have stopped her, Sire. (Not that she would have listened. Her doctor tells us he begged her to stay in bed.) When I left that afternoon, she seemed to have worsened. Although her doctor assured us that she had no fever and was not in danger, she was having difficulty speaking. I think this was on the Monday, which would make it the twenty-third of May. The next morning she woke with pain in her throat. Dr. Horeau administered a purgative and tried to persuade her to stay in bed. She refused: the Tsar and the Russian Grand Dukes were expected for dinner. She rallied, but partway into the meal was forced to excuse herself. I saw her to her room.

Wednesday she woke covered with a rash. She'd had a terrible night, Mimi told me: pains in her chest, fluxions of the stomach, a shivering fever. The rash did go away in the evening. Even so Hortense insisted that a plaster be applied to her throat.

On Friday the Tsar sent his own doctor, Sir James Wylie—a Scot, not an Englishman. All three doctors were concerned: the back of Maman's throat was dark crimson. That night her fever raged. A blister was applied between her shoulders, and mustard plasters to her feet.

But it was too late, Sire. We were losing the battle. Saturday morning her fever was high and it was hard to feel her pulse. She breathed with difficulty and was in pain, slipping in and out of delirium. In a futile effort to save her, the doctors applied a plaster to her chest. Hortense brought her boys, but Maman became agitated for fear the air in the room would harm them.

Whitsunday, May 29, the doctors told us there was no hope.[†] We sent for the curate to administer the last rites. He wasn't home, so Hortense's tutor, Abbé Bertrand, was summoned. At eleven Maman received the last rites. When Hortense and I appeared in the door, she held out her arms to us, but was unable to speak. Oh, the love in her eyes! Hortense swooned and had to be carried to her chamber.

---

*\* Out of sympathy (and friendship), Tsar Alexandre arranged for the child to be entombed in the chapel of Hortense's château at Saint-Leu.*

*† An autopsy on Josephine's body revealed an inflamed trachea with a gangrenous spot on the larynx. The lungs were choked with blood.*

*At that moment Mimi cried out to me in alarm. I rushed to the bed. Maman slumped against me and I knew she was gone. I held her thus for a time, feeling her spirit like a brilliant light all around me.*

*Mimi told me to go to Hortense—she would put Yeyette to rest, she said, weeping. Hortense was in her room, still insensible. She roused herself, took one look at my eyes and began to weep. "At least you'll have each other," Maman had told me several weeks ago. I hadn't been listening, Sire. She was saying farewell, and I hadn't been listening.*

*Soon after, Hortense and I left for Saint-Leu. We are here now. Hortense is still overcome. It will take time.*

*As you can imagine, the citizens of this nation are overwhelmed with grief at the news that their "Good Empress Josephine" is no longer with them. I was told by old Gontier that the gate could not be opened for the mountain of bouquets piled high there, that the long road from Paris to Malmaison has been thronged with people with tears in their eyes—peasants and aristocrats alike.*

*She was placed in a double casket. Over twenty thousand people came all the way out to Malmaison to pay their last respects. Astonishing. Even the gate here at Saint-Leu is covered with bouquets and letters of sympathy. Really, Papa, it touches us deeply to see such an outpouring of love.*

*"Tell him I am waiting," Maman told Hortense a few days before her death. Fever talk, we thought at the time, but now it all seems so clear. Mimi, who was with her through that last feverish night, says her last words were of you.*

*Did she know how much we loved her? If Maman's death has taught me anything, Sire, it is that one must speak one's heart when one can. I love and honour you as my Emperor and commanding general, but above all as my father. Bon courage, as Corsicans say. May God be with you. I know her spirit will be.*

*Your faithful and devoted son, Eugène*

## *Epilogue*

Napoleon escaped from the island of Elba one year later and returned to France, chasing out the Bourbon King Louis XVIII and the Royalists, including Talleyrand and all the others who had betrayed him. (Fouché, who stayed, betrayed Napoleon as well by sending his war plans to England.) This was the period known as the Hundred Days, which ended with Napoleon's defeat by the British and their allies at the Battle of Waterloo. This time Napoleon was banished to St. Helena, a remote island off the southern tip of Africa. He died six years later at the age of fifty-one—of stomach cancer, some say; of poisoning, others claim. His pleas to his mother and Uncle Fesch to send medical help were dismissed by them as a British ploy. They had been convinced by a mystic that Napoleon was perfectly well. On his deathbed Napoleon is reported to have said, with emotion: "I have just seen my good Josephine. She told me we were going to see each other again and that we would never again be separated. She promised me."

All the members of the Bonaparte clan were banished from France.

Madame Mère, who retired to Rome with her half-brother Fesch and daughter Pauline, refused to speak to Caroline after Caroline's betrayal of Napoleon. She died after a fall at the age of eighty-six.

Joseph emigrated to the United States as "Count de Survilliers," making a considerable amount of money on speculative ventures. He died in Florence at the age of seventy-six.

Lucien returned to France to help Napoleon during the Hundred Days. He was refused permission to join Napoleon on St. Helena, and lived out his life in Italy with his wife and eleven children.

Elisa fled to Italy as "Countess de Campignano." She died of a fever near Trieste at forty-three.

Pauline also fled to Italy, where she lived from time to time with her mother in Rome, and even, at the end of her life, with her estranged husband Prince Borghèse. Of all the Bonaparte siblings, Pauline was the most loyal to Napoleon in exile, even managing to visit him on Elba in spite of her delicate health. She died in Florence at the age of forty-five, dressed in a ballgown, with a mirror in her hand.

After abdicating the throne of Holland, Louis settled in Italy, leading a quiet life as a gentleman of letters. He wrote a melancholy novel (*Marie*, about a man who is forced to marry a woman he does not love), poetry and various works relating to Holland and the Empire. He died of apoplexy at the age of sixty-six.

Caroline, deposed Queen of Naples, was considered too dangerous to be allowed to live near any members of her family, and died in isolation in Florence as the "Duchess de Lipona," an anagram for Naples (Napoli). Her husband, Joachim Murat, was executed by a firing squad at the age of forty-eight, clutching portraits of his children. Foolhardy as ever, he had attempted to recover his kingdom of Naples with only thirty men.

Jérôme settled first in Switzerland and then in Italy. He returned to France eventually and lived to see the reign of Napoleon III (Oui-Oui). It is through Jérôme that the Bonaparte name exists today.


The Empress Marie-Louise, object of a deliberate plot on the part of the Austrians to keep her from joining Napoleon, succumbed enthusiastically to the sexual prowess of Count Neipperg, the chamberlain assigned to her for just that purpose. She became indifferent to the fate of her son by Napoleon. The boy—Napoleon II—died of tuberculosis at the age of twenty-two, without issue. ("My life would have been different," he reportedly said, "had Josephine been my mother.") Marie-Louise died in Vienna at the age of fifty-six.

Hortense came to Napoleon's assistance during the Hundred Days, and consequently was exiled after Waterloo. She settled in Switzerland, where she died at the age of fifty-four. Her eldest surviving son, Napoleon-Louis (Petit), died in battle at the age of twenty-seven. Louis-Napoleon (Oui-Oui) was elected to the presidency of France after the Revolution of 1848, becoming Emperor of the French under the name Napoleon III.

Hortense's lover, Charles Flahaut—believed to be Talleyrand's illegitimate son—asked Hortense to marry him, but she refused because Louis was opposed to a divorce, and ultimately Flahaut married another woman. Their illegitimate son, Charles Auguste Demorny, was prominent in the government of Napoleon III, his unacknowledged half-brother.

On condition that Eugène never take up arms again (which prevented him from coming to Napoleon's aid during the Hundred Days), Eugène was offered the title Duke de Leuchtenberg by Tsar Alexandre. Eugène, Auguste and their children settled in Munich, living happily and quietly. He died of apoplexy at the age of forty-three.

Of seven children, six grew to maturity. Each married into royalty:

Josephine married the Crown Prince of Sweden (son of General Bernadotte and Eugénie-Désirée Clary—Joseph and Julie's nephew), becoming Queen of Sweden.

Eugénie married Prince Frederick Hohenzollern-Sigmaringen, a German prince.

Augustus married Queen Maria II of Portugal (but died shortly after).

Amélie married the Emperor of Brazil.

Théodelinde married Guillaume de Württemberg, a German count.

Maximilian married Grand Duchess Maria, daughter of the Tsar of Russia.

Through Eugène, Josephine's progeny live on in most of the royal houses of the world today.

# *Chronology*

March 9, 1800. Napoleon and Josephine's fourth-year anniversary.

March 29, 1800. Napoleon meets with Royalist agent Cadoudal.

June 18, 1800. The Marquis de Beauharnais dies at Saint-Germain-en-Laye at the age of eighty-six.

October 10, 1800. The Opéra plot: revolutionaries attempt to assassinate Napoleon at the Opéra.

December 24, 1800. Royalist assassination attempt by exploding gunpowder nearly succeeds.

February 9, 1801. Lunéville peace treaty is signed with Austria.

July 7 to August 5, 1801. Josephine goes to the spa at Plombières to be treated for infertility.

January 4, 1802. Hortense and Louis marry.

March 27, 1802. Amiens peace treaty is signed with Britain.

April 18, 1802. Concordat with the Church is celebrated.

June 15 to July 12, 1802. Josephine returns to the spa at Plombières to undergo another treatment for infertility.

| | |
|---|---|
| August 2, 1802. | Napoleon is declared First Consul for Life as the result of a popular vote. (Fouché opposed.) |
| September 14, 1802. | Fouché is demoted. |
| October 10, 1802. | Hortense and Louis's first child is born, Napoleon-Charles. |
| November 1 or 2, 1802. | Pauline Bonaparte's husband, Victor Leclerc, dies of yellow fever in Saint-Domingue (Haiti today). |
| March 14, 1803. | Josephine's Aunt Désirée dies. |
| May 1803. | Josephine's goddaughter, Stéphanie Tascher, fifteen, sails from Martinique on *Le Dard*. |
| Shortly before May 18, 1803. | *Le Dard* is captured by the British. |
| May 18, 1803. | England declares war on France. |
| August 18, 1803. | Stéphanie arrives in France by ship from England, after being held hostage. |
| February 4, 1804. | A Royalist plot to kidnap Napoleon is discovered. |
| February 19, 1804. | General Moreau is arrested. |
| March 9, 1804. | Georges Cadoudal is arrested. |
| March 15, 1804. | Duke d'Enghien is arrested in Germany. |
| March 21, 1804. | Duke d'Enghien is "tried" and executed. |
| March 27, 1804. | Fouché makes a motion in the Senate inviting Napoleon to make his glory "immortal." |
| April 7, 1804. | Napoleon and Josephine ask Louis if they can adopt his son. (Refused.) |
| May 18, 1804. | A new constitution based on the Civil Code is proclaimed. Napoleon is proclaimed hereditary Emperor by a national plebiscite. |
| June 28, 1804. | Cadoudal is executed. General Moreau is banished. |

July 10, 1804. Fouché is reinstated as Minister of Police.

July 30–September 11, 1804. Josephine goes to Aix-la-Chapelle to take a treatment for infertility.

October 11, 1804. Hortense and Louis's second son, Napoleon-Louis, is born in Paris.

November 25, 1804. Napoleon receives Pope Pius VII at Fontainebleau.

December 1, 1804. Josephine and Napoleon are married by the Church.

December 2, 1804. Coronation at Notre-Dame. Napoleon and Josephine are crowned Emperor and Empress of the French.

May 26, 1805. Napoleon is crowned King of Italy in Milan.

June 7, 1805. Eugène is named Viceroy of the Kingdom of Italy.

August 1 to August 30, 1805. Josephine goes to Plombières-les-Bains for yet another treatment for infertility.

October 21, 1805. Battle of Trafalgar. The French fleet is defeated.

December 2, 1805. Napoleon scores a decisive victory in the Battle of Austerlitz.

January 14, 1806. Eugène marries Princess Auguste-Amélie of Bavaria in Munich.

June 5, 1806. Louis and Hortense are formally proclaimed King and Queen of Holland.

December 13, 1806. Caroline's reader, Éléonore Denuelle, gives birth to a son, Léon, thought to be fathered by Napoleon (but possibly by Joachim Murat).

May 4, 1807. Louis and Hortense's eldest son, Napoleon-Charles, dies.

July 27, 1807. Napoleon returns after an absence of ten months.

| | |
|---|---|
| April 21, 1808. | Hortense and Louis's third son, Louis-Napoleon, is born prematurely. |
| December 1808. | Eugène intercepts a letter revealing a plot to put Joachim Murat on the throne should Napoleon be killed in battle. Napoleon is alerted. |
| January 23, 1809. | Napoleon returns to Paris from Spain and, shortly afterwards, Talleyrand is demoted. |
| End of September 1809. | Countess Marie Walewska becomes pregnant by Napoleon. |
| November 30, 1809. | Napoleon tells Josephine that they must divorce. |
| December 15, 1809. | Formal divorce ceremony. |
| December 16, 1809. | Josephine moves out of the Tuileries Palace. |
| March 27, 1810. | Napoleon and Austrian Archduchess Marie-Louise meet for the first time at Compiègne. |
| March 29, 1810. | Josephine moves to the Château de Navarre at Évreux. |
| April 1, 1810. | Napoleon and Marie-Louise are married at Saint-Cloud. |
| May 4, 1810. | Napoleon's mistress, Countess Marie Walewska, gives birth to a son in Warsaw. |
| March 20, 1811. | Napoleon and Marie-Louise's son, François-Charles-Joseph-Napoleon II, King of Rome, is born. |
| September 15 or 16, 1811. | Charles Flahaut and Hortense's son is born. |
| December 17, 1812. | *Le Moniteur* prints the XXIX Bulletin, outlining the massive losses of the Grande Armée in Russia. |
| August 10, 1813. | Austria joins the Allies. |

August 26–27, 1813. Napoleon defeats the Allies at the Battle of Dresden.

October 16–19, 1813. Battle of Leipzig. Napoleon's army is defeated and reduced to 40,000.

November 22, 1813. Speaking on behalf of the Allies, Auguste's father, King Max of Bavaria, tries (unsuccessfully) to induce Eugène to abandon Napoleon.

February 15, 1814. Joachim Murat makes a declaration of war against Eugène.

March 28, 1814. Empress Marie-Louise and the Bonapartes make a decision to abandon Paris. Josephine gets an urgent message from Hortense: flee.

March 29, 1814. Josephine leaves Malmaison to go to Évreux.

April 1, 1814. Hortense and her two boys arrive at Évreux with the news that Paris has capitulated.

April 6, 1814. Napoleon abdicates.

April 16, 1814. Tsar Alexandre visits Josephine at Malmaison.

May 14, 1814. Tsar Alexandre visits Josephine, Hortense and Eugène at Saint-Leu. Josephine catches a chill.

May 29, 1814. Josephine dies at noon.

February 26, 1815. Napoleon escapes Elba.

March 21, 1815. Napoleon returns to Paris

June 18, 1815. Napoleon is defeated at Waterloo.

June 22, 1815. Napoleon abdicates a second time.

October 15, 1815. Napoleon arrives at Jamestown, St. Helena.

May 5, 1821. Napoleon dies.

# *Characters*

Agathe: Josephine's scullery maid.

Arberg, Countess d': Josephine's second lady of honour, replacing Chastulé.

Auguié, Adèle: Madame Campan's niece and Hortense's closest friend, as well as her maid.

Avrillion, Mademoiselle: Josephine's mistress of the wardrobe.

Bacchiochi, Elisa Bonaparte (Princess of Piombino, Grand Duchess): Napoleon's eldest sister; married to Félix.

Beauharnais, Eugène (Viceroy of Italy): Josephine's son by her first husband; married Princess Auguste-Amélie of Bavaria and had six children.

Beauharnais, Fanny: Josephine's aunt through her first husband; poet and eccentric.

Beauharnais, Marquis de: the father of Alexandre, Josephine's first husband; married to Josephine's Aunt Désirée.

Bonaparte, Hortense Beauharnais (Queen of Holland): Josephine's daughter by her first husband; married Napoleon's brother Louis and had four sons (little Napoleon, Petit and Oui-Oui by her husband; Charles Auguste Demorny by Charles Flahaut).

Bonaparte, Jérôme (King of Westphalia): Napoleon's youngest sibling; first married Elizabeth Patterson (annulled), then Princess Catherine of Württemberg; one child by his first wife, four by his second.

Bonaparte, Joseph (King of Naples, King of Spain): Napoleon's older brother; married to Julie Clary, by whom he had two daughters.

Bonaparte, Letizia (Signora Letizia, Madame Mère): Napoleon's mother.

Bonaparte, Louis (King of Holland): Napoleon's brother; married Hortense and had three sons.

Bonaparte, Lucien: Napoleon's brother; disowned by him; first married Christine, with whom he had two children; widowed, he married Alexandrine, with whom he had eleven.

Bonaparte, Napoleon (Emperor of the French, King of Italy): first wife, Josephine; second wife, Marie-Louise, by whom he had one son, Napoleon-François-Charles-Joseph.

Borghèse, Pauline Bonaparte (Princess Borghèse): Napoleon's sister, renowned for her beauty; first married to Victor Leclerc, then widowed; subsequently married Prince Camillo Borghèse. Dermide, her son by Leclerc, died at the age of six.

Bourrienne, Fauvelet: Napoleon's first secretary.

Cadoudal, Georges: Royalist agent, convicted of conspiracy.

Cambacérès, Jean-Jacques de: Second Consul, Arch-Chancellor.

Campan, Madame: schoolmistress and former lady-in-waiting to Queen Marie Antoinette.

Caulaincourt, Armand de: French Ambassador to Russia, Minister of Foreign Affairs. Josephine had known his family since before the Revolution and had helped them during the Terror.

Chimay, Thérèse Tallien (Princess de Chimay): Josephine's close friend. Divorced from Tallien (who died indigent, likely suffering from venereal disease) and the mother of a number of illegitimate children by the financier Ouvrard. Ostracized by the court and polite society, she nevertheless married Prince de Chimay. One of her sons by Chimay married a woman whose biological father is believed to have been Napoleon.

Constant: Napoleon's valet.

Corvisart, Dr. Jean: Imperial doctor to Napoleon and Josephine for many years, then doctor to Empress Marie-Louise. He conspired with the Austrians to help keep Marie-Louise and her son from joining Napoleon on Elba by telling her that her health was not strong enough for such a voyage.

Denuelle, Éléonore: Caroline's reader, Napoleon's mistress. Her claim that Napoleon was the father of her son, Léon, was later substantiated.

Désirée, Aunt: see Montardat.

Despréaux, Monsieur: dance master.

Duchâtel, Adèle: Josephine's lady-in-waiting; mistress to Napoleon, courted by Eugène.

Duplan, Monsieur: hairdresser.

Duroc, Christophe: Napoleon's aide and Hortense's first love.

Fesch, Joseph (Archbishop of Lyons, Cardinal): Napoleon's uncle by marriage.

Flahaut, Charles: Hortense's lover and father of her son Charles Auguste Demorny (raised by Flahaut's mother, the romance novelist Madame de Souza, with financial help from Hortense).

Fouché: Minister of Police, at various times; intriguer.

Frangeau, Madame: midwife.

Gazzani, Carlotta: Josephine's reader and Napoleon's mistress (briefly).

Georges, Mademoiselle: actress, Napoleon's mistress.

Gontier: Josephine's elderly manservant.

Grassini: Italian singer, Napoleon's mistress.

Horeau, Dr.: Dr. Corvisart's student; Josephine's physician at the time of her death.

Isabey: portrait artist, art teacher, Josephine's make-up artist.

Junot, Andoche: Napoleon's aide; Governor of Paris; Caroline's lover.

Lavalette, Émilie Beauharnais: Josephine's niece by her first husband; married to Lavalette. After Napoleon's second and final defeat, Émilie disguised herself as a man and took her husband's place in prison (where he'd been condemned to death), allowing him to escape to Bavaria. Tragically, while in prison, she suffered a miscarriage and lost her sanity. Pardoned in 1822, Lavalette returned to his wife in France, but she did not recognize him. However, his attentive care partially restored her memory and their last years together were happy ones.

Leroy, Monsieur: fashion designer.

Méneval: Napoleon's secretary, replacing Fauvelet Bourrienne.

Mimi: Josephine's childhood maid; a mulatto from Martinique, formerly a slave. She married one of Napoleon's cabinet guards and during the Hundred Days gave refuge to Hortense.

Montardat, Désirée: Josephine's godmother and aunt; first married to Monsieur Renaudin, who was suspected of trying to murder her. Her second husband was Marquis de Beauharnais, the father of Josephine's first husband. Shortly after the Marquis's death, she married Pierre Danès de Montardat ("Monsieur Pierre"), the mayor of Saint-Germain-en-Laye.

Moreau: popular general convicted of conspiracy; exiled to America but returned from exile to join the Russian forces. He was killed by a French cannonball at the Battle of Dresden in 1813.

Moustache: Napoleon's courier.

Murat, Caroline Bonaparte (Duchess de Berg, Queen of Naples): Napoleon's youngest sister; married to Joachim Murat, with whom she had four children.

Murat, Joachim (Duke de Berg, King of Naples): Caroline Bonaparte's husband.

Rémusat, Claire ("Clari"): lady-in-waiting to Josephine.

Rochefoucauld, Chastulé, Countess de la: Josephine's distant cousin and lady of honour.

Roustam: Napoleon's Mameluke bodyguard.

Talleyrand: Minister of Foreign Affairs and traitor.

Talma: the most renowned actor of his day.

Tascher, Stéphanie: Josephine's niece and goddaughter.

Thérèse: see Chimay.

Walewska, Countess Marie: Napoleon's Polish mistress, the mother of his son Alexandre.

# Beauharnais Genealogy

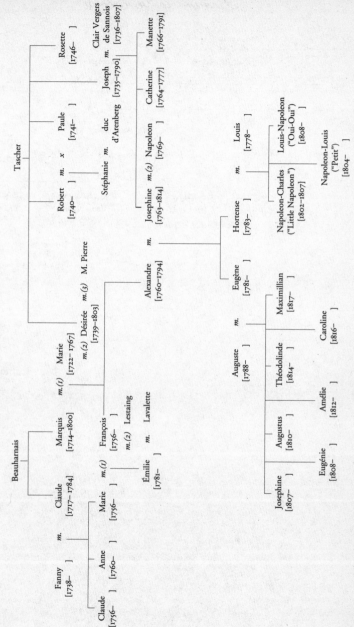

# *Bonaparte Genealogy*

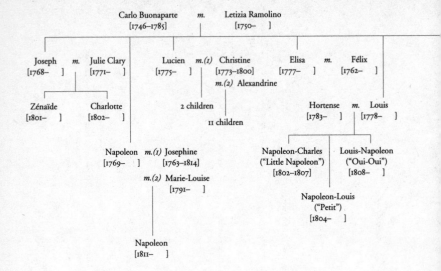

Carlo Buonaparte    *m.*    Letizia Ramolino
[1746–1785]                 [1750–  ]

Joseph    *m.*    Julie Clary          Lucien    *m.(1)*    Christine          Elisa    *m.*    Félix
[1768–  ]         [1771–  ]            [1775–  ]           [1773–1800]        [1777–  ]        [1762–  ]

                                                 *m.(2)*  Alexandrine

Zénaïde           Charlotte                    2 children                              Hortense    *m.*    Louis
[1801–  ]         [1802–  ]                                                           [1783–  ]           [1778–  ]

                                                 11 children

            Napoleon    *m.(1)*  Josephine                          Napoleon-Charles        Louis-Napoleon
            [1769–  ]           [1763–1814]                         ("Little Napoleon")     ("Oui-Oui")
                                                                    [1802–1807]             [1808–  ]
                        *m.(2)*  Marie-Louise
                                 [1791–  ]                                      Napoleon-Louis
                                                                                   ("Petit")
                                                                                  [1804–  ]

            Napoleon
            [1811–  ]

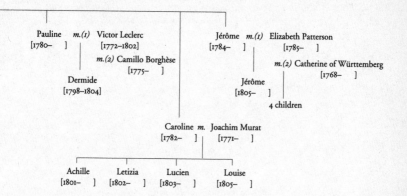

Pauline    *m.(1)*   Victor Leclerc
[1780–   ]       [1772–1802]

        *m.(2)* Camillo Borghèse
            [1775–   ]

   Dermide
   [1798–1804]

Jérôme   *m.(1)*   Elizabeth Patterson
[1784–   ]        [1785–   ]

        *m.(2)* Catherine of Württemberg
            [1768–   ]

   Jérôme
   [1805–   ]

      4 children

Caroline   *m.*   Joachim Murat
[1782–   ]      [1771–   ]

Achille      Letizia      Lucien      Louise
[1801–  ]    [1802–  ]    [1803–  ]    [1805–  ]

# *Selected Bibliography*

Anyone who ventures into the Napoleonic Empire is quickly over-whelmed by the vast number of books that have been published on all aspects of the period. After over a decade of immersion in this moment in history, I still feel I have only scratched the surface. My bibliography now lists almost four hundred titles; I will note only a few.

Researching this novel, I was highly entertained—"diverted" is a suit-ably eighteenth-century word—by the many memoirs of the period: those of Mademoiselle Avrillion, Fauvelet Bourrienne, Las Cases, Constant, Madame Ducrest, Baron Fain, Fouché, Madame Junot, Méneval, Madame Rémusat, and especially Hortense. In all cases it was necessary to judge the veracity and objectivity of the author (who was, in many cases, a ghost writer), making the search for "truth" rather like trying to find one's way through the hall of mirrors at a fun fair.

For information about Josephine, my mainstays have continued to be: *Impératrice Joséphine, Correspondance, 1782-1814*, compiled and edited by Maurice Catinat, Bernard Chevallier and Christophe Pincemaille (Paris: Histoire Payot, 1996) and *L'impératrice Joséphine* by Bernard Chevallier and Christophe Pincemaille (Paris: Presses de la Renaissance, 1988) as well as Ernest John Knapton's *Empress Josephine* (Cambridge, Massa-chusetts: Harvard University Press, 1963). An award-winning biography was published as I was in the final stages of this work: Françoise Wagener's *L'Impératrice Joséphine (1763–1814)* (Paris: Flammarion, 1999).

It is difficult to select one particular book about Napoleon: there are so many. Although decidedly pro-Napoleon, Vincent Cronin's *Napoleon*

(London: Collins, 1971) remains one of the best, in my opinion. At the very least it is highly readable and captures the spirit of the time. Frank McLynn's *Napoleon: A Biography* (London: Pimlico, 1998) is a recent and balanced account I consulted frequently.

Other books of note: Joan Bear's *Caroline Murat* (London: Collins, 1972); Jean-Paul Bertaud's *Bonaparte et le duc d'Enghien; le duel des deux Frances* (Paris: Robert Laffont, 1972); Hubert Cole's *The Betrayers: Joachim and Caroline Murat* (London: Eyre Methuen, 1972) and *Fouché: The Unprincipled Patriot* (London: Eyre & Spottiswoode, 1971); Émile Dard's *Napoleon and Talleyrand* (London: Philip Allan & Co., Ltd., 1937); Walter Geer's *Napoleon and His Family: The Story of a Corsican Clan* (London: George Allen & Unwin Ltd., 1928); Carola Oman's *Napoleon's Viceroy: Eugène de Beauharnais* (New York: Funk and Wagnall, 1966); Jean Tulard's *Fouché* (Paris: Fayard, 1998) and *Murat* (Paris: Fayard, 1999).

Three books in particular provided a wealth of wonderful detail: Bernard Chevallier's award-winning *L'art de vivre au temps de Joséphine* (Paris: Flammarion, 1998); Maurice Guerrini's *Napoleon and Paris: Thirty Years of History* (New York: Walker and Company, 1967); Frédéric Masson's *Joséphine, Empress and Queen,* (Paris and London: Goupil & Co., 1899).

I am often asked to recommend a non-fiction book on the subject of Josephine and Napoleon. Evangeline Bruce's *Napoleon and Josephine: The Improbable Marriage* (New York: Scribner, 1995) is excellent—a highly readable and generally accurate account of both personal and political worlds.

In closing, a word of caution: this subject is addictive.

*Note*

With the exception of the letter of March 12, 1810 (to which information has been added), Napoleon's letters throughout are edited versions of those he actually wrote to Josephine. The police reports (pages 245–46) are likewise authentic, as are Hortense and Émilie's account of the journey to Plombières (pages 48–49), Napoleon's instructions to Eugène on how to rule Italy (pages 196–97), and Josephine's letter to Napoleon (page 318). The translations are my own, with help from Bernard Turle.

The illustration on page 62 of minuet notation is from *The Art of Dancing* by Kellom Tomlinson, published in 1735. The illustration on page 146 showing how to bow is from *Chironomia; or A Treatise on Rhetorical Delivery* by Gilbert Austin, originally published in 1806. The map on page 312 is based, with permission, on a map by Hyperhistory Online.

# Acknowledgements

There have been times over the last three years when I felt that the spirits were putting roadblocks in my path, that there was a conspiracy to prevent this book from drawing to a close—a conspiracy in which I was, no doubt, an unconscious accomplice, for this hasn't been an easy book to finish. It ends a decade of daily interaction with Josephine and her family, closes a curtain on a world that has become home to me.

Perhaps the most difficult part of writing this novel was having to simplify a very complex narrative. Many delightful characters and fascinating stories had to be cut: readers familiar with the period will miss Fanny Beauharnais's granddaughter Stéphanie (*another* spirited Stéphanie); the several Tascher boys sent from Martinique to take advantage of the caring protection of their Empress aunt; Talleyrand's marriage to the delightfully clueless Madame Grand; General Bernadotte and his wife (Napoleon's first love, Eugénie-Désirée Clary), who became King and Queen of Sweden; the colourful Spanish royalty, most especially the unforgettable Prince of Peace. Any of these people could easily be the subject of a novel.

But most of all I have felt inadequate to the task of properly portraying Napoleon, his strengths and weaknesses, his vision and blindness, his heroic accomplishments and grievous failings. As well, the political picture—so vast and so complex—had to be simplified. Notably missing is the story of Toussaint's defence of Saint-Domingue (Haiti today) and his tragic death in France, as well as the story of the arrest and imprisonment of the Pope. This novel represents only the tip of the iceberg.

Of those individuals I have chosen to include, my apologies to their descendants if I have misrepresented them in any way. I hope my respect and love for them shows, even in their villainy.

Researching this book in Europe, I owe special thanks to Yves Carlier, the curator of Fontainebleau, who took me on a tour behind the scenes of that amazing château, and the staff of the Archives Municipales in Évreux. And, as always, I owe a special thanks to Bernard Chevallier and Dr. Catinat at Malmaison. Dr. Catinat has happily answered my numerous questions for almost a decade. His knowledge and perception of "notre héroïne" have influenced me greatly.

Special appreciation is due to all those on various Net history forums who took the time to give me specific information, notably: Bruno Nackaerts, Beryl Bernardi, Cori Hauer-Galambos, Yves Martin, and especially Tom Holmberg, who made perceptive and helpful suggestions after reading an early draft. Military historian Dr. Margaret Chrisawn not only answered my frequent questions, but combed the final text for errors (those errors that remain are entirely my responsibility). My debt to her since the inception of this trilogy is immense. Historian Dr. John McErlean kept me posted of new publications and developments; Irène Delage at Le Souvenir Napoléonien helped find obscure references; John Ballantrae provided tarot expertise; hemp activist Robert Anderman provided an interesting perspective regarding the Russian campaign; and Marshall Pynkoski and Jeannette Zingg of Opéra Atelier opened my eyes to the intricate world of eighteenth-century dance.

The members of the Algonquin Book Club (Penney Carson-Mak, Shirley Felker, Bonnie Ference, Catherine Lee, Rhoda Levert, Joanne Paine and Cathleen Sullivan) gave an exceptionally helpful critique of an early draft. My hard-working readers proved invaluable yet again: Peggy Bridgland, Janet Calcaterra, Thea Caplan, Dorothy Goodman, Marnie MacKay, Jenifer McVaugh, Carmen Mullins, Fran Murphy, Robin Paige, Chris Pollock, and especially my parents, Robert and Sharon Zentner. Kristine Puopolo at Scribners made very helpful suggestions. The sensitive work of Fiona Foster, a talented editor, is apparent on every page. A "triple salvo of bravos" to Judy Holland, who read two drafts and each time gave me the benefit of her considerable expertise as an editor, writer and teacher.

Thanks to Jan Whitford, whose early faith has at last been rewarded, and to my "home team" at HarperCollins Canada: Karen Hanson, Roy Nicol, Magda Nusink, Lorissa Sengara, Rebecca Vogan—and especially, especially, *especially* my editor and publisher, Iris Tupholme, who wept reading each draft.

And, as always, I thank my husband Richard, who picked me up when I fell down, brushed me off and gently but firmly turned me back in the direction of the eighteenth century.